C000231445

This is a love story beautifully
It reflects the complex ethnic,
Malaysia and beyond—all made ..... through the experience
of characters, movingly depicted, and the exciting action,
which carries the reader briskly from page to page.

—Dato' (Dr) Erik Jensen,
Author of *Where Hornbills Fly*

"Tautly written, Chan Ling Yap's second novel is a powerful
story of the problems of intercultural marriage that can
arise from family interference. With a superbly woven plot,
Bitter-Sweet Harvest leads the reader through a minefield
of cultural, ethnic and religious conflicts. Compelling and
gripping, I found I could not put down this tragic saga of
missed opportunities for the lovers. A poignant love story
that is highly recommended!"

—Professor Bill Edeson,
Professorial Fellow, University of Wollongong

"Chan Ling Yap's latest book *Bitter-Sweet Harvest* is a worthy
successor to *Sweet Offerings*, her first novel. I couldn't read it
quickly enough to find out the next step in this exciting story.
I wasn't disappointed."

—Kate Mazdon,
President, Princes Risborough Women's Institute

Reviews for *Sweet Offerings*:

A very down-to-earth book with down-to-earth characters that you cannot help but be drawn to. It has certainly been an absorbing and enjoyable read.

—Review from *Choose and Book*

The dramatic personal stories of Mei Yin and Nelly, first and second wife to the same man, are the best reasons for giving this book a go—not forgetting the mother-in-law from hell.

—Review from *Whichbook*

The book is a great read with real emotion and such detail as one can almost smell the atmosphere coming from the pages. Also I cannot recall ever reading a book where the very last word carried so much meaning for the future.

—Chris Allen

Just loved this book from start to finish—the characters come alive and the reader becomes totally involved in their lives. A book that is impossible to put down, and can't wait for the sequel.

—Anna Odlin

BITTER-SWEET HARVEST

HARVEST

Chan Ling Yap

mc Marshall Cavendish
Editions

Published in 2011 by
Marshall Cavendish Editions
An imprint of Marshall Cavendish International (Asia) Pte Ltd
1 New Industrial Road, Singapore 536196

Other Marshall Cavendish Offices:
Marshall Cavendish Ltd. PO Box 65829, London EC1P INY, UK • Marshall Cavendish Corporation. 99 White Plains Road, Tarrytown NY 10591-9001, USA • Marshall Cavendish International (Thailand) Co Ltd. 253 Asoke, 12th Flr, Sukhumvit 21 Road, Klongtoey Nua, Wattana, Bangkok 10110, Thailand • Marshall Cavendish (Malaysia) Sdn Bhd, Times Subang, Lot 46, Subang Hi-Tech Industrial Park, Batu Tiga, 40000 Shah Alam, Selangor Darul Ehsan, Malaysia

Marshall Cavendish is a trademark of Times Publishing Limited

National Library Board Singapore Cataloguing in Publication Data
Yap, Chan Ling.
Bitter-sweet harvest / Chan Ling Yap. – Singapore : Marshall Cavendish Editions, 2011.
p. cm.
ISBN: 978-981-4351-68-3

1. Interracial marriage – Malaysia – Fiction. 2. Interfaith marriage – Malaysia – Fiction. I. Title.
PR6125
823.92 -- dc22   OCN748613740

Printed in Singapore by Fabulous Printers Pte Ltd

To my husband, Tony,
with love

Bitter-Sweet Harvest is the sequel to the novel *Sweet Offerings*.
The stories can be read in any order and are complete in themselves.

Acknowledgements

I would like to thank Kate Mazdon and Ruth Deraed
for their useful comments on my manuscript. I am also
grateful to Maxine Chow for her helpful observations
and careful reading of those parts of the book that
involve legal matters.

Thanks also go to my husband for his patience
and support throughout the writing of this book
and to Lee and Hsu Min, our children,
who have looked at the manuscript.

Prologue

On 13 May 1969, following the results of the general election in Malaysia, violence broke out between the country's ethnic groups. Many people were caught in the violence. The riots were confined mainly to the capital Kuala Lumpur in the state of Selangor, but tension spread throughout the country. The Government declared a state of emergency and imposed a curfew immediately throughout Selangor. Parliament was suspended, as was the press, and the National Operations Council was set up to run the country. Over a period of two months, order returned and while curfews continued, these too were gradually scaled back. In February 1971, Parliament was re-established and The Constitution (Amendment) Act of 1971 was passed.

Part One

Chapter 1

The rain splattered on to the windowpane, the huge drops creating rivulets of water that flowed down the glass. *Smack, ping,* the sound resonated in the hushed silence of the room. Outside, plumes of dense lilac bent low under the relentless force of the pelting rain and peonies folded their silken petals.

An Mei slid off the wide window ledge. She shivered, involuntarily pulling her cardigan tight around her. "I have to tell my brothers," she announced. "My parents are coming to Oxford. They haven't set a date, but it looks like it might be soon."

Hussein stood very still. A frown settled on his normally good-natured face. "Why are they coming to see you now just when you've finished your studies and we are planning to go back?" he asked.

"They are not coming for a visit." She paused letting her voice trail off, her gaze straying into the distance. Then she looked directly at Hussein, reproach in her eyes. "They have decided to leave Malaysia for good, to emigrate to where they believe they will have a better and more secure future. For them, England is a natural choice because my brothers and I are already here." She looked away again, unable to meet his eyes as she tried to quell her rising distress.

"But why?" he repeated. There was a catch in his voice; he could not conceal a mounting anxiety, a premonition of something bad to come. He sensed her change of mood.

"Read these letters," she said, thrusting a sheaf of papers into his hands. "They are disillusioned. All the senseless hate that people have for each other. We have been watching the race riots and their aftermath in Malaysia for over a week now on the TV. Somehow, seeing the turmoil on television allowed me to distance myself from the situation. Reading these letters, I can't do that anymore — I can feel my father's anger. I feel my parents' pain."

She turned to face him. Her eyes flashed, their soft amber brown turning to hard agate. The resignation and despair that had shown on her face earlier gave way to a resolute expression as she reflected on the situation now confronting her loved ones. "They have worked so hard to rebuild their business. My father was almost made bankrupt some years ago... And now this! His shops vandalised, torched!"

"And you? What will you do? Will you stay here in the UK?"

"Of course! Where else can I go? I will have no home to go back to in Kuala Lumpur."

"But what about us? You know I have to go back. My father will expect nothing less than my immediate return, especially in light of these new problems. I came here to be educated and groomed to go into politics, to take over from him. I *can not*," he stressed, "not return. But I do not want to go back without you. Come with me. Please?" he pleaded.

He took her in his arms. He could feel her body, unyielding, stiff. "You have to tell your parents about us."

"No! Not now. Not when they are already so troubled."

"Is that the only reason?"

She hesitated and cast her eyes down. "No. But you must know the other reasons."

He tightened his arms around her. "I don't. Tell me. I want to hear them from you."

"Because," she said, looking up at him, her eyes a limpid pool of pain, "because we are separated by race, religion, custom and practically everything I can think of, except a shared education in Oxford and a shared birth place. We are Malaysians. But you are Malay. I am Chinese. You are a Muslim, I am... I am a Christian!" Rolling up her sleeve, she thrust her pale arm against his bronzed dark brown skin. "Look at the difference in our colour! Need I say more?"

She pushed away from him. Holding herself at arm's length, she challenged him. "What about you? Have *you* told your parents about me?"

"No!" he admitted, embarrassed. "I have told my aunt though. I thought that it would be the best way for them to know. She would be able to choose an opportune moment to break it to them gently and to persuade them to accept the situation. After all, she is a good example of how an interracial marriage works. Aunty Jenny is Chinese and she married my uncle and adopted Islam as her religion. She is on our side. She is also your mum's friend! In fact, I would say, her best friend."

"So!" An Mei fell silent after that single exclamation. It hung like an accusation in the air. She was disappointed that

Hussein had not told his parents. Wasn't he the one who had said their parents should be told? She lowered her arms and walked back to the window. She did not tell Hussein that she too had confided in Jenny, hoping that she would tell her mum and find a way to break the news to her father, Ming Kong. She had placed such hopes on Jenny because it was she who introduced her to Hussein in the first place.

An Mei recalled her early days in Oxford. Jenny was in London, on one of her short trips to shop in the city while her husband tended to matters of state with the British authorities. Jenny had invited her to go up to London and join her for lunch at the Savoy Grill on the Strand. During the visit, while chatting with Jenny in her hotel room, An Mei had confided that she was thoroughly enjoying her studies but was finding it difficult to make new friends.

Bustling with energy, Jenny had said immediately, "*Sayang!* What a pity! You are too shy. People think you are proud and aloof!" Then, with the spontaneity her mother had told her was typical of Jenny, she had immediately picked up the phone. "I know just the person to look after you in Oxford. My nephew! Hussein. He is in Balliol studying politics. *Aiyah!* He is so handsome! Curly hair and eyes like Omar Sharif! Only make sure you don't fall for him. His parents have many plans for him-*lah!* He will be a big shot when he finishes his studies."

"An Mei, speak to me!" Hussein pleaded again, breaking her reverie. "I will tell my parents now if you want."

"No, not now," she replied almost in a whisper. "Not now. It's too late."

She moved further away from him as if to escape his all pervading presence. She did not wish to be persuaded. "I too have spoken to Aunty Jenny," she confessed. "The matter is not so simple. She's in London now on one of her trips. She is coming to Oxford tomorrow."

* * * * *

Sunlight streamed through the tall stately windows of the Randolph Hotel, turning the gilded frame of the massive mirror above the fireplace into a burnished ring of gold. They sat around a low Regency-style table in Jenny's hotel suite, the silence broken only by the tinkle of cups and saucers and the sound of starched linen brushing by as a maid moved busily around them. Finally, the last cup of tea was dispensed.

"Do you require anything else Madam?" the maid enquired solicitously, her voice hushed as if intimidated by the quiet of the room. She could sense her presence was unwelcome. The lady had consulted her wristwatch twice during the short time it had taken her to lay out the tea service.

"Fine, fine, thank you," Jenny replied with a quick smile and a nod. She was impatient to speak to her two charges.

"What have I done," she had chided herself over and over again on the journey from London to Oxford. "To bring these two children together and expect that nothing would come of it other than a platonic friendship. What was I thinking?"

Now, sitting with them, she was filled with remorse. Expectations and hope were painted on their faces. They looked to her to bring good news from their parents in Malaysia. She had none to give.

"Things are very bad back home." Her voice was solemn. "The streets are virtually empty, businesses have come to a standstill. The curfew, short though it may be, has made people jittery. Confined to their homes even for a short time, they have imagined the worse. We are plagued with endless rumours. On my way to the airport to catch the plane, I had to drive through the KL city centre. I could hardly believe my eyes at the damage. Such mindless destruction! Malays against Chinese, Chinese against Malays! Then the Indians! Unbelievable that people can live in peace and harmony one day, and then the next descend into such hatred and mistrust. I just cannot believe it," she repeated. "*Bagaimana*? How did it happen? We don't have the racial conflict that you have in England. The calling of names, the bullying in the streets, the aggression ... yet ..." Her voice trailed off.

"What does it mean for us?" asked Hussein. He did not wish to hear any more about the violence. He had followed every detail and discussed every scenario with friends and fellow students. He had no doubt that these were matters that would involve him on his return home. At that moment, however, he was keen only to know where he stood with An Mei and his parents.

"This is not a good time to tell your parents." Jenny shook her head vehemently to emphasise her words. "Not even, perhaps, a good time to walk together in the streets in Malaysia."

"Father has decided that I should return to Malaysia and I had hoped that An Mei would come back with me."

"No! That would not be a good idea. Her family is moving here to England. She should stay and wait for their arrival. She cannot abandon her family, just as you cannot abandon yours. We have duties to perform." She looked away, not wishing to catch the eye of An Mei, not wanting her to guess that these were the words An Mei's mother, Mei Yin, had said to her.

An Mei, unknowing, listened silently, perplexed by Jenny's reaction. She had expected her to provide more hope for their plight.

"What about you? Can you walk in the streets with uncle?" challenged Hussein. He, too, had not expected such an answer from Jenny. He was disappointed and felt cheated.

"I don't *walk* out with him," Jenny retorted in exasperation. "In fact, if you want to know, I hardly go anywhere public or important with your uncle, even now after years of marriage. We move within a circle of friends that accept me. I dress Malay-style and I speak Malay. I have become a Muslim and I toe the line." She felt a surge of anger, anger that she had been placed in a position where she felt forced to reveal her feelings and long curbed resentment of her own situation; an anger that made her turn suddenly to lash out at An Mei. "Do you know that you have to become a Muslim, An Mei, if you want to marry Hussein? That is, if his parents even agree. Do you know what becoming a Muslim entails? Do you know that you have to be circumcised?"

An Mei blinked and she shook her head. It was not something she had given much thought to during the months she had been with Hussein. She had managed to persuade herself that it was an ordeal she could avoid somehow.

"From what I gather, Hussein's parents are not in favour of him marrying anyone other than someone from an important Malay family who would help his political career, and certainly not a Chinese girl. Don't keep comparing your situation with mine, Hussein. It is a different era and your uncle had only himself to answer to. He had no living parents. Even then, his decision to marry me cost him and it took years for his friends to accept me. You, Hussein, can you say that you answer only to yourself? You, the only son and heir?!"

In response, Hussein took An Mei in his arms. He placed his lips close to her ears. She felt his warm breath, compelling and insistent. "Don't listen to her," he whispered. "She is only trying to frighten you. Circumcision in Malaysia is symbolic, just a tiny prick to release blood. See, does she look as though she has suffered any mutilation? In any case, we can get around it. Trust me."

* * * * *

Jenny sat in the room long after An Mei and Hussein had left. The fire crackled casting a warm glow. She sank deeper into her armchair. She was aghast that she had revealed all the resentment she subconsciously harboured. It had escaped out of her like pent-up foam from a freshly opened can of beer. Her outward persona was always one of a confident, carefree and satisfied woman. She was ashamed of her bluntness and lack of tact, but she had promised Mei Yin she would put an end to An Mei's hope that things would somehow work out between Hussein and her. Jenny picked up the phone. She dialled. "Operator," she said, "Kuala Lumpur please. Telephone number..."

The minutes passed. She looked at the clock impatiently. A click sounded at the other end. A faint voice asked hesitantly. "Yes! Who is it?"

"Mei Yin? Is that you? I have spoken to An Mei. I have told her to stay in Oxford and await your arrival. And I think I have said enough to convince her."

Chapter 2

An Mei paced the floor. Stuffing her hands into the pockets of her trousers, she stared guiltily at the flight indicator board. "Any minute now," she mumbled to herself, "they should be at the arrival hall." She looked around to check that she was stationed in a spot where they would be able to see her easily, close by the neon-lit sign for the meeting point. She had been biting her fingernails and they were raw and tingling. How was she going to greet her parents with these hands, she thought to herself. It was an old habit, a habit that grew out of those very troubled times when her parents were separated. She sighed. At least, she thought, they were all back together again as one big happy family. Could she dare risk doing anything that might cause the family to split apart again? An earlier short conversation on the phone with her brother, Wei Han, had given her little cause for comfort. "You must not think only about yourself in these very troubled times, not when father has lost so much of his business," he had said. Accusing her of being selfish, he had slammed down the phone but not before saying that he would be coming to Oxford as soon as he could get permission from his professor. Now pacing back and forth with growing anxiety, An Mei acknowledged that she had been selfish. How could she have been so thoughtless to even consider loading them with another worry?

At that moment, a flight announcement boomed out. Groups of people began to filter through the barrier. She felt a sudden crush of bodies around her as people struggled to get the best view of the exiting passengers. Some broke free to rush forward, arms flung out in embrace; others were more reticent in their reception. Where were they, she wondered anxiously She suddenly felt a rush of longing and love. She could not contain her excitement. She had not seen her parents for nearly a year, not since last summer.

"An Mei!"

She turned towards the source of the voice. "Aunt Nelly," she broke into a run. "Oh Aunt Nelly, how are you?" she asked in Cantonese. She embraced the little rotund lady dressed in a quilted jacket with a Mandarin collar so vigorously that she knocked her spectacles askew. She remembered the jacket. A 'Mao Tse Tung' jacket, her aunt had claimed when she bought it back from Hong Kong some years ago. "Very fashionable!" But she had not remembered her aunt as being so short.

"Fine, fine. I came through first," she responded in Cantonese, her spoken English being rather poor. Your mother and father will be here shortly. They had to wait for the luggage. I left them to it. I'm no use with bags, too old and too weak to even try," she said chuckling. Wrapping An Mei's arms around her waist, she continued, "And, I want a word with you first. Your mum asked me." She held on to An Mei. "Don't talk to your father about Hussein. Jenny told us. Just don't. We'll work something out. We, your mum and I, would like to meet him and then we'll talk."

Even as she said these words, Nelly was not sure what course of action might be possible. What could she say? Ming Kong had been distraught when he found his stores vandalised and torched. She felt that nothing would ever persuade him to let his daughter marry a Malay man. "Things will never be the same after May the Thirteenth," he had said. "I'll not trust them again. I thought they were my friends. I worked with them!"

"But Aunt Nelly," An Mei began to protest.

"Promise me. Not a word until we have sorted things out," admonished Nelly. They saw Mei Yin and Ming Kong coming towards them, pushing a trolley piled high with suitcases.

"Here they are. Remember what I had just said. Shhh," she added for caution.

An Mei broke free from Nelly and ran to her parents, all thoughts of Hussein momentarily wiped from her mind.

*****

Mei Yin stepped eagerly into the hallway. A steep, narrow, carpeted stairway led up to the two floors above. She inhaled deeply the potpourri of scents, vanilla and rose vying with the unmistakable whiff of new paint. "So delightfully cool," she said. "The air feels fresh. Everything feels fresh, even the smell of paint." She followed the weak ray of sunlight that had seeped through to the hallway from the door on the right, and entered the living room. "I like it," she exclaimed, her eyes wide, taking in the bare wooden floor and the white-washed walls of the long narrow room.

Relief showed on An Mei's face. "I know it is small, but Mum, you did say to find something that was... that is inexpensive. This is a Victorian terrace cottage. They are rather long and narrow. But it is well located. We can walk into Oxford within minutes. The house backs on to a playing field and beyond that, is the river. There is a wonderful river-side walk that takes you through a park."

Mei Yin turned to look at An Mei, her eyes lingering with affection on her daughter. "Yes, dear girl I like it and very much so. Don't apologise. There is no need. It is certainly wonderful to be able to move into a house so quickly and certainly better than the small hotel we stayed at when we first arrived."

"I thought that you might not like the house. It was a mess before when it was let out to students, but the owner has renovated it completely. Just here," An Mei pointed to the middle of the room, "there was a wall. He had it taken down to make the room more spacious."

They did not notice that Ming Kong had followed them into the room. He looked around him, taking stock of the length and width of the room. "It will certainly do for the moment." He strode over to the bay windows that looked over the road and peeped out. The narrow road was lined on both sides with parked cars.

"It's not bad. Not bad at all. Good job An Mei," he said approvingly, ruffling her hair. "I know it was a tall order to ask you to find us accommodation in the time we gave you. Anyway, you have chosen well. Location is important when buying properties. And this is good: within walking distance to the town centre. Tightening our belts and economising again will not be a bad thing in our new situation. We have to start afresh once again."

An Mei slipped her arm around her father's waist and smiled, two dimples dipped and her lips parted.

"Good girl," said Nelly crowding into the room. She was proud of her charge and reached out her hand to stroke An Mei's face.

"Hey, I am twenty-four years old and have been here in the UK for over two years! Right now, I feel like a child again with everyone addressing me like I'm ten years old!" She felt a surge of affection for her parents and her aunt Nelly.

She moved to the front window and looked out. Not many people were around. A group of young mothers with pushchairs and prams had gathered to chat, taking up the whole of the narrow pavement. She reflected on the hushed conversation she'd had in the hotel with her mother and aunt just after their arrival. A shadow fell across her face and tears glistened in the corner of her eyes. Quickly she dabbed them away. She felt her mother's hands on her shoulder and she leaned back towards her, luxuriating in the comforting warmth of her mother's arms. "I'm alright," she said. "Come, I'll show you the rest of the house."

* * * * *

Mei Yin ducked and bent low to avoid hitting her head on the low doorway that led into the converted roof space. Once in the room she straightened up. The room stretched from the front of the house to the back. The ceiling sloped down at one end. Windows flanked both ends of the room, filling it with light. "We can probably make this into a bedroom with a study area at the far end. The three larger rooms in the middle floor below will be the bedrooms. The fourth is just a box room, so it could probably be made into a storeroom or a small office. What do you think?" She looked at her husband, noting the puffiness round his tired eyes. She wished she could inject some enthusiasm into him.

Ming Kong nodded absent-mindedly to Mei Yin's ideas for the house. He was engrossed in his own plans of how to start anew in England. His mind twirled and turned over the meeting schedules already lined up with his business associates.

"Fine, fine. I'll leave it to you." He walked out of the room and headed to the stairway. A flurry of footsteps caught his attention. He caught a glimpse of the fast retreating back of An Mei. The bathroom door slammed behind her. Then the hurried, urgent sound of bolts drawn tight.

"Hmm! Must have eaten something bad!" He hesitated and then called out. "Are you okay?"

"Yes, yes", came a muffled reply.

Ming Kong nodded and made his way down the stairs.

Inside the bathroom, An Mei sat on the side of the bath. She listened intently to her father's receding footsteps. She had received an urgent message while her mother and father were touring the house. A young boy, no older than eight years old, had rung the doorbell, checked who she was and then pushed a paper message rolled up in a ball into her hands before rushing away. Now, sitting on the bath, she unrolled the dirty piece of paper. "Meet me at noon tomorrow at The Bear," it said.

* * * * *

She stepped into The Bear. A group of students were huddled in a corner, engaged in serious conversation, their faces animated by the force of their arguments. Almost all the tables in the pub were filled. Young couples, old men, shoppers and office workers — with drinks in hand — were seated at the scatter of wooden tables and trestles that gave it an almost rustic charm. Cigarette smoke filled the air; the odour mingled with the stale smell of fermented hops and malted barley.

An Mei remembered what her friend, Casey, had said when she first brought her, together with Hussein, to the pub. "This is one of the oldest pubs in Oxford. Put your nose to the table and you can smell the years of ingrained alcohol. Have you had beer before?" immediately thrusting a foaming mug at An Mei. "You have to practise." An Mei smiled recalling her failure to like beer and her lack of tolerance to it. "You are red as a boiled lobster," Hussein had said rescuing her from her beer drinking ordeal and drinking it all in one gulp.

Someone tapped her on the shoulder. She started, flustered and on edge.

"It's me. I am sorry I'm late. Let's go and sit there over in the corner where we can talk," Hussein said, ushering her towards a round corner table set at the far side of the fireplace.

"I don't have much time," An Mei said. She spoke rapidly, her words spilling out of her. "They are unpacking and arranging the house. I came out to get some food for lunch. Aunt Nelly is with me, but she has gone ahead to the Chinese takeaway at the corner. I hope she'll be there for some time. She might, because she misses home and speaking Chinese; so she will most likely take the chance to chat, but we need to be quick."

"Slow down, slow down," he said. "Take a deep breath." He waited as she tried to calm herself and to catch her breath.

"I came to tell you that it has been decided," said Hussein. "I have just a week left before I take the BOAC flight to Kuala

Lumpur and then home to Kemun. I have bought an open ticket for you. Take it."

A lock of hair fell over his eyes and he pushed it back impatiently. His ponytail swished as he turned abruptly to look behind before he urgently drew his chair closer to her. "Please come. I'll look after you. I will talk to my parents and persuade them. It cannot be as bad as Jenny says. My parents have never refused me anything."

He took her hand and continued, "This fight between the Chinese and Malays is a temporary madness, stirred-up by unscrupulous politicians. It will not last and things will be as before. There will be peace, prosperity and progress in the country. This is what I have studied so hard for. Remember how well we work together as a team? Remember the march in London against America's bombing of Vietnam and how much we achieved in sending someone over to Chicago for the first American national women's liberation conference? We'll work together again and, together, we'll re-build trust among the peoples of Malaysia."

His eyes shone with conviction and An Mei felt herself mesmerised by his words. She knew his charisma, his ability to hold a crowd, the eloquence he'd shown so often in debates, but these words were now for her and her alone.

"Maybe you are right," she replied. She was confused, as she switched between the horrors her parents and Nelly had described to her and the optimism of Hussein's words. "I just don't know how to break it to my father."

He placed his other hand over her tightly folded ones and turned them palm up. He unfolded the tightly clenched fingers and drew them up to his lips. He kissed the fingers one by one. An Mei could not bear to look up, to let him see her tears or to look into his eyes.

"Come back to Malaysia," he repeated. "I need you."

An Mei sat silent. Her mind was muddled with conflicting desires. She wanted to be with Hussein, but she also wanted to please her parents. She withdrew her hands and pressed her fingers to her temple. "Don't! I want to be with you, but I just do not know how it can be achieved."

"Would you like me to talk to your parents?"

"No!" Her voice rose in panic. "I'll speak to you later. I must rush now." She stood up, toppling the seat behind her. Someone caught it. She turned guiltily. "Aunt Nelly!"

"Is this Hussein?" Nelly asked in Cantonese, her eyes taking note of the slim, tall, dark young man before her and cringing at the sight of his ponytail and flared trousers. Jenny had described him well, she thought, A wry smile pinched the corners of her lips. He was definitely good-looking but Ming Kong would certainly object to the hairstyle.

"I've heard so much about you from An Mei," Hussein said as he held out his hand, hesitant and unsure of his reception.

Nelly grasped it and cautiously returned his smile. An Mei had told her about Hussein. She talked about him through the early hours of the night in the attic room they now shared. An Mei had always confided in her. There was little doubt that An Mei was distraught over the likelihood that she would have to give up her first love, the boyfriend who had become her soul mate over the past two years.

"My aunty," said An Mei for a lack of any thing to say. "She has looked after me since... since I was a baby."

"I know. You've told me many times," replied Hussein. "Please help us out," he appealed to Nelly.

Hussein could not read Nelly's face. He grabbed his jacket from the chair, rising, "I'll go now. I will be waiting for your answer." He leaned over to kiss An Mei and then checked himself. He knew that it would be considered an act of impropriety, an act of disrespect for elders, something just not done in Malaysia, and Nelly had only just come from Malaysia. He groaned in frustration as he made his way out of the pub. He realised that was how their future would be in Malaysia — the constant need to keep their feelings in check and not show them in public. Little had his father realised that in Oxford he would pick up western customs and ways that would not please him.

* * * * *

An Mei's face was a bright red. When Hussein leaned over, she had panicked and had turned her face away. Now walking home with Nelly, she noted the casual way in which couples linked hands and kissed on the streets. She glanced sidelong at her aunt, noting her surprise and disconcerted expression. She remembered her first kiss. She had exclaimed, "Not here! Someone will see us."

"And so?" Hussein had asked, his eyes twinkling with amazement. He gestured to a couple sat at a bench some paces away from them. "Look at what they are doing!"

"Universal campus behaviour," Casey her friend had commented as she showed An Mei around the University. "I know, it is not like this at the University of Malaya, but it does not mean that they are not doing it. Just not in public."

An Mei slowed her pace to match Nelly's and took from her the bag of carefully packed silver-foil containers, all marked in Chinese characters: *siew yok, tai har, boh choi,* roast pork, large prawns and spinach. "I'll have to remember to walk slower," she said, tucking her other arm around Nelly to give her a hug. "Will you help us?"

"*Aiyah!*" exclaimed Nelly. "*Tai see yew man-man seong.* Such big matters really need careful thinking," she said, tapping her head, "and I cannot think in the street. Anyway, I must consult with your mother. I've not had time to really talk to her."

Since last night, and especially after seeing the two of them together in the pub, Nelly had wanted to ask An Mei a question that she found difficult to phrase with delicacy. "An Mei," she said softly, slowing her steps until they were standing by the iron railings that skirted the botanical gardens. "Are you ... have you slept with Hussein?"

An Mei gulped, almost dropping the bag of food. Her knees buckled and she leant against the railings, the cold hard grills digging into her back. Her eyes clouded with fear and shame.

"*Chan hai cham-loh!* This is really bad! What would your father say? *Aiyah!*"

"Are you going to tell him?"

"No, no I cannot; I must not! He is already a broken man despite the brave front he puts on. His fortunes have gone through so much upheaval that it is wearing him out. No, I can only talk this over with your mother."

* * * * *

Dusk drew in, casting long murky shadows over the back of the house. Nelly made her way to the rear of the narrow garden, threading carefully around the unfamiliar plants and foliage that spilled over on to the path. A profusion of roses in full bloom, with big, almost cabbage-like petals, perfumed the cool night air. Mei Yin followed. She slid open the bolt and the door swung open, its rusty hinges creaking in protest. They stepped out on to the single track that separated the garden from the playing field beyond. Further on was the path that would lead them to the riverside. They had not been there before. The sky darkened perceptibly, enveloping them in darkness. Mei Yin's face was cast in doubt.

"Are you sure? I am not particularly keen to go for a walk at this time of the evening."

"No, I am not sure, but this was the only way I could explain why we are stepping out. We are not really going for a walk, just somewhere to talk. I thought that the playground with the swings and see-saws at the end of the path would be as good a place as any. It is far enough not to be in view of the house. I could not tell Ming Kong that we are going to a child's playground. I was surprised that he did not ask why we would want to walk along the river at this time of day. I had my answer ready though. I would have told him that we always took a stroll after dinner when we were at home, I mean in Kuala Lumpur, as it is the coolest part of the day. He is so distracted. I doubt that he has even noticed that it is not just getting cooler in the evenings here but really cold." She drew her heavy cardigan closely around her. "Imagine! Such a cold wind! If this is summer, I am not sure how I can survive the winter," Nelly complained as she huddled further into her cardigan.

"I like it. I don't mind the cold. You need to wear warmer clothes. A light cotton *samfoo* is just not warm enough in the evening if you are not used to this weather, even if you wear a cardigan over it," said Mei Yin. She tugged at Nelly's sleeve to cover her arms. "Let's sit on this bench."

Both women sat down, Mei Yin turned to look at Nelly. The flood of light from a nearby street lamp lit her face. Nelly saw the creases of worry on her forehead and the anxiety in her eyes.

"Should we help An Mei to go back to Malaysia with Hussein?" asked Nelly, mixing English and Cantonese in one breath.

Mei Yin opened her eyes wide with surprise. "Why the change? I thought we had decided that we should persuade her to stay on here with us."

"She pleaded with me. I was against it at first. Of course, I wanted her to stay here with us. After all, it would be the first time the whole family could be together again. The boys are still at school and university, but during the holidays they can come home. Also, having An Mei here with us would be such a help. We don't know the country and its ways. Ming Kong will find comfort in her presence. And, I thought that she could be weaned off Hussein. I assumed it to be puppy love. But, I am not sure now. You know," she stuttered. "I told you..."

"That she has slept with Hussein, you mean?" asked Mei Yin, indicating together with hand gestures to her ears that there were other people around and that they should stick to Cantonese. Three women with a pushchair sauntered passed. One stopped to light up a cigarette. She glanced at the two Chinese ladies, curious, and then turned away to resume her stroll with her friends, talking softly.

"*Aiyah! Chan hai mm gong tak chut.* I can't bring myself to say it out loud. Surely, it means she should, must marry Hussein?"

"Virginity might not be a big issue like it was in our days. I pray that it is not. Remember my wedding day? My mother-in-law insisted that I lie on white sheets and have them delivered to her for inspection after our nuptials so that she could be assured of my virginity. I hope, I am sure, it is not done like that in Europe." Mei Yin nodded vigorously to emphasise her conviction.

"I suppose we should not let it cloud our decisions," Nelly conceded. She let out a huge sigh. Then, her voice changed suddenly from one of resignation to one of indignation. She burst out, "I am angry, angry that he has taken advantage of her and I am so cross that she has done the very thing we warned her against; all the time I spent warning her of the danger of being alone here has gone to waste. For once in my life, I feel like giving her a good shake."

"Nelly, Nelly *fan do suk le*. The rice is cooked, there is little to be done. The thing that we should consider is if Hussein is the right person for her and whether they would be happy together."

"*Dim chee?* How can we tell? Relationships change. They look very much in love now, but it could be just *sun so-pah!* A new broom sweeps well! How can we tell?" Nelly repeated. "All I know is that although I am cross, my heart bleeds for An Mei. The poor girl is distraught. She is terrified that her father will find out."

"Then should we tell Ming Kong?" asked Mei Yin. "If we do, would you do it? He listens more to you than me." She blushed at her own cowardice; after all she was An Mei's mother.

"Me? No! I can't." Nelly stopped to consider. She pulled her cardigan even tighter around her like a protective cocoon. "But if we don't and we help her," she continued, "it would mean deceiving him. Perhaps I should go back with her. She will have to see for herself how things are in the country and may be then she would come to her senses."

Nelly's voice was now little more than a whisper. Mei Yin had to bend close to hear her. She placed an arm around Nelly's shoulder. The two women huddled together for comfort and warmth.

"We have to give her space to think and decide for herself," Nelly concluded. "If we force her to stay on in the UK, she'll resent it and she will be always hankering for what might have been. She has to make the decision herself. I remember how when we were young, everything was decided for us. We were told to swallow our bitterness. We cannot ask An Mei to do the same. She has an independent mind; she has been taught to think for herself. Just the other day, she told me that at her University, marks are not awarded for just regurgitating facts, but for expressing thoughts and opinions. Think! When were we ever asked for our views when we were young? If we force her, she might succumb to our pressures now because she loves us, but she will resent and might even hate us later."

"Yes, I agree," replied Mei Yin. She thought of her past and how she had to obey every single instruction given to her by her mother-in-law. She would not wish the same fate on her daughter. "But how will you convince Ming Kong to let you go with her? What justification can you offer him? I am sure he will want you to stay to help him set up his business. After all you are his right hand in business. And what if it backfires and she decides she'll remain with Hussein?"

"I don't know."

Both women fell silent. Night drew in and the shadows lengthened over the playground; the silence of the night was broken only by the distant sound of a barking dog.

* * * * *

"Casey?" An Mei grasped the phone tightly. She angled her body so that her back faced the street. The phone booth reeked of cigarette smoke. Graffiti adorned the glass panes. Outside the booth, people hurried by loaded with shopping bags. There were brown paper bags, green, yellow and red ones, each advertising the shop that had supplied them. Students on bicycles weaved their way through traffic and pedestrians. "Mayhem," Nelly had commented the other day when a young man pushed past her on a bike.

"Casey, I need your help. Would you cover for me? I am going to tell my parents that I have to meet up with you early this evening. I have to see Hussein. We have to work things out. It is his last day, he is leaving for Malaysia."

A pause followed. An Mei fidgeted, worried that Casey might refuse. "Please," she whispered urgently into the phone.

"Just this once," Casey replied. "Don't get me into trouble. Otherwise, I'll be in trouble with your mum. Remember your mother was my mum's best friend when they were children and I am supposed to be looking after you in Oxford. Not helping you to have secret trysts with your boyfriend."

"Thanks a million. Will you call me at home? That way, they will be more likely to be persuaded to let me go."

Casey laughed. "I didn't know that you were that scheming. All right. I know how it is. Even though I have been on my own here for so long, the minute my mother comes to visit, she thinks that she has to know my every move. So out of pity, I'll cover for you."

Chapter 3

"**W**here is she?" Ming Kong demanded. He pushed away the array of bowls and chopsticks that had been carefully laid out before him.

Mei Yin and Nelly sat silent. They stared at the clock on the wall. Its ticking seemed obscenely loud. The clock-hand edged slowly round the dial, but there was still no sign of An Mei. They looked at the dishes in front of them, dishes that they had prepared together, their first home-cooked meal in Oxford. During their first week they had eaten nothing except takeaways and hastily made sandwiches until finally Nelly complained. Clutching her tummy, she protested against the grease and the sweetness of the food. "Sweet and sour! Everything sweet and sour! Everything with mayonnaise! We have to have something simple. Let us have something steamed, *ching-ching*. We'll cook this evening. We will be able to now. We have almost completed the unpacking and cleaning." So she and Mei Yin had gone to the small Chinese grocery next to the Chinese restaurant in Hythe Bridge Street to stock up with *tofu, choy sam,* lotus roots, ginger and spices. Now the dishes of *tofu* and bowls of lotus root and spare ribs soup lay cold.

Nelly got up and gathered the bowls and crockery together. "Better get these out of the way," she said, stealing a look at Ming Kong's face. His expression alternated: sometimes thunderous, sometimes fearful. It was nearly ten o'clock!

"She probably forgot. She has not been out with her friends for the entire week. So maybe she is just catching up," Mei Yin consoled. Inside her, fear was brewing, a fear that was so strong she felt her stomach contracting into a tight ball. "It cannot be that An Mei has done something silly. I spoke to Casey myself," she whispered to Nelly as they both made their way into the kitchen with the various trays and dishes. "Should we call Casey and ask her again. I called earlier and asked to speak to An Mei. She said she had already left for home."

"You wait here. I'll pop out to the phone booth." Hastily, Nelly untied her apron, grabbed a jacket from the kitchen door and went out.

Mei Yin went back to the dinning room. Ming Kong was cradling his head in both hands, his elbows dug deeply into the felt lining of the tablecloth. He looked up, his eyes weary. "What is wrong with An Mei? She is not herself. Is she in trouble? She seems so out of sorts, so distant some times and so affectionate and tearful at other times."

Mei Yin busied herself at the sideboard. Cautiously, she ventured an explanation. "She might be anxious. She wants to find a job here now that she is not going back to Kuala Lumpur. She does not want to be dependent on us, especially since our economic circumstances are not what they were. She knows that her brothers still need to go to university and there are fees to be paid." She lifted her head to look at her husband.

His head was still buried in his hands. She prayed that Ming Kong would not ask any more questions. What she said was true up to a point. An Mei had initially appeared reconciled to staying in Oxford, but she had not been herself since the day Nelly met Hussein.

* * * * *

An Mei stood to one side. She watched Hussein make his way to the check-in desk, wheeling his luggage on the red carpet for first-class passengers. They had been talking for hours and still nothing had been resolved. She had argued her case fervently. After days of talking with Nelly and her mother, she had reeled off all the reasons why they could not, and should not, be together. Now, close to the final moment of his departure, she was filled with doubt. "Have I made the right decision? How can I live without him?" The pain in her heart felt like a physical wound. She stared at his back. She shrugged deeper into her anorak and dipped her hands into its pockets. With a shock, she came into contact with a small booklet. Her passport! The passport that she had grabbed unthinkingly before she left home from the drawer at Hussein's persistent urging to bring it with her. Her fingers tingled as they closed over it.

Hussein turned and looked at her beseechingly. "Come with me," he mouthed silently. Then, almost half running, he reached her and gathered her in his arms. "Come with me, now," he repeated urgently. She felt her resolve — to break-up with Hussein and remain with her parents — crumble. Without thinking she nodded vigorously. He caught hold of her hand and ran back to the check-in desk ignoring the indignant remarks of other passengers. "Two seats," he said retrieving the open ticket that An Mei had so firmly pushed back into his possession two hours ago. "Two seats," he repeated, his voice triumphant with joy.

* * * * *

The doorbell rang. It was still early in the morning, just 8 o'clock, but the summer sun was already a bright ball of light. Mei Yin rushed to the door. She opened it. A woman with a girl of An Mei's age stood outside.

"Mei Yin?" the lady asked hesitantly. "Mei Yin? Is it really you? I am Siew Lin, Casey's mother. Don't you recognise me?"

Mei Yin did not answer. Her face crumpled in disappointment. She had hoped and prayed that by some miraculous intervention it would be An Mei coming back.

"I know we have not met each other since we were children, but we have been in touch these past few years by phone and through letters and photographs. Can't you recognise my voice at least?" she asked the distraught Mei Yin.

Mei Yin nodded. Her eyes were so swollen that she could hardly see, her voice, so hoarse from crying that she could hardly speak. It was near midnight when she had received a call from An Mei telling her that she was boarding the plane for Kuala Lumpur with Hussein. Then a muffled sob and the line went dead. She had stood for what seemed like an eternity holding the phone until Nelly wrested it from her and made her repeat what had been said. Ming Kong had stood at the dining room doorway, hands clutching his hair, his face grey with anguish as he struggled to understand just who Hussein was. Finally he had turned and headed upstairs shouting,

"I have no daughter. Don't mention her name in this house again." The house reverberated as he slammed the bedroom door shut.

Mei Yin moved to one side and motioned Siew Lin to come in.

"I am so sorry," Siew Lin said embracing Mei Yin in a tight hug. She felt the tension in Mei Yin's body; every muscle seemed to have contracted into a tight knot.

"Casey told me of her part in this terrible, terrible..." Words failed Siew Lin as she tried to calm a sudden trembling in Mei Yin's body.

"I have tried squeezing every word out of Casey when she called me from college last night. I brought her with me to apologise to you. What a shame to see you after all these years in such circumstances. I only flew back yesterday and I have come to see you as soon as I could."

Nelly came forward. She could see the distress on the lady's face. "Mei Yin, you should ask your friend to come in and not just keep her standing here," she said softly.

"Sorry, sorry to make you stand in the hallway," said Mei Yin. "Please come in."

"Yes, do come in. Don't stand in the hallway," reiterated Nelly. She had followed Mei Yin to the door in response to the sound of the doorbell. She too had hoped against all odds that it would be An Mei. She still could not believe that An Mei had left. Hiding her disappointment, she continued, "Come into the kitchen. I'll make you a cup of tea."

"Aunty Mei Yin, I am truly sorry," said a contrite Casey. Anxious to make amends, she followed the ladies into the kitchen. "I did not know, when I covered up for An Mei, that she was going to run away with Hussein. She told me that she only wanted some time with him to talk before he left. It did not seem so unreasonable. Please forgive me."

"How could you do such a thing!" scolded Siew Lin. "You were supposed to look after An Mei, not lie for her."

Turning to Mei Yin and Nelly, Siew Lin asked, "So what will you do?"

"What can we do? Ming Kong won't let us get in touch with her. He has disowned her. We don't even have an address or telephone number to contact. We don't know much about Hussein. Nelly met him just once."

"Where is Ming Kong?"

"Upstairs. He will be down any minute."

"I am already down," said Ming Kong coming into the kitchen. He too had come down in response to the doorbell and the murmured conversation that followed it. "And you? Who are you?"

"I'm Siew Lin, Casey's mother."

His face grew red, suffused with blood. Two deep ruts appeared in the area between his eyebrows, pushing the eyebrows together. "So what do you and your daughter have to say? I want to have nothing to do with either of you. If she," he said pointing at Casey, "had not lied, we would not be in this dreadful predicament." He found it difficult to bring himself to say An Mei's name. He could not forgive his daughter for leaving without so much as a word when the family was already dealing with so many problems. "*Mo sum kon*. Heartless wretch! And all for a Malay boy! The very people we are fleeing from!"

Mei Yin went to her husband; she laid a hand on his arm. She could feel the rage coursing through the muscles of his arms.

"Please Ming Kong, Siew Lin was my very best friend when I was a child. Her mother sent me to school. It was her mother who introduced me to your family. Had it not been for her, I would certainly not have married you. So for that at least, please hear what she has to say."

"Yes, yes! Do not come to hasty conclusions. We are all upset and tend to say things we do not mean and will regret afterwards," cautioned Nelly. "I'll get you a cup of tea, why don't you sit down," she said ushering him towards the kitchen table before rushing to pour out a cup of green tea for him.

Mei Yin sat down next to Ming Kong. She took his hands in hers, caressing them gently until they relaxed their tight hold. "Remember, when we were young, we too were rash in our actions. The most important thing now is for us to help An Mei, to make sure she knows that she can come back. What would cutting her off from the family achieve? Nothing! Not for her, not for us. Please reconsider. Jenny will be coming soon. Let's see what she can do. At least through her, we'll be able to trace An Mei's whereabouts."

Ming Kong looked at Mei Yin and then Nelly. Nelly nodded encouragingly. "We all make mistakes. It is still not too late to persuade her to return."

Chapter 4

An Mei stepped out of the plane into the hot blazing sun. The heat hit her with a ferocity that she had almost forgotten. She stood still for a moment on top of the mobile stairway before turning quickly to Hussein. He smiled at her, nodding at the same time towards a small group of people gathered on the sizzling tarmac. "They are here to meet me. Let's not keep them waiting."

She was nervous. She ran her fingers through her hair to bring some order to the strands that flew across her face. "Are you sure it will be alright for you to introduce me to your parents without notice? I must look terrible. I feel so grubby after 16 hours on the plane," she said. Her eyes pleaded with him. Hours of crying on the plane and sleeplessness had left them red and swollen. "Can't we wait? I can make my way like the rest of the passengers to the airport terminal and meet you later."

"Nonsense! You look fine. They will be delighted when I introduce you to them. Come!" He felt his smile tighten. Jenny's words of warning flashed through his mind.

They made their way down the stairway and walked towards the group of brightly clad men and women gathered on the red carpet. Their garments of exotic silks, colourful batiks and silver woven sarongs competed in the blazing sunlight. Hussein strode quickly forward to embrace a plump middle-aged woman dressed in a purple silk *baju kurong*, a sarong and sheath top that reached below the knee, and nearly knocked away the matching umbrella that a turbaned guard was holding to protect her from the sun.

"*Emak-mak!* Mother!" Hussein said lapsing into his childhood endearment for his mother. He bowed low before embracing her, gathering her into his arms in a tight bear hug.

"*Adoi! Jaga!* Careful! *Anak saya!* My child! It is so lovely to have you back! How are you? Come! Come! Let's get out of the sun. The car is waiting. Your cousins are here."

Faridah looked at her son, her face flushed with pride. "Also I would like, in particular, for you to meet Shalimar, *Tengku* Shalimar, to be precise. You've not seen her since she was twelve."

She rushed on oblivious to Hussein's discomfort and sidelong glances at the Chinese girl who was standing just behind him.

"Don't you think that she has grown up to be a beautiful young woman?" she chuckled, pointing to a young girl standing near them. "We'll sit at the back of the Mercedes and the rest can use the other cars." Faridah beamed, her hands waving expansively, flashing the diamonds and sapphires on her wrists and fingers. "Your father is waiting. *Mari!* Come! Come with us Shalimar."

"Wait mother. I'd like to introduce An Mei. We were at Oxford together."

Awkwardly, An Mei stepped forward. She did not know what to say. Should she shake her hand? She had totally forgotten to ask Hussein how she should address his mother. All she could think of during the plane journey was her parents' pain, her guilt at the way she had left, and her own heartache. She knew vaguely that there were complex titles and customs to observe when greeting someone of importance in Malay society. So An Mei stood silent, head bowed, her dress crumpled, her hair wind-blown and her face tear-stained, wishing with all her heart that she had followed her instincts and gone with the other passengers to the air terminal.

Faridah took one glance at An Mei and her face fell. Her eyes narrowed to bullet points. "*Siapa ini?* Who is this?" she snapped, wondering what her son could see in this chit of a girl! She glared at An Mei; then her eyes swept away almost instantaneously without acknowledging her presence. "Come, let's go," she said to Hussein, her voice cutting. "If she is coming with us, she can go in one of the other cars."

An Mei turned and made a dash for the terminal. Hussein ran after her. "Wait, wait! Come back!" He ran until he overtook her and ignoring the gasps and titters from the people gathered on the red carpet, he took hold of An Mei's hands and marched her firmly back to his mother. "She is coming back with me." Faridah stared at her son, her eyes unbelieving, shocked. She knew better than to argue in public. She did not wish to give people any more cause for tittle-tattle. She would deal with her son's lack of manners and respect for his elders later. Not now in front of the girl. Without a word she took Shalimar's hand and headed for the Mercedes.

* * * * *

"I'm sorry," Hussein whispered as he held on to An Mei's cold hands. She was shivering in the blast of cold air from the air conditioner of the car. "It's my fault. You were right. I should not have subjected you to this. It has also not been fair to my mother. I should have prepared her."

"So what do we do now? Where will I go? I cannot go back with you to your parents' place, not like this. They will not like it, despite what you say," said An Mei in a voice so soft that he had to bend low to hear her. She kept seeing the contempt on Faridah's face and the vision of Shalimar's large soft eyes and heart-shaped face, shrouded in a *hijab*, a headscarf, of luminous silk.

"Just give me a chance to sort this out. You can stay in the guesthouse for the time being. I'll get the caretaker to prepare the room. I'll come to you later this evening after speaking to my parents. Please?"

* * * * *

Hussein stood before his parents. He had been talking for two hours: explaining his relationship with An Mei; his wish that they would accept her as his bride; his love for her; who she was and her family background. But it was all to no avail. Their minds were already made up. They wanted nothing to do with An Mei. They warned him of the precariousness of his future.

"It is simple. Do as you wish and you will break our hearts," said Faridah. Her voice grew louder and coarser as her vehemence grew. She glared at her son. "We cannot, and *will not*, accept her into our family. Think of your future. She will become your baggage. Such a marriage just leads to bad publicity. And what if you have children? What will they be?

We have great plans for you. You had great plans for yourself. Remember? So what will become of them? Think!" She turned to her husband for support. "Rahim, *Chakap dengan–nya*! Rahim, speak to him!"

"Yes," said his father, his voice reasonable and modulated but firm. "The world is within your grasp if you will only put this madness aside. Doors to important positions will open and it will be just a matter of time before you are leader of the party or at least as near to the top as you can possibly be at your age. A few years further down the line I guarantee you will be at the top. The party needs young blood, intelligent and educated young blood."

Rahim was desperate that Hussein should not let him down. His eyes bored into his son's, holding his gaze. "Marry her and I can guarantee you will be as good as lost to us."

Hussein looked beseechingly from one parent to the other. "Mother! Please..."

Faridah brought both hands to her face and cried-out, "*Adoi! Hati sakit!* You wound my heart!" She slammed her clenched fist on her chest. "You cause us such pain and all because of a Chinese girl. Have you lost your senses? Marrying a Chinese girl would not be good at the best of times, but at this particular moment, it will be suicidal as far as your career is concerned."

"You are wrong. It will demonstrate our impartiality and pave the way for a harmonious relationship between the races," Hussein replied. He dropped his voice. He knew the futility of his argument. He could see the grim determination in their faces. His mother's chin, square and resolute, was quivering with rage and ready for battle. His father, face thrust forward, glowered at him, all semblance of moderation gone.

Hussein dropped his voice. "At least let her stay here. She has nowhere to go."

Faridah exchanged a look with her husband. Hussein could not fathom what passed between them although he saw his father nod in agreement.

"Alright," his mother conceded with a great show of reluctance, "she can stay in the guest house here in Kuala Lumpur. But tomorrow, you are coming home with us to the east coast, to Kemun. Don't say no. The whole family, aunts, uncles, cousins, nephews, nieces, are all waiting. A feast has been prepared to welcome you back. You have a duty to the family. This is what we want in return for letting her stay here.

Chapter 5

An Mei made her way to the French window. She slid the glass panel open and stepped outside onto a terrace. Within minutes, the panel was covered with condensation and she closed it hastily behind her. She padded barefoot to the rattan armchair and sat down. Not more than ten steps away from her was a pond. Groves of bamboos cast a dappled shade over the glistening water. Their sturdy straight stems sprouting straight out of the white pearly pebbles strewn around the edge of the pond. Brightly coloured iridescent dragonflies flitted hither and thither, their wings lightly skimming the water surface.

She looked at her watch and then at the garden. "A picture of peace and tranquillity," she whispered to herself, "but I can draw no peace from it. Where is he? When is he coming back?"

It had been five days since she was taken to the guesthouse and four days since she had last seen Hussein. He told her he would be back soon. "We'll talk then," he had promised. But each day dragged by and still there was no word. Where was he, she fretted, drawing her loose shift dress tightly about her body. The steady drone of insects and the unaccustomed heat made her feel light-headed. She was cut off from everybody. She had no money to go anywhere. Food and garments magically appear in her quarters, brought in by silent unobtrusive servants who, while taking good care of her, said little in reply to her questions. Her request for access to a phone fell on deaf ears. She had tried to look out of the fenced compound, peeping through the gaps in the panelling. She succeeded to some extent. The streets were empty and recalling the car journey here and the devastation of the recent riots, she did not dare venture out. She longed for the hustle and bustle of Oxford, the noise, the smell, even the rain and dampness. "Anywhere but this utter stillness and loneliness."

"You can have all of it," a voice said. She turned. A man was standing behind her. He bowed, his traditional headgear, an egg-shaped dark velvet cylindrical hat, the *songkok*, in hand. "*Selamat petang*, good evening," he said. "I am *Tengku* Ahmad and I bring you word from Hussein. May I?" he asked pointing to the empty rattan chair. Without waiting for a reply, he sat down and carefully crossed his leg, arranging the short, beautiful silver woven sarong that he wore over his pale green loose trousers.

An Mei, alarmed and taken aback by the unexpected intrusion and the stranger's familiarity, stared at him.

"I have just come from the mosque," he said, "hence my clothes. Don't you remember our Malaysian dress code anymore?" he asked, a sardonic smile on his lips. "Two years away from your motherland and you forget! *Bagaimana*? How could you?" His voice was teasing, but the accusation behind it was clear.

"Who are you?"

"I am, as I said before, *Tengku* Ahmad. Hussein's mother, *Datin* Faridah, asked me to see you."

"Not Hussein? I thought you just said you brought word from Hussein. Where is he? When will he be back?"

"One thing at a time, *perlahan-perlahan*! Slowly! Can we pursue this conversation in *Bahasa* Malay or have you also forgotten your national language?" His tone of voice was unmistakeably sarcastic.

An Mei, stung by his tone, shrank in her seat. His presence, manners, and his undisguised insolence both upset her and made her feel uncomfortable. "Of course I remember," she said. Her guard was up. She recalled Jenny's recounting of the tension in the country. "I just lack practice. We studied Malay in school but didn't get much opportunity to use it outside the classroom. And, I have been away in England for quite a while."

"Well," he drawled, "it just shows the kind of people you have been mixing with. Obviously not your fellow Malaysians and certainly not those proud to speak Malay."

"Hussein always spoke to me in English," she countered.

Ahmad frowned and his eyes flickered over her, sizing her up, as though seeing her anew. Checkmate, he thought, he had to be careful. She was no walkover.

He leaned forward and with his finger drew a drop of condensation from the side of the glass onto the table, painting a circle on the glass top. "Yes, Hussein," he murmured gravely, "that is why I am here now to tell you about Hussein. He is at this very moment, preparing to get engaged. His fiancée to be, as you might have guessed by now, is Shalimar, my sister. Their marriage is something both our families have been looking forward to since they were children. Now that my parents have both passed away, it is my duty to oversee this union. A marriage between them would be a marriage made in heaven. It will put a seal on all our ambitions and plans."

"No! That cannot be!" exclaimed An Mei. Her face was bleached white and her lips, bloodless. She felt her heart lurch and her whole being plunge into an overwhelming sense of despair. "Let me talk to him. Please let me have a phone. I would like to hear it from Hussein himself."

"It would be absolutely futile to talk to him. It has all been decided. I am just the messenger. I can offer you this much as a gesture of goodwill. I can give you a one-way air ticket to London to join your family and provide you with transport to the airport. And," he said taking out a wad of notes, "money to see you through. That is all. We do not wish to see you here again. Your insistence to be part of Hussein's life will only destroy him. Surely this is not what you want?"

"Destroy Hussein? Me?" she asked, springing to her feet. Incredulous, her eyes, dulled with despair only a moment ago, now blazed with fury at the injustice of his accusation. "All Hussein and I have talked about is how I would work with him to achieve his goals."

"Don't be naïve!" he exclaimed, standing up, not wishing to lose the advantage that he thought he had over her.

"I had expected some opposition from Hussein's parents, but Hussein had told me that it would be only a matter of time before he would win them over."

Ahmad snorted. "Only some opposition? Hah! I leave you to mull over the offer. When you come to your senses, tell one of the servants to contact me." He turned to leave. An Mei caught hold of his sleeve.

"Please let me speak to Hussein."

He shrugged her hand off. "*Tak malu!* Shameless! Chasing after him, throwing yourself at him and expecting me to help you. Who do you think I am?" He snorted again before striding off.

Left alone, An Mei crumpled to the floor. She felt ashamed, ashamed that she had let herself, her parents and her aunt down. She did not know how she could ever bridge the gulf created between herself and her family. She was in no doubt that she had done wrong. She had gone against the filial piety that her parents expected of her. She had convinced herself that it was for love; because Hussein loved her. Now even this seemed doubtful. Why hadn't Hussein been in touch? She was not sure if there was any truth in what Ahmad had relayed, but she felt humiliated by his taunts. Was she really throwing herself at Hussein? she wondered.

Chapter 6

In Kemun, Hussein paced up and down the length of the drawing room in his parents' palatial home. He ignored their entreaties to sit down and relax. His parents were sitting on a settee with other members of the family around them. He looked at their colourful clothes, their opulence and lavish styles; he saw them talk and laugh without a care and felt completely apart from them. He had rushed back from Oxford in response to his father's plea and the crisis his homeland was facing. But it appeared that the crisis did not bother his family. He had forgotten just how many family members he had. He felt stifled by their presence — their eyes following his every movement. The only respite came from speaking to his friend Ahmad. Yet even there he was disappointed. Ahmad had explained to him gently, but in no uncertain terms, that his parents would cut him off if he continued his relationship with An Mei in the brash manner he had done so far. He would not get a penny and would have to make his own way in the world. He had answered defiantly that this was precisely his intention and what his education had prepared him for, but Ahmad had brusquely pushed his bravado aside.

"How naïve you are and how out of touch. You might have the qualifications and of course that helps, but no doors will be open to you without the support of your parents. This is how things work here. Who would dare risk their displeasure by taking you on?" Ahmad placed his arm around Hussein's shoulders and, in a conciliatory tone, continued. "Let me speak to An Mei. Don't try to contact her. It will only upset your parents. Trust me. I will see what I can do."

"Can you tell her what is happening here? I have been trying to call her every day, but no one seems to know where she is. She must be frightened." Hussein was tortured by his inability to keep the promise he had made to her. "I don't want her to think that I have abandoned her. I wanted to go back to Kuala Lumpur but have been thwarted each time. You know my parents have taken away all my cash and even my cheque book?" When he protested, they said he had no need of them because everything was provided for. And at that point, as never before in his life, he understood the true meaning of independence. To be independent, you needed to have money and he had none. All that he possessed, or thought was his, had been taken away in a single swoop. He felt trapped and completely powerless.

Ahmad laughed. "Yes! Of course! Don't worry. Just go and sit over there with your parents and try to win their favour. Whatever you might think, they want the best for you. I'll see how I can bring both of you together without upsetting them."

Hussein looked over to where the party was congregated and caught his mother's eyes.

"Come, come over and join us. We are planning what to do tomorrow. Tomorrow is Shalimar's nineteenth birthday." Faridah patted the seat next to her. "Sit by me, my son. And stop looking so glum. *Apa ini?* What is this? I have had enough of your requests to leave us for Kuala Lumpur. We have only just arrived back home and you want to go away."

With the other hand, she waved to Shalimar to come forward. "Sit here, next to me." Taking Hussein's hand from one side of her and Shalimar's hand on the other side of her, she joined them together holding both on her lap. "We shall have to make plans for your engagement soon. Give it some thought. Make use of the time to get to know each other. Understand?" she said looking from one to the other.

Shalimar, her eyes firmly cast down, refused to look up. Her headscarf slipped forward, shielding her from view. Hussein looked desperately for Ahmad. He struggled to remove the hand that his mother had placed firmly on Shalimar's.

"*Ibu, jangan!* Mother, don't! Don't force me!" He could feel Shalimar's hand limp below his.

"What do you mean? Have you forgotten that you were already informally betrothed to Shalimar when you were children and until now you have never shown any objections."

"But mother, we were just children, playing — it was never meant to be serious. Anyway I have not seen her since she was twelve. And since that time, you have never really brought it up. Isn't that so Shalimar?"

Shalimar nodded, still silent, still looking down. Tears, however, fell from her eyes wetting her sleeves.

Did she agree with him? Hussein wondered. His heart leapt feeling a ray of hope that he was not alone in his opposition to his mother's plan.

"Look what you have done. You have hurt Shalimar," his mother scolded.

Hussein looked at Shalimar and saw her tears. Abashed, he gripped Shalimar's hand, which lay under his, and said, "Do you wish to talk? Shall we step out to the garden?"

Faridah broke into a big smile. "*Bagus! Pergi-pergi!* Good! Go! It will do both of you some good."

They got up and walked to the terrace and into the garden. Faridah nodded to Ahmad and indicated that he should follow the young couple. Ahmad shook his head. "Leave them be," he mouthed silently and smiled.

Outside in the warm night air, Hussein apologised. "I am sorry if I upset you, but what I said was true. Don't you agree? We may have played at getting married when we were children, but since then we have never been together. Surely, you must be as much against this marriage as I am?"

"*Abang*, elder brother, speak softly. Walls have ears. I am not free to speak my mind." Shalimar drew her headscarf tighter towards her face, half covering her mouth. When she looked up at him, her eyes were luminous.

"You can tell me. I won't repeat it to anyone."

She looked around anxiously before saying. "I have no choice. I cry because I have no choice. Don't you understand? I am to marry you — someone who has no wish to have me as a bride."

"You have a choice. You can say no!"

"You have no idea," She lowered her voice further.

"Tell me. I promise on my honour that I will not tell anyone."

She looked at him for a long time, her eyes searching his. "You swear to this?"

He nodded putting the palm of his hand to his heart.

Finally, she whispered. "I love someone else too. He is our gardener's son. My brother said that he is a thief and that he caught him stealing. He threatens to put him in prison if I do not do as he bids. Your parents do not know of my circumstance. They believe that I have agreed to the marriage willingly."

Hussein smiled a mirthless grin. He realised then why Ahmad had proposed to be his and An Mei's intermediary. He said to Shalimar, "We have to put our heads together and see what can be done." He held out his hand and she took it.

Faridah watched them from the window and smiled indulgently.

* * * * *

Two days later, Hussein went with Shalimar to Faridah. He held Shalimar's hand in his. "Mother, Shalimar and I would like to go to Kuala Lumpur. I would like her to see some of my favourite haunts and perhaps do some shopping." Turning to Shalimar, he asked gently, "You would like that, wouldn't you?" She nodded demurely in response.

"Yes! Go," beamed Faridah. "But you have to be chaperoned. And Ahmad is not here to go with the two of you. He has left for Kuala Lumpur and has not returned. "

"Can the driver take us to Kuala Lumpur and be our chaperone?" asked Hussein. Seeing her reluctance, he added, "You might wish to appoint Shalimar's maid to come as an additional chaperone. In any case, if Ahmad is in Kuala Lumpur, I am sure that he will look after Shalimar there."

Faridah's heart sang. She felt a change in Hussein's attitude; she liked his solicitous and caring manner when he spoke to

Shalimar. She recalled how he sought Shalimar's company after dinner last evening. However, there remained the problem of An Mei. She was still in the guesthouse in Kuala Lumpur and Faridah did not want Hussein to see her. She would have to get rid of the girl somehow.

With a broad confident smile, she said to Shalimar, "I leave him in your hands. See that he does not go astray. And buy something pretty."

She watched as Hussein and Shalimar left the room. Then she sprang up and with a speed that belied her age went into the adjourning library. She locked the door securely behind her and paused for a moment with her back pushed against it. A determined look crossed her face. She strode to the huge desk at the corner and picked up the phone, her fingers nimbly dialling before speaking into the mouthpiece. "I don't care how you do it, just make sure that she leaves the country. Take her by force if you have to, I want her put on the first available plane to the UK. I don't think we will have much trouble with Hussein. He seems quite besotted with Shalimar. He will be leaving for Kuala Lumpur with her tomorrow morning."

Chapter 7

Jenny rushed up the path and banged on the dark red door. Not satisfied, she lifted the brass letterbox to peep into the house before releasing the catch with a clash and a bang. "Come to the door. I have news," she shouted, breathing heavily. Her bosom rose and fell rapidly from the effort of running all the way from the car park.

"We're coming. Wait a minute," shouted Mei Yin.

Mei Yin wrenched open the door.

Jenny could see the top of Nelly's head, just the forehead and eyes, over Mei Yin's shoulders. Both women had obviously been crying.

Mei Yin took hold of Jenny's arm and ushered her into the house. "Tell us! What news? Do you know where she is?" Her voice rose. In her anxiety, she banged the door shut.

"Shhh! Slow down both of you," warned Nelly pointing with her finger to the floor above them. "Ming Kong is asleep. You are not going to get anywhere by shouting. It's always like this when the two of you get together. All you will succeed in doing is waking up Ming Kong and having him rush down. You know as well as I do that it would best for us discuss this calmly before getting him involved."

Jenny stopped mid-stride and turned to Mei Yin. She remembered Ming Kong's animosity towards her. He thought her a bad influence. There was even a time when he had forbidden his wife from seeing her. What would he do now if he knew that she had been instrumental in introducing Hussein to An Mei?

"Are you sure it is alright for me to stay?"

Their answer was to lead her into the kitchen. Nelly closed the door gently, wincing at the creaking sound it made. "Quick, tell us." Both women moved closer to Jenny.

"Hussein took An Mei to his parent's house in Kuala Lumpur. He left almost immediately with them for his hometown on the east coast. Poor An Mei was left on her own for days in the house. Then, according to the servants, she vanished. They could tell me nothing."

"Did you ask Hussein?" Nelly demanded.

"It took me a long time to get hold of him. At first no one seemed able or willing to get him to the phone. I felt I was bashing my head against a brick wall. One of the servants eventually told me that Hussein had returned to KL. So I called again and managed finally to speak to him. He had little to add to what I already knew about An Mei, but he did admit reluctantly that his parents were against An Mei. I had warned him that would happen, but he chose to ignore me."

"So where is our daughter, what has become of her?"

"I'm so sorry, but I just don't know," admitted Jenny. She was at a loss as to what to say. Her sources had told her of Faridah's antagonism towards An Mei and of Ahmad's visit.

She did not wish to alarm her friends of her own suspicion. It could be nothing.

Mei Yin looked unconvinced. She saw the guilt in Jenny's face. "You are hiding something from us," said Mei Yin.

"I don't really know. I... I just heard that Hussein's mother wanted An Mei out of the house before Hussein returned to it."

"How do you mean? You mean they've kidnapped her, harmed her?

"I don't know." She regretted her words and tried to calm Mei Yin and Nelly. "It might be that they just forced her to leave the house."

"Who are these people? How could they turn a young girl out onto the streets, particularly at a time like this, when it was their son who invited her?" asked Nelly turning to Mei Yin, bewildered. "What has An Mei got herself into?" And as Jenny explained Hussein's family and the ambition they had for him, both Mei Yin and Nelly fell silent. They held on to each other's hands, finding comfort in the contact. They could not understand why this had happened. They felt as though something precious had been wrenched violently from them. They had lost a daughter. An Mei's short phone call to say she was leaving without any prior warning had left them distraught. It came as a complete shock that she could behave in such a callous way. Now it seemed that even this thin thread of connection leading to KL was broken.

"Can you do something, Jenny? Please help us to find her."

Jenny took their hands in hers and shook her head, unable to bring herself to say *no*. She felt guilty for introducing An Mei to Hussein, but all her pleading with her husband to intervene had fallen on deaf ears. "*Datuk* can't help. He said he does not know how or what to do."

Chapter 8

When Ahmad left, An Mei had remained huddled on the floor. Feelings of shame and anger had coursed through her mind. It drained her of energy. Slowly she picked herself up, every movement an effort. She felt lifeless and heavy. Every sinew in her neck was taut, painful. She returned to her room and lay on the bed, unsure what to do. She closed her eyes. A sense of utter loneliness enveloped her.

She felt a presence in the room. Frightened she sat up abruptly, swinging her legs to the floor. "Who is there?" she asked.

From the shadows behind the canopy of the bed, a figure appeared. An Mei heaved a sigh of relief. It was the young maid who normally brought her meals and clothes. "Why are you hiding there?"

"Shhh," the girl signed, pointing to the door and to her ears. She came forward and whispered. "*Saya mari tolong.* I have come to help you."

An Mei looked at her suspiciously.

"You know *Datin* Zainab?" asked the girl.

An Mei shook her head.

"I mean," the girl hesitated, not knowing if she could be so familiar as to use the Datin's name, "*Datin* Zainab, Jenny?"

An Mei smiled, her first in many days. "Yes! Yes!" she said. It came back to her that Zainab was Jenny's Muslim name when she converted, although she never used the name with her friends.

"She called and asked for you. We told her that you had vanished. We were instructed to say that."

"By whom?"

The girl backed away. She looked terrified.

"I can't tell you. But I overheard that you are not wanted here and that you are to disappear. *Datin* Zainab said that she would reward me if I could find you and keep you safe. I replied that I knew nothing about your whereabouts or your situation. I was frightened. But I have thought it over since. I will help you to leave this place."

"How? How will you help me?"

"But first will you promise to put in a good word for me if you see *Datin*? Say that it was Fawziah who helped you. She will remember me. She recommended me to this job."

An Mei was not keen to make the commitment. She hardly knew the maid, but she detected the urgency in her voice, the fear in her face. What choice had she? She remembered Ahmad's visit, his threats and insinuations. She nodded.

"We will leave now. First let me do something with your hair." Gathering An Mei's hair into a coil, she roughly pinned it into a knot at the base of her neck. "Now put this *hijab* on." The maid thrust a thin green coloured headscarf into An Mei's hands. "Draw it close around your face. Like this." She demonstrated tugging the cloth around An Mei's neck. "Here, let me help you put on this sarong." She wound the sarong round An Mei's waist and secured it with a thin belt. "Leave your shift loose on top. It will do as a makeshift Malay dress."

Leading her into the corridor, she made An Mei stand and wait at each corner while she did a quick recce before motioning her to go forward. "This is a good time to leave. Most people are at their prayers. Do you have a place to go to, someone you trust?"

"I have an aunt and uncle in Kuala Lumpur. They used to live in the Sun Chuen area. I believe they still do although I am not sure. The city has changed so much since I was here two years ago."

"I know where you mean. Just around Kampong Hijau. There was terrible destruction there during the disturbances: two settlements, one Chinese and the other Malay, side by side. I do not know what you might find there. First, however, let's concentrate on getting you out of here."

They crept soft-footed along the marble corridor to a side door that led out to the back. "Stay here. I'll take a look first," Fawziah instructed. A few minutes later she returned. Beckoning An Mei to join her, they ran quickly to a little side gate. "This is the gate that servants and tradesmen use. We are not allowed to use the front entrance. I have the key. Quick! I hear cars coming into the front driveway."

* * * * *

An Mei stared out from the window of the mini bus. Here and there, the burnt façades of a few buildings could be seen, ugly, desolate reminders of what had happened during the riots. Hardly any people were about in the street.

"Hurry, hurry! This is your stop. Remove your head scarf and hide it away and walk quickly," said Fawziah, gesturing to An Mei to leave the bus. "We are in Sun Chuen now and you will not need a headscarf. It is probably best, in fact, not to wear one here. I won't go with you. It is not safe for me. You will have to make your own way to your aunt's house."

"Thank you. I will never forget what you have done. Will you tell Hussein my whereabouts?"

Fawziah did not know if she should do more, but she nodded after a moment's hesitation. "Go," she commanded, "the bus will not stop here for long."

An Mei got down quickly from the bus. She stood for a moment to wave to Fawziah as it pulled away. The warnings from Fawziah made her uneasy and frightened. She walked rapidly as instructed. Leaving the main street, she turned into a smaller side road. Residential houses flanked both sides of it. They seemed relatively untouched. A few had scorch marks, big black streaks that told of attempts to torch them, but the damage was superficial. Here and there, the road tarmac also bore marks of burning. Fawziah had told her that even though the curfew had been lifted and most shops had re-opened, the street atmosphere had changed. The criss-cross singsong parlay of the different ethnic groups was singularly absent. In Chinese dominated areas, no Malays were to be seen and, similarly, in Malay dominated areas, there were no Chinese. People went out only when absolutely necessary.

A man passed her pushing a cart. He muttered to her crossly. '*Ni mn moi mang, qi ki hang!* Don't you want to live? Walking alone! Go home girl!"

She shrank away from him and hurried to the other side of the road. She was, desperate to be away from him, away from his ominous warning. She looked left and then right, but did not recognise the houses. The road looked different from when she had last been there. Single-story terrace houses stood on one side of the road. Facing them on the other side of the road were double-storey link houses. A hundred metres on, she saw another turning. A sign indicated that it was a dead end. The double-storey detached houses on it look familiar. She half ran towards the cul de sac and saw, nestling in the shade of the Angsana tree, her Aunty Kai Min's house. She picked up speed, her legs pumping fast, not stopping until she was in front of its gate. She grabbed hold of its grills and called, "Aunty Kai Min, open the door. Please open the door." Her legs gave way as she rattled the gates. The fear she had suppressed in the previous days rose like bile in her throat. She retched.

* * * * *

Kai Min tucked a cushion behind An Mei's head and applied a hot towel to her face. "Hold this over your face and breathe in the warmth. It should help refresh you. Now, put some of this tiger balm on your forehead. Here, I'll do it for you," she said taking over the jar with a label showing a pouncing tiger. She dabbed her finger into the jar and took out a big blob of translucent pungent ointment and rubbed it into An Mei's temple. Not satisfied she added a small dab under An Mei's nose. "There, this should do the trick."

Tears appeared in An Mei's eyes as she inhaled the fumes. "No more. I'll be alright."

Kai Min's husband, Tek San, had joined them and watched silently as Kai Min administered to An Mei.

"Why are you here?" he asked. "Your parents left Malaysia about a month ago to join you in England. What happened?"

An Mei told her story. Kai Min and Tek San sat motionless until she finished.

"Why didn't your father and mother tell us? We may have had our differences, but we are still family," asked Tek San, irate that they had not been told earlier.

"They must have been so embarrassed that they chose to ask Jenny for help instead of us. Otherwise, I am sure they would have called," said Kai Min in an attempt to soothe her husband. "But you," she jabbed her finger at An Mei, "what were you thinking? I thought that you were an intelligent girl. You must be mad to run away with a Malay boy at the very time when the Malay and Chinese communities are at loggerheads. How could you even think that it would be alright? Didn't you think about what it would do to your family? Your father and mother were reunited not that long ago. I am sure your father will blame your mother and aunt for all of this. How could you?"

An Mei cringed under their reproachful gaze. Yes. How could she have done all the things she did? she wondered. It all stemmed from that one insane moment at Heathrow when Hussein had turned to her beseechingly and mouthed the words, "Come with me."

"We'll have to call them. To tell them that you are at least safe."

"Then what, Aunty Kai Min?"

"That will depend on what your parents say."

"I don't want to go home without first speaking to Hussein."

"Enough! Enough, I say!" shouted Tek San. He jumped up from his seat. "You selfish, stupid girl! If he had cared for you, he would not have left you alone in KL. He would not have left you at the mercy of that rascal Ahmad. I have heard of him. He is renowned for throwing his weight around and that Hussein of yours is obviously weak."

"We'll call your parents now!" said Kai Min picking up the phone. "You deal with it," she said thrusting the phone at An Mei. "It is your mess and your parents may not want us to interfere."

* * * * *

An Mei sat on the bed and drew her knees up until she was hunched into a tight ball. She plucked at the bed cover, crumpling the starched cloth in her fist at random until the sheet was a mass of little hillocks. Tears ran down her cheeks and on to her blouse. Everything had been decided for her once again. She was to return to Oxford, alone, without Hussein. She must never see him again. Her father had said that this 'little' incident, as he put it, would never be mentioned again. Her mother and aunty Nelly were overjoyed. Their happiness reflected in their voices, "Come home! *Suen le! Suen le!* It is over! It is over! We'll not talk about it again. It's already forgotten." Their joy had moved her and she felt once again the intense guilt that had haunted her since she left for Malaysia with Hussein. Now as she sat on the bed, the feeling of guilt and self-contempt was overtaken by anger. She doubled over, hands pressed into her tummy. The hurt in her heart was like a physical pain.

"Why? Why Hussein? Why have you let me down?!" she moaned.

Chapter 9

In the opulent surroundings of his parents' home in Kuala Lumpur, Hussein sat in awkward silence with Shalimar. He was spent from the furious exchange he had just had with Ahmad. He was exhausted, worried, frustrated and helpless. He had accused Ahmad of kidnapping An Mei and demanded to see her. He had got nowhere.

"*Bukan saya*. It is not me. I have nothing to do with her disappearance. Ask any of the servants here. Of course, I wanted her to leave, but I did nothing," Ahmad had protested, blustering with righteous indignation.

Hussein did not believe him nor did he believe his mother and father when they too protested that they had taken no part in An Mei's disappearance.

He did not understand how she could have vanished without anyone knowing. Panic rose in him. He feared for An Mei's safety. He got up and walked towards the door, only to retrace his steps until he towered over Shalimar. "Did Ahmad let slip any clue as to the whereabouts of An Mei?" he asked her. She stared blankly at him. It irritated him that she did not seem to share his concern for An Mei. "Think! What did he say to you?" he shouted.

"*Minta maaf!* I'm sorry. He did not say anything to me," she replied. She poured out a cup of tea, found it cold and beckoned Fawziah to come forward. "Please bring us fresh tea. This is cold."

"Stop fussing with the tea. Go, go if you cannot help," he yelled venting his anger on her. Once alone, he felt ashamed. He wanted to make amends.

"Fawziah, please would you tell *Tengku* Shalimar that I apologise for my outburst." Every minute that went by weighed on him like a millstone; he feared and imagined the worst.

"May I speak to you sir?" Fawziah asked softly. "I have something important to tell you."

Hussein who had been re-making his way to the door stopped in his track. He turned to look at Fawziah, a glimmer of suspicion and surprise in his eyes. "Go on, tell me."

She looked around the room and then out of the window. She went to the door, peeped out and then closed it gently behind her. Hussein stared in amazement at her strange behaviour, but felt compelled to wait. Perhaps...

"I know where *Cik* An Mei is."

He stood frozen for a second and then a torrent of questions spilled out of him. "Where? How did she leave? Was she forced to go? Is she safe? Can you get me to her?

"Shhh! I will explain, but first I have to get fresh tea and go to *Tengku* Shalimar otherwise she might look for me and think something is amiss. I will tell her that you apologise for the outburst. Wait here. I will take you to *Cik* An Mei. I work in shifts and this afternoon I am supposed to go home to my family. No one will miss me then."

"You mean I can see An Mei this afternoon?"

"As soon as I can arrange for transport."

"Then, tell Shalimar that I have gone to my bedroom for a nap and do not want to be disturbed. Tell her I will see her at dinner. That should avoid her seeking me. Will that give us enough time?"

"Yes!" the maid replied and hurried away.

* * * * *

Hussein followed Fawziah out of the servants' entrance at the back of the house. Five hundred yards down the back lane they turned into another lane lined with small houses; most of them no more than one room huts on stilts. Groves of banana trees and coconut palms were dotted between the houses. The scarlet flowers of a scattering of hibiscus bushes gave colour to an otherwise dull domain of dirt. Chickens scratched desultorily in search of food in the dark orange lateritic soil. They bent their heads low to peck at the soil, jerking them up once in a while to survey their surroundings, their beady eyes opened wide in a perpetual expression of surprise. Skinny dogs lay on their sides, thumping their tails at the hovering flies, their skins festering with wounds. Rainwater lay in stagnant pools until a cart or bicycle ran over them, stirring and splattering the murky water over any bystander unfortunate enough to be too close.

"It is very quiet here. Is there no one around?" asked Hussein.

"They are indoors. Normally, everyone would be out here in the courtyard. Children would probably be playing in the puddles and women would be drawing water from the well or washing. Sometimes, they even cook together in the open, sharing a pot to save on fuel. See those strings of *ketupat* hanging in that veranda? They boil the rice wrapped in leaves in that caldron over there. But these days, people prefer to stay indoors. They are frightened. The curfew was lifted only recently. And we hear so many stories. Come, my cousin is waiting."

They hurried on ignoring the stares of the few people who had dared to peep out of their houses or venture on to the verandas of their homes. But Hussein did not attract their attention for long. He was dressed in a pair of shabby trousers and an old long-sleeved shirt. Once they saw that he was with Fawziah, they returned to what they had been doing. They walked on until they came to a man standing by a ramshackle car, an old black Morris Minor. He was wrestling with one of the car's indicators. It was jammed and stuck out in defiance of the man's attempts to push it down.

"I didn't know that they still allow such old cars on the road," commented Hussein. He stopped aware of his rudeness. *"Minta maaf,"* he said immediately. How stupid of me, he reprimanded himself. Of course, everything was old and decrepit in this little village even though it was just a few minutes away from his palatial home. Wasn't this one of his reasons for returning to Malaysia? To help iron out the inequalities that had emerged even amongst the Malays.

For her part Fawziah was not fazed by his remarks. "It works well enough," was all she said as she opened the door for him. He slid into the car. "Mind the seat," she warned, as his hand connected with stuffing from the torn upholstery. "I won't come with you. My cousin has helped me find where *Cik* An Mei is staying. Before she left she gave me the name of an aunt who lives in a Chinese village called Sun Chuen. He will drive you right to the house so you will not need to walk into the settlement. It could be dangerous for you. Try to keep a low profile."

"*Terima kasih!* Thank you! How can I repay you? Won't it be dangerous for him?" he asked looking at Fawziah's cousin.

"We'll talk about it afterwards, but do not bother yourself about my cousin. He is willing to take the risk and I have taken the liberty of promising him that you will reward him well. He knows quite a few families in the village from the days when his car was in better shape and he was a taxi driver."

"I don't have money on me," replied Hussein.

"Don't worry, it's fine. He knows you will pay him later. Go! Go now before he changes his mind."

* * * * *

The shutters were half drawn to keep out the sun. Kai Min sat in the sitting room, nursing a cup of tea in her hands. She held the cup close to her lips and blew gently into it, enjoying the waft of light perfume rising from the rose tea. She closed her eyes. Peace, at last. She did not like the commotion and arguments that had followed An Mei's arrival. She was no longer used to it. Her children had all left home and she valued the feeling of peace in the house. It gave her space. It made her calm. The ceiling fan whirred above her. She closed her eyes.

In the days following the civil riots, she had kept to herself at home. She did not dare to venture out, not even to buy fresh provisions. She was thankful that they were so well stocked with canned foods from her husband's stores. She had been very sorry to see her brother Ming Kong leave with his family for England but had accepted it. She missed them and she was hurt that they had not called her for help. She sighed. Would she have done the same thing if one of her girls had run off with a Malay boy? Perhaps she too would not have wanted the other family members to know. She supposed Jenny had to be involved because she was the link to this Hussein. She should not be upset and jealous over it. Children, she mused, they were such headaches.

She heard approaching footsteps and felt someone touch her arm lightly.

"*Siew nai,* mistress, please come. Someone is blaring his horn and shouting for your niece, the one who arrived yesterday. I do not know who it can be. The car is very old. *Aiyah lan cheh*, a complete wreck of a car."

The maid sniffed dismissively. She ran to the window and lifted the shutters to look out. "Oh! Oh! The car has left. A *Malai chai*, a Malay boy with a ponytail is outside. He is shouting for An Mei. Who can the *sooi chai*, bringer of bad luck boy, be?"

"Mind what you say, Ah Foong," chastised Kai Min buttoning up her tunic. She did not appreciate being so rudely disturbed by her maid and she certainly did not appreciate someone calling loudly at her gate for her niece.

"An Mei," shouted Hussein, rattling the gate. "Open up. Let me in. I know you are there. I can explain."

Kai Min went out to the gate, her temper rising by the minute. All signs of the peace and tranquillity that she had been enjoying earlier wiped away from her face.

"Tell An Mei to come down," she commanded the maid. But An Mei had already heard and was scrambling down the stairs. "Hussein, Hussein," she cried, breaking into a run. She ran past her aunt and went straight to the gate, grabbing the grill. "Please," she cried to Ah Foong, "please open the gate."

The maid turned to Kai Min uncertain what to do. She waited for instructions, but kept glaring at Hussein muttering, "*Nooi yan ying*, like a woman, wearing his hair like that!"

Kai Min gave a brief sign to the maid to open the door. Surprised, the maid took the bunch of keys that hung from her waist band with a great show of unwillingness and brusquely told An Mei to step aside, "*mn ho chou qi sai*, don't block my way." She pulled open the gate with much force and clanging. "What will the neighbours say if they see us consorting with a Malay man," she muttered.

Hussein came in and reached out to take An Mei in his arms.

Kai Min immediately stepped between them. She pushed Hussein away. "Hey, this is my house. Remember your manners. Who do you think you are? An Mei, go in." Addressing Hussein, she said. "You can come in only if you behave yourself."

"*Aiyah*, he is a Malay boy, Mistress," said the maid disapprovingly, her upper lips curled into a sneer. "This is what happens when they go overseas. *Mo-kah gow*. They lose all their family teachings."

"This is not for you to say," scolded Kai Min. "Go to the kitchen!"

An Mei and Hussein followed Kai Min into the house. They stood waiting for Kai Min to sit down, not daring to sit themselves.

"You might as well sit down," said Kai Min with a sigh, feeling that she was fast losing control of the situation. She wished that Tek San was there with them. She looked disapprovingly at Hussein and immediately thought of her brother, Ming Kong. He certainly would disapprove of his hairstyle! And a Malay! Even if he was the son of an important man, a *Datuk*. I bet my brother would say, those titles were a dime a dozen, she thought to herself. She frowned at An Mei.

"I can explain everything," said Hussein. Turning to An Mei, he explained how his attempts to get in touch with her had been thwarted and how Fawziah had helped.

Kai Min snorted. "Do you believe him? A tall story, don't you think?" She tried to convey her disapproval and disbelief by fixing her eyes on An Mei with a look of pity, challenging her niece to disagree with her.

"His parents did not put him in chains, did they? So why is it that he can come to Kuala Lumpur so freely with this new girlfriend and couldn't do the same on his own earlier. Listen, whatever it is, your father would not agree. Do you want to hurt your parents and disappoint them yet again?"

An Mei, stung by the sarcasm, looked desperately at her aunt Kai Min. Her mind was in a whirl. She turned to Hussein. "Promise me you are telling the truth?"

"Yes!" he said, his eyes looked into hers, willing her to trust him.

An Mei turned to Kai Min. "I believe him." A gasp came from the kitchen.

"Ah Foong, mind your own business and stay in the kitchen," Kai Min reprimanded her maid. She did not know what to do. An Mei was not her daughter; she was twenty-four years old. She got up. "I must speak to your mother. I'll call her right now."

Chapter 10

The house was quiet. Oxford was steeped in darkness, broken only by the soft glow of the streetlights and the headlights of the occasional car that was still about in the early hours of the morning. Peace reigned.

Mei Yin eased herself out of the bed, careful not to wake Ming Kong. It was four o'clock. Barefoot, she tiptoed out of the room. It was dark. She made her way to the top of the landing feeling for the banister. The phone rang; its sharp shrill sound echoed through the house. She retraced her steps quickly to a wall phone in the adjacent corner and snatched up the receiver. By the time she had heard what Kai Min had to say to her, she was shaking. Just when she thought it was all settled and An Mei would be coming home, everything was up in the air again. She did not know what to say. She wanted An Mei to be happy but she was not sure if Hussein was the right person for her, especially in the present climate of mistrust and division in Malaysia. Her voice was barely a whisper, "Can I call you back? I need to discuss this. Can I speak to An Mei now?"

"Mum," An Mei's voice sounded faint.

"An Mei, are you sure about Hussein? You know all the consequences. We talked about it for days when you were with us and I thought you had come to your senses when we last spoke."

"Mum, I love him." An Mei's voice broke. "Please can you and Aunty Nelly think of a way out for me. We'll wait for your answer. I won't do anything silly; I promise I won't do anything without consulting you and Aunt Nelly."

"I don't know. Your father will not forgive you. Do you want to risk that?" She heard sobbing at the other end, a big gulp, and then, "Yes, mother, but I hope it will not come to that. Please, please help me."

Mei Yin felt a surge of tenderness. She remembered herself at such a crossroad just a few years ago. She felt the familiar prickle in her nose and the wet warmth that welled up in her eyes. "Let me first talk to Nelly. I'll call you back. Thank Kai Min for me. It has been hard on her. We have put her in an awkward position."

She placed the phone back on the receiver intending to go to Nelly's room, but she was already on the landing waiting. She gestured to Mei Yin to go into her room.

"Not good news?" she asked, once she was sat on the edge of her bed.

Mei Yin sat down on the other twin bed, the one that An Mei used to occupy. "No! Hussein has found An Mei and has convinced her of his love. He has explained how his attempts to reach her had been thwarted. She believes in him. She does not want to come back."

"She is sure she loves this boy?"

"She believes she does."

"We cannot tell Ming Kong. Have you noticed how terrible he looks? One minute his face is pallid, the next bright red. According to the doctor, his blood pressure is dangerously high. Last night, he complained of a dull ache in his heart and shortness of breath. Did he hear the phone ring?"

"I don't think so. He took a sleeping tablet last night. He has not been sleeping well for days."

"Neither have you?"

"Never mind about me," replied Mei Yin. "More important at this point is what should we do?"

"Let me think this over. You go back to bed. No! Better stay here with me. Then you won't wake Ming Kong up with your tossing and turning. "

Mei Yin laid down on the bed and closed her eyes. Tired as she was, she could not sleep. She pressed her fingers on her temples in an effort to reduce the tightness in her head. Her eyes grew heavy but when she drifted off to sleep, she would wake up with a start. Nelly stroked her hair tenderly.

Mei Yin sighed. "Thank you Nelly. Remember those days when I was young and petulant and you came to my rescue. I... all of us, do not know how we could have managed without you." Responding to Nelly's ministrations, Mei Yin finally fell into a deep sleep.

Nelly continued stroking Mei Yin's hair. She was full of her own thoughts. Time went by. Finally, she left Mei Yin sleeping and went back to her bed. She laid down, pulled the duvet up to her chin and wriggled under the cover until she was comfortable. That's what I'll do, she decided before she too drifted off to sleep.

* * * * *

At the first streak of dawn, Mei Yin woke up. She reached over to Nelly's bed and tapped her gently on her arm. Nelly grunted and opened her eyes. They were bleary with fatigue.

"I'm sorry. Can we talk about An Mei again? We didn't quite finish. What shall we do?"

Nelly sat up, swung her legs over her bed and gathered the duvet around her shoulders with a shudder. "*Dong seh yan! Yow lang, yow sup!* Such cold; it kills people! Cold and damp! I don't like the climate here. I miss the sun. I will return to Kuala Lumpur. And that, among other things, is what I'll do. I'll tell Ming Kong this evening."

Mei Yin sat up and looked at Nelly with dismay. "What!" she exclaimed, "you can't do that. Ming Kong will be really upset. You have always helped him with his businesses. You are his right hand. How would that help him? And how will that help us with An Mei?"

"You do not need me here. You can be his right hand. You have mastered English and you are much younger. He will need you now. I am not much use here. I can be a greater help in Kuala Lumpur. Remember we still have two stores left in KL because we could not sell them before we left. Maan *sook*, uncle Maan, is helping out in the stores until we find a buyer but, really, we should have our own people at the helm. Tek San promised to keep an eye on them, but he has his own business to run. I was always responsible for managing the stores in the past and I feel I can play a better role back home than here. I do not speak English nor do I know the English system and people."

She buttoned up her pyjama top and smoothed her hair down. "You, however, would or should get on fine here. You have your friend, Siew Lin. She is already charting out business contacts for you. Her family is well established in Soho. Then, you have Jenny. Both are more your friends than they are mine. Here in England, you would be a bigger help to Ming Kong than me."

Mei Yin looked disbelievingly at Nelly. But she was flattered. "You think so? My experience is much less than yours. I've managed only a small part of his business, producing and selling cakes. That is not enough surely."

"Yes, I think it is and it was not such a small operation," Nelly replied emphatically, pushing her spectacles up her nose and staring at Mei Yin intently through her bifocals. "In any case, Ming Kong will be taking the lead and making most of the decisions. Unlike in KL where he had a finger in every pie and needed to delegate, he is starting from scratch here. He will definitely have to focus his energies and won't leave you to manage on your own."

Mei Yin was doubtful. She looked at her hands, examining her fingers and the palms of her hands as though she was trying to read her future in them. Nelly took the hands in hers and placed them on her lap. "Think!" she said, "we are not sure how the business will develop here in England; it is such an uncharted territory for us. If we liquidate the two stores, give up everything in Kuala Lumpur and then fail here, the consequences could be dire."

Mei Yin pulled her hands away abruptly. "I thought we were talking about An Mei," she said. "How would your return to KL help?" Suddenly she grew cross at how Nelly seemed to have side-tracked her proposed discussion on how to help An Mei with business talk. "I am surprised at you! Why are you thinking about business now, putting such considerations before solving the problems of An Mei?"

"I am not," exclaimed Nelly, "how could you accuse me of that when you know how much An Mei means to me?" Her voice rose and her face grew red with exasperation. She felt hurt and misunderstood.

"You asked me how I could justify returning to KL and abandoning Ming Kong. So, I am explaining to you the reasons I would give him for returning, reasons that he should find acceptable. I would propose that An Mei stays in KL to help me out and keep me company. I need an English-speaking help in KL to take the place of Ming Kong and who better than his daughter?" Her voice rose in excitement. "This way, we'll buy time and An Mei will be able to remain in KL. We will have to take it from there, one step at a time. If she really loves Hussein, then there is nothing we can do to stop her. Who knows, with time Ming Kong might come to accept the situation. If she falls out with Hussein, then she will not have burnt her boat with her father. He would think that she is staying in KL because of me. We are buying time for her so that she does not have to make rushed decisions and, just as important, so that Ming Kong does not make any hasty resolutions such as disowning her."

Exhausted by her outburst, Nelly laid down on the bed again pulling the duvet over her. "Ming Kong will probably hate me if he finds out. This will be the first time I would not be telling him the whole truth and nothing but the truth," she whispered, shocked at her own proposal.

"Oh Nelly," said Mei Yin ashamed of her earlier outburst, "thank you. I have never been as good a mother as you have been to An Mei all these years. And now, it is still no different. You are truly her wonderful mother; I am nothing more than her biological mother," said Mei Yin softly. She realised how much it had cost Nelly to make her decision. She knew her loyalty to Ming Kong. She lay down next to Nelly and cuddled her close, feeling the warmth of Nelly's face. Two women, both wives to the same man, who over the years had become like siblings sharing a profound and lasting love for their family.

Chapter 11

Hussein hurried along the path through the village and retraced his steps back to his parents' house. He was late. When Fawziah's cousin arrived to pick him up from Kai Min's house, he had not finished explaining his plans to An Mei because of the continuous interruptions. Despite Kai Min's promise to give them time alone to sort out their problems, she had been in and out of the sitting room monitoring their movements. She made all kinds of excuses: she had forgotten her spectacles; she had mislaid a book she was reading. Then she needed something from the cupboard and rummaged through its shelves, all the while throwing anxious glances at her niece. When they returned her stare with an exasperated plea for privacy, she had retorted with a firm shake of her head. "Mei Yin will never forgive me if you misbehave in my house. Sorry! I cannot give you so much time that you could behave badly." Her maid, Ah Foong had been indignant when Kai Min had first left the two young people on her own, warning her of her mistake.

"Aiyah, nei you cheong sut hui. You have to guard them closely. These young people, you cannot trust them. They have different morals after studying in the west. They forget themselves," she had grumbled at Kai Min until she felt obliged to abandon the latitude she had earlier given the couple. So when the car arrived to pick up Hussein and blared its horn, Kai Min sighed with relief and hurried him out of the house. "Go! Go before my husband comes back!"

She had been taken aback by Tek San's vehemence when An Mei first told them of Hussein. Her normally docile husband showed a side of him she had not seen. It must have been the result of all the stress he had been subjected to following the riots, the curfew and the reintroduction of Emergency rules, she had surmised. "Don't even mention May Thirteenth," he had warned his wife. "It could be construed as being anti-government, anti-state. You can be imprisoned." Throwing his hands in the air, he cried, "How can I continue to run a business in this climate? Who would want to shop? Perhaps Ming Kong was right to leave!"

Hussein, fresh from Kai Min's vigilant household and the distinctly unfriendly attitude of its occupants, was even more determined that such insane racial prejudice be wiped out of his own household. He hurried through the marble hallway, saw Fawziah and was about to call out to her when she pointedly pretended not to see him. She scurried like a mouse, looking at the floor, until she came within a metre from him. Without looking up, she bowed low and went her way, announcing softly that his parents were within.

He went into the large sitting room and greeted them. He pretended surprise at their presence.

"Where have you been?" they asked. "Shalimar said that you were taking a rest and we sent someone to your room. But you were not there. So where were you?"

"I have been to see An Mei."

There was complete quiet following his announcement. He could see that they were taken aback.

"So she was not kidnapped by us!" Faridah said sarcastically, breaking the silence. She was surprised that her son had found An Mei and displeased at the turn of events. Her voice grew even more strident. "Don't you think you should have more trust in your parents? Apologise even. Where is she? And how did you find her?"

"She is safe with her uncle and aunt."

"How did you find her?" Faridah persisted observing his discomfort. "Who led you to her and how did she leave here?"

"We did not discuss how she left. I did not ask," answered Hussein, desperately looking for a way to avoid his mother's questioning. "I found An Mei because I followed my intuition. I knew she had relatives here in Kuala Lumpur. She told me about them when we were in Oxford."

"Well, if she is safe, we can wash our hands of her and leave her be where she is now," said Faridah, brandishing her arm as though she was swatting a fly. "We can concentrate on Shalimar and your marriage plans."

"No mother. I would like you to reconsider your views about An Mei."

"What about Shalimar? I thought you liked her. Things were going so well between the two of you before you came back to KL. What has happened?"

"Mother, Shalimar understands that I do not wish to marry her. So can we please discuss An Mei and me?"

"No! No! Stop this nonsense," demanded Faridah. "I have said all that I wish to say on this matter. The answer is no!" She brought her hand in one big downward arc, crashing it on the table with a loud thud. "We will never accept her. She will destroy all your chances of a political future."

"How could you say that? I believe the opposite will happen. It will show us as moderates. Look at our Prime Minister, *Tengku* Abdul Rahman. He had a Thai Chinese mother and a Chinese wife to boot. That has not destroyed his career. People love him. He is *Bapa Kemerdekaan*, Father of Independence."

"Huh! But remember, even he had to relent. As prime minister, he is married only to Sharifah Rodziah. She is the First Lady. By then he was free of his previous Chinese wife and his English one as well, if you remember. In any case, times have changed. He is on his way out," said Faridah.

"Yes, Hussein. He has been heavily criticised recently," his father confirmed.

"What political leader escapes criticism? He is still loved by the people. They trust him because he has a clear view of what is best for the country. People trust him because of his fairness towards the different races and his background," replied Hussein. "We need to be more like him. And like him, I do not think that we should allow ethnic origins to divide us. We are all Malaysians irrespective of race. For that reason I believe my marriage to An Mei would be a source of good — an advantage — rather than a hindrance."

His mother glared at him, her eyes angry and incredulous. "Talk sense into him," she said turning to her husband. "Make him see what is good and what is right. At this moment, he has nothing between his ears except that girl. Bah! *Bodoh*! Stupid! What good is this western education?"

She stormed out of the room leaving Hussein alone with his father.

Hussein watched his mother's departing figure. He turned to his father, his eyes pleading for understanding. He thought that his father would see his point of view. But Rahim showed no sign of it as he stood up and came close to him.

"Your mother is right, Hussein. Have her as a girlfriend or a mistress if you must, but not as a wife. There is no future in that. Besides, you will not find a more lovely, devoted *and* devout girl than Shalimar. She is the sort of girl who will enjoy public approval." Seeing the look on Hussein's face, he added. "If this girl An Mei loves you, she will accept you on any condition. Why not put her to the test?"

"You don't understand. She is a good girl from a rich family, a family whose roots in the country go back for generations. Her family would not let her accept such a proposition."

"Yes, I know all about her family." Rahim waved his hand dismissively. "We had her checked out, the minute you came back with her. Her father deserted Malaysia, his own country, for another when times became bad. He showed little trust and belief in his own birthplace. How would people here react when you marry her? How do you think that sort of marriage would improve your chance in politics?"

"But it is not quite how you put it. He only left because of what happened to him; his shops had been ravaged by the mobs. Place yourself in his position. Imagine what you might do if you came home to a burnt out shell. If you put him in such light, then anything can be distorted to look bad. Your sending me abroad to study instead of letting me study in the local universities could also be misconstrued, for example, as a mistrust of the national curricula, the national education system. In fact, one could say that An Mei's father showed more trust in our local education system because he sent her to the University of Malaya before she went to Oxford for her post-graduate degree."

Rahim snorted and then turned his back to Hussein. It would seem it was not for nothing that his son had been sent overseas for education. He certainly spoke and argued better than most of his peers, he thought. Aloud though, he said, in a voice tinged with boredom, "I'm not going to argue with you. I just ask that you think about it. Ask your girl if she would agree to be just a girlfriend, mistress, whatever, without status, or not have you at all." He walked briskly out, holding his hand up palm outward as a gesture to silence any protestations that might come from Hussein. "And, while you are at it, cut off that damn ponytail! I would like to see you at prayers in the mosque this evening, minus that tail."

Chapter 12

Nelly folded the last of her clothes and packed them in the suitcase. Her movements were slow and mechanical. She felt detached and listless. She observed how her hands were able to function even when her mind was not on the task. She wrapped two pairs of shoes and tucked them into the corner of the case. "There," she sighed, her voice resigned, "that's it, all my life possessions once more in two suitcases and, in a couple of days, I'll be back in Kuala Lumpur." She sat down with a thump on the bed, causing it to sag under her weight.

"You don't have to do this," said Mei Yin, stricken with guilt, "you don't have to sacrifice yourself. You can still change your mind."

"Then what about An Mei? She won't have an excuse to remain in KL and that would mean Ming Kong would disinherit her because she will certainly refuse to come back. Besides, there is that crucial other matter of minding the shops and keeping the business going until we are sure we can survive here. I meant all that I said the other day."

"Oh how I wish that we could all go together. It just doesn't seem fair on you." Mei Yin sat down on the bed beside her.

"It is not about fairness. It's about practicality." Nelly stood up again and fussed around her suitcase before closing the lid with a finality that reflected her thoughts. "I have decided. Ming Kong has agreed. An Mei is happy. That is all there is to it."

"I cannot believe even now, how easily you persuaded Ming Kong to let you go," Mei Yin exclaimed.

"I think that deep down he too is worried about cutting off all ties with Malaysia in case it doesn't work out here. And I am sure he feels that giving An Mei responsibilities will snap her out of what he considers to be her infatuation with Hussein."

"Do you think that it might also be him trying to give An Mei a chance — by letting her stay on in KL to work out for herself what she really wants? I still cannot believe that he would fall for your suggestion that An Mei will be useful to you in KL."

"Why not? She speaks excellent English and Malay, which I do not. That is essential for business nowadays." Nelly stared into the distance deep in thought.

"Maybe you are right," she said after a while. "Ming Kong has changed. There might be a grain of truth in what you say. Maybe, it is his way of letting An Mei work it out herself without showing that he has conceded. We will never know unless he chooses to share his thoughts with us."

"Well right at this moment, he is busy with his plans and meetings. We are going this afternoon with Siew Lin to Soho's Chinatown to look at some premises that might be suitable for a restaurant. You are coming as well, are you not?" asked Mei Yin.

"No, you go. This will be for you and Ming Kong to decide. And don't worry about An Mei and me. Things will work out."

* * * * *

Mei Yin stared out of the taxi that they had taken from Paddington station. It had taken them an hour's train journey from Oxford. Her face was pale. In the month they had been in England, she had lost her tan. Thinking they must be tourists, the London cab driver insisted on giving them a running commentary of the sights: Baker Street, the home of Sherlock Holmes; Hyde Park with its renown Speaker's corner; Park Lane and the famous Dorchester Hotel; and then down past the entrance to Buckingham Palace, home of the Queen. From there they went on to Trafalgar Square and Nelson's column. People were milling around the square, some snapping photos, others feeding the seemingly thousands of pigeons gathered there. Suddenly a flock of pigeons rose into the sky, their wings flapping noisily amidst squeals of delight from the children.

Ming Kong looked at Mei Yin's face, examining the lines and planes of her cheekbones and long neck as though he was seeing her anew. His eyes softened and he felt a tremendous rush of love for his wife. She was still beautiful he thought, even after all these years. He reached out and held her hand in his. For the first time since he landed in England almost a month ago, he felt that he was getting somewhere and that something positive was about to happen.

The taxi finally reached the crowded streets of Soho and dropped them off at the entrance to Chinatown. Brightly coloured signs with Chinese calligraphy greeted them. Mei Yin sniffed the air and smiled, her mood brightening up.

"Even the air smells different here," she remarked, "so much like Chinatown back in KL, perhaps even brighter and more densely packed. Look at the number of restaurants." She pointed with delight at the roast ducks and meats hanging from hooks in the windows, their red-brown, gleaming skin offering a promise of succulence and crispiness. They made their way along the street until they reached a building on a corner where Siew Lin was stood waiting for them.

"This is it." Siew Lin gestured towards the building. "We could have a good Chinese restaurant here. It has great possibilities because this spot is virtually a junction for three streets so you can get customers from three different directions, all business flowing into this catchment. Good *feng shui*, water and wind, the balance of the elements bringing harmony and prosperity." She clapped her hand in excitement. "It is difficult to get such a spot. I had a *feng shui* expert check it out."

Mei Yin looked uncertainly at Ming Kong. "Siew Lin, can I have a word with Ming Kong?"

"Of course! Take your time," replied Siew Lin before disappearing into the premises.

"I'm not sure about this *feng shui* business. It is, however, in a good location," said Ming Kong. "But do we want to start a restaurant here?" exclaimed both Ming Kong and Mei Yin together as though reading each other's thoughts simultaneously. They broke into laughter.

"When you first broached the subject of restaurants, I had thought of an eatery serving Malaysian food, like a noodle bar, much like the hawker stalls back home where food is cooked in front of the clients, but instead of different stalls under different ownership, it would be under one management. I don't think that Soho needs yet another Chinese restaurant serving the same dishes. Look how many there are, just on this one street. There is too much competition here."

"Yes, I agree. By contrast, as far as I can tell, there does not appear to be many, if any, Malaysian restaurants here. Mind you, if we succeed, there will be many in the future. I think we have to go back to the drawing board. We ought to look elsewhere, perhaps consider university towns that have large Malaysian populations. We might still come back to this place because there are lots of Malaysians living in London.

"If we do take this place, I think we can make use of our experience of food stores by using part of the premises to display and sell Malaysian ingredients and pre-packed foods. The remainder could be the eatery. Eat, taste and buy ingredients to cook good Malaysian food at home, might be the sales pitch we could adopt. Few shops in London stock food ingredients from Malaysia. We can get Tek San involved. He can supply them to us," said Ming Kong recalling Tek San's food chains in Malaysia. His face grew animated; he was pleased with Mei Yin and her acuteness in sussing out the situation. "You have learnt a lot from running the cake business at home," he complimented her. "Nelly was right."

Mei Yin blushed with pleasure.

* * * * *

In the house at Oxford, Nelly sat opposite Jenny in the sitting room. Jenny had arrived without warning and Nelly felt awkward and shabby in her presence. Eyeing the beautifully cut suit Jenny was wearing, she tugged at her own *samfoo* top, recalling Mei Yin's plea for her to give up wearing Chinese clothes and to put on the pair of trousers and shirt blouse she had bought for her instead. "You won't stand out a mile and besides you will be warmer," she had advised.

"I'm sorry you have missed Mei Yin. She is out with Ming Kong. You have only me." She was not at ease with Jenny whom she viewed as more Mei Yin's friend than hers. "She won't be back until late, perhaps very late."

"It's okay. I can speak to you," said Jenny. She made herself comfortable, plumping a cushion and placing it behind her back. Relaxing into the sofa, she draped one arm over the back and crossed her legs. Her black leather pumps glimmered and shone.

Nelly had little to say to Jenny. They had few things in common. She fiddled with the cups of tea she had brought out from the kitchen, making a big show of placing them correctly, adjusting the cup handles this way and that as though it was of utmost importance to do so.

"Are you okay?" asked Jenny sensing her discomfort.

"Yes! Of course."

"Have you heard from An Mei?"

"I am going to see her. I am leaving for KL in a couple of days' time." Nelly did not wish to say any more about An Mei.

"What? You are leaving?"

"Yes, just to take care of bits and pieces at home and to look after An Mei."

"For how long?"

"I don't really know. It depends."

"Oh dear!" said Jenny. "I had hoped that I would see more of you in Oxford, now that I am to spend at least three months here. I so wished to get to know you better."

Nelly's scepticism must have shown because it prompted Jenny to explain herself. "I realise," she said, uncrossing her legs and leaning closer towards Nelly, "that in the past, we have had very little to do with each other because I am closer to Mei Yin, but I would like to change that."

Jenny wanted to make amends. She recalled how she had treated Nelly in the past. She blushed to think of how mean she had been.

"Such a shame," she continued. "In fact, I want to say how sorry I am that I do not know you better, because you have been such a pillar of support for Mei Yin. If there is anything I can do to help out in Kuala Lumpur, please let me know. Even if I am not there physically, I am sure I can help with a few phone calls."

Nelly looked out of the window and her eyes glazed over. She had an idea. "Perhaps," she said slowly, "perhaps you can help me. There is something I have to do for myself."

"Tell me."

"I am trying to trace a family in Singapore. The mother is someone called Mary Woo. She has two children, a boy and a girl. They will be quite old now, in their late 20s."

Chapter 13

Nelly threw open the window. The hinges groaned and creaked. Just over a month of absence and they had already turned rusty. Hot humid air rushed in filling the room with an all-pervading damp mustiness. She could feel the sunshine on her face, a blistering heat that turned her face instantly red, erasing the pallor of her skin, the result of a month of weak English sunshine. She breathed in deeply, enjoying the warmth that filled her lungs. "Home," she murmured contentedly, "at last, we are home. We are so lucky that Maan *sook* was unable to sell our house."

She rushed from window to window, throwing shutters open. "Help me An Mei. We have to get some help to give the house a good clean. Look at the dust! And cobwebs! Tomorrow, we will go to our shops and see how things are."

"Aunty you have only just arrived. Why don't you take a few days of rest to get used to things?"

"Rest? I have had enough of rest. I feel renewed vitality; the warmth has woken up my old bones." Nelly smiled, rubbing her eyes. "I admit I am a little sleepy and jet-lagged, but a nap will cure all that. Come, come and talk to me."

Together, they went up the stairs to the bedroom, trailing their fingers on the banisters, penning the thin veneer of dust into shimmering snakes. They threw open the bed covers and, pushing them aside, crept into the bed. Nelly put her arm around An Mei, patting her shoulder softly in the way she had done ever since she was placed under her care as a tiny girl.

An Mei buried her face deep into the pillow, her back was towards Nelly. "Aunty Nelly," she said, her voice somewhat muffled, "thank you for doing this for me. I know you have made a big sacrifice for me. I can't bring myself to return to Oxford. I love Hussein. I want to be here for him."

"Tell me, An Mei. Have his parents agreed to his marrying you? "

"No, his parents are still opposed to it. Hussein said that for the moment, we cannot be married, but we can carry on as we were before. Only this time, we will have to be more discreet..." Her voice trailed off. Nelly could hear the disappointment in her voice and feel her shoulders going limp under her enfolding arm. She held An Mei tighter, as though she hoped to absorb some of her pain. "By that," An Mei continued, her voice filled with hurt, "it means we do not go anywhere important together. See," she continued assuming a false brightness, "just like Aunty Jenny. I'm to be like her, someone who I have ridiculed in the past."

"Are you sure this is just temporary, for the moment, as he puts it? Would there be a chance in the future that he could, would marry you? I cannot put off explaining or telling your father forever. If Hussein cannot marry you, then you should think of your other options. Perhaps, go back to Oxford, find a job and start life again. You are young. At the moment, your father thinks that you are staying on only to help me out and that you have ended your relationship with Hussein. I have given my word that I'll look after you and I am sure he has interpreted that to mean that I will see to it that you no longer see Hussein."

An Mei turned to face Nelly. "I'll stay for a while," she said. "Perhaps, I can find work here. I'll help out in the shops," she added hastily, "but I would like to find my own work. Hussein too wishes to find his own feet. And if he can, I am sure we will be married. He would be able make his own decisions then and be less constrained by his family. At the moment, his wings are clipped. He has no money of his own. He is totally dependent on his parents. They wield such power over him. We need time to work things out."

"Can't he find a job on his own?"

An Mei recalled what Hussein had said to her. "In theory, yes. With his qualifications he should be able to get a good position. In practice, it would be difficult."

Nelly leaned over and planted a kiss on An Mei's wet cheeks before withdrawing her arm. She turned on her side. "Let me sleep and think about it."

*****

A week later, Nelly travelled to Singapore. She boarded the train at the Kuala Lumpur railway station. The station's mixture of neo-Moorish/Mughal architecture brought back sharp memories of her hasty departure from Singapore many years ago. It was here in this very station that she was directed to Penang and it was in Penang that she had met Ming Kong.

She sat alone as the train rolled forward, each jolt, each sound it made took her nearer to Singapore. Little had changed on the train, but so much of her life has been transformed. Her thoughts flew from one episode to another, but one scene kept coming back to haunt her. It was the day she abandoned her children to escape the incessant beatings of her former husband, Woo Pik Soo. The longing to hold them in her arms was like a fresh wound. She felt the sudden flood of warmth around her eyes as she recalled the scent of her children when she held them for the last time. She looked out of the window to avoid the curious stares of other passengers. Palm oil and rubber plantations rushed by, their orderly alignment seemed to mock the chaos in her life. She looked at her own reflection on the windowpane, seeing the change in herself. When she boarded the train all those years ago, she was slim, youthful with long black hair. Her reflection now showed an old, plump, grey-haired lady.

"I have to find them," she said aloud, waking the dozing passenger sitting next to her. His lolling head shot up abruptly as he looked with a confused expression at Nelly.

"Were you speaking to me?

"No!" replied Nelly.

"What-*lah*! Woke me up," he barked, clearly annoyed. "Don't do that again!" With that he dug deeper into his seat and turned his back to her and closed his eyes.

* * * * *

Clutching a piece of paper and her handbag, Nelly got out of the taxi at Bukit Timah, a leafy hilly suburb in Singapore. Huge houses with equally large gardens stood on either side of the road. The chatty taxi driver had told her that the hill, *Bukit*, had been originally named after the Temak trees that grew in abundance in the area but it had been wrongly pronounced during the colonial days as *Timah* or tin and the name had stuck. "See," he had waved his hand expansively, "no tin but it is still called Tin Hill! No tin but still rich. Only rich people live here." He eyed Nelly as she fished out her purse to pay him, hoping that his acknowledgement of the rich would bring him a big tip.

The taxi had stopped in front of a mansion, the size of which dwarfed even the other substantial surrounding buildings. Nervously, she checked the house number and then made her way to the mansion's gate, a massive wrought iron structure, painted green with sharp spear-like tops gilded gold. She buzzed the bell and within minutes the gate opened like a well-oiled machine opening its jaws to claim her. "Please enter," a voice echoed through the intercom. "Our mistress is expecting you."

Nelly mopped impatiently at the perspiration on her forehead and walked briskly forward. Shimmers of heat steamed up from the black tarmac. It enveloped her feet making them swell. Her legs grew heavy and she felt faint. She had become unaccustomed to the heat, even in the short time she had been in England. But she persisted, increasing her pace in her haste to reach the mansion. "I cannot run away this time," she told herself. The thought of seeing her children again made her forget her age, her weight and her lack of fitness. She hurried forward, puffing. She saw a servant in uniform coming down the steps of the mansion carrying a parasol.

"*Siew Nai,* mistress, wait! I have this shade for you. It is too hot to walk so fast." She saw the sweat that was pouring down from Nelly's face and thrust forward a waxed paper parasol painted with yellow chrysanthemums. Bamboo spokes, splayed out from the stem handle, supported the fragile fabric of the shade.

"Let me, let me," the maid said, holding it high above Nelly. "I will hold it. I am Ah Kuk's replacement. She died last year."

Nelly stopped in her track. For a moment, she was speechless. Already the unexpected had happened. She thought she would see Ah Kuk, and was looking forward to the reunion. Ah Kuk had been Mary's maid and had been so good to her. She had helped her look after her children.

"We should not stand under the sun. Mistress Mary is within. She is waiting," coaxed the maid, anxious to go into the house and escape the relentless heat.

They walked up the flight of steps that stretched the entire length of the terrace in front of the mansion to reach the entrance. By this time, Nelly was puffing hard. She paused at the top of the steps; her hand went to her heart to still its wild beating. She took a few deep breaths and then slowly, with great trepidation, she entered the house. Standing in the middle of the expansive hallway was an old lady, her hair almost pure white, her face a cobweb of wrinkles radiating from her eyes and her cheeks. Flanking her on either side were a man and a woman. He was very tall and she diminutive and slight. Nelly checked herself. She looked in bewilderment from one to the other; she pushed her spectacles up the bridge of the nose and looked again.

"Mary, Chai-chai and Mei-mei?" she asked hesitantly.

Nelly clasped her hand to her mouth, the motion, involuntary and clumsy. In all her dreams, she had pictured her children as they were when she left. She knew that after well-over twenty-five years, they would be adults. Yet in her mind, she held only an image of them as children, taller, bigger, yes, but nothing resembling the two adults standing before her. She could not recognise them. She turned to Mary.

"Mary? Is it you?" she asked again.

"Come, let's go and sit down. You are in shock." Mary smiled and, at that moment, Nelly saw, behind the wrinkles and shrunken outer-shell, the person who had helped her escape from her plight and who had looked after her children, her confidante, the woman who had been her previous husband's first wife. She took the hand extended to her and they went into the sitting room.

"This is your mother," said Mary to the man and woman beside her.

"Please, I have not come to claim them. I have lost all rights to call myself their mother," protested Nelly. "I just wanted to see them." She was shocked that Mary had spoken in that way. It was totally unexpected. When she had left all those years ago, she promised Mary that she would never come between her and the children and Mary had welcomed that promise.

Mary waved her hand dismissing Nelly's protest. "I have told them and I have explained everything. I made up my mind to do so after your friend, Jenny, called. I am getting old. I might not have much longer to live and I believe they have a right to know."

Nelly kept her gaze on the floor, apprehensive of the scorn and even hate that her children might show her. Her eyes were tightly shut, but this could not prevent the tears from oozing in a continuous trickle from their corners. She felt an arm around her shoulders, then, someone clasped her hand. She looked up at her two grown-up children, so different from what she had imagined but all that she had hoped and prayed for. "Forgive me," she asked.

"There is nothing to forgive," they replied in unison. "Mother, uh Mary, has explained everything."

"Please, you have to continue to call Mary, mother. Just call me *sum,* aunty." She lowered herself to the seat. She looked at Mary, seeking with her eyes, her permission. Mary nodded in encouragement and Nelly said, "Tell me about yourselves. Start from the very beginning. I want to know and share everything.

* * * * *

Nelly spent the night in Mary's house. The following day, she returned to Kuala Lumpur. In the short time she spent with her children and Mary, she learnt about all that happened after she left Singapore well over twenty-five years earlier. Several years after her departure, Woo Pik Soo, her husband and tormentor, had died of a massive heart attack. Mary and the children were in Johor when the Japanese first started bombing Singapore and were able to escape the worst of the damage. After the war, the Woo's business flourished and both children excelled in school and eventually went on to study first at the University of Singapore and then later on in Australia.

It was clear to Nelly that both Chai-chai and Mei-mei were close to Mary and viewed her as their mother. They spoke without rancour because they understood how their birthmother, Nelly, needed to escape from the continuous beatings and abuse of their father. But she sensed in their tale that they did not miss her because in Mary they found the mother they had always believed they had. Nelly recalled her hurt when she first learnt that her children did not remember her. She could still recall that one occasion when she tried to make contact. They had looked at her without a flicker of recognition when she had gone to the school playground to see them. Over time the hurt had eased, replaced by an understanding and acceptance that the shift in affection and affiliation was inevitable. In fact she welcomed the outcome for their sake.

They had exchanged news late into the night until exhausted they went to bed. Nelly felt a renewed bond with her children. However, with a sharp twinge of guilt, she realised that this bond was not as strong as the one she shared with An Mei. It was at that point that she could see herself in Mary's place. I am to An Mei what Mary is to my own children. Yes, I will maintain contact with Chai-chai and Mei-mei, but I will still keep some distance to give Mary space. She deserves it, she thought. The guilt that had plagued her for intruding into their lives after her abandonment of them seemed to dissipate after this decision. She sensed a real physical relief. They did not hate her. A serene smile crept over her face. Both children had pointedly asked her to stop calling them by their childhood nickname when in company.

"It would not do," said Mary "for you to call them by their childhood names. Professionally Chai-chai is Dr. Jeremy Woo and Mei-mei is Dr. Jane Woo. Jane is a medical doctor; Jeremy has a PhD in economics. They both adopted English names when they were studying abroad. They experienced such problems when they used their full Chinese names that eventually they gave in to the demands of their friends to have 'proper' names!"

"Jeremy, Jane," she whispered to herself, "*hai ho tang*, good sounding names."

* * * * *

"Where have you been?" An Mei asked the minute Nelly stepped from the train on to the platform in Kuala Lumpur. "Let me carry your holdall," she said taking the little grey bag from her aunt. "Why all that secrecy? Maan *sook* said that you turned up in the office and went out immediately leaving only a message for me. And what a message! 'I am going to Singapore and will be back shortly.' This is not like you. Why did you go? What is wrong? What happened?"

"What about a hug first?" replied Nelly, her face beaming with joy.

An Mei dropped the bag on the floor and hugged Nelly tight. "I missed you. I was so worried that father would call while you were away."

"Well," said Nelly, "it did worry me a bit, but I had to go. Let's get into the car and I'll tell you all about it."

Chapter 14

An Mei wove her way between the chairs, desk and boxes of samples in the tiny office, arranging and re-arranging them. She could not settle down. She had tried calling Hussein but could not reach him and he had not called back. She could not bear the silence and felt herself wavering between the decisions open to her. What if he changed his mind under the pressure of his parents? Was he not there because he did not want to take her calls? Doubts crept into her mind. Then there was the phone call from her father asking how Nelly and she were getting on in the shops. He had not asked specifically about Hussein. He was, as Nelly had pointed out, pretending that nothing had happened. But the unspoken question was there. She felt it in every nuance, every question he asked. Nelly's sudden revelation on her return from Singapore added yet another dimension to her confusion — her aunt had a separate family of her own! How could that be? She could not bear sharing Nelly, even if it was with her own children.

Nevertheless her curiosity drove her to devour the photographs Nelly had bought back with a voracity that surprised even her. The young man, Jeremy, was tall and slim. His face had little of Nelly. She observed the strong chin, the determined mouth and the pair of steady eyes under thick eyebrows that spoke of strength and commitment. Involuntarily, she compared him to Hussein with his handsome brown face and charismatic charm. In Jane, she saw what Nelly might have been when she was young, with calm almond eyes, beautiful in their serenity and pale, pale skin. "She has such beautiful hair," she had complimented her aunt and was taken aback by the happiness and pride in Nelly's face. She felt a pang of jealousy and then remorse over her own selfishness.

Nelly watched her from the corner of the office. She had a stack of files in front of her and was going over the books and accounts. "Sit down or you will wear down the floor. I need you to help me out and learn this. You will take this over eventually."

"Are you going to tell father?" asked An Mei.

"You mean about my seeing Jeremy and Jane. Yes, but not right now. When I first met your father, I told him of my previous life. So, he knows about them."

"What should I do?" asked An Mei switching to her own immediate concerns. "Hussein is not returning my calls."

"Perhaps he does not know you called. When is he supposed to come to see you? Is he back on the East coast with his parents?"

"I believe so. I was so sure of what to do but now, after days of not hearing from him, I am confused once again. My resolve weakens each time I speak to father on the phone. I feel so guilty. I feel like I am cheating, lying to him."

"What you need is interesting work. With work, you will be able to focus your mind on something that has a beginning and an end. It leaves you less time to brood."

"Tell me Aunty Nelly. Am I right to come back to Kuala Lumpur to be with Hussein? Am I right to hurt my father with my selfishness, to involve you in this deception?"

"We've been through all these questions. There is never a clear right or wrong. But it is certainly wrong if Hussein is not prepared to commit himself. Then all the sacrifices you have made would be meaningless. You will have hurt your family for nothing. If that is the case, you should think of going back to Oxford before your father learns of our deception."

An Mei did not like being reminded that she might consider returning to Oxford. Her face changed from fretful to glum. She was so torn. When she was with Hussein, things seemed so much clearer, but away from him, one thought chased after another until she became completely muddled.

"Perhaps you need a more challenging job to keep your mind occupied," continued Nelly. "When I mentioned to Jeremy your interest in looking for work, he said that his bank's office in Kuala Lumpur is looking to recruit a banking executive. If selected, you will be trained. From what I understand from him, new recruits have to undergo rigorous training programmes. Then in the evenings, you could help me out with this," she said, pointing to the files of correspondence and accounts, "it would not be such a deception on my part because you will still be helping me out. I can say so with conviction to your father. You will also be too busy to fret like you are now." Nelly smiled to take the edge off her words. "Fretting is not going to get you anywhere. Perhaps, this will cheer you up. Jenny is back in Kuala Lumpur. She flew back yesterday. She was curious to know what happened at my meeting with my children and she has cut short her stay in Oxford. We are meeting her for dinner."

* * * * *

An Mei dressed with extra care that evening. She looked at the image in the mirror and for the first time in days, she smiled. The new hairstyle suited her. Nelly had sent her to the hairdresser, having failed to get her to settle down in the office. Her hair swung freely, a sheen of black descending to her bare shoulders. Nelly had given her a pair of gold and ruby stud earrings to wear with her simple white cotton shift, caught at the shoulders with two thin shoe string straps, and white high-heeled sandals. Her eyes shone with excitement. She had caught the sun and her skin glowed with health. Jenny had called again to say that she had managed to get hold of Hussein and had persuaded his parents to let him accompany her to a function. They were not in the East coast. They were in Kuala Lumpur because Hussein was being considered for a post in UMNO, the main Malay political party. An Mei could feel her heartbeat quickening. All thoughts and doubts as to why he had not called when he was in Kuala Lumpur temporarily left her mind.

* * * * *

Jenny gently nudged Hussein towards the sofa. She sat herself down. "We have time to talk before we meet up with An Mei and Nelly," she said looking up. "Do sit down," patting the seat adjacent to her. "It is such a strain to have you towering over me." She had collected Hussein from his family home and driven him to her house rather than the restaurant where they were to meet An Mei. "Now tell me everything."

He looked sheepish; he recalled the way he had answered her when she warned him of his parent's likely opposition. He had been rude, even insulting. He walked away from her and sat down on an armchair.

"You were right," he admitted, shrugging his shoulders, "my parents are dead set against our marriage. Father has conceded that I can continue seeing An Mei, but only if we are discreet and quiet about our relationship. At least for the moment, marriage will be out of the question unless I ignore my parents. This, however, would mean that I would have to sever my relationship with them and to tell you the truth, I am reluctant to do that."

Afraid, more likely, she thought to herself as she saw the nervous tick at the corner of his mouth. She was surprised at the change in him. The confident young man she knew in Oxford had all but disappeared.

Hussein pressed both his hands into his temple, ruffling his hair, feeling its unaccustomed shortness. He had cut his hair as his father had ordered. He could not bear to have Jenny staring and appraising him. He felt himself slipping away. The stranglehold of his familial ties had wiped out all the independence he had felt in England. The bravado he had shown to Jenny when he challenged her advice was long gone and in its place he could only offer excuses.

"I am so confused. They have packed each day with so much activity in the name of advancing my career that I have hardly any time to myself. I have not even been able to call An Mei," he confessed. "My parents are with me every single moment of the day. Can you help? Talk to them?"

"I would if I could, but I doubt they would pay much attention to me." Jenny paused, her brow etched with concern. "An Mei will be devastated. Have you told her the truth, that you cannot marry her? You have to. Otherwise, she will be deluded into staying and waiting for you."

"I tried to but she is convinced that, if I can find my own way and she hers, we will be able to marry once we are financially independent and that our parents would eventually reconcile themselves to the fact that we are in deeply in love."

"And you? Do you feel the same way?"

"I don't really know."

*****

An Mei and Nelly were already seated at the table when Jenny and Hussein arrived. They made their way to the far corner of the dimly lit restaurant, threading carefully between the scatter of seats and tables around the central floor space that had been kept clear for the evening's entertainment. Despite the return to normality, few of the tables were occupied. People were still wary of going out. A Malay folk dance group was promised as the night's attraction and already the drums and cymbals were laid out. A tinkling of chords sounded and suddenly, with a roll of drums, the dancers took to the floor. Lights flashed and as they flexed their bare feet and stamped to the music, jumping deftly between clapping bamboos, their anklet bells tinkled. Hussein seemed transfixed by the stylised gestures of the dancers, their brightly painted faces and elaborate hairstyles and costumes.

"Come, they are waiting for us," said Jenny impatiently, sensing his reluctance to move. She was determined that Hussein should tell An Mei the truth. Hussein's changed manner alarmed her. He was nothing more than a shell of the once dynamic young man at Oxford.

Hussein was even more nervous than he had been moments ago in Jenny's house. When they reached the table, all he could do was say hello to An Mei and Nelly. He looked at An Mei and then guiltily turned away to address Nelly. An Mei's face tugged at his heartstrings; he just could not bring himself to look her in the eye. He could not focus his thoughts; he fretted over Jenny's insistence that he should tell An Mei the truth. He smiled weakly. His eyes caught An Mei's briefly, and then, almost abruptly, he looked away again.

The smile on An Mei's face vanished. She was puzzled by his behaviour. The excitement and anticipation that had led her to make such an effort with her appearance were extinguished as rapidly as they had arisen. Her shoulders sagged. Nelly, who was sitting next to her, could sense her changing emotions. She grasped An Mei's elbow, squeezing it gently to instil strength and give her support. She felt An Mei straighten herself imperceptibly.

"Let's order and get that out of the way," Jenny said, gesturing to the waitress to take the orders. "Then, we'll talk. Hussein wants to say something to you."

Hussein started. "Now?"

"Yes, now," answered Jenny, her voice firm and uncompromising.

Irritated by Jenny's insistence, his resentment at being manipulated by everyone surged. He felt betrayed by Jenny, when he thought she should help him out. "All right, I will, but not here. And not in front of everyone," he said, all traces of the uncertainty and guilt that had clouded his face earlier, gone. "Come An Mei, let us get out of here."

So saying he took her hand and, half dragging her to her feet, ushered her out of the restaurant without a backward glance at the two older ladies. Once they were outside in the courtyard, he turned to An Mei. His eyes that had been waxing and waning in guilt and confusion suddenly came into focus. And An Mei saw the decisive Hussein of old. Yet, something had changed. She could not place it and withdrew her hand from his tight grasp.

"I love you," he said in a rush. "I want you to share a life with me. Isn't it enough to be with me and to share in every aspect of my life? Is marriage so important that you would rather relinquish our being together for its sake? You will be my wife in every sense of the word, except officially. Wouldn't that be enough?"

The words poured out of him, the same words that his father had said to him day in and day out for the past week. He had insisted that Hussein could have An Mei as his soul mate so long as it was not official. "If she loves you," he had said, "that should suffice for her. If she loves you," he had repeated, "she would do this for you and she would understand. Test her." Gradually, Hussein's original views weakened. He felt that the only way he could have An Mei was to do as his father bade him. Jenny's insistence that he told An Mei the truth to set her free angered him. He wanted An Mei and the more he spoke the words of his father to her, the more convinced he became that this was the best way out of his dilemma. He had no doubt about his love for An Mei, but equally he was in no doubt that he would find it hard to make a life of his own without the support of his parents. And if they were to be actively against him, all chances of his making good in politics would be gone. To be part of the ruling political party was now within his grasp and already he could see himself rising in its ranks. To deal in politics in Oxford, surrounded by peers and teachers who hail independence of thought and freedom of speech, was entirely different from the real world of politics. It was, as his father and mother kept reminding him, not a question of how qualified you are, but how many strings could be manipulated to help you.

An Mei tried to pull away from him. He reached out to restrain her, accidentally catching her shift dress at the waist. There was a sound of tearing as the shoulder strap gave way under the strain of his tug and her pull.

"No!" she cried out, drawing the bodice of her shift closer to her. The sharp sound and her cry brought two waitresses running out to the courtyard. Already puzzled by the earlier commotion when Hussein unceremoniously marched An Mei out to the courtyard, they had been hovering by the door to follow what was happening.

"Can we help?" they asked looking at An Mei's distraught face, worried that the restaurant would become caught up in a dispute between the couple. They knew from recent events that what seemed like a quarrel between lovers could turn into an ugly fight when people of two different ethnic origins were involved.

Hussein turned to them in fury. "Go! This does not concern you. We are just having a discussion."

"No! Don't go," An Mei called to the two girls. Turning to Hussein, she said, "I have nothing more to say to you. You have changed. You were the one who persuaded me to come back to KL with you. I defied my parents for you and broke their hearts. I thought we had agreed that we should make our own way and marry and that we should then win over our parents into accepting our marriage. You have reneged on all we agreed. Go! If anyone is to go, it should be you." She turned, brushing his hand away from her and, holding her dress strap, began heading back into the restaurant.

Hussein ran after her. "So you don't love me enough. My father is right."

Tears of self-pity gleamed in his eyes. An Mei halted mid-stride. She brought her hand to his face, wiping his wet face with her palm and whispered, "It is *you* who do not love me sufficiently."

"Please don't say no. Think about it," he pleaded.

The anger in her was fast subsiding and pity grew in its place. He was not as strong as she had thought. She would have to be strong for the two of them. She realised that deep down she still felt Hussein was part of her.

"In England, people do not necessarily marry to be together. Can we not adopt this attitude, so that we can be together at least? I love you," he pleaded.

"This is not England," she replied, but with each word her will weakened and when he put his arms around her and clasped her to him she felt her resolve losing ground.

"Let me think about it." Pushing him away, she walked back into the restaurant.

* * * * *

"No! No! Don't do it. I have some hope of persuading your father to accept the situation if you were to marry, but I have no hope at all if you just live together." Nelly was furious with Hussein and frustrated by An Mei's seeming inability to defend herself against him. She wanted to shake some sense into her.

She wanted to take Hussein by the collar and slap him. Her voice, normally low and quiet, rose. She brought her fist down on the table like a cleaver.

Jenny, startled by Nelly's unaccustomed violence, stood up, toppling her seat behind her. "I am going to speak to Hussein. But please keep your voice down," she said before hurrying away to look for him.

Unheeding, Nelly continued, "What an insult! How could Hussein ask you to hang around, be here for him, while he offers you nothing in return? Think, An Mei, your father will not agree to this and he will disown you. You will break his heart. And what about your mother and me? We will be placed in an impossible situation. I cannot continue with this lie and keep you here for Hussein under such conditions. Will you risk losing your family for someone who does not even want to share his name with you?"

People turned in their direction, attracted by the loud voice. Waitresses flocked around the table, keen to hear what was being said. An Mei bowed her head with embarrassment. "Please, can we leave?"

* * * * *

Once back in the house, An Mei ran up the stairs and into her bedroom. She bolted her door. Abandoning all attempts to hold on to her dress, she let go of the strap. The shift fell immediately to her ankles and she stepped out of it. Pulling the bedclothes off her bed, she draped them around her and went out onto the balcony. The night air was warm, but she shivered as it came into contact with her bare skin. She sank down on the floor, the tiles cold against her buttocks. Cross-legged, she sat covered by the clothes she had gathered around her and inhaled deeply on the night air. A rich, almost over-powering perfume of Jasmine filled her lungs.

She sat there for a long time, upright, her face turned upward to the night sky, eyes closed, oblivious to the pounding on the door and Nelly's anguished voice asking her to come out and talk with her. The pounding ceased. There was a scuttle of footsteps as she went away. Then, she returned and she spoke again, but much softer this time, "I am sorry. I spoke too harshly. I've left a glass of water for you outside the door. I will be in my bedroom, when you are ready to talk. *Yeong-yeong to yow tuk seong leong*. All things can be discussed and solved."

An Mei heard her footsteps receding, and then all was quiet except for the sounds of the night. The humming of insects filled her ears, interspersed by the *chik-chak* calls of the geckoes. She dropped her head to the palm of her hand and wept, the hot tears seared through her skin.

"God, please help me. What shall I do?"

She sat still, her face wet with tears that just would not stop flowing. The darkness grew, lights faded as households went to sleep. Still she sat there. Hours passed. Dawn broke. The first glimmer of sunlight peeped through the strata of clouds on the horizon, breaking into thin wavelengths of colour: orange, mahogany red against a background of clear bright blue. In the distance, a cock crowed, dogs barked. Then imperceptibly, almost without notice, the cool dampness of the night air gave way to the growing heat of the sun. An Mei got up. Her legs could hardly bear her weight after the long hours of being twisted in a wedge under her body. She made her way to her bed, crawled into it and fell asleep.

Chapter 15

An Mei opened the door of the study quietly and peeped into the room. Nelly was sprawled on an armchair; her head lolled to one side of the backrest. Her eyes were closed and her arms hung loosely on either side of the chair. The maid had warned An Mei that Nelly had been up the whole night waiting for her to come to speak to her. When morning came and there was still no sign of An Mei, Nelly had tried to break open An Mei's bedroom door. Failing that, she then tried positioning a ladder on the flowerbed below to climb up to the balcony to check on An Mei. Finally succumbing to the restraints of the cook, she had run from one room to the other like a mad woman, until, exhausted, she had fallen asleep on the armchair.

An Mei tiptoed to her aunt and knelt down beside her. She placed an arm around her aunt and laid her head on her knees. Nelly woke up and immediately clasped An Mei to her, bending her head to kiss An Mei's.

"I know what I should do," said An Mei. "I will keep myself occupied with work, as you suggested. I will stay on in KL, help you out in the evenings and get a job during the day. I need that to be independent. That way, we will fulfil our commitment to father. I won't be Hussein's mistress because that is essentially what he is offering me. Instead I will wait for him to find himself and change his mind about marriage. Until then, I will not be his."

"Dear girl, you are not proposing to wait for him forever, are you? You have a whole life before you."

"I am taking things one step at a time. I cannot give him up at this point. But, who knows, I might give him up with time. Until then, I will just wait."

Nelly drew An Mei to her feet and stood up. "I am sorry for all those harsh words. I know I was wrong to try to force you into my way of thinking. I was so angry with Hussein. I was so frightened for you. I have such hopes for you."

"I know. You are right. Malaysia is not England. I will not be able to start again to find a life partner here if I were to so freely and publicly give myself away. I am not sure that this might not be true even in England amongst the Chinese community. The Age of Aquarius has certainly not arrived in this country. I feel tainted, dirty. Perhaps in a few years' time, things might change. All I wish to do for the moment is to achieve something for myself."

"You are not tainted," protested Nelly. She lowered her gaze briefly, recalling her conversation with Mei Yin when she had voiced her fears about society's views on sex before marriage. "You are right. Perhaps, time will solve things for us."

"Can we talk to your son, Jeremy, about the job?"

Nelly's face brightened. "Yes. He has already offered to help."

"Does he know about Hussein and me?

"That has not entered into our conversation."

* * * * *

A uniformed, turbaned footman, complete with gold-fringed epaulettes, opened the huge glass door. Jeremy stepped aside to let An Mei enter before following her into the foyer. A black marble floor tinged with woven gold and red stretched from one end of the room to the other.

"It's on the first floor. Let's take the stairway," he suggested, pointing to a central staircase that wound upwards hemmed in by ornate railings to the next floor.

They walked up the steps in silence, the tapping of her high heels echoed in contrast to the soft fall of his leather shoes. She felt a sense of vertigo. Everything was huge, enormous even, in the building. Two years away from Kuala Lumpur and things had changed. Buildings seemed to have become bigger and the high rise blocks even higher. Wealth it seemed was measured by size, and success by the ability to dwarf neighbouring buildings.

"This way," he said pointing to an exquisitely carved door to the right of the stairway. "I have spoken to them about you and they are expecting us. I am sure you will be fine. I had a look at your curriculum vitae and it was impressive."

Nervously, she acknowledged his encouragement.

"After the preliminary introductions, I will not be taking part in your interview. I will not be involved in the final decisions." He felt the need to explain as Nelly had said how keen An Mei was to get the job. "It is an American bank and the board's decision is solely theirs."

"Yes, I would not expect otherwise. Thank you," An Mei replied, slightly amused at his discomfort.

* * * * *

"We'll meet up with Kai Min and her husband Tek San tonight. Kai Min is An Mei's aunt, her father's youngest sister. I'll introduce you, Jeremy. I am sure you will like them. They are very forthright and keen to meet you," Nelly said, leaning forward from the back seat of the car to pat Jeremy on the shoulder. He was driving.

She turned to An Mei, at her side, "And we must also tell them about your new job, An Mei. *Gong hei, gong hei!* Congratulations! It is such a pity that Jane cannot be with us." Bending closer to An Mei, she whispered in her ear, "We have to make an extra effort with your uncle Tek San. Relations between your father and Tek San are still a bit awkward because of past misunderstandings and business rivalry. Your mum's failure to ask for their help when you fled from Oxford has only added to the tension. Kai Min has always considered your mother, Mei Yin, as her best friend so she is miffed. She is coming around though. I have primed her about your decision to stay and have extracted a promise that she will keep it between us."

"Where are we going?" asked Jeremy, unaware of what was being said. He steered the car through the congested streets. "It would seem that things are beginning to settle down at least in this part of Chinatown. People seem to be going about their day-to-day business," he observed.

"Tek San said to meet at his favourite *kopitiam*. I have forgotten its name. He said it has been five months since he has eaten there. It is a coffee shop in Chinatown, near the Rex cinema. It is a grotty place in an old alleyway. Do not be surprised to see rats scuttling by," she teased. "Tek San is always going on and on about the good old days and the flavour of food in the past."

They turned into a brightly lit street. A neon display with the caption *Rex Cinema* loomed large.

"Look, we have arrived. Park over there."

They got out of the car and walked over to the corner coffee shop. Bright neon lights lit up the 'open-plan' eatery. Where there should have been walls, individual food stalls were set up instead, separating it from the roadside. Wooden tables with rickety stools were set in the middle of the coffee shop as well as by the roadside. Jeremy looked at the stained floor and walls.

"Where should we sit? Inside?" he asked, looking at the tables in the room and the slowly revolving fans on the ceiling. He could feel the simmering heat from the hot cauldrons and pans in the stalls. "Perhaps not. Outside?" he asked turning to look at the tables by the roadside.

"Not much of a choice. It seems to be between smouldering heat inside or car fumes outside," said An Mei. Despite herself, she could not help but smile at his discomfort. "But the food will be good, perhaps not as hygienic as one might have wished, but Aunty Nelly will see to it. Just watch." Nelly had told her of Jeremy's fear of getting food poisoning.

"I am not worried," he replied pretending indifference. "When you are in Singapore, I'll take you to Bugis Street and you will see that I am not at all unfamiliar with such set-ups. Singapore may have had a big clean-up campaign but there are still lots of the old places left."

"Bugis Street! What are you thinking off? Don't you dare take An Mei there. *Ham blan do hai kai tai, hang lei, hang hui!* It is full of transvestites, men dressed as women walking here and there," cried Nelly.

Both An Mei and Jeremy laughed. "That is why it is worth a visit! Plenty of entertainment and eating stalls."

"*Choi! Choi!* Bad luck! Bad Luck! Who wants to eat in such a place?" muttered Nelly darkly. But she was pleased. It was the first time since her return to Kuala Lumpur that she had seen An Mei really smiling.

"Well, let us take this table on the kerb. It is cooler here," she suggested and drew up a stool and sat down. An Mei and Jeremy followed suit. Immediately, youngsters, dressed in ill-fitting shorts and tee shirts, some no older than twelve, and all in various degree of grubbiness, surrounded them each demanding that they order food from them.

"*Char Hokkien mee*, fried Fukien noodles," one shouted. Another, not to be outdone, proclaimed, "the best *Chui yuk chok*, pork balls congee!" This was followed by another loud voice coming from the back, "*Sui gow tong*, prawn dumpling soup!" The children gathered around the table, repeating their offers by rote until Nelly told them, "Wait. We are meeting someone. Just bring us tea, a big pot and it must be boiling hot, and also a small basin and some bowls. Then, we'll order."

An Mei looked at Jeremy, her eyes twinkling, and mouthed, "Just watch."

A big enamel pot, chipped in places, arrived with small China teacups and bowls. Nelly immediately poured the boiling hot tea into the basin and rinsed the bowls and chopsticks that had been set earlier in a holder in the centre of the table. Satisfied that they were clean, she then fished out tissues from her bag and wiped each utensil carefully before placing them back on the table. "Germs," she said very seriously. "Can never be too careful. Another pot of tea, please," she added to the urchin waiting for her order,

An Mei placed her hand over her mouth to stifle a giggle.

"I'm no stranger to such treatment of germs," Jeremy said, keeping a straight face and determined not to be outdone. "In Singapore, Mary does much the same thing." He mimicked Nelly's vigorous cleaning of the chopsticks. More children gathered around the table. They too laughed. No one was offended. "Yes," they chorused, "germs."

An Mei looked away. A shadow crossed her face. Thoughts of Hussein intruded into her mind. He would not have been able to join in such revelries in a place like this, she thought, looking at the meats and poultry hanging at each stall. Every dish had pork, that essential meat for Chinese dishes. Even the fat used was likely to be pork lard. And, of course, nothing was *halal*. She did not know how she could have deluded herself into believing that they could be together when so many things, even common everyday things, divided them.

Nelly saw the sadness on An Mei's face. She wanted to reach out and comfort her but refrained. Distraction would be the best remedy. She saw two figures walking towards them. Her face brightened. She stood up and placed a hand on An Mei's shoulder.

"They are here. Kai Min and Tek San!" Nelly took two more stools from a neighbouring table for them. "Please sit. Let us order first. I'll introduce everyone later. The poor children are getting impatient. You know, they have to go to school tomorrow and probably need to find time to squeeze in some homework between serving guests." Turning to An Mei, she explained, "They are probably the stall owners' children. They work hard to earn enough money to send their children to school. Some even manage to send them overseas for education. But the children are expected to do their share."

"*Hokkien mee* for me," said Tek San promptly as he hitched up his trousers to sit down. "I love the dark-sauced, fat noodles fried with pork, prawns and squid. Black paradise!"

"I'll have the same," said Kai Min, "but with white rice vermicelli, please. Less fattening than those thick yellow noodles that my husband likes," she continued, patting Tek San on his girth before turning to Nelly. "Tell me, is this Jeremy, the son you spoke of on the phone?" she asked quietly, her eyes examining him. "You have still to introduce us."

Jeremy heard and looked at Nelly expectantly. With a quick glance around the table, Nelly introduced Jeremy immediately. Her face was filled with a mixture of pride and apprehension. She had already explained over the phone to Kai Min about her rediscovered family after she had called Ming Kong. Kai Min, taken by surprise, had demanded detailed background and explanations, exclaiming that she had no inkling of Nelly's past. Nelly had told her then and had no wish to dwell on her affairs in public again. Instead, she told them of An Mei's success in getting a job with Citicorp.

"Congratulations!" Tek San said. "So you will stay on in KL. What about...?"

"Kai Min will tell you later," Nelly cut in. "Do you want to hear about An Mei's job?"

"Yes, tell us," said Kai Min, kicking Tek San's shins under the table.

Chapter 16

Mimi walked into An Mei's office. She was flustered." It's that Mr. Hussein again," she announced. "He has called you three times this morning. He is now waiting in reception. He insists on seeing you, even when I said that you were busy and that he needs to make an appointment. He would have barged in if I had not stopped him."

An Mei feigned a nonchalance she did not feel. "Give me five minutes and then send him in please," she instructed her secretary and continued with what she was doing, her head bowed low over the desk. Mimi opened her mouth to speak, but checked herself. It was not her business, but the man had been calling persistently every day this week. She walked out of the room to do as she was told.

An Mei kept on with her writing until the door closed behind Mimi. She put her pen down and leaned back in her chair. It had been some ten months since she had taken the job with the bank and in the last couple of months she had begun to take some of Hussein's telephone calls. But she had not answered them this week. They intruded too much into her peace of mind. She was settling in to her job and her boss was full of praise. "A hardworking, capable and trustworthy employee with a quick and innovative mind," he had written in the last review.

In the evenings, she carried out her promise to help with her father's business. She kept every minute of her time occupied. The pain and hurt she felt had not eased, but she had successfully pushed them to the back of her mind, at least, until nightfall and bedtime. Resolutely she worked hard to fill her days with activities. If she had any time after she attended to Nelly's needs, she went to her old University campus to play netball or badminton. She longed to join a gym and attend keep-fit classes, but these were not widely available. "Girls don't go to the gym; gyms are only for men," was Nelly's comment. Despite Nelly's misgivings, An Mei had started jogging in the park early in the morning before work. She would return home, wet with sweat and her leg muscles taut from the exercise, to take a quick hot shower before going to the office. She had grown toned and brown; her large almond eyes were alert and bright. The slightly apprehensive and unsure expression of the past was replaced now by one of confidence and determination.

Although she would occasionally have a faraway, wistful look when Hussein intruded into her thoughts, she was always able to get a grip on herself and address the situation at hand. Even so she found Hussein's persistent calls wearing her thin. She could not afford to let him find a chink in her armour. She regretted taking that call two months ago and agreeing to see him. She was determined that this first meeting with him would also be the last. Straightening her pencil-slim skirt, she crossed her legs and placed the writing pad in front of her in an attempt to find something, anything that could occupy her if things got tricky. She felt her heart beating almost uncontrollably; *thud, thud, thud.*

The door opened and Mimi put her head in to announce Hussein. He did not wait for her to finish. He strode in, weaving from behind her without a backward glance, leaving Mimi aghast at his boldness. She hovered for a minute and then left, quietly closing the door behind her.

An Mei saw him approaching. She sat frozen in her seat. She was determined to keep some distance between Hussein and herself. She motioned him to the seat in front of her desk. He ignored her and walked purposefully towards her, skirting around the desk.

"No, please take a seat." She had difficulty controlling her voice. It came out high-pitched. Her face was grave as she waved him back to the chair. She did not smile. She felt a smile would be her undoing. She remained very stern even while she greeted him and went through the formality of asking how he was. Her expression gave no inkling that her legs felt like jelly and that, if she had stood-up, she would not have been able to remain standing. She examined the face that had been so dear to her in her memory. Her heart continued its wild flutter. This would be the last time she saw him, she told herself.

"An Mei, why have you stopped taking my calls? Have you nothing more to say to me than mere pleasantries?" He stood up and made as though he was going to come round the desk to her again.

"No!" she said sharply, panic in her voice. "No, stay where you are. I do not have much time. I have a client coming to see me in five minutes. So please say what you have to say. We should not see each other again. I took your calls only because

I felt that I should be polite, and I wanted to know how you were. I know now and what else there is to learn I can read in the newspapers. You are doing well. You are making a mark in politics. It is what you wanted."

"An Mei, have you not heard what I have been saying to you all this time. I love you. Will you marry me?"

Taken aback, she went death-pale. She grasped the edge of the table.

"Why?"

"I have always wished us to marry. It is just circumstance that did not allow it."

"And these circumstances have changed?" she asked. She could not avoid the sarcasm that crept into her voice.

"Yes, my father has agreed to our marriage." Hussein dropped his eyes. He let out a sigh. Linking his fingers and clasping both hands together as though in prayer, he brought his forehead down towards them. He stayed in that position, head on the clasped hands, both elbows resting on his knees, looking at the floor. He could not bring himself to look at An Mei because he was not telling her the caveat his father had attached to the agreement. "You are a Muslim. You are entitled to four wives. She should know her position. And I expect you to take at least another wife, this time a true Muslim girl, a Malay girl, preferably someone with good connections. You can divorce An Mei after you tire of her. So have her, if you must. It seems that this is a price I have to accept in order to get you to focus on your career."

He kept his head bowed, muttering to himself that he would never do this to An Mei. That he would not take another wife. He convinced himself that there was no reason to tell An Mei and upset her when he had no intention of doing what his father had demanded. All he could think of was to be together with An Mei and the immediate gratification of having her to himself.

An Mei misunderstood his posture; she thought he was not able to look at her and kept his head bowed because he feared losing her and regretted his past actions. She stood up and went to him. She knelt next to his chair; she placed her head close to his and without thinking, kissed the top of his head. And the very next moment, she found herself in his arms.

She pushed him away. "Wait, wait, not here. Please go." She rushed back to sit behind her desk. Everything was going too fast and contrary to all that she had planned. She could not deal with it. She could not absorb the situation fully. She was alarmed, appalled even at her own actions.

"I'll see you later, but not at home. Aunt Nelly will not allow it. Meet me at the Lake Club after work."

He made as though to go to her. She shook her head. "No! Go! Please," she pleaded.

*****

Hussein walked into his parent's residence with barely a glance at the tall columns in the entrance, standing incongruously in the tropical surrounds. The columns, huge and imposing, were inspired by the 'wedding cake' in Rome's Piazza Venezia, the famous *Monumento Nazionale a Vittorio Emanuele II*. His parents were awed with what they saw in Italy and made a grand building of similar design a 'must have' in their list of things to acquire. He had tried to talk them out of it, but they ignored him. "Son, you do not know of such things. A building of such size and grandeur is bound to impress people," they had replied. "It will be a wonderful place in which to entertain and will soon become the envy of everyone in Kuala Lumpur."

His father and mother were waiting for him in the drawing room. They sat facing the French windows with their heavy gold damask curtains draped artfully on either side. His mother had her back to him as he entered the drawing room. His father, who was sat at a half angle facing the window turned, cocked his eye questioningly, and asked, "*Sudah?* Done?"

"*Sudah,*" Hussein replied.

"Then, let us get on with the planning in preparation for the next party meeting. We will put you forward as the candidate for the ministerial post."

"Isn't that a bit presumptuous? I am still new and learning the ropes. Shouldn't we wait?"

"Leave it to us," Rahim replied, waving away Hussein's protestation with impatience. "Get *Tengku* Ahmad to join us. He is in the library," he instructed the servant, before turning to address his son. "We need young people like you with new ideas. Have you not heard our new Prime Minister's instruction? He said he needs young leaders who are grounded in the Muslim faith and Malay culture, and who can debate both in English and Malay, to take up ministerial posts. Wouldn't you say you fit the bill? Or have I wasted my money sending you to Oxford?"

Hussein could only shrug his shoulders. He felt that to argue with his father would just be a waste of energy. It was far better to go along with what he said. He was also feeling increasingly tired, a lethargy that seemed to sap his very lifeblood. The oscillations between energised jubilation and extreme lassitude were becoming an all too frequent occurrence. He fought to shake off his fatigue and put on a smile.

"Of course! Not a problem at all," he said brightly. He tried to instil in his voice an enthusiasm that he did not really feel. "Of course I can debate. I was President of the Oxford Union, one of the world's most famous debating societies. I just thought that as I have only been recently..." His voice trailed off. He knew that his father was not listening and any protestations would fall on deaf ears. Already his father's attention was switching to Ahmad who had entered the room.

"Here, study this," said Ahmad, handing him a folder. "It contains some of Lee Kuan Yew's speeches. Singapore idolised their Prime Minister for his oratory skills and, I am sad to say, even people in this country do as well." Ahmad had caught Hussein's pronouncements that he could debate. He smiled in amusement at his blustering, drawing comfort from his discomfort. He had not forgiven Hussein for reneging on Shalimar. "See what you make of it. It might serve you well if you are to be our champion in parliamentary debate."

"We'll get someone to draw up your next speech to your constituency. Jot down some ideas and we'll work on it. You may go, unless you have something to say. That is, something other than to do with your preoccupation with that girl, An Mei."

* * * * *

"He is besotted! All he can think of is the girl!" Faridah exclaimed after Hussein left the room. She was exasperated with her son. "I have enlisted the *bomoh* to see if this Chinese girl has cast some evil charm on him. I suspect so. Why else can he not give her up? We present him with Shalimar, such a beautiful girl, and he refuses her. *Minta maaf*, apologies,

Ahmad, but we have even lined up other equally beautiful girls who he has also steadfastly refused. I see nothing in this Chinese girl. Nothing!" She waved her hand dismissively.

Hope stirred in Ahmad. Perhaps all was not lost and there might still be a small chance that Hussein could be persuaded. He kept a low profile, bowing his head to maintain a humble attitude that he knew pleased Faridah.

Unchecked by both men, Faridah became even more expansive and outspoken. "The *bomoh* has given me some potions to undo her evil charm and I will see to it that it is infused in his drinks." She sniffed in frustration, her nose creased up at its bridge, before exclaiming, "*Kepala sakit!* Headache! Let us hope that he recovers from this malady. Otherwise, we will have to go ahead with this sham marriage."

Rahim broke his silence. He was tired of his wife's meddling with charms and potions that had become increasingly costly and senseless to him.

"Remember," he said, "it is such an opportune time to launch his career now with a new Prime Minister that we should let him marry her if only to get him to settle down to some serious work. You have spoilt him, giving in to his whims all the time since he was a little boy. That is why he expects the same now. I say, let him have her, tire of her and then we can get on. In any case, it is too late to obstruct this marriage. I have given my word. Your role is to make sure she converts to the Muslim faith. She is to be presented in the future as a devout Muslim imbibed with our culture. You make sure she learns it."

"No! Let me try one more time to make him see sense."

"And I say, let him have her. It will not last. It is just *gatal,* an itch that will pass. You make sure that the wedding preparation goes to plan."

"*Adoi!* All I get is the hard work. Do you know how many ceremonies are involved?

"Get a wedding planner," retorted Rahim.

"You are good at it, *Datin*," said Ahmad. He was bitterly disappointed, but he hid his feelings behind an affable smile. "I will help if you need me."

"How I wish my son was a bit more like you," Faridah responded.

Chapter 17

The wedding took place in Kemun, his hometown and the constituency that he hoped to gain in the next election. Hundreds of people congregated in the grand hall of his parents' house to participate in the *bersanding* ceremony. The residence was open to the public for the special occasion.

An Mei sat next to Hussein on the *pelamin*, a raised ornate dais, beneath a canopy of drapes and silk flowers of different hues, yellow, blue and gold. She looked down at her feet. She felt nothing, a coldness clutched at her heart. She stared at the *Mehndi*, the intricate light orange and deep brown, henna-stained patterns on her hands and feet. They were a symbol of love and fertility, she had been told. The artist had spent hours patiently grinding the dried henna leaves, mixing oil and water before painting them. People came to the dais, chanting blessings and prayers, scattering *beras kunyit*, rice stained with tumeric, *bertih*, fried rice grains and *tepung tawar*, scented water, around her. The music was unending as was the queue of people who came. Young and old, some with their entire family, people from the surrounding villages and towns, trooped in with their gifts. Still she sat, detached, the custom as alien to her, as she was to them, her *hijab*, an unfamiliar constraint.

The wedding was rushed. Things moved quickly from the time Hussein proposed to her. Her mother-in-law who had been dead set against the marriage worked at breakneck pace to speed it up. She had not softened in her stance towards An Mei. She hardly looked at her other than to give her cutting glances. "I just want it over and done with," she would say. The various complex stages of a traditional Malay wedding were reduced to two. Nor did Faridah, her voice, loud and brusque, hesitate to say why it was so. "If you had been one of us, the *Akad Nikah,* the signing of the wedding contract, and the *Bersanding* or wedding ceremony would have been in your family home; needless to say, we have had to pay for everything."

Yes, my family or the absence of it, An Mei thought. She'd had so little time to prepare her parents. She looked to where Nelly sat and caught her eye. Nelly, despite her father's threats, had flown to Kemun from Kuala Lumpur to be with her.

Hussein sat next to her, resplendent in a silk top, a beautifully woven sarong tied over silk pants, a *songke*t headgear and the traditional silver dagger, the *keris,* at his waist. "It will be soon over. I'll make it up to you," he whispered, sensing her sadness. His voice was drowned by the start of loud recitations of the Koran and blessings. An Mei almost jumped at the loud intrusion. She closed her eyes tighter, reminded of the *Khatam Al-Koran* that had been conducted in the mosque the previous day. Surrounded by women folks, she had recited the last few pages and verses of the Koran. It signified that she had completed reading the Holy Book and that she, An Mei, now renamed Noraidin, was transformed into an adult responsible for bringing up her own children and family in the Islamic way. She trembled in memory of the Imam's interrogation. She had lied about her circumcision. With the support and agreement of Hussein, she had betrayed the faith even as she had professed to grasp it. Hussein reached over and held her hand. Gritting her teeth, she steadied herself, taking deep slow breaths.

Throughout the ceremony, her thoughts flitted to the events that followed after she accepted Hussein's proposal of marriage. One in particular kept coming back to haunt her.

* * * * *

"Why the hurry?" Nelly had asked. "Why this sudden change in mind? I have no time to prepare your father. An Mei, have you really thought it through? It is not just about love and being with Hussein. It is also about giving up all that you have worked for, including your family, culture, religion..."

"Yes, yes, I have. We have been through it all. I promised that I would give him up if he did not marry me. But now that he has proposed... Aunt Nelly! You did say that you would help turn father around if we were to marry."

"But not suddenly. Can't you wait? Give me time to prepare him."

"I can't. Hussein, even his parents, seems to be suddenly anxious that we get on with the marriage."

Nelly had then sat down in the armchair, giving out a sigh so loud it seemed that all the air had been forced out of her. She sat deflated, defeat etched deeply into every feature of her face, both hands at her temple. "Yes, I did promise you. I suppose, now is as good a time as any if we are to do everything in a rush." She had then got up and walked over to the phone. She moved slowly, her steps heavy as if weighed down by her legs. The ten or so feet passage to the study seemed to be a major excursion. Eventually she had reached the phone, picked it up and dialled.

"Hello, Ming Kong? This is Nelly. I have something to tell you."

An Mei had kept very still. Smatterings of loud curses filtered through to her. She could see from the doorway her aunt's face, wan and apologetic. She could see her opening her mouth to try to explain the situation only to close it again as the tirade over the phone continued. Her fingers and knuckles grew white with clutching the phone. Still the rant continued. Finally, Nelly had put the phone down. "He does not wish to see you. He said that we have deceived him and that he will never forgive us. He blamed me."

Except for one occasion when An Mei was a small child, Nelly had never cried in front of her. That evening she did. Her face crumpled and she dissolved into tears that rolled down tracking the lines and planes of her cheeks. "Your father blamed me," she repeated. "I have failed him. I am to be blamed."

* * * * *

An Mei came out of her reverie. From her dais, she looked across the gathering at Nelly. She smiled and Nelly smiled in return. With an imperceptible nod of her head, Nelly gestured and mouthed, "I love you. You look beautiful. Everything will be all right. Don't worry."

* * * * *

The wedding was over. The guests had all left, including Nelly who, unlike Hussein's other family members, had not been invited to stay. An Mei had wanted a quiet moment with her aunt but there was no opportunity. The ceremony had gone on and on, and she felt herself glued to the dais like a doll on display. In her mind, the wedding had been surreal; the music, the recitations, the formality, the guests she did not know or recognise. She felt disconnected from it all. She was ushered like a puppet on a string through each stage. She felt like an onlooker even up to the moment of their departure for the honeymoon.

"Look after yourself," Faridah said, embracing Hussein tightly, her back to An Mei. "We will see you back here in a week."

They were standing just outside the residence doorway, at the top of the flight of steps that descended down to a magnificent domed portico. A fleet of black limousines were lined up waiting like a row of shiny black beetles, their polished coachwork reflecting the splendid livery of the chauffeurs and attending valets.

"No, *Mak*, a fortnight," Hussein reminded her.

"And call us," Rahim added. "We have work to do. Come back here. I don't want you to go to KL. "

They did not look at An Mei. It was as though she did not exist. She stood aside, alone, looking on. She wondered where her aunt Nelly was and wished she was there with her.

An Mei waited until Hussein's farewell to his parents ended. She stepped forward hesitantly and bowed. "Good bye, *Mak, Pak*," she said, following Hussein's informal address of his parents. She was not sure if she should embrace them. She stood with both her arms limp by her side. They did not look as they though they wanted to be embraced by her. They looked forbidding.

Faridah turned away pointedly as though she had been insulted. Rahim replied with a curt nod, his eyes sweeping over her summarily. He saw her hurt and his face softened momentarily. "*Selamat jalan*, safe journey," he said.

"*Jangan beri dia muka!* Don't give her face!" An Mei heard Faridah reprimand her husband. She turned to face An Mei and for just once that evening looked at her.

"Just remember to behave like a good Muslim girl. And keep your *hijab* on in public. We do not want you to flaunt your face in public."

An Mei, stung by the remark, stepped back. A blush spread from her neck to her cheeks, colouring them as though she had been slapped.

"Mother, the *hijab* is not compulsory. Lots of women, even those in high office, don't necessarily wear them," protested Hussein.

"Well, we do. On the east coast, we do."

"Come," Hussein said to An Mei, "let's go." He took her hand and guided her down the steps to the waiting Mercedes. "Don't worry. Give them time. Mother is deliberately taunting you. The etiquette is not as alarming as she makes it out to be."

Faridah overheard him. She shouted to their departing backs, "If you aim to be in high office, it is exactly as daunting as I say."

Chapter 18

An Mei got out of the pool and made her way to the sun lounger. She sat down and draped a robe around herself. The brilliant white of the robe stood out in sharp contrast to the azure-blue water behind her. She had swum about ten laps. Invigorated, she raised her face to the sun and sighed. "I'm so happy. And you?" she asked turning to her husband.

He was lying on his back on the lounger next to hers, his lanky body half-sprawled, his brown legs placed carelessly on the rolled up towels at the tip of the extended chair. His hair had grown out during the two weeks of the honeymoon.

"Of course," he answered, with a smile. "You swim well."

"Yes, I had a lot of practice in Oxford. Casey and I used to go to the Oxford City Swimming Club at the Temple Cowley Pool. She introduced me to sports and I have tried to keep at it whenever I can."

"You can certainly keep it up here. No problem," he assured her. He traced his fingers gently on her arm, drumming little butterfly tattoos.

"I know. But we are in Bangkok and this is the Dusit Thani Hotel." She looked around the pool and at the people perched or sprawled on the towel-covered loungers. Drifts of English, American, Australian and the occasional German conversation reached her ears. "But what about when I am back home?"

He looked away. Two deep furrows appeared on his forehead. "Let's not talk about it on the last day of our honeymoon."

"But we must."

"Before I went to Oxford. I do not recall that there were problems with girls swimming in public pools in Malaysia," said Hussein. "Perhaps I took it for granted. I did not consider a girl by her race. They were all girls and if they swam, they swam. Apparently things have changed quite a bit, perhaps not so much in Kuala Lumpur but back home in Kemun, it is definitely more conservative, particularly so for Muslims."

"So? Does it mean that I will always have to wear the *hijab*? Does it mean that I must not swim because a swimsuit is considered indecent or play netball because I would be wearing shorts?" An Mei shuddered. Faridah's words still haunted her.

"Perhaps, we will have to be careful when we are with my parents but you would probably be fine in KL. The conservative dress mode has still to catch on there. People generally wear what they want." He swallowed hard as he said those words, remembering his mother's caution: "You are expected to be a good Muslim, pray five times a day, and your wife as well. Modesty is the most important thing for a woman and your wife should best follow my example."

"What about when I go to my office? Can I wear skirts, an office suit, like I did before?"

"Perhaps, if they are long, to the ankle, like the *Baju Melayu*," teased Hussein, tapping her foot with his own. He wanted to lighten her mood and not spoil the last day of the honeymoon with a discussion of how a Muslim woman was expected to dress. He had not given much thought to clothes until An Mei reminded him. He did not consider it an important issue.

"But do you still want to continue working? I had thought that you would give it up," he continued.

An Mei looked at him in surprise. She had taken it for granted that she would continue to work. When they were in Oxford, they had always discussed the careers that they had in mind. She reached out and tapped him playfully on the shoulder. "You are pulling my leg. You are, aren't you? Of course, I want to work. You have never said I should give it up. What about you? Are you going to continue to work?"

"Of course! Didn't you hear my father? He has already set up a rota of meetings for me immediately on our return."

"Well then."

"Work if you wish. I just thought that you might want to be with me and support me in my role as a budding politician," he countered. He grinned and she smiled in response, but in those few minutes both saw the chasm that separated them.

"It will be alright," he assured her again. "It would be good for you to continue working because I will be busy myself. Let's take things as they come and not spoil this last day with worries about the future." He leaned over and kissed her. "Come," he said, drawing her to her feet, "siesta time." He grinned.

* * * * *

Nelly opened the door. An Mei stood at the doorway for a moment looking lost and sad. She dropped her briefcase and went to Nelly, bending over to rest her head on Nelly's shoulders. "Can I stay the night?" she asked.

"Hussein is not around?"

"No!"

"Well then!" Indignation and resignation were reflected in that one exclamation. "Let's take this upstairs," she said, picking up the briefcase.

"I'll take it," said Ah Kun, the maid, taking the briefcase from her. "Shall I get you tea and bring it to the sitting room? I have opened the French windows and lit the incense to keep mosquitoes away so it should be more comfortable than the study. Mistress Nelly does not like having the air-conditioner on," she explained to An Mei. "I'll prepare your bedroom."

"I don't mind the warm night air. It relaxes me, and my muscles don't tense up as they do when we have the air-conditioning on," Nelly said as she led the way to the sitting room.

They sat down, Nelly in an armchair, An Mei on the sofa. Feet tucked under her, An Mei looked around the familiar room. Table lamps, stood on side tables and sideboards, cast a warm glow around the room, touching each piece of furniture with a soft golden light. A duck blue celadon bowl, filled with dried rose petals and cinnamon, sat in the middle of the coffee table. She inhaled its perfume. "I love this room," she said. "I love coming home."

"When is Hussein coming back to KL? It has been many weeks since he left you after that brief honeymoon in Bangkok."

"Yes, five weeks and three days," said An Mei, her eyes cast down. After the honeymoon in Bangkok, they had flown to Kuala Lumpur where Hussein had taken a connecting flight to

Kemun to go back to his parents and his duties. An Mei had not gone with him; she had returned instead to his parents' house in Kuala Lumpur. She recalled their awkward parting at the airport lounge. She had wanted to cling to him and ask him not to leave, but she held back.

"I do not like being alone in KL in Hussein's parents' house. It is huge and empty; it is not home. I call it their residence," said An Mei. Her fingers were busy trailing little loops on the cotton throw left on the chair. Then impatiently, she placed both feet down on the floor and leaned over her knee to rest her chin on the upturned palms of her hands.

Nelly regarded her charge from behind her spectacles; she tried hard to contain her sympathy. It would not be welcomed.

"There is so much marble that I believe my every movement, my every footstep rings empty to mock me. I feel spied upon. The place haunts me. Every moment I am in that house, I relive the utter loneliness and helplessness that I experienced when I first returned with Hussein. Only Fawziah, who helped me escape, is friendly and she is very guarded because she fears that any sign of friendliness would be reported to my in-laws. How they must hate me," she sighed.

"Give them time. It must be a shock for them. Jenny said they had very different plans for Hussein."

"Yes! Time." An Mei twirled a corner end of her shirt blouse that had become un-tucked at the waist. A flash of anger crossed her face.

"And father? Have you spoken to him? Does he need time as well to accept my marriage?" Her voice was bitter. She needed to blame someone, to vent her anger at the injustice of it all.

"Have you tried to call him?" asked Nelly. "You have to eat humble pie. We are at fault because we did deceive your father."

An Mei pretended not to hear. "And what of mother? Any word from her? You cannot say that we deceived her as well. We did keep her informed."

"Stop this! Stop trying to put a wall around yourself by making out that it is their fault."

Nelly drew herself up and sat up straight in her chair. She pushed her spectacles up her nose then bent closer towards An Mei.

"Put yourself in their place. And tell me how you would have reacted. And don't blame your mother. You know how things are. She would not have been able to fly over to be with you at the wedding and abandon your father at the best of times." Nelly stopped abruptly, undecided whether she should say more. Then she took a deep breath and continued. "At this moment, your father is ill. There, I have said it. He is ill. I did not want to tell you, to protect you so that you do not have to add guilt to the emotions you are already suffering. But I cannot accept the attitude you have adopted."

Horrified, An Mei slid off her seat and knelt by Nelly. "When did you hear this? How ill is he?"

"Yesterday. Your mother called to tell me and asked how you were. He had a heart attack about a week ago and had to be rushed into hospital. He is recuperating. The doctor says that he has to take it easy. So your mother is managing the business. She has a lot on her hands. The restaurant has only just been opened. Her time is split between the hospital and the restaurant."

"I'm so sorry. I was hurt and I said things to wound the very people who are already hurt by me." Appalled at herself, An Mei crept closer to Nelly. "What's wrong with me?" she asked. "I wanted to call father but my silly pride held me back. I blamed mother, but I should have known better."

Nelly shook her head. "It's unhappiness," she said. "It is unhappiness that is the engine of your bitterness. Only Hussein can cure you of it, I am afraid."

*****

She came out of her boss's office closing the door gently behind her. She walked to her own office, a large room not quite as big as the one she had just left, but significantly larger than the one she had previously. "A reflection of your promotion," Jeremy had told her before she got married. It seemed like a lifetime ago. On her desk was a message left by her secretary. It read: 'A gentleman by the name of *Tengku* Ahmad is here to see you. He is in the Blue Room.'

Panic seized her; the same fear that struck her each time his name was mentioned. She left the form she was carrying on her desk and walked rapidly to the waiting room. She had meant to arrange her air travel to see her parents as soon as her boss had granted her leave. That would have to wait.

Ahmad had his back to her when she went into the Blue Room, a room reserved for VIP visitors. He was alone. He turned when he heard her footsteps. His eyes scrolled down her body, registering every detail, before returning to stare insolently at her face.

"Ah! Noraidin," he said, his voice, soft, menacing but as smooth as silk. *"Tetapi, bagaimana tak pakai Baju Negara? Apa-lah terjadi tudung awak?"*

She did not reply. His lips curled. "Let me repeat in English in case you do not understand. Why are you not wearing your *baju*, your National dress? What has happened to your headscarf?"

She ignored his questions. "Where is Hussein? Do you bring news of him?"

"Has he not called you?" Ahmad pretended to be surprised. He shook his head feigning pity but his voice was loud and insolent. "I am not here to bring you news of him. If he had wanted to give you news of himself, he would have contacted you directly. I am not your lackey."

He turned his back on her, reflected a moment before facing her again. "I bring word from *Datin* Faridah. She has learnt that you have been spending many nights away from the residence and that you have driven out on your own without letting the staff know your whereabouts."

"That is not true," she protested. "I told them that I was spending the night with my Aunt Nelly."

"*Datin* Faridah has asked me to check on these rumours that have come to us: your night-time activities! Flaunting your face and body in public!"

"I am wearing what others wear to the office."

"I will report accordingly," he said and walked out with a flourish.

She stood in the centre of the room, deflated. She knew it was useless to even try to explain. She made her way back to her office. She had tried to call Hussein but he had not returned her calls.

Chapter 19

Villagers came out in full force. Farmers, field hands, car mechanics, traders jostled and reached out to touch him as he walked with his entourage through the village. They chanted. "Hussein! Hussein! Hussein!" Fists pumped up and down, pushing like pistons into the hot humid air above the heads of the crowd.

Hussein caught their fervour and, in turn, was stirred to even greater action. He jumped up nimbly onto the makeshift stage erected in the square. He put both arms up and smiled, acknowledging their enthusiastic welcome. He thanked them. A silence descended upon the crowd. He began his oration. He spoke of his vision for greater equality, the pursuit of redistributing wealth to the poor. He promised them access to education, scholarships. He spoke of their rights to greater economic achievement. "You! *Bumiputra*! Sons of the soil! You are the source of our wealth. You will be the ones to reap the benefits of this New Economic Policy." His face was animated. His eyes sparkled. The crowd cheered. They clapped.

His bodyguards grouped around him. They descended with him from the stage and cleared a way to the car. He waved and the crowd, drawn to his magnetic charisma, roared their appreciation in response. At last, here was someone who cared for the rural people, for this village in particular, that had been left neglected while the rest of the country advanced and grew wealthy.

"Share! A greater share!" they roared. "*Insha Allah!*"

The car accelerated as the crowd parted to make way for it. Hussein slumped back in his seat. Exhilaration and exhaustion took over. He grabbed the drink handed to him by Ghazali, his secretary and drank, long and full.

"That was good. They loved you," Ghazali said. He was busy: his writing, spidery long elegant strokes, scrawled across pages and pages of a report for Rahim.

"We have already covered over ten villages within the constituency and it has been one success after another. You have them in your pocket, Sir. You will be elected."

Hussein continued to lie back, his eyes tightly closed. He did not see the paddy fields rushing by, the wooden houses on stilts or the waving bystanders. All he could feel were the beads of sweat brimming over his forehead; his *songkok*, the headgear he wore to these forums, was drenched. Quickly, he sought a handkerchief to mop his brow. Lately, it had been like this for him, exhilaration followed by doubt. Would they be able to deliver the promises they were making? he wondered. His shirt was also soaked with sweat and the blast of cold air from the car's air-conditioning caused him to shiver. He needed food, perhaps even those nutritious potions that his mother had been giving him recently to revive his health. They had not had time to eat.

Ghazali handed him a fresh shirt and he stripped and put it on, tucking the shirttails into the short sarong he wore over his trousers. He inhaled slowly and deeply to calm himself. Minutes passed before he asked, "So where to next?"

"To the town of Kemun, a short rest in the quarters that have been set aside for our use, and then you will be opening a shopping complex in the town. This will save us some time; it will be more convenient than going home to your parents."

"Then?" asked Hussein.

"Then, there will be a dinner to follow and you will deliver a speech. I have it ready here for you to look at," said Ghazali, waving the sheaf of papers in his hand. "I will arrange for any amendments that you might have. There will also be entertainment of some sort, perhaps, some local dancing girls, at the end of the evening."

"Never mind about the entertainment," said Hussein, taking the papers from Ghazali. "Have you called Noraidin for me? Did she tell you why she has not answered my calls nor returned them. When will I be free to talk to her in the midst of the mad schedule that you have arranged for me?"

He had tried calling An Mei late in the evenings and was alarmed that she was not at home.

"We did try but could not reach her. Ahmad has gone to KL to check."

"And? What did he say?"

"I don't know. He didn't tell me. He said he would report to your mother. She will tell you."

Hussein looked at Ghazali and, sensing his unease, made up his mind to contact Nelly. She would probably give him a fairer account than his mother. But his thoughts kept returning to the failure of An Mei to return his calls.

* * * * *

The room was quiet except for the soft footfalls of the maid preparing the bed. Faridah sat in front of the dressing table and looked into the mirror. She hardly registered the image of the woman reflected in it. Behind her, in the dressing room, her husband was putting the final touches to his dressing for the reception. A manservant stood by, his hands holding out a velvet tray on which a range of cufflinks were displayed. Rahim pointed to a pair with dark blue sapphires.

"That pair. They should go well with my white silk shirt and blue *songket* sarong." He looked up to where his wife was in the adjacent room.

"Hussein did well today," he continued, holding out both his wrists to the manservant, his words breaking into Faridah's thoughts. "Ghazali has sent in his report. We should succeed in getting him into *Dewan Rakyat,* the House of Representatives, if he continues like this."

"Not if that minx is still his wife." She regarded her husband through the reflection in the mirror. "She's up to no good. She is not wearing her *hijab*, she stays out late and does not even return to the residence some nights."

"You have to talk to her. We cannot allow her behaviour to drag down Hussein's name in this critical period. It is fortunate that she is in KL and not here in Kemun. Perhaps, you are right. We have to get rid of her."

"But how? Our son is still besotted." Faridah thought for a moment. "The only way we can get rid of her is if Hussein himself wishes to do so. If he would only tire of her; I'll ask Ahmad for his advice."

* * * * *

The wind blew, its force whipping the casuarina trees into a wild frenzy. Coconut palms bent under the force, their fronds trailed on the white sand sweeping up clouds of fine debris. In the distance, purple storm clouds were gathering, masking the daylight and wiping out all signs of the horizon. Suddenly, thunder reverberated, followed by streaks of lightning, their brightness, urgent and violent, pierced the blackness of the sky.

Shalimar stood by the window, her face transfixed as she watched fishermen make for the shore, dragging their long boats behind, and desperately tying them to anchors on the beach. She sank to the floor to sit on her haunch, legs folded beneath her, her forehead pressed to the windowpane. Silently she wept, her hand went to her cheek, feeling the heat of the slap that had been landed there.

"You have failed once!" Ahmad had accused her. "Don't fail me again if you wish me not to charge that useless whelp you are in love with. Remember I am your brother, your guardian. And I have the power to send him to prison."

She had begged him on her knees. Furious, he had swept his hand back and landed a resounding blow on her face. For a few seconds, even he was astounded by his action.

"There, look what you have made me do! Clean up. Repair the damage to your face and make yourself ready for tonight."

With that he had departed with barely a glance at her crouching form.

Shalimar rose. She made her way slowly into Ahmad's room. It was empty. She walked to his desk, made her way round it and sat on his chair. Her eyes were bleak, bitter. She reached into a drawer. The coldness of the metal startled her; she grasped the handle and brought the *keris* up, turning it almost lovingly before a sudden revulsion took over. She placed it hastily on the desk, pushing it away from her, her fingers stinging. Then, with a quick deft movement, she grabbed it once more; bringing it up firmly with both hands she turned its jagged edge towards her heart. She trembled.

"*Jangan!* Don't! *Tengku* Shalimar! It will not help the one you love. He will be blamed and it will not be just imprisonment," came a cry from the doorway.

* * * * *

An Mei sat on her bed, clasping her knees close to her. She had shed her clothes and cast off the *hijab* that Faridah had instructed her to wear when she went out. She ruffled her hair and shook her head until the hair bounced in glorious defiance after the enforced restriction. She sat, chin on knees, savouring the cold air on her skin, the cold air pumped in by the air-conditioner. She could hear its reverberation as it too sang its protest against the enforced churning of hot air into cold. The house was empty. Perhaps, she thought, Nelly would come to visit or I can go over to her and stay the night. But pride made her inert. Eyes closed tight, she contemplated her marriage; her thoughts went back to Ahmad's visit. She had regretted her earlier rashness of not wearing the *hijab* if that was the one thing that might bring her closer to her mother-in-law. For a week now, she had gone to the office dressed as instructed. She had ignored the stares and sudden hush of conversation when she passed. Her boss understood her situation, though privately he admitted with a wry smile that he was not delighted, amused may be. She had put off going to England to visit her father and had called her mother to explain the situation.

"Come when you can. His condition is stable," Mei Yin had said. So An Mei stayed on and waited. Yet, Hussein had not called nor could she get hold of him.

A whole gamut of emotions passed over her: fear, hurt and worries. They left her thoughts in a maelstrom. She sat, motionless. Finally, she decided to go to Kemun. She would leave immediately to see Hussein and to find out why he had not been in touch and then she would leave for Oxford. She must see her father.

Chapter 20

The driveway was jam-packed with limousines. Crowds of people milled outside the gate; photographers with cameras held high snapped pictures, men and women pushed each other to see what was happening beyond the gates, their hands grabbing at the metal bars that separated them from the residence.

"What is happening?" wondered An Mei, her face pressed to the taxi's window as it turned into the driveway.

"*Berhenti!* Stop!" commanded a guard.

She wound down her window and flagged the plastic disc that Hussein insisted she carried.

"*Minta maaf*, I beg your pardon," said the guard. He clicked his heels to attention and stepped back hastily waving the taxi on.

An Mei tapped on the glass panel that separated her from the driver.

"Stop over there," she instructed. She paid the driver, got out and walked up the steps to the entrance of her in-law's house, waving her identification card at the guards who stepped forward to block her progress. They all retreated hastily, bowing their heads in the process. They did not recognise her. They were not expecting her.

"I'll ask," said a guard. He went to the phone booth. He picked up the telephone, a black clumsy heavy instrument in his white-gloved hand. "*Puan* Noraidin is here. What do you wish me to do?" He listened in silence; his brow creased into a puzzled frown, then he hung up. He marched smartly to catch up with An Mei.

"This way, please," he said. They walked through the splendid hallway, past the stately official rooms and into the glass covered courtyard. She stopped. Seated in an alcove of carefully arranged bamboo was Hussein, his head dropped into the palms of his hands. Next to him was Shalimar, her tear-stained face jerked up at An Mei's entrance. Her eyes beseeched An Mei's. Facing Hussein and Shalimar, their backs towards An Mei, were Rahim, Faridah and Ahmad.

"I am sorry but this was exactly what I found when I went to my sister's room," An Mei heard Ahmad say. "Hussein was on her bed and my... my sister, damn her soul for the shame brought to my family, was in his arms. Her bedclothes were dishevelled and he, he was naked!"

Hussein's head shot up. He did not see An Mei. "I do not know how I came to be in her bed. Believe me. I did not go to Shalimar. I have no recollection."

An Mei saw his bloodshot eyes, the fear and bewilderment in his face. Her own heart was thumping.

"What?" Ahmad shouted. "Are you accusing my sister of seducing you and forcefully taking you to her bed. If you did not go to her, then somehow she must have forced you into her bed! Do you wish to add more shame to my family?"

Hussein turned to face Ahmad and as he did he caught sight of An Mei standing at the entrance. His face turned a bright red. "Please, you have to believe me," he appealed to An Mei, "I do not know how I came to be in Shalimar's bed. I remember nothing."

Desperately, he reached out for Shalimar's hands. He shook them. They lay limp under his.

"Tell them the truth. Tell them nothing happened."

Shalimar remained silent. She looked up at her brother, Ahmad. An Mei saw the fear in her eyes before she turned her gaze towards the floor.

"*Malu!* The shame!" cried Faridah clasping both hands to her ears as though she was trying to block out the unpleasantness. She placed her head on her husband's shoulder and sobbed. "Do something," she cried.

"If I can make a suggestion," said Ahmad to Faridah and Rahim. "I do not wish any unpleasantness. All I want to do is restore the honour of my sister, the honour of my family. Betroth them."

"No!" cried An Mei. "You can't do that. We have just got married."

"A mistake," snarled Faridah. "Yes, a bad mistake. If you love him, why don't you stay with him here in Kemun and stand by what he does? Why do you abandon him to his loneliness? The consequence of your actions is before you. And you dare to protest and refuse him the chance of rescuing himself from this... crisis... dilemma."

"I did not abandon Hussein. I was waiting for him to join me in KL."

Hussein jumped up. "I told An Mei to stay in KL to be out of your way and your displeasure. I was, in any case, to spend half my time, if not more, in the capital to attend to matters of the House once I am elected. That is why she remained in KL."

"Look, I do not care about the issues between yourselves. I would like the matter of my sister's honour resolved," interjected Ahmad. He stepped between Hussein and his mother. He did not want a standoff between mother and son. It would not help his cause. He glared at An Mei and Hussein. He was bristling with self-righteous indignation.

"The house is surrounded by the paparazzi outside, waiting for news. What do I tell them? Do I tell them that my sister has been molested... raped... or do I tell them that she is to be married to Hussein?"

"How do they know? Who sent for them?"

"At the moment, it would seem they know nothing. But someone must have alerted them that a story is about to unfold from within these walls," said Ahmad. "I will, of course, tell them nothing if things are resolved amicably.

The security guard looked guiltily from Ahmad to Faridah and her husband to Hussein and Shalimar. Ahmad had instructed him to alert the reporters that an important announcement was to be made at the residence that evening and he only did as he was instructed.

Five pairs of eyes turned towards An Mei.

"Will you agree to this? Under Muslim law, your agreement is essential for a husband to take another wife. Of course, he must treat all of his wives equally," explained Rahim. "My son's future lies with you."

* * * * *

The crowd was dispersing. Slowly, people were drifting away. Cameramen, tired of waiting lowered their cameras. Some were already packing away their equipment while others were lighting up cigarettes to mark an end to a busy day of waiting for a drama to unfold.

An Mei released the drapes, allowing them to fall back to their original position to block her view of the front drive, the gates and beyond. Her voice was cold. "So they have been fed the news that they have been waiting for," she surmised.

"No, they were promised that they would be the first to know, once we are ready to give them news of an important occurrence. We have not told them anything yet," replied Hussein. He sat dejected, humbled by his recent experience. "I meant what I said earlier in the courtyard. I have no recollection and do not know how it happened."

She burst into a giggle, a harsh hysterical gurgling driven by desperation, disbelieve and hurt. There was no humour in her face when she turned to him.

"No recollection of a consummation of an act of love? Shalimar will be insulted!"

With a sudden change of mood, she went to him. She pummelled his chest, hitting him with all the force she could muster.

"How could you? How could you? Why didn't you answer my calls? Why if you were so desperately lonely, didn't you ask me to come to you? I would have. I would have. Instead, I waited for you." Her body shook uncontrollably.

"But I did call. You were not in, even in the early hours of the morning. Where were you?"

"I was with Aunt Nelly." She pushed him away. "How dare you try to pin the fault on me. How dare you doubt me? Does it give you an excuse to go with Shalimar?"

"Listen someone is trying to separate us," he said. He caught hold of both her hands and held them to him.

"The more I think of it, the more I believe that the whole thing has been fixed," he said. "This has all the makings of what happened previously... before we got married."

She struggled, but he maintained his grasp.

"My not being able to get hold of you, nor you me," he said. "I did not go to Shalimar. In fact, I have not even had time to speak to her all these weeks in Kemun. I was just going from campaign to campaign. I was exhausted at the end of each day, so much so that mother had to concoct all sorts of strengthening potions to revive me. All I remember was going to the opening ceremony of this shopping complex in the town, participating in the dinner as a guest of honour and being driven home. I do not remember the journey and I certainly have no recollection of being driven to Ahmad's house or of seeing Shalimar. I must have blacked out in the car."

She snatched her hands away and turned to leave. She walked, her back straight and proud, but two steps away, she turned back to face him.

"At this moment, all I know is that you will have a second wife! And I cannot bear it."

She could not check her tears. She did not want to cry, but it was like a floodgate over which she had no control. It rose from her chest and came out like a moan that shook her very being.

"What will you have me do? If I don't take her as a wife, Ahmad will see that I am finished." He pulled her to him. "Please believe me."

She shook her head. She felt numb. She felt she would drown under the weight that had gathered in her heart.

"I don't know," she confessed, "I don't know what I should do."

*****

Nelly sat silently listening to An Mei. They were in Nelly's house. An Mei had gone directly to her after flying back from Kemun. When An Mei finished she clasped her in her arms, rocking her gently, soothing her with little kisses.

"*Yow mang, yow tak ta seong,*" she said. "If you have life, you can think and find a solution. Do not despair."

They sat cradled together with Nelly rocking gently forward and back, as though putting a child to sleep, and with time An Mei's sobbing ceased. She felt a calm descend on her. She felt her eyes, heavy and swollen, close. She heard Nelly's voice, soft and soothing.

"You will have to try to make the best of a bad situation. Do you love Hussein? Do you believe in him?"

An Mei nodded. She believed in Hussein; she could not believe that he would betray her in such a way. Yet at the same time, she was angry and held him accountable for the situation. Why did he allow himself to be manoeuvred in such a disastrous way?

"Then, you might well have to accept his marriage to Shalimar," advised Nelly. "Don't make a rash decision. But also don't let your actions be governed by pride and hurt."

Nelly was profoundly shaken by the turn of events. She felt An Mei's hurt as if she was the one who had been cheated. A sigh escaped her as she took An Mei in her arms again. "A marriage is sacred; it is not a union to go into and discard the following day. But it also shouldn't be a millstone that ties you until death if it is clearly not working. You have to think about it carefully for yourself. Go to your father and mother. Away from it all, you might be able to think more clearly what to do."

"Thank you, Thank you for not saying, I told you so," whispered An Mei.

Chapter 21

Mei Yin tucked the blanket firmly around Ming Kong's knee, released the brake of the wheel chair, and pushed it towards the newly extended arrival hall in Terminal 3 at Heathrow. Throngs of people were heading purposefully in the same direction. She wheeled the chair suddenly to the left to avoid three young children running helter scatter after their parents.

"You shouldn't have come. She would not expect it. It is too soon after your heart attack. Really, Ming Kong, you should take it easy."

"I'm fine. Don't fuss. I am not dead yet. I owe her that much. All these weeks in the hospital and at home, have given me time to think and mull over the hurtful things I have said to her. Nelly and I had a long conversation on the phone. Well, you were part of it, so you know. She made me realise the folly of my action. Perhaps, if I had listened and not just set the rules and expected them to be followed, all this would not have happened."

He fell silent brooding over the role he might have inadvertently played in An Mei's headlong rush to marry Hussein. Mei Yin sensed her husband's sadness.

"Don't blame yourself. I am sure it was not Nelly's intention that you should blame yourself. I think An Mei would have married Hussein whatever we might or might not have done. It is a new age. Our children, and I am not speaking only of An Mei, but also the boys, cannot be handled the way children were handled in the past." Mei Yin spoke quietly; uncertain as to how Ming Kong would respond. Despite her newfound confidence and Ming Kong's mellower manner, she still half-expect him to burst into a temper. He disliked being proved wrong.

Ming Kong reached up and patted her hand. "You are right." She did not see his smile. "I'm excited. I have so much to say to my daughter, but I fear I will not be able to say them."

"Me too," agreed Mei Yin. They arrived at the terminal and headed for the flight arrivals screen. She watched the screen change.

"Her flight has landed. We'll wait over there, the same spot where she met us," said Mei Yin, excitedly. She pushed the chair to the meeting point and stood, one hand steadying the chair, the other firmly on her husband's shoulder. She knew how much it had cost him to eat humble pie. She looked around her; noted the casual manner in which people hugged one another; the kisses exchanged; the cries of endearment, "darling", "love", "sweet-heart". She knew that Ming Kong was not comfortable with such shows of affection, but Nelly had told her not to hold back. "If you do, it will make An Mei feel you do not love her," she had said. "Hug her. She needs you."

She could hardly hear the arrival announcement for the noise in the hall. She saw An Mei, her head shrouded in a hijab, looking in search of them. She looked different, older and thinner. Her eyes were wary. Ming Kong made a movement; he was attempting to rise from the wheel chair.

"No!" Mei Yin said. "Wait! She has seen us. She'll be here any moment now."

An Mei was half running towards them now, her shawl flying behind her, her hair loosened; her long skirt made her stumble. She checked herself, hitched up her skirt and continued towards them, pulling her suitcase behind her. The case wobbled, spun left and right and then righted itself. Still she ran.

"Mama! Papa!" she cried coming to a stop in front of them. She was breathless, her chest heaving, her eyes questioning. A moment's hesitation and she was in Mei Yin's arms. No words were exchanged; no words were needed. An Mei dropped to her knees and embraced her father, shocked at his appearance, surprised that he had come. Mei Yin looked on, her eyes bright. Nelly had been right. A deed was better than words in expressing how they felt.

* * * * *

Ming Kong got up from his bed and made his way to the window. He drew the curtain aside to look out. It was dark and the street deserted. The street lamps cast an eerie glow, lending a mystical air to the houses alongside them. Shadows formed and broke. A cat meowed; a dog barked. Then stillness.

"Can't you sleep?" asked Mei Yin, pushing herself up to a sitting position.

"No! I did not mean to disturb you. I thought I was keeping very quiet."

"You were. I couldn't sleep either. I keep thinking of An Mei."

"Ahhh... me too! I am so full of anger," he said, rubbing his chest as though to ease the pain. "I am frustrated by the inability to do anything to help. Did I drive her to marry Hussein?" he asked Mei Yin. "I had no idea that she was so much in love with him. I had no inkling. In my eyes, she was my little girl. I just could not adjust to the fact that she is a grown woman. I could not accept that she could really be in love with someone. I was so angry and so wrapped up in my own grievances; my mind just would not accept her loving a Malay."

"I know," she said, "but it's no use blaming yourself."

"Why? Why him, of all people?"

"You might as well say why you and me?" Mei Yin replied.

"I hate what they did to my girl. I can't bear to think of how she has been treated." He looked at Mei Yin; his eyes full of pain.

"Shhh! You will wake her."

"We have not even seen Hussein. What kind of man is he?" Ming Kong continued. He was furious although he knew he was not in a position to pass judgement on Hussein considering his own infidelity in the past. It was not something he wished for his own daughter. "Should we return to KL, meet him and his parents?"

Mei Yin thought for a while. "Jenny knows them. I am not sure if our going would help. It might make things worse." She thought of her husband's temper and what Jenny had told her about Hussein's parents.

She got out of bed and went to him. She laid her head on his shoulder. "An Mei is happier and calmer, just knowing that she has our support, that you are not cross with her." Holding his head to her, she kissed his cheeks and then his eyes. His tears were salty on her lips.

*****

Mother and daughter weaved their way along the uneven path alongside the river. The grass at the side of it was almost knee high. It was the height of summer. Plumes of grass seeds swayed; bees droned as they dived from flower to flower in search of nectar.

"I love this part of the river Thames. Casey and I used to row along here," said An Mei.

She was looking more like her former self, observed Mei Yin. There were some colour in her cheeks and she was wearing trousers and a tee shirt.

"There! Over by that turn in the river, where the ducks and swans are, that was where our boat capsized. We were lucky it is quite shallow. I had no idea how to row and Casey kept saying in Mandarin, *jia you, jia you*. At that time, I didn't know what 'add oil' meant. I did not realise that she wanted me to speed up. So I desperately flung my oar towards the bank to stop the boat and over we went."

An Mei laughed. Mei Yin could see that her mind was delving into her happy student days. It was such a contrast from her present situation. Her heart ached for her daughter.

"So how did you get on with your father?" Mei Yin asked her.

"Good," An Mei replied. "He was very supportive and understanding, but I have to make my mind up myself. Aunt Nelly said as much. But knowing that I have made amends with both father and you helps me. I am not so bound by guilt as before. Now I can focus on the problem."

They stopped and sat down on the bank. Mei Yin noticed the abrupt change in her daughter's demeanour. She looked downcast, the energy and joy that were there only moments ago had vanished.

"I have to return to KL tomorrow. I am frightened."

"You are a strong girl; a bright girl. You will make the right decision," comforted Mei Yin. She saw the doubt in her daughter's face. She wondered what she would have done in her place; if she were young, like her, again. She recalled her own rashness, her own foolhardiness and the mistakes she had made.

"Remember, you are young. What might seem so impassable and impossible can easily change. If you make a wrong decision, it can be undone. Don't look back. Look forward."

An Mei plucked at the grass. She ran her fingers through the feathery flower heads. She plucked a dandelion seed head looking like a ball of cotton. She blew softly on it sending a cloud of little fluffs drifting into the air around them.

"I think Hussein will have taken Shalimar as his second wife by now. Ahmad was in such a hurry to seal things and my mother-in-law, well, she would be pleased. I did not want to know the details. I decided to run. I flew here because I did not want to participate in their wedding ceremony. It makes a mockery of my marriage. What I have to decide now is whether I still want to be his wife."

She plucked more dandelion heads, tearing them from the bank; she blew and blew as though her life depended on it. Tears splattered down, staining her tee shirt.

"I still do not know if Hussein was an unknowing, unwilling participant when he..." She could not complete her sentence. "At times I believe in him. I told Aunt Nelly I believe him.

Now I am not sure. I have been thinking night after night. Can I believe him, when all evidence suggests otherwise?"

She shrugged her shoulder. "See I vacillate. I told Aunt Nelly I believe in him and now I have doubts again. Sorry! I keep repeating myself."

"If you do not believe in him, it would be a very bad basis for a marriage. You are young. You can end it." She saw her daughter's reluctance. "Is there anyone that can help you find out the truth? Would knowing for sure help you decide?"

Mei Yin sighed, frustrated by her inability to help her daughter. "What about Shalimar herself? You said that she had originally been unwilling to marry Hussein. What about Fawziah, the maid who helped you before? Servants have ears. They know a lot."

Chapter 22

Hussein walked into the bridal bedroom. The servants closed the door behind him and hurried away. They whispered amongst themselves and remarked on the mournful expression of the bride.

"Face like a bitter gourd! *Alamak!* Like quinine," they remarked of Shalimar.

"He does not look too happy either. If I had a chance to have a second wife, I would be so happy. I would be jumping for joy." The young manservant grinned from ear to ear, revealing a row of crooked teeth. He jumped up high and clicked his heels to demonstrate his joy; his short sarong ballooned like a jellyfish before he landed with a thud on the polished wooden floorboards.

"Shut up! Do you want to be sacked?"

"Quiet! You two! Stay here in the hallway. Not too near the door but close enough to see. *Datin* Faridah has instructed us to keep a close eye on the young couple."

"You mean we have to stay awake throughout the night?"

"We'll take turns. We'll come back to relieve you in three hours."

"*Tolong!* Help! What if I need to go the bathroom?"

"Stay where you are! Or you know the consequences."

* * * * *

Inside the wedding suite, Hussein regarded his bride with disquiet. "You did not want this. You said so. So why can't you tell me what really happened?"

Shalimar refused steadfastly to look at him. Instead, she looked at her hands. She kept silent.

"Or was it a ploy and not having succeeded the first time, you and your brother conspired for this to happen?"

He lost patience. Her stubborn silence irritated him. He marched up to her and dragged her to her feet.

"Tell me!" he demanded, shaking her by the shoulders.

She shook her head and looked away.

"Tell me," he repeated, taking her face and squeezing her chin so that her face was tilted towards him.

Still she would not answer. He let out a sigh of exasperation. Releasing his hold, he turned and strode to the sofa.

"You can have the bed; I'll sleep here," he announced.

"No! Please!" she pleaded, "I have to... I have to sleep with you."

"Have to? You don't have to. I don't want you to," he shouted.

"I have to," she pleaded again, running to his side. She held on to him, and slid down on the floor. She kissed his feet. "Please come to bed."

She was willing to do anything to consummate the marriage. She tore at her *baju*, the lace top of her wedding garment. She had been warned. If she were to fail her brother again, Ali, her lover would be charged with a crime so severe that a death penalty was guaranteed. She saw again in her mind's eye the raw welts on his body, the purple bruises on his face, his swollen eyelids.

Hussein stood, frozen. Shocked at what she was doing. He realised that something was wrong. He could not believe that Shalimar would stoop to bare herself if he refused her. Not even after what she had obviously done with the connivance of her brother.

"Don't," he said gently this time.

She stopped. Still on her knees, she hung her head in shame. Her hair was dishevelled, her body was half bare, the lace sleeves of her dress hung, armless; the *baju* top, still partly intact, hung around her neck. Desperately, she covered herself.

He turned and walked away, keeping his back to her to give her time to dress. Then he went over to her and led her gently to the sofa.

"Tell me why you are doing this. Tell me the truth so that Noraidin, An Mei, will believe in me again. Mend my relationship with her and I will be eternally grateful."

She did not speak.

"I promise that you will remain my wife at least in name and I will not inflict on you the shame of divorce. Look, I couldn't anyway. My parents believe in Ahmad. Our marriage has made headlines. I could not retract even if I wanted to. Just help me to salvage the little happiness I have with An Mei."

Still she maintained her silence.

"You should know that you have the power to deny whatever you tell me in this room. It would be my word against yours. And, as I said, my parents believe in you and Ahmad. They want this marriage. You have nothing to fear. I just want to know for myself so that I can tell An Mei, without any doubts in my own mind, that I am innocent."

Shalimar kept her head bowed, but the tension in her body relaxed. He saw it in the easing of the tendon cords in her neck and the way her spine soften.

"Come, tell me."

In a small voice, she whispered, head still bowed low. "In turn, I have a favour to ask of you. Help me. Help me save Ali. If he can be moved safely away from here to a place where they cannot reach him, I will be able to act according to my conscience."

"Ali? Who is Ali? What are we talking about?"

* * * * *

The next morning they came down hand in hand. They smiled at each other; she looked shyly into his eyes and he into hers. Breakfast was served in the middle terrace leading out to the lawn. They took their time, aware that they were being closely scrutinised. They stood for some time admiring the garden. A peacock strutted by, his tail fanned out in gaudy splendour; he shimmered his feathers, rippling deep greens and royal blues. At a distance, a peahen stood indifferent, pecking the ground.

"So! You are up! Come and join us for breakfast," said Rahim. He looked at his wife Faridah, smiled and with an imperceptible nod that seemed to say 'I told you so,' waved the young couple over.

"Looks like we won this round," said Faridah softly to her husband, smiling at the approaching couple all the while. "The servants told me all went well last night; they certainly look contented enough. Ahmad is right. And I am glad we went with his plan. I must confess I had my doubts for a moment because of Shalimar's strange behaviour, but Ahmad said that it was all due to nerves. He assured me that the poor girl has always been in love with our son, but was just too shy to push herself forward."

Servants rushed forward to pull chairs out for the approaching couple.

"Sit! Sit! You look very pretty this morning," Faridah said to Shalimar. "And my son, you are well?" She examined his face, raising one eyebrow in quiet concern when she saw the shadows under his eyes.

"*Selamat pagi*! Good morning!" Hussein replied. He grinned. "I did not have much sleep last night."

Rahim laughed. He whispered to his wife, "What do you expect?"

Shalimar blushed. Both had not slept much. They had spent the night talking and working out their plans. They decided that they had to present a picture of contented love to convince his parents and Ahmad. They would be able to carry out their plans only if Ahmad and Hussein's parents dropped their vigilance and stopped following their every move.

"Well, take the next couple of days off, but I regret to say that is all the time we can spare you," announced Rahim. "We are right in the middle of an election campaign and we have gained so much ground that we cannot afford to lose momentum."

"Thank you, that would be wonderful," Hussein replied.

"And, son, you will find that the swing towards you will be even greater when you go back onto the election trail. Your marriage to Shalimar has already improved your standing among the people. We have heard from villagers, all along the coast of Kemun, and even in the hinterland, that people approve. People here are still old fashioned. They do not wish to see their leaders completely westernised, and with a Chinese wife to boot! You will find a big contrast from before. Noraidin is pretty, but she is not one of us."

* * * * *

Hussein left the village hall, a simple wooden structure with a plain cement floor. The last of the voting booths were being cleared away and they could see the ballot boxes being carried to the adjoining offices. Hussein turned to the *penghulu*, the village headman. "*Terima kasih*, thank you," he said, clasping both of the older man's hands in his own before touching briefly his heart, a gesture of respect and gratitude.

"It is my honour to serve you," he replied.

"No, the honour is mine. I will remember your support and you can count on me to do the best for the villagers here. I bid you farewell for now, but I will be back." Hussein bowed once more; his humility so touched the older man's heart that it evoked tears in his eyes.

Ghazali smiled, noting how easily his boss won people over. People had expected a brash, pushy westernised young man. Hussein's adherence to tradition pleased the villagers.

"Congratulations!" Ghazali said, opening the car door for Hussein, before sliding in next to him. "The votes are not all in; two other villages have yet to finish, but all the indications are that you have won a landslide victory. Here, I have received a letter from KL. You are invited to see the PM. This must be good news."

Hussein laughed. He was elated. It had been all that his father had predicted.

"Good!" he answered. "When do we go? This will give me the opportunity to go to KL. Have you called Noraidin for me?"

Hussein had been so rushed that he had not had time to lift up a phone. He depended on Ghazali to do it for him.

"One day," he continued, "we will have a phone that we can carry around with us, instead of this mad rush to find a phone and then spending time dialling a number over and over again. But before we have this miracle, we will have to rely on land lines."

"I am sorry," replied Ghazali, his voice was reproachful. "We are not in KL; telephones are still not that widely available in the villages of Kemun, and the lines are not good. I find it difficult, in fact I would say impossible to rush in search of a phone and be with you at the same time. You have to tell me your priorities."

"I know, I know. I will do it myself. Let me have the letter."

Hussein read the letter and then read it again. A smile broke out on his face, transforming it.

"Yes, I have done it! If the votes swing my way, the ministerial post is mine."

He felt a surge of adrenalin course through him; his doubts, his worry that the sacrifices he had made in pursuit of politics might not be worthwhile, fell away.

Chapter 23

An Mei's eyes strayed to the clock; measuring each miniscule movement of its hands as though her life depended on it. Perhaps it would speed up if she were to close her eyes, she thought. She squeezed her eyes tight; she willed the clock hands to move faster. "Hurry, hurry," she whispered. Yet the minute hand lingered, making each little movement a reluctant jerk forward.

"Seven o'clock will arrive soon enough. No amount of blinking and mumbling will make it go faster," teased Nelly. "Go and make yourself beautiful."

She blushed. "No! I am just being silly, conjuring up a game I use to play as a child. I'll go through this correspondence for you and then I'll change out of my day clothes."

"You will do no such thing. I am going and I will leave you to do what you need to do. I will take these with me. They can wait. You have worked like a demon ever since you came back from Oxford. You will be worn out soon if you are not careful."

Nelly took the folder away from An Mei and walked to the door.

"Fawziah will see me out, and then I'll send her back to you." Impulsively, she turned and walked back to An Mei to give her a kiss. "Everything will be alright."

"I hope so," An Mei replied, but she was already lost in thought, reliving the day she returned to Kuala Lumpur. The memories of what happened flashed through her mind as they had done so often over the past few weeks in Kuala Lumpur waiting for Hussein to come back.

* * * * *

She had returned from Oxford without telling Hussein. She had taken the Kuala Lumpur airport limousine and driven straight from the airport to her in-law's home in the capital. Stepping out of the car, she had made her way up the grand entrance to the foyer. She could still recall the sharp shaft of light shining down from the dome window that overlooked the foyer. It had lit up the whole expanse of marble, light reflecting light. Standing in the midst of this, were a group of people, their backs towards her. They had turned abruptly at the sound of her footsteps. Taken off-guard, they had stared at her. She could still recall clearly the surprise and shock in their faces. Her mother in-law Faridah had uttered just one sound, "Huh!" before she turned her back on An Mei and resumed talking; there was no acknowledgement that she had seen or knew her. Her father-in-law Rahim had not lifted even an eyebrow. He had looked through her. Only Shalimar had come forward, followed quickly by Hussein.

And only Shalimar greeted her. "Welcome back," she had said, her face tinged red. She could not meet An Mei's eyes.

An Mei rubbed her arm, involuntarily as she recalled how Hussein had grabbed hold of her, his fingers digging deep into her arms.

"Why didn't you tell me? Why did you leave without saying a word?" he had asked.

"Leave her alone. She has only just arrived home," Shalimar had intervened on her behalf.

An Mei had shrugged off his hand, her anger boiling over. "Don't you know why I went away? Do I have to spell it out for you? How unfair can you be to make out that it was me who left you?"

"Please do not quarrel. He is upset because he missed you."

"And you! I trusted and befriended you and this is how you repay me. I want to have nothing to do with you," An Mei had said to Shalimar. She could not, even in her anger, but notice how beautiful her rival was, dressed in a hand painted silk batik of gold, bronze leaves. Her heart contracted recalling how she must have looked in comparison, rumpled and hot after the long flight. Just like when she first came back with Hussein from Oxford.

But neither Shalimar nor Hussein had time to answer An Mei. Both had been summoned.

"Tell Hussein and *Tengku* Shalimar that we are waiting for them," her mother-in-law had called out aloud to a servant. "We are late! We have to leave right away!" The family, making it known to all that she, An Mei, was the odd one out, unwanted, not part of the 'we'.

* * * * *

An Mei sat motionless, deep in thought, after Nelly left, unaware that the door had opened and that she was not alone in the room.

Fawziah closed the door softly behind her, pressing against the door with both palms flat against it. She watched An Mei wipe her eyes furtively. She walked quickly towards her and knelt down sitting on her heels.

"Please *Puan* Noraidin, I have been sent by *Puan* Nelly to help you dress, to prepare for *Encik,* Master Hussein's return. This is not the time for sadness. Don't think back. I have told you all that I know and have found out. *Encik* Hussein and *Tengku* Shalimar are not living together as husband and wife. You have to believe in him," she reminded An Mei.

"Yes, I have to believe and continue to try to win my in-laws over and in particular to retain my husband's affection," she said. But her heart sank at the enormity of the task. It was like confronting a tidal wave that threatened to rear up and crash down on her.

In the weeks following her return, she had seen little of Hussein. Rahim had commanded his son to leave the following morning to Kemun in order to continue his election campaign. They made it clear that An Mei was not to follow. "You will spoil all the progress he has made," they had warned.

In the very short time she saw Hussein, he had explained everything to her. The maid attending Shalimar had supported his story. She also learnt from Fawziah how Hussein was carried, almost unconscious, to Shalimar's room, the night he was supposed to have spent the night with her.

"He has not been unfaithful to me," she had told Nelly. "They have forced him to take on a second wife, but I shall not give him up."

Sitting in her room, she remembered her brave words. She looked at Fawziah, her only ally in this hostile house of her in-laws. She wondered if her brave words had not been foolhardy.

"He will be here soon," said Fawziah. "Why don't you bathe and I will do your hair. It will make you feel better, give you more confidence in yourself."

* * * * *

He came alone. An Mei ran down the stairs and was on the landing when he bounded up the staircase, two steps at a time, to reach her side. He crushed her to him.

"Where are they?" she asked Hussein. "They did not come with you?" she asked again, full of disbelief. She smiled. "Is this real? Is it possible that we are alone?"

"Yes! My mother and father think it safe enough to just let Shalimar accompany me because they believe that we are in love. But I have left Shalimar with the nurse who brought her up," he said. "And she is very happy with the arrangement." He grinned, his brown eyes shone with mischief. "And I am to spend a whole week here. Can you bear it?"

"Bear it?" she asked, nestling into his arms.

* * * * *

Much later. She sat up in bed. Drawing her knees up, she pulled the bedclothes to her chin and turned to look at her husband. She reached out and traced a pattern over his cheeks and down to his neck. He caught her hand.

"I wish you could stay longer," she said.

"Not this time. But when, if, I get the ministerial post, I will be able to spend more time with you in KL."

"Have you considered that if you did not get the ministerial post, in fact if you were not involved in politics at all, you could stay in KL and find something else to do?"

He turned away. He raised his arm and placed his thumb and index finger, a miniscule distance apart.

"I am that close to achieving what I have always aspired to do. Would you deny me that?"

"Of course not!" she conceded.

He failed to notice the catch in her voice. He buried his face behind the small of her back. She could feel his sharp intake of breath. Her body responded.

"Shall I give up my job and come to Kemun to be with you?" she asked. She was drunk with recklessness and the emotion of the moment.

"Yes!" he said without a second's hesitation as he pulled her to him.

Chapter 24

An Mei and Hussein returned by car to Kemun. The driver stole a glance at his rear mirror then quickly looked at the road ahead. What a tale he had in store for his friends, he thought to himself, one man and two wives, one on either side, in harmony. He looked again. Perhaps not quite in harmony, he surmised. He had gone to fetch *Tengku* Shalimar the day before. He had met up with the servants of the household. *Tengku* Shalimar, they had told him, was not happy. No wonder, he thought to himself. The other wife, Noraidin, was a picture of contentment and it had done something for her. Changed her appearance! He had never seen her looking so beautiful before. Next to her, perhaps *Tengku* Shalimar was a tad pale.

Hussein caught his eye on the rear mirror. The driver quickly averted his gaze to the road ahead. Five hours later they arrived in Kemun.

They drove into the driveway. Ghazali and the security guard in the escorting vehicles were already striding towards them. They opened the door.

"Do you wish me to accompany you sir?" asked Ghazali, brief case in hand.

"No! Not now. Business can wait. Just arrange to have the suitcases sent up to our quarters and please instruct the servants to prepare *Puan* Noraidin's rooms. We will go to see my parents now and break the good news to them."

"Shall I send someone to run ahead to tell them that you are on your way?"

"No! We'll surprise them," Hussein replied.

They made their way slowly up the stairs, walked through the hallway, passed the maze of staterooms and entered the private glass-covered courtyard. An Mei recalled the earlier scene she had witnessed there; she breathed deeply to calm her nerves.

"Do we go to your parent's quarters now or should we first go to ours?" she asked Hussein hoping to postpone meeting with her in-laws.

"I am sorry," said Shalimar. She had not spoken throughout. "I wish to go to my room. I don't feel well."

"Then go. Rest," Hussein said not unkindly, "but, An Mei, we should go straight to my parents and let them know. We should not give them too much time to prepare their confrontation with us." He took An Mei's hand. "Come along," he coaxed, leaving Shalimar standing on her own, totally oblivious to the distress on her face.

They walked through the glass-domed courtyard with the potted ferns and bamboos and entered another part of the mansion. An Mei had never been to this part of the house before. She had never been invited to the private quarters of her in-laws. She slowed her pace, her trepidation increasing by the minute. A maid spotted their entrance.

"Good afternoon," she said. "Welcome back. I'll tell *Datuk* and *Datin*."

Hussein stopped her. "Shhh," he mimed with a broad smile, "we want to surprise my parents."

Hussein held on to An Mei's hand and together they entered the room. It was a large room that spanned the entire length of the wing. Light flooded in from the windows. Rahim and Faridah were in deep conversation with Ahmad. They did not hear their entry. An Mei stumbled, her toe caught the corner of a chair; Hussein reached out to steady her. All three turned: Faridah's eyes widened; she was surprised to see An Mei with Hussein. Rahim, rose from his chair; Ahmad followed suit. To An Mei, their movements were a record in slow motion, a film reeling slowly forward.

"Mother, father. We are back," said Hussein, his voice shattering the silence. "And we have good news. I've got the post. I am now a Deputy Minister. An Mei, Noraidin, has resigned from the bank and has come to Kemun to be with me. Isn't that great?"

They stared at him, speechless.

"Aren't you going to congratulate me?"

Ahmad was the first to recover. He extended his hand. "Of course! What good news though we knew from the start you would succeed. Even then, the speed with which you have advanced is outstanding. Everyone is talking about it."

Faridah and Rahim took Hussein in their arms, taking turns to whisper words of praise. No one commented on An Mei's presence. They ignored her completely.

"And Shalimar?" Ahmad asked. "Where is she?" He kept his smile firmly on his face, but he was furious. His sister had once again failed in her responsibility.

* * * * *

Once Hussein and An Mei had left the room, Faridah turned on Ahmad furiously. "Send for your sister, this very moment. Where was she when all this happened?"

Ahmad blustered. "Don't ask me. I thought she was with Hussein all the time in KL."

Faridah turned impatiently to the hovering servants. "Tell *Tengku* Shalimar to come here at once!" she said.

"Hussein and Shalimar had looked so in love when they were here in Kemun. What happened?" asked Rahim. He too was bewildered by the speed his son seemed to have switched his allegiance from one wife to the other.

"Noraidin, that Chinese minx put a charm on him, that is what happened," replied his wife. "That brazen hussy. Otherwise, how could my son change so completely?"

"I am not keen to have An Mei, I mean Noraidin, here," said Rahim. "She will distract Hussein from his work and I am not at all sure that his popularity with the electorates will not suffer as well. It would be a shame; the people have responded so well to his marriage to Shalimar."

"I will have to consult my *bomoh*. I'll get him to undo her charm," said Faridah.

Her belief in magical powers was not a thing that Rahim would like the public to know. He did not believe in them and he did not approve of her use of what was tantamount to witchcraft. He had left her to her own devices just for peace.

"Maybe it has nothing to do with magical charms," he muttered. "Remember the potions you gave him? They did nothing for our cause; they did, however, make him very ill. Hussein had such extreme changes in mood, fluctuating between elation and depression, smiling and laughing one minute and in a cold sweat, the next. Leave him alone. For goodness sake!"

He was irritated and made to leave the room, but he could not refrain from making a parting remark as he left. "Now that Hussein has achieved this success, I am less concerned about who he prefers as a wife. As long as Noraidin keeps to the background, out of sight, out of mind. I just don't want him to be distracted at this critical stage of his career."

Faridah rounded on him venting her anger. "And you tell me that we should take a long view," she said, wagging her finger after him as he left. "In politics, you can be in one minute and out, the next. His recent success might be a distant dream in the future, if people here in Kemun realise that he has dumped Shalimar for Noraidin, someone who has no roots here and is not even a practising Muslim."

"*Datin*," said Ahmad, "You are so right, but *Datuk* Rahim makes a fair point as well. The only way we can create a serious rift between them is to isolate her, make her life such a misery that she will wish she had never decided to come here to Kemun. But it will have to be done in a clever way; Hussein must not be aware of our intentions."

Faridah rewarded Ahmad with a small smile. She looked impatiently at the grandfather clock. "Where is that girl we sent to fetch Shalimar?"

"I am here. *Minta maaf*, so sorry I did not make my presence known earlier but I did not wish to interrupt." The maid, a slightly built young girl, was clearly frightened. Head bowed low, she whispered, "*Tengku* Shalimar *sakit*."

"Huh! Ill, you say? Too guilty to face us more likely! Well, I will have to leave it to you, Ahmad, to do what is right and necessary."

Chapter 25

Jeremy took Nelly's arm and led her to the corner seat in the café. Nelly protested, "*Aiyah!* Just call me Nelly or Nelly *sum*. As I said on the first day we met, you should call Mary your mother. I feel so bad. Like a... a usurper!"

"I shall call you mother. I will also call Mary mother. And when the two of you are together, I shall find a way of distinguishing between the two of you." His tone was firm, but his eyes twinkled with amusement. In the short time he had known Nelly, he had come to realise that she was the gentlest of persons, who always placed others first.

"But I have not flown in from Singapore to discuss this," he said, "I came because of An Mei."

The twinkle in his eye was gone in a flash. His face was grave. "I had a call from our office in KL. Her boss was completely flabbergasted. You know she has resigned?"

"Yes! She has gone with Hussein to Kemun and now that she realises he was set up, she is determined not to give him up. I didn't want her to give up her job but she has to do what she feels is best. She cannot possibly keep it and be in Kemun."

"Well, this time, perhaps we should have tried to persuade her against resigning. She might find herself in need of it in the future. If only I had been around to dissuade her."

She looked up sharply, surprised by his wistful tone. "Why do you think she would need the job in the future?" she asked, worried. "Tell me," she demanded.

"I just have this gut feeling. You must have heard of all the new policy ideas that have been bandied about under the New Malaysia Five Year plan. Does Hussein agree with them? The Plan aims to give Malays greater access to universities and employment by extending the special quota systems to guarantee their entry. I am uneasy about all this talk of increasing the percentage wealth of the Malays. How can it be achieved except through redistribution from the other ethnic groups?" His hand shot up and he ruffled his hair in exasperation as though it was his hair that bothered him.

"How well does An Mei know Hussein, I wonder?" He paused to think, wrinkling his nose and screwing up his forehead in the process. "Of course I may be biased," he added, "after all I am a Singaporean. But you know, I got to know An Mei quite well in the short time we spent together, or at least I thought I did, and I feel sure her views will clash with Hussein's. So how can she live with him daily and support him in the implementation of policies that, to me, discriminate between one ethnic group and another, policies that she probably disagrees with?"

"Well, we do not know if she agrees or disagrees. They were very like-minded in Oxford. It is your conjecture. But what do you have in mind?" She looked seriously at her son as she tried to fathom his true feelings beneath the words. She began to wonder whether he might have a soft spot for An Mei.

"Nothing much. But I would like to save her job. It would give her a fall back position. Do you think I should do it without letting her know? I might fail but I would just like to talk to her boss. I know him quite well. Get him, the bank, to propose to her that she takes leave without pay for a finite period."

* * * * *

Shalimar sat on her bed with her shoulders hunched; her head drooped forward in abject defeat. She heard the distant soft sound of footsteps approaching her room and she shuddered in the expectation of what must surely follow. Yet, she remained seated, still as a mouse, frozen in fear. She recognised the footsteps as they grew closer and louder. Each step seemed more menacing than the previous. Her hands darted up to clutch her blouse. The door opened. She saw his silhouette, dark, faceless against the bright light that shone from the corridor behind him. He closed the door softly behind him, an act so unlike him that it seemed to suggest some even greater threat of what would come. She decided there and then that she would agree with whatever he wanted. It was the only way out for her. She had examined every alternative route since she seen her old nursemaid in Kuala Lumpur. And every one of them she had found wanting.

"Ahmad," she said rising to her feet.

Chapter 26

In the stately drawing room of her house in Kemun, Faridah sat laughing and talking with the friends who had gathered around her. They were women from her various clubs and associations. High society women, all clad in brightly coloured silks, congregated to discuss the latest fashions, their charities and to gossip. The sound of their chatter drifted across the room to where Shalimar sat alone embroidering. Her needle pushed and pulled with speed and deftness through the cotton, stretched out tight over the circular tambour frame. Blue, pink and yellow threads mingled and flowed to form a forest of flowers. Her head bent low, she was completely focused on her work.

From across the room, she heard her name mentioned. Then, a cackle of laughter followed. She could sense the women looking at her, but still she worked. Her fingers flew nimbly on.

"Shalimar," called her mother-in-law, "come over here. I have been telling my friends of your good news. Come, come sit with us."

Faridah turned to her friends. Her eyes gleamed.

"You are the first to know," she said. "I have not, rather Shalimar has not told Hussein yet. So please keep this to yourself. He is away in Kuala Lumpur. Since his appointment as Deputy Minister in the PM's office, he has to be there very often."

She paused, her nostrils distended in indignation. "And that minx, that Chinese witch! She does not let him alone so she is with him. I am afraid my gentle Shalimar lets her get away with blue murder."

"*Sayang!* Pity! *Tengku* Shalimar must learn to fight her corner. Surely she has a better claim than Noraidin now," remarked one of the ladies.

"I would have thought that *Tengku* Shalimar has a better claim than this commoner, even without the pregnancy," added another.

Shalimar face turned a bright pink. She heard a shuffle and looked up. The maid, Fawziah was looking at her puzzled. Shalimar turned away and dropped the tambour frame into the basket.

"Would you please excuse me, I need to go to my room to rest. I feel tired," she explained to Faridah.

"Go! Go and rest," Faridah replied. "Fawziah, you attend to *Tengku* Shalimar."

"She is such a good, obedient girl. You are lucky."

Faridah smiled. "*Nasib baik!* My good luck!" she said.

* * * * *

They were in the car. A stack of papers in blue and red binders sat between them. Hussein reached over and took An Mei's hand in his before resting their hands lightly on the papers.

"What is in them?" she asked, eyeing the files.

"Draft outlines of the different measures mapped out under the New Economic Policy."

"Can I have a peek?"

"Better not. It is an early draft and we are still debating some of the issues."

"I overheard some of the debate during the cocktail party. Are you supporting this New Economic Policy? There is considerable unease in the country. In fact, Jeremy says that..."

"Stop quoting Jeremy to me. It is none of his business. He is not even a Malaysian. Anyway, you should not involve yourself with this."

She withdrew her hand and sat up, her back stiff like a ramrod. Her face was a bright red. But she could not keep silent for long.

"Hussein!" she exclaimed. "What are you saying? Isn't that what you want? My involvement? That was what you have always said to me, even when we were in Oxford together, and, when we came back here, you have said over and over again, that we should work as a team."

"Ah! But things have changed and I was naïve. It is not what I want. It is what the party wants. I have to toe the party line. I cannot go against it and I cannot involve you in any major way. After all, you are not the elected officer. Come, surely we have better things to discuss than politics."

She was shocked. She turned away to look out of the car window. The low humming of the engine was all that could be heard, but the air was filled with a tension that had not been there before.

"I know I am not the one who is holding office," An Mei said, breaking the silence. "It has never been about my holding office in competition with you. But in the past you have always talked about your views and told me what you were thinking. We discussed things. We bounced ideas off each other. Your silence cuts me out. I hear and learn what you are thinking only through your conversations with others. And they are not changes and ideas that I recognise; ideas that I believe could have originated from you. What is happening, Hussein?"

He shrugged his shoulders, his face, impassive.

"Mother has called," he said instead, "she asked that we return to Kemun as soon as my work in KL is over. A break from this incessant chatter of policies will help us to redress our thoughts."

He leaned over and kissed her cheek. "Cheer up. Don't fight the tide of history."

But her cheek was unyielding. She remained unresponsive to his overtures.

* * * * *

An Mei stood alone in her bedroom in Kemun looking out of the window to the lush green beyond the driveway. Clipped hedges, almost ten foot high, marked the boundary of the grounds. Tall red-barked bamboos grew all along the hedge, their vibrant textured stems and leafy fronds softening the stark outline of the hedge. She could see staff hurrying to and from the car parked directly below as they unloaded the luggage. She had come directly to her rooms, leaving Hussein to go to his parents. It was not what she had wanted to do, but they had received instructions that Hussein's parents wished to see him alone. She sighed. "When will they accept me," she asked herself. "Perhaps never," she answered the question herself.

She felt the silence of the house and her own complete isolation from its residents. But it was not this that troubled her. It was the conversation in the car that worried her. Hussein had always used her as a sounding board for his ideas and views, but over these past few months, she had heard less and less from him. Conversation between them had become frivolous, even as the opposition parties became more and more vocal. She learned about political developments from the local papers not from him. She blushed a bright red as she corrected herself. They were not local papers; they were newspapers left in Nelly's office by Jeremy. She wondered if Hussein distrusted her. "No! That can never be," she said aloud. "I have never given him any cause not to confide in me."

She sat down on the edge of the bed. Suddenly, she straightened up and rang the bell. "Shalimar," she whispered to herself. "Perhaps she knows. I shall get Fawziah here to find out where Shalimar is."

She paced up and down the room waiting for the maid. Her eye caught the open page of a newspaper on the reading desk. It was the *Berita Kemun*, Kemun Times. She looked uncomprehendingly at the headlines in bold red: AN HEIR FOR DEPUTY MINISTER HUSSEIN AND TENGKU SHALIMAR!

* * * * *

Hussein stood in front of Shalimar, arms akimbo, feet wide apart and his lips quivering with anger. He glared at her until she dropped her gaze.

"What is this? What is this that I hear from my parents? How can you be expecting my child when nothing has happened between us."

Shalimar shrank away from his reproach, but her face remained determined. "I am expecting," she said. "It is... it is your child."

He flopped down onto the armchair nearest him. "How can that be? I have never been near you."

"Remember the night you were found in my bed. That was when our child was conceived," she said. She kept her eyes on the floor, unable to meet his direct gaze.

"You vouched that nothing happened. You helped me, connived with me to allow me to be with An Mei. Why would you do that if you were bearing my child?"

"Because I did not know," she answered. She looked up. That part of the answer was true. She did not know that she was bearing a child then, a child that she had to protect with everything she had. A child that she would lose on top of losing her lover, if she had not agreed to go along with her brother's suggestion. How could she admit to having her lover Ali's child when she was married to Hussein, a Minister? It would not only be the end for Ali but also for her unborn baby. She had to maintain, swear even in the name of Allah, that it was Hussein's baby. She knew the pain it would cause An Mei, but her mind was made up. This was for the sake of her child; her hand went involuntarily to her abdomen. "It is our baby," she insisted once again. "I did what I did because you loved An Mei and I did not want to destroy that."

Hussein held his head in his hands, clutching handfuls of hair in desperation. He felt the entire world was slipping from his grasp. Then he looked at Shalimar. He did not know what to believe. He saw the tears in her eyes and, against his will, he felt compassion. Perhaps, he thought, she was telling the truth. In truth, he had no recollection of what happened that night.

Perhaps, she was willing to share him with An Mei because she was placed in this wretched position. Only by becoming his wife could she protect her reputation and give a name to the child that he had fathered.

"Your father and mother are very happy. Please tell me that you are also happy. I will make it up with An Mei. I will explain that it was an outcome of... of your intoxication; that you did not know what you were doing when you were brought to my bed. That you thought I was her."

* * * * *

In the fern-filled, glass-covered courtyard, Faridah and Rahim were holding court. Tea had been laid out. The long table that the servants had earlier carried with great difficulty into the courtyard was resplendently covered with a white damask tablecloth; its intricate weave of silk, linen and cotton gleamed richly. The table groaned with food; plates piled high with cakes sat next to savoury offerings. Glutinous rice cakes filled with coconut shavings cooked in dark molasses competed with tureens of curries served with turmeric rice. Their aromas mingled: sweet, spicy with hints of heat to tickle the tired palette.

"High tea! High tea!" Faridah exclaimed to her guests. "To celebrate our good news. In a few minutes, my son and his wife will be here to join us, but do eat. *Tak payah tunggu*. Don't wait. We are very informal." Her excitement was evident in her pink cheeks; her eyes glittered as she searched the room to engage her guests in her joy.

"By wife, she must mean *Tengku* Shalimar. She can't stand the other one, the Chinese one he brought back from England," whispered one of the guests to another.

"Hush!" replied the other, "she is here."

The room went quiet. All eyes turned to stare at An Mei.

An Mei stood awkwardly for a second and then turned hurriedly. She had not realised that there was a celebration, a party. She had come into the courtyard in search of Hussein. Now, blindly, she turned unaware that Hussein was behind her. He had also entered the courtyard with Shalimar trailing after him in search of An Mei. He held her for a moment, and then released his arm.

"Come, come, just in time for tea and our celebration. Sit, sit," commanded Faridah beckoning her son and Shalimar to come into the room. Her eyes, as usual, swept passed An Mei without acknowledging her presence.

"No, mother. Later," said Hussein. He ushered both An Mei and Shalimar out of the room, gripping their elbows firmly.

"Please excuse my son," said Faridah nonplussed. She quickly recovered to hint darkly that something was amiss, her eyebrows lifted in an arch, like a question mark, and nodded in the direction of An Mei. "Jealous," she remarked.

* * * * *

"Let go of my elbow," An Mei hissed, seething with anger. "Don't you dare touch me!"

"We'll explain. Come into this room," he pleaded, pushing the two ladies into a room. It was the study. He locked the door behind him and leaned heavily on the closed door.

"I am sorry that you had to learn about this in such an unpleasant way. I did not know myself. I had no idea," he said.

"No idea?" An Mei asked, her eyes incredulous. "No idea?" she repeated. "That you have fathered a child?"

"I don't," he replied. "Shalimar now says that I am the father, but I have no recollection, none at all, as to what happened the night I was found in her bed." He looked to Shalimar, his eyes pleading for help.

Shalimar felt ashamed but could not retreat from her course of action. She could not bear to look at the two people before her, the only ones to befriend her in her time of need.

"He thought I was you," she said. "He was feverish, calling your name; he did not know what he was doing. He seemed so intoxicated, so drugged. I... I... could not fend him off." Shalimar's eyes remained focused on the floor. That part about Hussein's state of intoxication was true, but everything else was a lie.

"Please An Mei," begged Hussein. "I cannot vouch if what she says is true or false, but what do you want me to do? I love you. Even if it did happen, it was not a conscious act. It does not change anything between us."

"Please," pleaded Shalimar, "the baby is all that I have in this world. I will not intrude on your love."

An Mei looked from one to the other. She felt torn between compassion for Shalimar and jealousy; anger against Hussein combined with a desperate wish to believe in him. In all her tormented moments in Oxford when her thoughts reeled through all the pitfalls of a union with Hussein, she had not anticipated anything even remotely like this. To have to share him with someone else within months of their marriage, to be so hated, so isolated from the family that she had married into, and worse still to suffer Hussein's recent reluctance to share his thoughts with her. What chance had she, now that Shalimar was to have Hussein's baby, to redeem herself with her mother-in-law?

She stood rooted to the floor, unable to answer. Slowly, her legs gave way. She sank down to her knees and held her hands to her face and wept. Once she had begun, she could not stop. She felt utterly lost; what could she do? What future was there for her?

Chapter 27

Mei Yin rushed into the office at the back of the restaurant in Oxford. In her hand was the telegram that was delivered to her when she was in the foyer overseeing the arrangements for the day. Flowers had been delivered fresh from the covered market that morning and she had helped to arrange little posies of pink and white for the tables. Her next job would have been to see the cook in the kitchen to go over the preparations for the lunchtime guests. She would normally tick these against the menu for the day and go on to her task of tasting: sauces, soups, and stock broths, even the size and crunchiness of the thinly sliced vegetables did not escape her attention. It was while she was joking with the assistant cook, about how her waistline had expanded with her kitchen duties that the post boy came with the telegram. She took one look at the thin slip of paper that was handed to her and all semblance of joviality was wiped from her face.

She manoeuvred behind the desk and sat down on the wooden chair. She looked at the clock on the wall; it was just

10.45 in the morning. She reached for the phone. She made a quick calculation of the time difference. Nelly should be still in the store, she thought, but her staff would have left. They should be able to talk.

* * * * *

"She is absolutely devastated. *Seong sam do mo tak gong*, her heart is so wounded that she cannot speak. She just weeps," said Nelly. Her voice over the phone sounded hoarse as though she herself had been crying. "My fault, entirely my fault. If I had not come back and given her an excuse to stay back in KL, then this might never have happened."

"Don't blame yourself. As I said many times before, she would have married or gone with him anyway; she was so smitten, so in love. She would not have risked her father's anger by running away with Hussein otherwise. Who could have anticipated that his family would go to such extreme measures to push them apart? Why did Shalimar change her story? And can we believe Hussein? It seems... it seems..."

"A tall story? I too have my doubts, but I cannot say that to An Mei."

"So what is she going to do? Tell her we love her; that she can always come home."

"Are you going to tell Ming Kong?"

A long silence followed. Mei Yin struggled with her thoughts. They were in limbo. "What do you think?"

"Yes; this time we should tell him, but we must break it to him gently."

* * * * *

Ming Kong smiled as Mei Yin tucked the rug around his knees. This was the time of the day that he liked best; when she was back home with him, just playing a game of cards, watching television and eating the restaurant delicacies she had packed into a tiffin box for him.

"Is this the tiffin box that you used to bring food to Nelly when we had our first shop?" he asked. Cream and painted with red roses, the chipped three-tiered box had clearly seen better days.

"Mmm..." she nodded, "I brought it all the way here, as a reminder of how we started business; a humble reminder." She tried to smile back in return, but she couldn't. Her mind was busy, scrambling to find an opening statement to introduce the subject.

"You're back early," he commented, noticing her reticence. "How was it today?"

He loved her daily accounts of what went on in the restaurant, content to take a backseat, at least for the moment. He hoped that his lethargy would soon lift; he felt unaccountably tired. He could not explain it. On the business front, things were working out. Nelly was keeping the Malaysian side of his business going; in Oxford, Mei Yin seemed to be thriving. He was blessed with two wonderful women, more than he deserved, he acknowledged silently.

"Good, the day was good. The restaurant was full this lunch time," she replied. She saw that he sensed something was not right. He was looking at her intently, expectantly. She made up her mind to tell it straight. "I have news of An Mei. It's not good."

She took his hand and told him, leaving nothing out.

He sat quietly and listened. Once upon a time, he would have ranted and raved; he would have threatened and rushed out to make good his threats. Now he just sat listening, his face full of sadness. Like Nelly blaming herself, he considered himself responsible for the situation.

"Perhaps my sins are revisiting my child," he said softly, so softly that Mei Yin had to bend low over him to hear.

"Nonsense!" she said. "Completely different context. You were much worse!" she teased in an effort to lighten his mood. She was worried; his face had turned virtually grey.

"An Mei needs someone to talk to and perhaps it is not us. She needs to clear her head. She has to get away from Kuala Lumpur, from Kemun, and think and talk it over," she said.

"Casey!" he said suddenly. "She was her best friend in Oxford and seems to know Hussein. So what she says An Mei would not interpret as being biased against him. If it came from us, she probably would."

"You might be right. Casey is young like An Mei. Our way of thinking is different from theirs. Siew Lin, her mother, says she is level-headed. I'll speak to her."

Chapter 28

"It's a matter of grave concern," An Mei heard the man say. She glanced up and caught his eye. He smiled politely, bowing just a fraction to acknowledge her existence before continuing his conversation with the group of men standing by the bar. "It is not a matter that is covered in this conference and we are not here to discuss it, but informally..." he paused, casting his eyes around the room, "people are talking. Just like us. In the corridors, behind closed doors, people are commenting on the new directions. The long term results that surely must arise from such short term considerations." His voice droned on.

An Mei was aware of the glances in her direction, a lone woman in the room, distinguished from the other suited delegates by the lack of an official badge that would give her title and credentials. A large poster announced that an international conference was underway. She was waiting for Casey. Casey had said that she might be able to pop out to see her for a few minutes in order to arrange a reunion tonight. She warned she might be late because much would depend upon how the conference was going. As an interpreter, her hours were determined by the proceedings. But surely, An Mei reasoned, she should be able to get away now that the delegates were taking a break in the bar. She looked around the room uneasily. She felt like an intruder.

"You see that woman sitting there," she heard a delegate say, "look what she is wearing. It did not use to be like that here, but, increasingly, this is a common sight. A swing to ... to ... conservatism would you say?"

She knew instinctively that she was being examined and lowered her head to let her *hijab* fall forward to cover more of her face.

"An Mei?" a voice asked cautiously.

She looked up. "Casey!" she said, jumping up and grasping her friend's hands.

"Why are you dressed like this?" asked Casey. "I'm sorry, I shouldn't have said that," she apologised immediately. "I am late because of the working group responsible for drafting the report. There were some difficulties with some of the words used by the interpreters. Suddenly every delegate in the group became a self-appointed linguist. They combed each word to ferret out all possible nuances. We had to liaise with the translators preparing the report of the conference."

She paused for breath.

"Look! I can't stay," Casey continued, "I have to return immediately now the break is over because we have to be back in the interpreters' booths ready for the resumption of the session. Here, meet me at my hotel,' she said pushing a piece of paper into An Mei's hands. "It is wonderful to see you." Casey gave An Mei a hurried hug and rushed off, but her face was taut with anger. "How dare Hussein reduce her to this plain, shrouded woman, with fear and anxiety written all over her face."

* * * * *

An Mei stood in the middle of the hotel room examining the clothes strewn in chaotic disorder on the big bed.

"Find a place to sit, will you," Casey shouted from the bathroom. "Just push the clothes aside. I will be out in a minute. I just need to make myself nearly decent. There! I am ready."

She came out of the bathroom, wrapped in a big fluffy towel, a smaller towel wound round her hair like a turban.

Suddenly, An Mei felt like she was back in Oxford in the digs she shared with Casey. The hotel room was bigger, more luxurious, but there was the same chaotic assembly of clothes, books and paper. Even the smell of Casey's bath soaps and powders were the same. She could not help smiling.

"How did you manage to create such a mess in one day? You have only just arrived."

"That is why. I have not had time to unpack properly. Ah!" she said, eyeing An Mei. "I am glad you took that off. I was worried for a moment that you were going to keep it on even with me. Why have you taken to wearing a scarf round your head. You have such beautiful hair."

"My mother-in-law insists on it. I resisted initially, but it caused such havoc and unfavourable comment that I gave in. Anyway I have to think of Hussein. Apparently, it is important for him that I profess and practise the faith."

"Tell me all, that is if you are up to it. I shall order something from room service for us. You are free this evening, I hope?"

"Yes, I am back in KL alone."

* * * * *

When An Mei finished speaking, the atmosphere in the room descended into a haunting silence. Casey had let her speak without once interrupting. The dishes brought up by the hotel staff had long gone cold. The food lay congealed, uninviting on the plates. An odour of uneaten food filled the room.

Casey stood up. "I'll get rid of this," she said gathering the tray and walking to the door. "Shall I order something else?"

"I can't eat."

"Neither can I," admitted Casey, "and I was so hungry when you arrived."

"Sorry."

"What about?" Casey stood for a moment, hands empty of the tray she had left outside the door. "Come here," she said, hugging An Mei to her. They stood together, Casey towering over An Mei, her arms around An Mei's slight body in a tight hug.

"What shall I do?" asked An Mei as she extracted herself from Casey's embrace. "I just do not know what to do."

"Do you want me to see Hussein?"

"Yes! We can go to Kemun together. You might be able to judge better if he is changed. I can't. Nelly thinks I make excuses for him. She does not say it in so many words, though her face speaks volumes. First, I'll introduce you to Jeremy, her son. He is here in KL; he comes often to see Nelly."

"Ah! *The* Jeremy. What about Jane, her daughter?"

"She is in Singapore and her visits are few and far between. She is tied up with her work in the hospital. I think she has a boyfriend and does not want to leave him for long."

"And in Kemun, would I be able to meet Shalimar?" asked Casey.

An Mei nodded. "And you will see for yourself why I am so confused. She is the epitome of gentleness and goodness. I cannot bring myself to hate her. That's what makes it so ridiculous. I can't even hate her. I cannot believe that she would lie but if she hasn't, then..." She left the sentence unfinished.

"We should eat. You will feel better," Casey said looking at her watch. "If I am to go to Kemun, it will have to be this weekend, after the Conference. So shall we arrange to see Nelly this evening? We can have supper with her and then I'll get to meet Jeremy. She grinned. "I can't wait to see the man."

"Then get changed and wear something very informal. Nelly likes to shock people by going very local."

"Then, you must leave this behind and borrow my tee-shirt." Squashing An Mei's headscarf into a ball, Casey threw it across the room. It landed behind the armchair.

An Mei's sombre mood broke under her friend's influence. "All right," she said. "We are not going any place where I might be recognised."

* * * * *

The heat and humidity hit her the minute she opened the car door. An Mei half stepped out of the car and shivered as the damp air enveloped her; the car windows steamed up and mist covered the screen, partially obliterating the outside scene for a minute. Casey leaned over, stopping An Mei's exit, and rubbed the window glass vigorously with her handkerchief until the glass showed clear.

"Here! We are over here," a voice called from some yards away.

Still leaning over An Mei, Casey looked up and saw Nelly perched on a stool by a round wooden table. Next to her was a young man. He stood seemingly in search of something more substantial to sit on.

"That's Jeremy," said An Mei. "Will you please get out from the other side and let me get out of the car from this side?"

"You are right about Nelly's choice of a place to eat," said Casey shifting back to her seat before opening her side of the car door. She sniffed exaggeratedly.

"Mmm! Lovely! What aromas!" She eyed one of the stalls suspiciously. A man was busy flipping what seemed like a piece of thin round cloth over and over a hot flat iron stove.

"What's that?" she asked round-eyed.

"*Roti canai*, an Indian bread that is as thin as thin can be. See how it expands as he flips it over and over. It is a soft bread; you dip it in a sort of *dhal*, lentil curry sauce. Delicious! See the other guy. He is making another type of Indian bread, *dosai*. This is rolled into one big hollow crepe and is crispy."

"Gosh! I only know *naans* and *chapatis*. I did not realise there were so many other Indian breads."

"Yes, because you don't have such a varied Indian community in Hong Kong or England, the choice there is less than here. Northern Indians eat quite differently from their southern brothers. I suspect *dosai* and *roti canai* are eaten mainly in South India. But come, they are waiting for us." An Mei took hold of her friend's hand and walked over to Nelly. Surrounded by her friends and family, she felt almost happy, almost like her old-self.

"Come along, sit down," invited Nelly pointing to the stools around the table. "Take any of these. Jeremy," she said, turning to the young man, "this is Casey, An Mei's friend."

Casey stared at him, completely captivated. He smiled. She was taken by his broad warm smile. She smiled back and with a lingering glance, turned her attention to Nelly once again.

"How are you Aunty?" she asked politely. An Mei noticed that Casey's cheeks were a bright pink.

"Good, good. How is your mum? I met her just briefly in Oxford, but I have heard so much about her over the years from An Mei's mother."

Then, turning to An Mei, "I chose this place to eat partly because you cannot eat pork now and in this place, there are all sorts of Indian and Muslim curries and *halal* food. Anyway, I thought Casey might like to try something different."

"Take this chair," Jeremy said to Casey, "it might be more comfortable than the stool my mother offered you. Or perhaps, you might like me to show you what is available before you make a choice?" He got up extending his hand to her. "Back in a minute," he said to An Mei and Nelly.

He walked Casey over to the food stalls. "Has An Mei told you?" he asked.

"Yes, she has told me. I presume you are referring to her situation. I am going to Kemun to see for myself."

"You know Hussein?"

"Yes."

"Tell me what you see, what you think of Hussein, please."

Casey looked at him. Her heart did a little somersault. "Sure," she replied. She wondered why he would be so interested.

"Can we meet when you come back?"

"Sure," she said again, hoping that her heart would calm down. What an idiot he must think I am, she thought.

Chapter 29

The car powered forward, its engine purred smoothly, leaving behind Kuala Lumpur and its high rises en route for Kemun. Densely packed townships gradually gave way to one-street villages. Two-storey shop houses lined the road on each side, interrupted here and there by ramshackle outbuildings with piles of used rubber tyres and rusty wheels lying on the dirt ground. Potholes filled with brown muddy water and old abandoned cars dotted dirty courtyards. Brightly coloured posters with English and Chinese characters announced the business of the shops. They sold everything: plastic balls vied for space with enamel pails, tins of biscuits, milk powder, cooked food and fresh vegetables. Through the open doors of the shops they could see the goods packed in their dark interiors; there was no particular order in their arrangement and often they spilled out to the common frontage that linked the shops. Children played; some cried, others smiled; their pale faces covered with dirt as they jostled with each other or rode their bicycles.

"Missy! Missy!" they cried running alongside the road, wildly waving their hands.

Casey and An Mei spoke little, aware of the driver. An Mei could see his curious glances reflected in the rear mirror. Slowly the scenery changed. The two-storey shop houses gave way to small wooden houses set on stilts. Sarongs and brightly coloured shirts hung on clothes lines stretched between coconut palms; they waved like flags in the breeze. Old men and women sat in the shade, their brown skin burnt almost to a blackened nutmeg. Here and there, a table was set out in the blazing hot sun offering refreshments. Fresh coconut! A sign said: 20 cents per nut. Durians! said another, 4 for 2 Ringgit. The tables were not manned. Bees and flies buzzed. Nearby, a brown cow stood swishing its tail to ward off the insects. A cloud of dust rose and then settled. A desultory air prevailed. The momentum of life, it appeared, had slowed down to a snail's pace.

"*Mei you huan;* seems like not much has changed here," said Casey switching to Mandarin. "It is exactly like mum used to tell us about life when she was in Malacca."

Then, suddenly the scenery changed completely with the start of mile upon mile of plantations, palm oil and rubber, their orderliness contrasting sharply with the earlier scenes; the buzz and dirt in the small townships fighting for livelihood and the relaxed laid-back villages of stilt houses. The plantations' lush green formality shouted wealth.

"There is change. You have to know what to look for. There is a greater divide. And once you recognise it, you will always see it," said An Mei.

Casey looked at her friend puzzled. "That is quite a profound statement. Tell me more. Tell me what Hussein thinks."

216 Chan Ling Yap

An Mei made a face, looked at the rear mirror and grimaced once again.

"*Shuo putong hua*, speak in Mandarin," Casey suggested.

"I'll try but it won't be as good as yours. Remember I had only two years of private study in Oxford," An Mei replied. "When we were in Oxford, Hussein used to tell me his plans and ambitions. He was always so fired up with the idea of redressing any wrong. Remember his involvement in the women's movement and the protest against the Vietnam War? In the early months of our return, he was still full of enthusiasm. He wanted to help the poor. But his definition of poverty has gradually changed. Now it seems to be very much drawn on racial lines. He does not discuss it with me. When I try to point out that there is poverty amongst all the ethnic groups, he just won't discuss it. All he says is that he must toe the party line. It is this more than anything that hurts me. More than even Shalimar, because I still believe she was forced on him."

An Mei stopped and looked at her friend. "He has no need of me any more." Casey took An Mei's hands in hers. She squeezed them in reassurance. She could not comment. She had to wait and see for herself.

* * * * *

The marquee was over-flowing. People went in and out of it carrying plates of food. *Rongeng* music blared from one corner, lilting drumbeats and the string music emitted from the *gamelan* combined to give a haunting Malay tune that speaks of Arab-Indonesian-Portuguese-Chinese influence. A group of people danced bare foot to the music.

Hussein emerged from the tent with Shalimar next to him. They were immediately surrounded by well-wishers. They had come from all over Kemun to pay their respects and offer their congratulations to Hussein. They were proud to have him, so young yet already a Deputy Minister in no less than the Prime Minister's office, represent their state. They were effusive over Shalimar and her pregnancy. Prayers were offered on his behalf. Hussein's head reeled from their effusive messages. He smiled and bowed until he felt a twitch developing on one side of his face.

"Here," said Ghazali handing him a scented towel that he had taken from a passing servant. "*Tengku* Shalimar's pregnancy seems to have boosted your rating even higher. Look at them. They are falling over at her feet."

"See what I told you," a voice said over his shoulder. He turned around to face his mother. "If you were to let Noraidin go, who knows? You might be Prime Minister in the future. She is definitely baggage you can do without."

"Please, no more of this," said Hussein. He turned and stalked away only to bump into another group of well-wishers.

* * * * *

"Come, let's go over there," said Ahmad to his sister who was standing alone, temporarily abandoned in the crowd. She was watching her husband's retreating back.

Ahmad took her by the elbow and deftly wove his way through the crowd until they reached the pergola. "There," he pointed to a bench under the dark shade of a woody climbing plant overhanging it. Shalimar looked at the masses of pink blooms and leafy tendrils swaying in the breeze. She took a deep breath of the scent and sighed. She sat down; the seat was a welcome respite after hours of standing and small talk.

"You must be tired," he said. His tone was gentle; he seemed concerned. Her pregnancy was not obvious, not unless you knew.

She was surprised at his solicitous manner even though he had been almost kind ever since she had agreed to his plans. By default, they were her plans now. They were accomplices, she thought. She was amazed at how her life had suddenly improved as a result of that one promise, that one word, she had given to Ahmad. She was shocked by her own thoughts and her eventual acceptance of the situation.

"*Datin* Faridah is pleased," said Ahmad. "She wants you to work on Hussein. Make him feel good, needed. She wants you to flatter him, work your way into his heart. With Noraidin spending more time in KL, she feels you will succeed. And I think you will too."

He bent close to her ear.

"Remember, our family fortunes depend on you. We have lost almost everything except our royal connections. And your mother-in-law wants that connection to complete her ambition for status. Remember, your child depends on you. If Hussein casts you off that will be the end of your child's future. In fact, I cannot think how we would have been able to allow it to come into the world but for your marriage to Hussein; the shame it would bring on our family. You understand don't you? On no account can Hussein know that he is not the father."

He smiled and reached over to touch her head, gently tucking a stray lock under her *hijab*.

She felt overwhelmed by the gesture; she had never received even the simplest act of kindness from him since their parents died. Her hand strayed once more to her abdomen, as it had done repeatedly throughout the day. She needed to seek assurance from her child that she was doing the right thing; that she was doing it for this life growing within her. She bowed her head.

"I'll try," she said.

"It is not that difficult, is it?" he teased. "You like him, don't you?"

She blushed. Yes, she admitted to herself, it would not be difficult to love Hussein. Hussein's kindness had won her heart and if it were not for her love of Ali, she would not have objected to the arranged marriage. "Ali!" her lips moved to form his name silently. He was now gone from her. All that remained was his child, and she could have it only if she was with Hussein."

* * * * *

An Mei and Casey stood at the verge. They looked at the milling crowd, the band playing music and the dancing men and women. Their eyes surveyed the scene scouring it for a sight of Hussein.

"There he is," cried An Mei pointing to a figure leaving the marquee.

"That's him?" asked Casey in surprise. She looked at the man walking towards them. She saw little of the Hussein she knew in Oxford. Gone were the flamboyant flared trousers and ponytail. In its place, walking towards them, eyes anxious, was a man with short hair, resplendent in silk trousers and sarong; but a man seemingly with a burden. He walked slowly as though he wanted to gain time to collect himself.

Maybe she was imagining it, thought Casey, but in the past, he would have ran to them; at the very least he would have waved.

His progress towards them was slow. People continually went up to him. She observed how they greeted him. They shook his hand and placed theirs on their heart in return as a sign of respect.

No, she was not being fair, she concluded. Perhaps, his position did not allow it now. He had to show restraint, even amongst close friends. She must not allow any prejudice to colour her views of him.

They waited on the verge in silence. Casey could feel the tension in An Mei; she could almost imagine the thoughts that must be crossing her mind. She squeezed An Mei's hand.

"The last time I saw him was when I found out that Shalimar was expecting." An Mei's face turned red with shame. In her mind's eye, she saw herself again in the room with her husband and Shalimar; her feeling of utter dejection; her loss of control, and her total breakdown.

"It was just over a week ago, but it feels like a lifetime. Now, everyone is celebrating the event; this party was organised by the town people of Kemun for them," said An Mei bitterly.

Casey followed the direction of An Mei's eyes. She saw people part to make way for a girl in a green pastel silk ensemble. Even from where she was standing Casey could see her grace, her beauty. The girl went to Hussein and took his arm; she smiled up at him.

"Shalimar?" Casey asked An Mei.

An Mei turned suddenly to face Casey. "I cannot take much more of this," she cried. "I want to run, to run away and be free. Maybe it would be best, not only for me but for Hussein as well."

She looked towards her husband.

"To be free from a love that is so intense and meets with such adversity, a love that has devoured my existence for the past year." Her face was no longer a stoic mask; tears were coursing unchecked down it.

"To be free to think and do ordinary things, even something as simple as wearing a skirt to work. I look at you Casey. And I think of myself. My future is nothing in comparison, nothing but a waiting game for a husband who I share with someone else. I try, I try so hard to believe in him, to believe in us, but I am being worn down." She caught hold of her friend's arm. "Let's go," she said.

"Are you sure?"

"Yes! Yes! I am sure. Let's leave them to their happiness."

Hussein looked up at the sudden commotion. He saw their parting figures. He made as though to follow them. He felt Shalimar's hand tighten on his arm.

"Please," Shalimar beseeched him silently. He looked up and saw people looking at him expectantly. He saw Ghazali, his mother and father, their faces anxious, pleading. Let her go, they all seemed to be saying to him. A momentous silence followed. People held their breath. The seconds ticked by. Then he turned his back on the departing figures to face the crowd. A sigh of relief went up from the group of people around him. They began to clap.

Chapter 30

Casey and Jeremy met at the Merlin Hotel in Jalan Treacher. The coffee house was almost empty. A waiter hovered near their table waiting for their order.

"Coffee," they both said, anxious to get rid of him.

"Just coffee? Anything to eat? We have specials today. Durian cakes made just this..."

"Just coffee will be fine."

The waiter closed his note pad with exaggerated slowness and leaned over to rearrange the coffee cups and cutlery already laid out on the table. Casey looked at Jeremy and broke out in a wide grin. She waited until the waiter left, and then shook her head in amusement.

"I thought he would never leave us alone."

He returned her smile; but he was preoccupied; he seemed to be looking at her, yet she felt he was not seeing her. He had called her to set up the meeting.

"I am leaving for Rome in two days time. My time here has run out, so I have to go back to the old grind," she said. Please, she pleaded in silence, say you do not want to see me leave.

"I called to ask you what happened," he replied. He seemed not to have heard her say she was leaving. He was wrapped up in his own thoughts and distracted from all things except for the one thought on his mind; An Mei. She had not answered anyone's calls.

Hurt and embarrassed, Casey replied quickly. "Of course! We went to Kemun and it was while waiting for Hussein to join us that, out of the blue, An Mei announced that she did not wish to go on with the farce and that she wanted to be out of the situation she was in. I can't blame her. No matter whether Hussein has lied or not about his actual relationship with Shalimar, the future seems bleak for An Mei. The thing is I did not say that to her. In fact, I did not say much at all. I just let her talk it out of her system and, it would appear, that talking has enabled her to make a decision."

"Do you think she will stick to her decision? She has made similar ones before and each time he has been able to talk her out of it."

"An Mei is very, very hurt. She is also very proud. I think, this time, she has been pushed too far. If he had run after us as we were leaving, she might have had a change of heart. But not now; not when he publicly let her go."

Jeremy said nothing.

"Don't get me wrong. I didn't think that she was only trying to make a statement when she stormed out. She genuinely wanted to end it all. Even then, if he had run after us, he might still have stood a chance," continued Casey. "It was very painful for me to watch her vacillate; one minute she believes in Hussein and was making excuses for him, then the next, she was uncertain, even suspicious."

"It hurts me too," Jeremy said.

Casey looked up sharply.

"Only because I care for her; she was a daughter to my mother," he said quickly, conscious that he had to explain himself.

"Of course," said Casey. Her eyes did not leave his face.

"What was your impression of Hussein?" asked Jeremy. He was anxious to shift attention from himself.

"Obviously, I have little to report on Hussein. I did not have time to observe him, except that he is changed, at least in his dress and manners. Not the rebel he was in Oxford. On the contrary, quite a conformist."

Jeremy shrugged. "It is not important now. I know enough. You are quite right. He conforms; and that is why he is such a fast rising star. He is just made out to be a symbol of dynamism because he has the ability to talk. But what he says is all planned and mapped out for him."

Chapter 31

Nelly opened the door. She peeped in. It was dark in the room; the curtains were drawn tight. There was utter silence. She went straight to the windows and drew back the curtains. Not satisfied with the paltry light that seeped in, she threw open the wooden shutters causing them to rattle and creak. The window catch that anchored them shut swung loosely. Light flooded into the room and the curtains moved gently with the breeze that blew in. She took a deep breath and then turned to face the bed. There was no one in it. Alarmed, she looked to the other end of the room.

"Hello Aunt Nelly," said An Mei in a small voice. She was in a corner of the room in the armchair where she normally sat to read. But there were no books or magazines in sight. Her feet were drawn up and tucked under her. In her pyjamas, and with her hair, ruffled and loose, she looked young, lost and vulnerable.

"You have locked yourself in this room for the past two days, ever since you came back from Kemun. Ah Kun said that you rushed out yesterday and came back again in the afternoon and locked yourself in again. What's going on?"

"I needed to be alone. But I did come out and I did eventually unlock the door."

"Well, that's a good start." Nelly went over to An Mei and kissed her head. "Can you talk now?"

"Yes. I just needed to sort myself out. I just needed time to myself."

Nelly saw the empty tray on the coffee table and smiled.

"At least you have had something to eat," she said.

"Yes, I asked Ah Kun for food when she knocked on my door. You see I needed to eat."

"Of course you need to eat, silly girl," said Nelly holding An Mei's head to her bosom. "Shall I send for more food?"

"Later, I want to tell you why I needed to eat. Please, let me," she said as she saw that Nelly was about to interrupt. "I need to eat because I am expecting and I do not want to hurt my baby by starving."

Nelly grew very still. Her arms fell to her side. They hung lifeless. She sat down heavily on the pouf next to An Mei. "Are you sure? How did you...? When did you find out?"

"Yesterday. I was sick and suddenly I realised that my period was late. It never dawned on me until I became sick that I could be pregnant. I went out because I needed to see a doctor. We did some tests. He confirmed it."

An Mei was calm and collected; her face was serene and her gaze direct.

"I plan to have the baby."

"And Hussein? Are you going to tell him? Are you going back to him?"

Uncertainty showed in her face. "I have to wait and see."

* * * * *

In the weeks that followed, An Mei returned to work with the bank. Her daily routine assumed a normality not unlike before she was married. In an attempt to forget, she threw herself into her work both at the bank and in her father's shops. Hussein did not contact her. Through the media, she traced his rise in the government. Photographs of him and Shalimar featured regularly in the newspapers. Glamorous and exciting were the words used to describe them. Rumours abounded that he would soon become a full minister in the Prime Minister's department. Her acceptance of the inevitability helped her to accept that her marriage was over. She buried her sadness deep inside and, if she felt bitter, she did not show it. She directed her energies to the child growing in her. She was still not showing and hence invited little comment or questions. But she felt the change in her body. She examined it when bathing; she saw the filling out of her breasts, the little blue veins in them. A tiny bulge developed in her abdomen. She felt it timorously, caressing it with reverence and wonderment.

An Mei realised that as her womb expanded and the bulge grew, people would notice and word was bound to get back to Hussein and her in-laws. Still, she postponed telling Hussein because she did not know what she wanted to do. She knew what she did not want. She did not wish to have her child grow up in an environment where it could see its own mother despised by the family that she had married into. She did not want her baby to be the centre of a tug of war for affection. She also did not know if her parents-in-law would welcome her child when they were already expecting a grandchild from a daughter-in-law they favoured. She did not want to share her husband's love. Yet did she really want to give him up, now that she was having his child? So she waited for her mind to clear.

* * * * *

Ah Kun swept into the room, tray in hand, and closed the door with a flick of her foot.

"Your Aunt has asked me to prepare this for you; bird's nest soup. This is the best brand and the herbal shopkeeper, you know the one at the corner of Petaling Street, kept it especially for us. It took me the whole night with a pair of tweezers to get all the feathers out. We do not want to eat feathers do we?" she asked jovially. "This is very good for you in your condition. Tomorrow, I shall prepare another dish that is also very good for you; chicken with herbs, steamed for ten hours until it is almost blackened."

"Please, no more. I shall get fat," protested An Mei, getting up from her desk to take the tray from Ah Kun.

"Fat? No chance. You have been working so hard you are unlikely to get fat. You have to think of the baby. Do you good if you fit in some rest as well."

An Mei smiled. "What's this?" she said taking an envelope from the tray.

"For you. The postman delivered it this afternoon and I forgot to give it to you earlier. Remember! Don't let the soup get cold. I shall come back later to collect the tray." Ah Kun closed the door gently behind her.

An Mei sat down and took the tray from the coffee table and carefully balanced it on her knee. She lifted the lid releasing the trapped aroma and breathed in deeply. Mmm. Good! No bitter herbs! She took a spoonful, gulped it down expecting the worst, and then licked her lips in pleasant surprise. Ah Kun had used rock sugar to prepare the dish. She took another spoonful and then turned her attention to the envelope. She looked at the back; there were no indication of where it could have come from. She slit it open and took another spoon of the soup. Lazily she flipped open the one page letter. She looked uncomprehendingly at the scrawl.

I DIVORCE YOU. I DIVORCE YOU. I DIVORCE YOU. Large writing that stared out at her in obscene boldness.

She dropped the spoon. It fell with a loud clang against the bowl and bounced to the floor. It crashed breaking into smithereens. The tray slid off her knee joining the debris of broken ceramics. The commotion brought Nelly running in.

"What's the matter? What's the matter?" she asked. Her eyes went to the letter in An Mei's hand. She saw the bold writing, large prints and the scrawl at the end. "Hussein?" she asked incredulous. "Not even a single attempt to contact you, and then this?"

Numbly An Mei nodded. "I have no one to blame but myself, Aunt Nelly. At least, I have this." She clasped her abdomen. "Thank God, he doesn't know."

"Oh An Mei! Are you sure you wish to go through with the baby? Will you be able to keep the child under Shariah law?"

"Yes! I will go through with it. And, yes! I will keep the child, no matter what! That is why I am so happy Hussein does not know." The enormity of what she had to do struck her. She panicked. Wild-eyed, she clutched at Nelly, her fingers digging deeply into Nelly's arms. "We have to keep my pregnancy a secret. At least until after I have consulted a lawyer."

"I'll ask Jeremy if he knows of one. But if the matter is to be kept a secret, Jenny must not know because, for all her goodness, she is related to Hussein's family by marriage and she might let something slip. We must make your mother understand the need for secrecy; she is too trusting. She must not tell Jenny even if she is her best friend. This is too big a matter," said Nelly. "I'll warn your mother now."

* * * * *

Night fell. As the shadows lengthened, the neighbourhood grew quiet. The members of Nelly's household had gone to sleep one by one. Only An Mei was still awake.

She was sat on the edge of the bed. Slowly, she slid off it and dropped on her knees. She let herself fall forward and her forehead hit the floor. A muffled sob rose from her throat. A shudder went through her body. Twisting from side to side, she fought for breath; she sought to calm the overwhelming sense of loss she felt. She blamed herself for her own self-deception; to even tarry with the thought that a baby might change things. She told herself that she should have expected the break, even so the cruelty of seeing it in black and white emblazoned across an otherwise blank piece of paper had shocked her to the core. She sobbed convulsively. Gradually the sobs subsided. She got up and crawled into bed. I will call Casey and then Jeremy, she thought, and talk to them.

Chapter 32

The office was little more than a cubicle, a box room with wall-to-wall shelves, jam-packed with files and volume upon volume of books. On the desk were more papers and files. A phone stood balanced on a stack of journals. Pushed towards one corner was a mug of coffee, its contents long consumed and the dregs black and congealed. Cigarette butts filled a huge ashtray; smoke spiralled from one perched on the side. The whole room was filled with a hazy fog. The air conditioner, an old grey metal Carrier, clanged energetically in one corner, its frame shaking in protest, as it poured out tepid air.

An Mei looked at the chaos and then at the man behind the desk. The apprehension in her eyes seemed to amuse him. He smiled showing a row of teeth yellowed by nicotine. He had come highly recommended by Jeremy.

"He is a good man," Jeremy had said. "One of the best in his field. Don't judge him by appearances. He practises civil law, but he is also familiar with Shariah law. What he does not know, he will find out, but even so he may need to refer you to a specialist in Shariah law."

She swallowed hard and tried not to breathe in the fumes. Nelly held her hand, squeezing it reassuringly.

"Take a seat," the lawyer said, waving them to two chairs on the other side of the desk. "Thank you for coming in. Jeremy has given me a brief outline of your situation. Perhaps you can now fill me in on the details."

An Mei opened her mouth to speak only to end up coughing and spluttering. She tried to disperse the spirals of smoke coming her way. Nelly in her concern jumped up and took a wad of paper brandishing it vigorously to fan the smoke away.

"Sorry, sorry, I'll get rid of this," the lawyer said, taking the ashtray and tipping its contents into the over flowing waste bin behind his chair. He turned to face them again, a cigarette between his fingers. It was the one that had been perched on the ashtray earlier. He had stubbed it out.

"Apologies, I can't think without one of these. I will just hold it; I won't smoke. My name is Tan. People just call me Jay Tee."

An Mei remained silent. She stared at the cigarette poised in his hand as though mesmerised. Fear and exhaustion from sleepless nights seeped through every limb in her body. Then slowly, as though the words had to be dragged out of her, she asked. "Will what I say in this office stay in this office?"

"Client confidentiality? Absolutely!"

His eyes were steady. Jeremy had the utmost trust in him. They had been to school and later university together. "What you say will stay with him," Jeremy had said.

Yet she hesitated until Nelly prompted. "An Mei," she said. "Tell him."

So for the next hour, she described her situation to him. He did not interrupt her and despite his obvious addiction to cigarettes, he did not light up again. His forehead was a mass of creases as he concentrated on her tale; his eyelids were half closed, but when he looked up after she had finished, his eyes were alert, bright.

"Can he divorce me like this?" she asked showing him the letter. The words "I divorce you, I divorce you, I divorce you," scrawled across the page.

"Unfortunately, yes! You are a Muslim. Your case, which comes under family matters, falls under the jurisdiction of the Shariah court. Although the legal system in Malaysia is a dual system based on both English common law and Islamic law, the civil court has no jurisdiction over matters that fall under the Shariah court's mandate. If you were not a Muslim, the situation would be completely different. Under Shariah law, a Muslim man can divorce his wife in this way. It just has to be confirmed by a court. A Muslim woman, by contrast, has to prove her case before she can divorce her spouse."

"What about any children ensuing from the marriage?" asked An Mei, her face bleached of colour.

Mr. Tan stared at her, his eyes brimming with curiosity, his spectacles halfway down the bridge of his nose. He suspected that his client was not telling him everything. "It is fortunate," he said, clearing his throat, "that you do not have children from the marriage."

He paused to give An Mei time to clarify. But An Mei continued her silence. Her eyes cast down on her hands lying limp and lifeless on her lap.

"Divorces that involve children are always messy even in a civil court," said Mr. Tan, "but it is even more so in a case like yours. Under Shariah law, a mother generally has custody of a young child. By young, it means below seven to nine for a male child and nine to eleven for a girl. However, you have to understand that the father is considered to be the primary guardian under Islamic family law even though the mother has custody. If the mother is to remarry, the whole question of custody can be thrown open if there is uncertainty over the welfare of the child."

He paused to let his words sink in. He saw the fear and apprehension in An Mei's eyes. His suspicion grew. He watched her face closely.

"In your case, were you to have a child, the situation would be even muddier," he continued. "You were a convert to Islam. And you have embraced the faith for only a short time. I am pretty sure that to qualify for custody, you would have to demonstrate that you would be able to bring the child up to follow the true Muslim faith."

An Mei's hand flew involuntarily to touch her face. Her lips trembled.

His expression softened. He realised his suspicion was correct. He looked sympathetically at her.

"There is a general perception that mothers who have converted to Islam could not raise their children according to Islamic ways." He coughed and reached for his packet of cigarettes then checked himself. He drummed his fingers on the table, *rat-a-tat, rat-a-tat!*

"Without doubt, if you are found wanting, that is if you were found not to be practising the faith, you would be disqualified from having custody of the child."

"Any excuse could be used to say a woman is not practising the faith," she replied, her voice faltering.

He shrugged his shoulder and raised both hands to indicate that that could well be so.

"However," he said, his eyes fixed on her, "we do not have any such concerns because there are no children from the marriage." Mr. Tan paused. He had seen women like this before, his eyes swept over her discreetly. Perhaps, he thought, his words would spur her to tell him of her condition.

An Mei fell back in the chair. Until then she had been sitting upright, on the edge of the seat, hands pressing down hard on the sides, her knuckles and her fingers white and blotchy from the pressure. She had no doubt about what he was telling her even though he had not said so specifically. His expression said it all. She suspected he had worked out her condition. He must be warning her against telling Hussein.

Nelly caught hold of An Mei's hand. The atmosphere was tense and Nelly could sense it even though she could not follow fully what was being discussed. The fear in An Mei's face worried her. "What are you going to do?" she asked.

An Mei whispered, "I'll tell you later. Let's leave!" She got up from her chair and thanked Mr. Tan.

"There are other matters you will also have to consider, like alimony, maintenance..."

"It's alright. I do not intend to seek any alimony. I'll get Jeremy to get in touch with you. I am so sorry to cut short this meeting. Thank you so much for your time."

An Mei grabbed Nelly's hand and marched to the door. She went quickly down the stairs and walked out into the intense bright light of the street. She continued her brisk walk, marching Nelly along until they reached a corner shop selling dried fish. Sacks and sacks of dried anchovies, prawns, sole and even gingko nuts stood at its doorway, their odours mingling with the hot air and traffic fumes from the streets. An Mei turned to face Nelly. Her eyes were fierce.

"I have made up my mind. Hussein must not know, must not be told about the baby. I do not want to risk losing custody of my baby; I am sure I would not be given a fair chance if either he or his family get to know about it. He has a baby now of his own with Shalimar. This is my baby. I have to leave KL for a place where I can bring up my child in the best way."

Back in the office, a cigarette smouldered in Mr. Tan's fingers. He looked at the empty chair. If he had any doubts, her hasty departure had removed them.

* * * * *

Nelly took one last look at the store, a store that she had worked so hard for, her pride and joy. She walked its entire length, touching the shelves, the goods displayed; sometimes a little smile played on her lip; at other times, her eyes were filled with longing and regret. She was the only one in the store. Everyone had long left. Soon she would have to lock up and then drop the keys at her storekeeper's home. Maan *Sook* had been her right-hand man for a long time. He would see to the smooth running of the store just as he had done when she left for England with Ming Kong and Mei Yin. She sighed and dabbed at the corner of her eyes. Jeremy would help out and arrange for the eventual sale of the place. It would not be an easy task.

Ming Kong knew of the arrangement. In fact when he was told of the circumstances and the divorce, it was he who had suggested closing down the business immediately. He had wanted them to come back to England, but An Mei had other plans. "I just want to leave everything behind; everything that reminds me of Hussein. Oxford holds too many memories. I want to go to a place where I can start afresh," she had explained. "I have spoken to Casey. I am going to Rome, where she is; she will help me find a small apartment. I will have my baby there and then find a job with her help. She knows of several posts that are coming up in the two UN agencies located there and for which I might be suitable. Applications for posts, she said, typically take a long time to process so if I apply now, by the time they actually recruit, I would have had the baby."

"I'll come with you," Aunt Nelly had insisted.

Aunt Nelly you don't have to come with me. I know how much you love the store. Please stay in Kuala Lumpur. I will be okay," An Mei had protested not wishing her to sacrifice herself yet again on her behalf.

"Alright. But I shall come with you and stay until you are settled and the baby has arrived. Then I might decide to stay with Jane and Jeremy in Singapore at least for half of the time. We'll take it one step at a time and things will fall into place."

* * * * *

Two days later they flew to Singapore. Jeremy met them. He stood waiting behind the barrier in the disembarkation hall at the airport. He saw the two familiar figures appear. He waved. Without thinking, he fished out his camera and snapped a picture, two women wheeling their suitcases; An Mei looking thin, her eyes swollen; her soft floral skirt clinging to her legs; her little bump barely showed. Next to her was Nelly, his mother, looking up anxiously at An Mei.

"This photo will be a memento for you, An Mei," he whispered to himself. "A new beginning."

He hurried towards the two women; his arms wide open to embrace them. He dropped a kiss on their foreheads.

"We'll spend three days in Singapore, to give us a little time to settle things over here. What cannot be done will be left for later. The important thing is to get An Mei away. We will then fly directly to Rome. I have booked tickets for all of us. I am coming with you. Casey will be meeting us in Rome. She has made all the necessary arrangement at that end."

Part Two

(FOUR YEARS LATER ...)

Chapter 33

"*Vieni amore*! Come my love," called Adriana. She waved her arm encouragingly at the little boy paddling in the little makeshift rubber pool in the sandpit. "He'll be wet, *Signora* and then he'll catch a cold."

She ran to the boy, panting, both arms extended to catch him; her pendulous breasts heaved with the exertion. He ran from her, splashing water as he leapt out of the water to the sand.

"*No! Non mi prendi.* No don't catch me," he chanted, jumping up and down, a grin on his face, his dark eyes twinkling with mischief.

An Mei smiled. She dropped the pad she was scribbling on and went over to him. She scooped him up into her arms and smothered his face with kisses.

"Listen to Adriana, you little monkey. Don't make her run after you because you know she cannot run as fast as your little legs." With one arm, she hitched him on to her hips and said to Adriana, "I'll clean him up. I am going to take a break from my work anyway. After three hours of solid writing during the weekend, I deserve a break. Would you prepare something for supper while I bathe him?"

"What would you like, *Signora*?"

"*Spaghetti all'amatriciana*, a salad, some of the lovely pecorino cheese and your wonderful *casareccio* bread, would be wonderful. Signora Casey and her husband will be joining us."

"*Va bene*; okay," she replied and moved away, turning every now and then to wag her finger at Timothy. "Behave yourself," she warned rolling her eyes to indicate that she would be cross if he misbehaved.

An Mei carried her son into the house. The interior was cool; the terracotta tiles, polished to a glossy coppery red, gave soothing comfort to her bare feet.

"Mummy, mummy, see! I can go upside down," Timothy said, bending backwards to let his head hang down.

"Ouch! You are getting too heavy for mummy," she teased tickling him in the ribs. Immediately he bounced back like jack-in-a-box.

"Too heavy, too heavy. Mummy can't carry me," he mimicked.

She sat him down on a stool and filled the bath watching the steam rise from the tap.

"Hot! Hot!" he yelled, his little face screwed up.

"Yes, I know. I will add cold water and I will test the temperature with my elbow. See no more steam. Let's get you out of these clothes," she said, threading his chubby arms out of the tee shirt he was wearing. She drew him close to her and breathed in deeply his little boy scent. Fresh, lemony even, with a hint of sweat and sand. She felt her chest tighten with emotion. "I love you,' she whispered. He smiled revealing four little even teeth. She scooped his little brown body into the bath. Lazily she drew trails of water to dribble on him as he played with his bath toys. They floated around him; a duck, three men in a tub, a swimming frog that powered from one end to the other and a little rubber boat. Silently, she mouthed a prayer of thanks. She had been so lucky.

"There you are," a voice sounded at the back of her. She turned to see Jeremy standing in the doorway.

Behind him a voice interrupted, "Make way, I want to see that little devil," Casey popped her head above his shoulders. She shouldered her way in, pushing her husband exaggeratedly to the side and immediately went to the bath. "Let Aunty Casey wash your hair. Please may I?" she said in a little girl's voice.

"She is enamoured with Tim and if you trust her, we can leave her to finish the bath and go into that lovely den of yours and chat. Come, it has been an age since we've had a chat alone," Jeremy said, raising his voice to ensure that Casey heard.

"No hanky-panky!" she yelled.

"Yes! Madam," he saluted.

Once in the den, Jeremy took An Mei's elbow and guided her to an armchair. She sat down. She turned her face up to look at him. A pool of soft light from a table lamp lit up the contours of her face, accentuating its lines and planes. Her round cheeks were long gone; in their place was a face that spelled maturity, grace and softness. Her almond eyes were questioning as she looked at him.

"Is it Aunt Nelly you want to talk about?" she asked.

"She sends you her love. She can't come this summer. The journey is too trying for her. She is with Jane now."

"Is she well?" asked An Mei, her voice filled with concern. "I spoke to her on the phone the other day and she sounded cheerful. Has something happened since? I will be going to Bangkok to visit a project in the Menam Chao Praya and had planned to stop over in Singapore to see Nelly. The only thing is that she won't get a chance to see Tim because I can't bring him along with me; it's a working trip. So what do you think? Should I make a separate journey with Tim to see her?"

"Calm down! Don't fret. She is fine, just a bit tired of long hauls. It is nearly four years since she stopped running the business. Since then, she has been flying to Rome to see you every year. This year, she has decided that she would like to stay with Jane in Singapore. Also, Jane's household has an additional attraction for her. Jane's newborn."

"But no one can beat this baby," said Casey as she entered the room. She was cradling the struggling Timothy in a pair of pyjamas, and kissing him.

"Let me down," he wailed.

"Yes, unhand the poor boy and stop smothering him with kisses," her husband chided.

"Wait till I get my own. I will not let him go," promised Casey, putting Timothy down. "But when will that be?" she asked. She made a face at her husband. "We have checked and checked and nothing seems wrong with either of us and yet we are still waiting for our first child."

"It will happen. Don't worry," consoled An Mei.

"You sound exactly like Nelly. Come on! Let's see if Adriana has the food ready. My mouth is already watering with the smells coming from her kitchen. You are so lucky to have her."

"I am lucky all round," replied An Mei looking at the friends who had stood by her and made it all possible.

* * * * *

That evening after Casey and Jeremy had left, An Mei opened the album of photographs she kept by the side of her bed. She looked at the photos, each one a vivid reminder of the days that followed Hussein's renunciation of his marriage vows. Jeremy had taken them saying that they would be her keepsakes. "Look at them only when you are fully recovered from the pain and trauma you are going through now," he had said. So until a year ago, the album had been kept locked away.

The first photograph showed her arriving in Singapore. Nelly was with her. Jeremy must have caught them when they were just leaving the arrivals hall at the airport after their hasty departure from Kuala Lumpur. She looked thin. It was just three days after she had received the letter from Hussein announcing that he was divorcing her. She recalled her constant fear throughout those three days; how the three days had passed with a blur of frantic activity; how her heart had throbbed; how each little sound had made her jump. She turned the pages of the album, examining her own photos and those of her family, gathered to celebrate Timothy's full moon. One photo captured her attention. It had written under it, the caption "*Mun yuet!*"

She recalled how Nelly had said, "Tim is one-month old, which would be a year old if we counted his age the Chinese way, because it is measured from the time of conception." They had argued light-heartedly over the logic of making ten months into a year.

An Mei traced her finger on the next picture and smiled. She recalled how her mother, Mei Yin, had then bustled in with a large ceramic bowl full of boiled eggs that had been dyed red. "*Heh*!" she had announced with great pride, "this is for all your neighbours and friends to celebrate Tim's *mun yuet*. I also made this huge jar of pickled ginger to eat with the eggs. I just gave some to Adriana to test!"

She chuckled at the image Jeremy captured of them: the red eggs, pickled ginger, Adriana almost gagging and a very pained look on her mother's face.

She flipped through the pages until she found the one with Casey and Jeremy. Casey was in white holding a bouquet of creamy roses, their petals delicately curling against her arm encased in a pale white three-quarter length glove. Jeremy was looking at her with pride. She peered closer and saw herself standing to one side with her mother, father, aunt Nelly and Casey's mother. In her arms, she was holding little Timothy, barely a year old. The photographer had captured Nelly's questioning gaze. They were directed at her. Nelly had been uncertain whether she would be hurt by Jeremy's marriage to Casey and had asked her directly. "No! Of course not!" she had replied. "I love Jeremy as a brother. I am happy that the two friends who have helped me so much should find love and contentment."

She sighed. So much had happened in the past four years. She stood up and laid the album down by the side table. She slipped out of her clothes and took out her nightdress from the drawer. She slipped it on followed by her old dressing gown, a faded, pale rose-pink kimono with a wide silk sash that was his present to her. Padding bare-foot into the kitchen she put on the kettle. As the kettle sang and hissed, she heaped two big spoonfuls of cocoa into a mug and then poured the boiling water into the mug. She recalled how he had teased her over her fondness for cocoa made with water and just a dash of milk. "It should be made with hot milk," he had said. "Not where I come from," she had replied. "In Malaysia, when I was a child, fresh milk was not that easily available. I use to drink it with condensed milk!"

She took the steaming hot mug into the den and made herself comfortable in an armchair. She picked up a book. "Mark," she said aloud. "Mark should be home soon."

Chapter 34

Their meeting was accidental.

It was a blistering hot summer's day in Rome. The air was still. Heat radiated from the thick walls of the buildings lining the road. Mark walked rapidly down the cobbled street, weaving his way between the cars parked hither and thither at all angles along the street.

"No pavements!" he grunted. "We need pavements here for pedestrians, but of course that is impossible with so much history around us. I can't see anyone wishing to take these down just to make way for pavements." He looked at the massive old buildings on either side. Their grandeur and age never failed to astonish him. Despite the shade they provide, it was still hot. The air was close and the walls warm to his touch. A trickle of sweat fell from his brow; he wiped his forehead and pushed his shirtsleeves further up his arms. He had long relinquished his jacket and held it loosely over his shoulder. He stopped a passer-by.

"*Mi scusi*, do you know of a good restaurant around here?" he asked.

"*No! Niente qui*; there are none on this road; see there," his informant pointed to a turning, "Viale Mura Gianicolensi, try there."

Mark hid a smile. A twinkle gleamed in his deep-set brown eyes; his lips moved imperceptibly. He could not believe what he had just heard. No good restaurants on the street and that from a *Romano*!

"*Grazie, grazie*," he said to the man.

He turned into Viale Mura Gianicolensi. Immediately before him was the imposing building of the Salvator Mundi, a hospital run by sisters of the Divine Saviour. He saw a young woman emerge from its gate. She was just some fifteen yards away. She was crossing the street. Two boys on a scooter stopped in front of her. One of them dismounted and grabbed her bag, pushing her roughly aside while he scrambled back on the scooter before roaring off. Mark saw her stumble and he sprinted forward. He gathered her up. He could feel her shaking uncontrollably. Her hair, which had been tied back into a ponytail, had come undone. It streamed across her face. He placed her gently back on her feet and retrieved a shoe that had become trapped in the cobbles. He could see that she was heavily pregnant. Her tummy was a hard dome that protruded from her slight frame. He pushed her hair away from her face.

"Are you alright?" he asked. She looked at him, her large eyes apprehensive. His heart missed a beat.

"Yes! Thank you," she said.

"Have you just come out from the hospital?" he asked, his head nodding in the direction of the Salvator Mundi. "Shall we get you back there to check just to make sure everything is okay?" He was anxious for her. Her cheeks were drained of colour, and her lips were trembling. He looked at her bump; she looked away embarrassed.

"Sorry, I was just concerned, since... since..."

"Yes, I am almost due. In four weeks time, the doctor said."

In his usual brusque manner, Dr. Ginelli had wagged his finger at An Mei shaking his head in disapproval when she asked if she should continue to walk daily as part of her exercise regime. "*Signora deve stare attento*, take a little care; it is too hot to be wandering around the centre." But she had no wish to return home immediately and she had some last minute shopping to do. So she had stepped out of the archway of the hospital onto the cobbled street of Viale Mura Gianicolensi and then... It had happened so quickly.

"I shall be alright," she said, attempting to be put on a brave face, "but I have lost my handbag. I have no money with me to take a taxi home."

A crowd had gathered around them. A few women pushed forward. Mistaking Mark to be An Mei's husband, they hurled their advice at him.

"*Si*, take the *signora* home. It is too hot. Give her ice tea with a slice of lemon," they said. They looked at her sympathetically, muttering a range of curses against the thugs. *Figli di puttana! Stronzi!*

"Come," said Mark, "I'll take you home. If you can manage, we'll walk to that corner bar and we'll get you a cool drink. Then I'll go round the corner to try to flag a taxi."

"Don't leave me. Stay with me for a moment, please," An Mei said. The aftershock of the incident was still with her, every footfall behind her made her jump. "I had everything in my handbag; my address, my credit and identity card, my keys. They will know everything about me. What shall I do?"

"Shall I call your husband?"

"I live alone, that is when my aunt is away. She spends half of her time in Singapore. She is due to be back any time soon." She hesitated and then said, "I don't have a husband."

She watched his reaction, expecting some disapproval or contempt, but there was none. Instead he asked if she could get a friend over to be with her.

"Or perhaps you can stay with a friend," he added.

"Yes, I have friends, but they have just left for a long weekend." She looked desperate. She was the one who had encouraged Casey and Jeremy to go away for a long weekend. "Go! I'll be okay. I shall need you when the baby arrives, not now," she had said to them.

"Take this," he said thrusting a handkerchief at her. "Sit down and breathe deeply. You need to sit down and take a drink first to calm down. We'll work something out." He guided her to a chair and table outside the bar. "I am Mark, Mark Hayes. And you are?"

"An Mei. Ong is my surname," she replied.

"Pleased to meet you," he said extending his hand. He clasped hers. She felt the warmth of his hands seeping through her and she felt comforted. Slowly, her tensed shoulders relaxed and she managed a small smile, a little upward quirk of her lips that resulted in two dimples on her cheeks. The rush of emotion that he felt from that one smile shocked him. He relinquished her hand quickly. How could you, he thought to himself; she is expecting. Almost brusquely, to cover his feelings, he said. "You will have to report the incident to the *Carabinieri*."

"Now?" she asked. She sensed his change of mood; her smile vanished as fast as it came.

"I'll help you. I do not live in Rome, but I have been here often enough to have experienced some misadventures ... well, my car was vandalised so I know the ropes of reporting incidents to the police. It is almost a fine art. You have first to buy the paper to make the report on from the *tabacchi*." He smiled. "In Rome, you buy everything from the tobacconist; stamps, bus tickets, even salt in the past."

She listened, wide-eyed.

"After we've been to the *Carabinieri*, I'll help you change your door locks," he added and was rewarded with a smile that warmed his heart.

* * * * *

"What do you do? I mean why are you here in Rome?" asked An Mei.

It was their second meeting. Mark had phoned unexpectedly. "It is too hot to cook. Come down and join me for dinner," he had coaxed. "I am calling you from the *trattoria* opposite your apartment. If you look out of the window, I'll wave to you."

She had walked to the window in a state of disbelief and peered out. She saw him. A tallish young man in his late thirties with a grin on his face standing by a table laid out in starched white linen. He waved. She pulled a light cardigan hastily around her. It barely covered her bump. For a minute she hesitated, conscious that she was dressed in an old dress for comfort rather than for dining out. He would have to take me as I am, she decided. She descended the steep stairway from her apartment on the second floor, taking each step carefully.

Seated opposite him, with the table between them, she waited for his answer.

"I am a biologist turned freelance journalist," he said. "I am doing a piece on food for work and agricultural development for the *Observer*."

"What's food for work?" she asked.

"It is something that has proven to work well in many developing countries. Agencies such as the World Food Programme, WFP as it is often called, provide food in exchange for work on development projects. This has made it possible for the poor and hungry to devote energy and time to agriculture. It is a first step out of the hunger trap. And you? How is it that you are living in Rome? Do you work for a living?"

Something about this young beautiful Chinese woman in Rome, alone, pregnant and looking so vulnerable interested him. His heart did silly things even when his face was calm and collected.

She looked away. She took some time before she redirected her gaze at him.

"I came here to have my baby." She dropped her gaze. She had not wished to say any more than that. Fear that Hussein would discover her deception and would hound her for the baby, played on her mind. But she also felt a sudden urge to unburden herself to this stranger, who had helped her, who she would probably not see again after he had finished his assignment in Rome.

"You don't have to say anything if you don't want to," he said, placing his hand on hers. "I shouldn't have asked."

"I want to," she said. "I want to tell you. I need to talk to someone." So she told him. He listened in silence and when she had finished, he moved his chair closer to her.

"I know I should not be doing this, but I am going to." He took her face in both his hands and kissed her forehead. She felt her heart lift, a burden removed from her. Nearby a band of singers strummed their guitars and crooned. The waiter who had been hovering to take their orders and who had departed with disgust after several attempts to interrupt their conversation, returned with alacrity. He had seen the kiss.

"*Bene! Tutto a posto! Che volete?* Everything is okay now. What do you want?" He asked, fishing out his note pad. He reeled out his list: *Proscuitto melone, pasta e ceci, spaghetti alla vongole...*"

They looked at him and smiled.

Chapter 35

Mark sat with his head in his hands, his elbows on his knees. The long corridor smelt of polish; each square floor tile a rich coppery red. He looked up at the cross on the white wall opposite him and then at the clock at the end of the hall. As though on cue, it struck 6 o'clock. The first stream of sunlight was beginning to peep through the windows. Almost three hours had passed since their arrival in the early hours of the morning. Sisters rushed past him, their starched white pinafores over grey habits competing with starched white headdresses. They steadfastly ignored him. If they did deign to look at him, it was with dislike. They had asked if he was the husband. He had answered no and had explained that he was a friend. From there on they had looked at him frostily and then dismissed him completely, directing him to the hallway. Only immediate members of the family were allowed, they had decreed.

It had been 2 o'clock in the morning when he was woken up by the ringing telephone. He was cat-sitting for a friend who was away on holiday. It was a distraught An Mei asking for his help. Her labour pains had come unexpectedly early. She had thought that she had over two weeks to go.

"You don't have to explain," he had replied. "I'll come straight away. Just have your bag ready and call the hospital."

The sound of hurried footsteps came from one end of the corridor. He looked up. He saw a lady, plump, grey-haired with spectacles, panting as she walked and half-ran towards him. Two other people followed her, a tall man and a statuesque young woman. He waved. They must be Nelly, Jeremy and Casey, he thought. An Mei had told him that all three would be coming from Rome's Fumicino airport. Nelly was arriving from Singapore and Jeremy and Casey had gone to meet her. The plane had been delayed. That was why she had no one to turn to. "Please tell them that I am at the Salvator Mundi."

It took him the best part of two hours to get a Fumicino airport official to agree to search for them.

"Are you Mark? How is she?" Casey asked immediately. She had an arm round the breathless Nelly. Nelly's chest was heaving, her knees looked as though they were buckling from her exertion.

He nodded. "I don't know. The nuns have not told me a thing. Maybe you will have better luck. I think they disapprove of me; they think I am the errant father."

Nelly looked alarmed and turned immediately to Casey. "*Hui gong meh?* What did he say?" English was not her *forte* at the best of times, but she was completely confused by his accent.

Casey explained. She chuckled, amused by the nun's treatment of Mark, but it did nothing to relieve Nelly's anxiety.

"Sorry, so sorry," she blustered in Cantonese. "I should not have left her, but I had an urgent matter to attend to, we finally managed to sell off our business. I couldn't return any earlier because there were so many fiddly little details to complete."

"Calm down, calm down," said the man next to her, placing an arm round her. Turning to Mark, he introduced himself as Jeremy. "And this is Casey and this is Nelly, my mother," he added. "Thank you so much for helping out. We will ask the nurse if we can see her. If you want to, you can go. You must be tired."

"I'll stay," Mark replied. They looked at each other, measuring one another up.

Casey saw the look that passed between the men. She liked the look of Mark. Tall, well built, a solid, dependable sort of person, she concluded. Good looking too but not in the way Hussein had been. This chap looked like someone you could lean on. He had the weight of age on him. She saw how Jeremy was looking at Mark and it worried her. Was he jealous, she wondered? She turned to Mark and said deliberately. "Come with us. We'll ask the sister over there and then wait together."

* * * * *

Timothy was born two hours later. They trooped into the room to see An Mei and the baby. Mark excused himself and ran out to the bar a couple of hundred yards along the road. He ran back to join them, holding a bottle of *spumante* to celebrate. All eyes turned to look at him when he entered the room with the bottle held high in the air, a wide smile and eyes that held so much joy that Nelly was to say in later years, you would have thought he was the father. But Mark had no eyes for anyone.

He looked at An Mei, her face flushed, happy, and the baby in her arms.

"Congratulations!" he said.

"Would you like to hold him?" asked An Mei.

Mark leaned over and took the baby in his arms. He felt the smallness of the baby in his arms. He had never held a baby that small. He was perfectly formed. Mark smiled and then gently returned him to his mother. His hand lingered on the baby, stroking his head,

From the foot of the bed, Nelly watched with keen interest. She saw how comfortable An Mei was with Mark and he with her. She felt gladdened, glad that at last An Mei had made a new friend. She had kept too much to herself, carrying her loneliness like armour. Casey nudged Jeremy and threaded her arms around his waist, her fingers made a cross for luck. Jeremy caught hold of her hand and whispered. "Don't presume. Don't meddle."

* * * * *

By the third day, An Mei was well enough to return home. Mark was a regular visitor. He went to see her every day after work and during weekends, he was almost a permanent feature in the household.

It was the weekend following the completion of Mark's assignment in Rome. He had arrived late morning. Nelly said she needed to give the flat a good clean and asked if they would take the baby out for a walk. They manhandled the pram down the narrow stairway.

"Be careful," directed Nelly from the top of the steps, "don't drop the pram. Take care that Tim doesn't get bitten or stung by insects. There are loads in the park, especially bees at this time of the year. Insect bite-bite," she added the last words of warning in English for the benefit of Mark. "Lunch will be ready in two hours."

"Yes, we will be careful," replied An Mei smiling at Mark. Together they carried the pram outside and set it on the pavement.

"Let's go to that small garden over there by the monument," suggested Mark. "It is not too far to walk. These cobbled roads are not made for prams and are dangerous. At this time of the day, when the road is almost empty, it should be okay."

A *motorino* whizzed passed them.

"Perhaps I had better walk in front and you follow behind," said Mark changing his mind.

They walked single file, attracting the attention of passers-by. Women stopped to peer into the pram exclaiming "*Che bello il piccolo! Complimenti!* How beautiful the little one! Congratulations!" they said to Mark and An Mei mistaking them as husband and wife. He smiled, accepting their greetings, stepping into the role.

"I don't mind if you don't," he whispered turning to look at An Mei pushing the pram behind him. She blushed.

They came to the entrance of the garden, marked by a solitary statue. A tree lined pebbled path skirted its circumference. Wooden benches stood at intervals along the path. In the middle of the garden was a raised pond and around it were large terracotta urns. Flowers cascaded from them spilling on to the ground.

"So different from English gardens! But utterly charming!" Mark observed. "What makes it different is not so much the flowers, the trees and the structure and layout, but the light;

the sheer brightness of the Mediterranean sun and the absence of grey clouds. I'll miss this," he said.

"Are you leaving?" Her voice shook.

"Yes! I have to go home to England. My assignment is completed. I took a week's leave to stay on, but now I have to go."

She looked away. She had expected it, but she had willed thoughts of his departure away.

"I want to tell you something; ask you."

Her eyes were moist as she looked at him. She steeled herself for the worst.

"I have applied for a post with the World Food Programme, the UN agency that I do a lot of work for here. In fact, that is why I was asked to do the piece for the *Observer*. I am not sure if I will get it, but what I really want to know is would you mind? That is, would you mind if I am around?"

For a moment she was speechless. Then she found her tongue.

"Mind?" she asked, her hand grasped a bunch of lavender seed heads, bobbing by the side of the path. She needed to do something. She crushed the seeds rubbing them between her fingers to release its heady perfume. Her eyes shone. "Mind?" she asked again, looking up at him. Unabashed, she said. "These past few weeks have been my happiest weeks in Rome, the happiest, in fact, for a long, long time."

He gathered her into his arms, burying his face into her neck, lifting her off her feet. A chuckle of delight broke from him and he whirled her around. "Marry me!"

People passed, some delighted with the display of affection. "*Ma guarda! Amore!* Look at them! Love!"

Chapter 36

An Mei placed the book down and looked at the clock on the wall. She had not read a single line. Her mind had wandered and drifted. It had weaved in and out of time. She could smell the lavender as though the oil from the crushed flower heads still lingered on her fingers.

Mark should have been home by now, she thought.

She got up from the armchair and paced the room; she passed the table where she had laid the album, tempted to look at it again. She heard a car turn into the driveway; a roar of the engine and then silence. Headlights shone straight through her drawn curtains illuminating the room. She ran to the window, drawing the curtains aside to look out. A shadow emerged from the car hauling a bag. She knew it was him. With quick nimble steps, her feet tingling from the cool tiles, she hurried to the door. She drew the bolts and unlocked the door, flinging it open, shivering as the damp outside air, hit her. She drew her kimono close around her and stood waiting for him. He was soon with her. Dropping his bag, he took her in his arms and buried his nose in her neck.

"It's good to be home," Mark said. He relinquished his hold reluctantly. "You shouldn't have stayed up, but I am glad you did. Come, let's close the door and go in. It's chilly out here."

An Mei tucked her arm into his. "Good journey?" she asked. "Would you like a drink?"

"I'll have one later. How's Tim?"

"Come and see. I tucked him into bed early this evening."

They opened the door gently, pausing every now and then to break the sound of creaking hinges. Timothy was sound asleep; his eyelashes lay like a fan on his plump cheeks. They watched the steady rhythm of his breathing. Mark took her hand and brought it to his lips. "He is a beautiful boy," he whispered. He went over to Timothy and gently kissed his forehead. "I missed him even for the short time I was away. But we should leave him to his sleep."

"So how was England? How did the Conference go?" asked An Mei closing the bedroom door and tucking her arms once more into his.

"The Conference went well and I saw your parents in Oxford. Your mum is practically running everything now and the restaurant in Oxford is flourishing. The one in London is also doing extremely well. I went with your parents to have a meal and it was packed; a queue developed while we were there.

"What about dad? Is he well?"

"Your dad is well; thinner, much thinner. They would like you to visit them."

"I will. Perhaps when I come back from Thailand. You remember don't you that I have to go to Bangkok to our regional office for Asia and Pacific, FAO's RAPA as they call it, to backstop a project in the Menam Chao Praya?"

"Thailand! That is what I want to speak to you about. I will have to go to Singapore around the time when you are in Thailand." His face was bright with excitement.

"This unexpected travel is a result of the agreement reached at the Conference. Usually things take so long to happen after a meeting. But this time, the follow-up is moving at top speed. It is one of the conditions stipulated by a major donor in return for its agreement."

"What will you have to do?"

"I have to make the preliminary arrangements for a mission to be fielded in that part of the world. Basically I will do most of the paper work here in Rome, set up a series of meetings in Singapore from here, and then, when I am in Singapore, finalise the arrangements. Could we meet up in Singapore? I leave Rome for Singapore only towards the end of your mission in Thailand, so I can bring Tim along. Then if you take some leave after Thailand, and I do the same, we'll be able to be together in Singapore. I would need to juggle with some dates and the holiday might be in tranches. I have to work some days, but we'll be together."

"What a wonderful idea! Aunt Nelly would like that. She is not coming this year and I was already toying with the idea of going over to see her. This would be perfect. I shall get to see Jane's new baby; in fact, her other one as well. I have not seen any of them because I have not been back to Singapore since I left. I am excited."

She stopped, a frown appeared on her face. "It's alright isn't? I mean to go to Singapore with Tim?"

He thought for a while. "We won't be going to Malaysia and no one knows about him except for you, me and the family. Everyone here thinks of Tim as my son."

"Then let's call Aunt Nelly and tell her now; it should be early morning in Singapore."

Turning to her husband, a delighted mischievous smile on her face, she said. "Aunt Nelly will want to baby sit for us, I am sure."

Chapter 37

"Phew! To think I thought Rome was hot in summer," exclaimed Mark, mopping his forehead. It was gleaming with sweat. He donned his hat quickly. He could feel the heat washing over him. "Why is it that no one wears a hat to protect them from the sun in Singapore?" he asked looking around him.

An Mei followed his gaze. People walked by; there was not a cap or hat in sight.

"I have never given it a thought," replied An Mei. "We just don't. Farmers do, but city people don't. Perhaps, it is because we are used to the sun. It's the same in Malaysia."

A bus stopped and disgorged its passengers. They came down single file; the waiting crowd moved aside for the disembarking passengers. Mark looked on with surprise.

"How orderly! That is really impressive," he remarked, recalling his experiences of buses elsewhere in the region. "In India, you would have the bus so packed that people would be hanging on to it by their fingernails; and, of course, the scramble to get on and off a bus is just wild."

"Yes! Singapore is renowned for its cleanliness and orderliness." An Mei grinned. "There is a penalty for practically everything: littering, throwing away chewing gum, smoking in public places, even the flushing of toilets. It works but that does not stop Malaysians from making jokes about Singapore. You see Malaysians are proud of their more *laissez faire* approach to life. Did you know that the authorities here in Singapore frown on men with long hair? If you have long hair, you might not get served! Don't laugh! There was a campaign against hippy culture some years back."

She recalled Hussein's long hair and his refusal to cross the causeway from Johor to Singapore because he would have had to cut his hair. Her heart quickened. It had been a long time since she had thought of him. But coming to Singapore, despite it being different from Malaysia, brought back sharp memories.

Mark saw her sudden change of mood. "Are you okay? Cobwebs from the past?" he asked gently.

"I'm fine. Let's get you to your meeting. I will walk you there, do some shopping and come back here. See that hotel? I shall be in the coffee house on the first floor waiting for you at around 5 o'clock. Tim is with Nelly. We have the evening to ourselves. Why don't we do something different? I feel ... I feel..."

"Naughty? Wicked?" he suggested, looking at her impish grin.

"Yes! I have always wanted to go to Bugis Street. Jeremy told me about it when I first met him. Yes! That's what we'll do," she said, determined to enjoy their holiday. She propelled him gently forward.

"What's Bugis Street? What's there?"

"I will tell you, but after."

They arrived in front of a tall building.

"Here we are. I'll leave now. See you later. Remember 5 o'clock," she said waving goodbye.

An Mei turned and walked towards a side street. She waited at the kerb, gauging when she could cross. A car passed her. It pulled to the side of the road and came to an abrupt stop; she saw from behind the tinted window of the car, someone looking at her. She looked away and stepped quickly into the crowd of people, joining them in the march across the road. Once across, she looked quickly back to where the car was. It had gone. Just my mind playing games with me, she thought.

*****

It was dusk when they made their way to Bugis Street. Determined to play the perfect tourist escort, An Mei had bought a guide to Singapore and read up on it whilst waiting for Mark in the café.

"It's probably not as exciting as it once was," she said. "A campaign to clean up the place is being planned. Still, I hear it is almost mandatory for tourists to visit it."

"You sound very mysterious. I am getting more and more curious by the minute. Because you were so evasive, I asked some of the people at the meeting that I just attended, whether they've been to Bugis Street and what's there. I got quite a few glad claps on my back; they laughed and said, see for yourself!"

"It's called Bugis Street because a long, long time ago the Bugis, a sea-faring people from South Sulawesi in Indonesia, use to travel up the river that runs into this area to trade with the local merchants. The area has a chequered history. During the Japanese occupation, it was known for the nightclubs and brothels for Japanese soldiers. Now of course, it is famous..."

Before she could finish her sentence, a woman with a plunging neckline had sashayed right between them, her formidable chest crushed into Mark. She was beautiful; long black hair, perfectly moulded lips painted a bright red and large come hither eyes. She winked, her face brazen, suggestive. An Mei gulped, rendered speechless by the boldness of the woman, her voluptuous body and how she moved. Mark, taken by surprise, stepped back. The woman laughed. "Sorry," she said, her voice deep and husky, "you are occupied, I see. What a pity!" She walked away, her hips swinging. Heads turned, people whistled. She smiled and waved like a celebrity.

"She ... she must be one of those I read about. Look ... she is not a woman! She is..."

"A transvestite! *Malu!* Shame!" said a voice behind her.

An Mei turned, but no one was there. She looked keenly into the crowd and saw beyond them a car parked at the corner. She was sure that it was the same car she had seen earlier in the afternoon. She turned and grabbed Mark's hand. "I think we have been followed. That car there," she said turning to point. But there was no car. "It was a dark blue car, a Mercedes," she added lamely.

"Darling, you must not be frightened. There are many blue Mercedes in Singapore. You are a free woman. There is nothing to be frightened about. Come let's go home. We have probably seen all we want to see. This way, we'll still see Tim before he goes to bed."

"Sorry, I'm just jittery." She smiled. "All in my head."

* * * * *

The next morning they emerged from the white-fronted house with a little white gate and fence that separated the residence from the road. Timothy jumped and bounced with excitement. "Tiger garden! Ah Kun said I should go to Tiger Garden!"

"He means the Haw Par Villa," said Nelly. "I would advise against that," she said quietly to An Mei. "Too frightening for a young child; full of scenes of torture. I am going to tell Ah Kun off for even suggesting it. The Jurong Bird Park would be a better place, ideal in fact. Lots of ground for him to run about."

They were standing in front of the house, waiting for the taxi. Mark and An Mei stood on either side of Timothy holding on to his hands.

"Swing me daddy; swing me mummy!" Tim yelled. His laughter and voice carried over to the car parked a short distance opposite the house. It had been there since the previous night when it followed An Mei and Mark's journey home from Bugis Street. It looked inconspicuous; a driver was engaged in polishing its bonnet. The deep shade of the angsana tree, and the tinted windows of the car shielded the lone figure within. Hunched in one corner, he had slid low down in the back seat. The child's voice floated through the window that was wound some two inches down. He peeped out and started. His eyes widened in surprise. Rage ran through him, currents that tore at his insides. He looked at the man smiling down at the little boy, his pale hand grasping the little brown one. He knocked discreetly on the window, indicating to the driver to get into the car. They waited. They watched as a taxi arrived. They saw the three adults and child get into the car. "*Ikut-nya!* Follow them!" Ahmad said.

*****

Ahmad got out of the car and followed them, keeping a gap of some 20 yards. Once in the park, the child broke free and ran ahead. Ahmad saw that within seconds, the man they called Mark and An Mei had sprinted forward. They caught up easily with the little boy. They held on to his hands, laughing and playing, while waiting for Nelly to catch up. Ahmad bade his time; he stooped to tie his shoelace, hiding his face. He reconciled himself that it would be a long wait before the opportunity rose to do what he had just decided.

He followed them visiting one section after another: pelicans, parrots, flamingos, parrots, mandarin ducks, and the ibis. He saw Nelly flagging. Her walk became slower and slower. The crowd got denser as the day grew. He had no problem in camouflaging himself; at times he had to merge with others in the crowd and pretend that he was with them. He made sure that his face remained hidden, especially from An Mei. He felt confident that she would not recognise him. Not with this beard, he thought. There was no reason for them to expect him in Singapore. He listened to their chatter, his ears tuned to their voices. He watched, his eyes sharp.

Two hours went by.

He heard Mark say, his voice filled with concern, "Nelly would you like to sit on that bench and rest? You must be so tired. Here," he continued, lifting Timothy off his shoulders, "Tim can stay with you for a while; An Mei and I will just pop over to that little booth and get some refreshments. What would you like?"

"Yes, what would you like?" repeated An Mei in Cantonese.

"Anything that is cold. I must admit that my feet are starting to swell up in this heat."

"Stay here with Aunt Nelly," An Mei told her son. "I'll get you an ice cream if you are good." She patted him on the head and left with Mark.

Ahmad stood to one side, one arm resting on the wooden barricade that separated the path from a gigantic birdcage. He kept watch on the little boy and Nelly, but always mindful to keep his bearded face turned sideways. Five minutes went by. He glanced quickly in the direction of the refreshment booth. A long queue had developed and he could see that Mark and An Mei were still some way behind their turn. He looked back at the little boy. He could see that he was getting restless and bored.

"Oooo I don't want to sit on your lap," Timothy yelled. His voice was loud and penetrating. "I want to see birds. I want to go to play there," he said pointing to the play area behind Nelly. He wriggled and pushed. "I want to, I want to." He bawled.

"Wait, wait a little. I too tired to run with you," Nelly wiped her brows to show that she was tired in case he did not understand her English. She pointed to her feet. "Painful," she said. "Be good boy."

"Don't want to be good boy," said Timothy, petulant. Big drops of tears rolled down his cheeks. He cried as though his heart would break; his face was red with the effort; his little cheeks scrunched up.

"*Ying sing!* Promise me you play in sand pit. Not go anywhere," Nelly said in a mixture of Chinese and English and demonstrating with her hands. She wiped his face and his nose.

He nodded vigorously; all signs of sadness were gone in a flash. Nelly smiled and hugged him to her before releasing him. He ran, his chubby little legs moving fast towards the sand pit. Ahmad followed him. He walked to a hibiscus bush a short distance from the sand pit. He was out of Nelly's sight. He watched. Ahmad caught the eye of the little boy. He beckoned, fishing from his pocket a brightly coloured marble. He threw it into the air and caught it in a flash. He nodded to Tim with a wide smile. He gestured to him, putting out his palm with the bright marble. He glanced nervously at the bench. Nelly was bent over rubbing her ankle. The boy walked towards him, hesitantly. He beckoned the boy again, thrusting forward the marble in his hand. The boy ran towards him. He caught him up in his arms and ran into the crowd and into the birdhouse.

* * * * *

"*Ah* Tim! *Ah* Timmy!"

An Mei turned abruptly at the sound of Nelly's voice. She saw Nelly; both her hands were cupped around her mouth like a horn; she could see the anguish in her face, even from a distance. An Mei dropped the cans of drinks and the ice cream cone she had been holding. Its contents splattered as it cascaded down on to the pavement. She ran towards Nelly. Her heart thumped; her stomach hollowed like a vice holding her tight. She heard Mark behind her, his feet gaining ground, closing in on her. Still she ran. A little boy of around eleven or twelve rushed towards them, gesticulating.

"Mam! Mam! I saw the man take boy," he said, pointing in the direction of the birdhouse.

"What man?" they cried, veering then in the direction of the birdhouse.

"Man with beard. A dark man," the boy yelled after them.

They ran into the birdhouse. People were standing everywhere obliterating their view. It was difficult to manoeuvre around the crowd. A sudden movement at the other exit caught their eye. They pushed through the crowd and ran in pursuit. They ran outside, the bright sunlight temporarily blinding them. A sudden stillness seemed to descend on the scene. It was surreal: people moving, laughing and enjoying themselves. Timothy was nowhere to be seen.

Chapter 38

Timothy lay limp in Ahmad's arms. His head lolled like a rag doll. Ahmad ran from the birdhouse. People turned to stare at the little boy, his neck seemingly out of control as his head flopped from side to side on the man's shoulder.

"*Dia sakit!* He is ill!" Ahmad explained without breaking his speed. "*Nak pergi hospital! Orang jahat ikut kita*. We need to go to a hospital. Bad people are following us. They did this to my son."

They made way for him, even as they saw Mark and An Mei emerged from the birdhouse. When they saw the desperate face of the young woman and white man, they were torn as to whom they should believe, but the instinct of self-preservation, of not wanting to be involved, prevailed. The child was without doubt not a European they thought. He looked more akin to the man carrying him. So they kept silent and went about their enjoyment as though they saw nothing and in that precious vital few seconds, Ahmad was able to get safely away to the waiting car.

"Drive on," Ahmad instructed the driver, pushing Timothy to one side of the seat and covering the little boy with the blanket he had used during the previous night's vigil when he had sat in the car outside Nelly's house.

Taken by surprise, and frightened, the driver looked uneasily at his rear mirror. He caught Ahmad staring at him. Ahmad snarled, his lips drawn back to reveal his teeth. "*Cepat!* Quick!"

The driver stepped on the accelerator, sure that something bad had happened, something even worst than he had anticipated when he was co-opted into the previous night's watch. He could smell chloroform. He glanced nervously again at the rear mirror and caught the grin of delight on his master's face. He had been driving Ahmad to Singapore almost every month in the past two years and had been sworn to keep the trips a secret. He had no problem doing that. Within a year, he knew all the main underground gambling dens in the island like the back of his hand. He did not care if Ahmad was infringing the rules that he so frequently expounded and preached to others: the evil of gambling. He was paid well for his duties. His duty was to drive and to keep quiet, but kidnapping! That was another matter. What else could it be but kidnapping? He asked himself even as he drove back to his master's house; a house that he was sworn not to tell to anyone about, a house that had to be kept a secret from all.

* * * * *

The car swerved into a yard hemmed in by tall trees and bushes. A bungalow, a bleak functional square building with shutters drawn tight, stood in the middle of it. There was an air of neglect about the compound and the bungalow. The ground was littered with fallen twigs and brown, spotted leaves tinged in places with yellow and khaki green like a diseased membrane. They blew and swirled in the wind before settling in little heaps only, at the next gust of wind, to be blown to settle elsewhere.

Ahmad threw open the car door and carried Timothy into the bungalow and into a bedroom at the back of it. He laid the little boy on a bed. Despite the dimness of the room, he drew the curtains tight as an extra precaution. After one impatient glance round the room, he closed the bedroom door behind him, turning the key in the lock and pocketing it. He turned to fix his eye on his driver.

"Aquino," he said, "you have been with me for the past three years. Have I treated you well?"

"Yes, sir. Very well."

"I would like you to keep this between us. You will be well rewarded. Remember, I can send you back to where you came from very easily. You do remember don't you?"

Aquino's mouth went dry. He remembered very vividly; the miserable boat journey across the rough South China Sea from Mindanao in the Philippines, battling against the monsoon as the boat tossed and heaved while he clung to his mother and siblings. The horror of seeing his family vanish, swallowed up by the churning waves. He had stayed afloat in the sea for days before ending in the confinement of a refugee camp. He shivered as he recalled his suffering at the hands of the guards and other immigrants. He could feel their hands on him, even after three years. "Please sir. Don't send me back. I will do as you say."

Ahmad swept his eyes over him, a gesture so dismissive that Aquino cringed with shame over his own helplessness.

"Keep guard outside. I will rest now. Make yourself something to eat, but I want you at hand," said Ahmad waving him away. Once Aquino left the room, Ahmad sat down on an armchair. He sat still for a long time, occasionally tugging violently at his beard as if to remind him of pain.

"My poor Shalimar," he said quietly to himself. It was all the fault of that bitch, he thought.

Again an insane rage rose inside him when he thought of An Mei. Even though they had managed to get rid of her, she continued to dominate their lives. "Bitch!" he said aloud. He had thought that Shalimar had won Hussein over when he divorced An Mei but, if she had, it was short-lived. Poor Shalimar. He had alternately threatened, cajoled and pushed her to win over Hussein. Little did he expect her to fall in love with him. His face grew thunderous when he recalled her suffering at Hussein's indifference.

He sighed. Shalimar was always weak, even as a little girl. Even so, he did not expect her to die in such circumstances; die while trying to bring a bastard child to the world; and spoiling everything in the process. Ahmad smashed his hand hard against the armrest. He was furious, furious with his sister for her stupidity, with her lover who got her pregnant, with Hussein who rejected her, and most of all with An Mei who he blamed for Shalimar's failure to win over Hussein. Following his sister's death, his position in Hussein's household had weakened. Hussein had told him in no uncertain terms that he would not be paying him the retainer Ahmad had thought was his right. And he desperately needed that source of income because the dowry from Shalimar had long been spent to meet his gambling debts.

"So what now?" he asked himself. He had not thought it through when he made the impulsive decision to take the boy. Instinctively, he knew that he could make use of the boy to further himself. He thought of Faridah and her sorrow at the demise of what she had thought was her grandchild. She would probably pay for the boy if he could prove that he was Hussein's child. He had little doubt that the child was Hussein's; he was his spitting image. But it was anger and rage, the desire to punish An Mei that drove him to take the boy. He wanted to make her suffer just as he had suffered as a consequence of Shalimar's death. His mind was filled with plans. He got up and went to the drinks cupboard and took out a glass tumbler. He poured himself a brandy; inhaled its deep aroma with appreciation before downing it in one gulp.

"*Arak!* Alcohol! Forbidden pleasures and so much more pleasurable because of it," he muttered to himself as he poured yet another shot of the brandy into his glass. He walked back to the armchair, sat down and placed both legs on the coffee table before him. He nursed the drink in his hands, his mind plotting his next steps, his facial expression ever changing, reflecting his thoughts.

Chapter 39

Some eight kilometres away, in a police station, An Mei sat with Mark and Nelly on a long bench that lined one side of a white wall. A policeman in a blue Dacron uniform had directed them to it.

"Wait," he had said before turning on his heels and disappearing into the inner sanctum of the police station. Beyond that single word, he had said little else to them.

An Mei sat cradling her head in her hands. Mark placed his arm around her shoulder and she looked up; her eyes were ringed with fatigue, exhaustion and despair. He kissed her forehead. From the other end of the bench, Nelly looked on. She opened her mouth to speak but could not find words to express what she felt. She blamed herself. Timothy's happy saunter away from her to the sand pit replayed in her mind. If only she had not been distracted ... to say any more would just add to everyone's pain. So they sat waiting. They waited and waited. Minutes ticked by as the slow hand of bureaucracy ground onward. Policemen ambled by; each

time a door opened, they jumped, half-rising in readiness
to be invited in only to discover it was still not their turn.
Unable to stand the wait any longer, An Mei stood up and
walked up and down the corridor. Frustration, despair and
panic took hold of her in turn. Mark sat by and watched
her, helpless.

Time continued to tick by, oppressive in its slowness. Mark
felt his utter sense of helplessness multiply. Finally, a door
opened and a policeman appeared. "We are ready for you now.
Come with me."

* * * * *

"How did it go?" asked Jane. She stood aside to let her mother
Nelly, Mark and An Mei enter the house. "Come, let's go into
the sitting room. I have laid out some tea and sandwiches. You
have to eat something to keep up your strength." She bustled
ahead to lead the way, a baby in her arms.

No one spoke. An Mei sat next to Mark, her face glum. He
placed his arm around her and she buried her face in his chest.
He could feel a surge of hot tears on his shirt. Her muffled sobs
tore at his heart.

"We can't tell you how it went," he said. "They took down
our details and we wrote a report of the incident. We answered
their questions, but we do not have any idea of how it went, or
how it will go. It was all very frustrating."

"Did they shed any light on what they intend to do?" Jane
asked.

"No," replied Mark, "they said they would do their best and
I believe them. It is not good publicity for their growing tourist
industry. But what does their best amount to?"

An Mei struggled to a sitting position. "The only lead is that blue Mercedes. I just feel in my bones that it has something to do with this," she said. "And I told the policeman. I wanted also to tell them of my suspicion. I suspect that the long hand of Hussein and his family is involved. I cannot believe that it is a coincidence that someone would choose to take my son out of the hundreds of children in the park."

"And did you tell them?" asked Jane.

An Mei looked at Mark. "I didn't," she replied, her eyes full of guilt. "I didn't in case I was wrong; for if I was wrong, then telling the police would alert Hussein and my former-in-laws to the existence of Tim."

She rubbed furiously at her swollen eyes with the back of her hands, not caring about her streaming nose. "I didn't know what to do. Have I done right?"

"If Hussein and his family are as important as you say, then accusing them without any real evidence is not likely to go down well with the police. We did have one good piece of luck. Remember the little boy, the one who saw Tim being bundled a way? Nelly had the presence of mind to ask him for his name when An Mei and I were busy giving chase. His parents also gave Nelly their address. He would be an important witness; he could identify the kidnapper. His details are with the police now."

"Well! That is important. We can't do much now, so why don't you take An Mei up for a rest. You both look absolutely washed out." Jane placed a hand gently on An Mei's cheeks. "Rest, please rest and you will see things clearer." She was making her way out of the room, when, suddenly, she turned. She looked guiltily at her friend and her hand flew to her mouth.

"I forgot. How could I?" she exclaimed. "An envelope, without any postage mark, was pushed through the post box

just before you came back. It is addressed to you," she said
to An Mei. "I meant to hand it you immediately but..." She
rummaged through the pile of letters at the sideboard and
handed An Mei a crumpled brown envelope.

With trembling hands, An Mei took the envelope. She tore
it open. A solitary piece of paper was in it. On it was written in
block capital letters: I KNOW!

* * * * *

Faridah held the phone to her ear. Joy, surprise and triumph
mingled in her face. Her eyes sparkled with wonder. Her
bosom heaved with excitement. She spoke little except for the
intermittent exclamations of "Yes! Wonderful! *Insha Allah!*"
She returned the phone to its cradle and stood absolutely still.
Then she walked quickly towards her husband's office, her beaded
slippers slapping on the floor in her haste. A servant followed. She
waved her away and pushed open the door without knocking.

"Rahim!" she exclaimed from the doorway, "Ahmad called."

"And?" he asked, laconically. Seated behind a desk and
holding a newspaper, he had not bothered to look up. She
slipped into the room and closed the door. She looked at her
husband, triumphant.

"He said that An Mei bore Hussein a son who she has kept
hidden from us. The little boy is a spitting image of Hussein."

Rahim lowered his paper abruptly. The pages crackled and
fell on his lap. He did not reply straight away. His face was
thoughtful. Then he shook his head in doubt.

"Are you sure that is what he said? Are you sure he is not
pulling your leg, punishing you — us — because we stopped
his payment."

"I am not deaf and I am certainly not mad! Of course that is what he said. He saw Hussein's son. Unlike you, I believe in Ahmad. I do not know what you and Hussein have against him. He has always been helpful to me. He is always respectful."

"How did Ahmad manage to see An Mei and the boy? Did she not leave the country?" asked Rahim. "It's been some years since she disappeared. From all accounts she is not in Malaysia."

"If Ahmad saw them then it must have been here in Malaysia."

For the first time since his wife entered the room, Rahim began to give the story some credibility.

"If this is true," he said cautiously, "then we can certainly apply to the court for custody. We will have a strong case, at least in our Shariah court, if she is not a practising Muslim. But we are jumping ahead of ourselves. Don't get your hopes too high. It could well be a hoax or Ahmad is mistaken."

"We don't have to resort to the courts. Ahmad has him."

Rahim jumped up crashing his chair to the floor. His hand gesticulated wildly, one finger pointing to his head.

"What!! Are you out of your mind? How did Ahmad manage to get hold of the little boy? Did he take him by force, kidnap him?"

"I don't know the details. All I care about is that he can bring him to us."

"And how much does he want? Where is he now?" asked Rahim. Over the years, he had seen through Ahmad. Hussein had opened his eyes to the cunning and manipulative nature of the man. They had bailed him out one too many times.

"He wants half a million. I don't care about the money. Just give it to him. All I care for is my grandson."

"I can't go along with this. I would love to have my grandson if the little boy is truly Hussein's, but I cannot condone kidnapping. We'll all go down. In any case, it might not be Hussein's son and we would have involved ourselves in a murky deed for nothing if we were to pay Ahmad."

"*Adoi!* I have waited so long for a grandchild. I had such hopes for Shalimar's baby, but it was not to be. What right has An Mei to deceive us, to cast us out of our grandson's life? I feel nothing for her. I don't consider it as kidnapping because how can we be accused of kidnapping our own blood?"

"Calm down. I don't see it like you do. If Ahmad wanted to help, he would have just told us and we would have got the law to track An Mei and the child down and we would apply for custody. She is now here, not in some far off country where we do not have jurisdiction. I assume that she is here in Malaysia, even in KL itself," he said.

Faridah shrugged. Ahmad had said very little except for describing the little boy as a lovely child who looked the image of Hussein. After that revelation, all she could think of was having Hussein's son in her arms.

She sat down, dejected. She had not expected such a response from her husband. She should have tried to find out more details from Ahmad, but she was so carried away. Even so she had not expected her husband to be so negative.

"Huh!" exclaimed Rahim, "he has not told you much has he? Typical! All he wants is money. If it were not for him, we would stand a better chance of getting our grandson legally. Now, the boy is being held against his will. Have you thought about that? How frightened your grandson might be, snatched from his mother?"

Rahim's words made sense to her. She now became concerned for the child who she believed with all her heart must be her grandson. "What do we do?" she asked. "Ahmad said he would call us for an answer this evening."

"We must tell Hussein."

* * * * *

"Are you absolutely sure?" asked Hussein. "An Mei made no mention of expecting a baby."

Hussein was elated. Yes, it was possible. He could not be sure, but deep down he hoped that it was true; he wanted it to be true, that he and An Mei have a son. He wanted the connection, the tie between them. Perhaps there was still a chance of reviving their love, now that Shalimar was gone. With a child, his parents might come round. He regretted giving up An Mei. He had not wanted the divorce. His parents' constant urging, his own ambition and temptation for its easy fulfilment, held in front of him like bait, propelled him to write those three words: *I divorce you.*

It was a moment of weakness, intense selfishness and utter callousness. He admitted to all that. If he could turn back the clock he would. He squeezed his eyes tight to obliterate the shame he felt. Unbidden, he let out a deep guttural groan. It took him by surprise. He sensed his parents looking at him. He pushed the thoughts away, took a deep breath, and the controlled outward face of the politician he had become took over once more. There were more urgent matters to attend to. His son might be in danger. If his mother does not come up with the money, what might Ahmad choose to do, he asked himself. Would he harm the boy? Should they inform the police about Ahmad? Would this provoke Ahmad to take desperate action? Where was An Mei? How did Ahmad get hold of his son? There were so many questions, so many unknowns. He picked up the phone and asked for Ghazali.

"Find out if a little boy of around three-and-a-half years old has been reported missing," he instructed his aide. "I am not sure where it might have occurred. It could be in KL, Malacca or in one of the tourist resorts; it could even be in Singapore. The best place to find out might be the newspapers. Use your contacts with the police. Don't leave any stone unturned."

By the time he had finished his conversation and replaced the phone, his calm demeanour had gone. In its place was again agitation, an agitation that made him scratch his neck until it left streaks of red. Talking about the various possible ways in which Ahmad might have taken his son, brought closer home, the danger he might be in.

"Father, should we report this incident to the police? We could pretend to go along with Ahmad and still make the report. We cannot keep it from the police."

'No!" cried Faridah, "If Ahmad suspects that we have told the police, he would harm my grandson. I cannot bear the thought of it. We cannot risk that."

"If we don't, we will be breaking the law and there is still no guarantee that he would release my son," warned Hussein.

"I doubt this will be Ahmad's last demand; he will return for additional ransom money. The next time it might be blackmail. Once we connive with him, he has his hands round our throat. And, how can we explain the child's presence if we do get him?" asked Rahim. He was determined not to refer to the boy as his grandson. He observed how quickly Hussein was assuming that the boy was his. He did not wish to challenge Hussein. He could well be right. If anyone would know, it must surely be Hussein. But for himself, he felt that he needed to remain detached. Referring to the boy as his grandson would make him emotionally vulnerable. He would be like his wife.

"I think if we do get my son back, we will first have to return him to his mother." Hussein looked from one parent to the other. He was trying to gauge how they would react. Slowly, tentatively, he continued. "Perhaps, An Mei would consider marrying me again. If that were possible then everything could be settled amicably."

"*Gila!* Mad!" cried Faridah. She could not believe what she had just heard. She appealed to her husband. Rahim, wrapped up in his own thoughts, did not hear what Hussein said nor did he take note of his wife's response.

"Let me get hold of my friend in the police force and asked him for his advice. He would keep it off the record for me, I am sure," he said.

Hussein agreed. "We have to be fast though. We don't have much time. I am sure An Mei will conclude that we have had a hand in the kidnapping and will point the police to us. Then it would look like we are conniving with Ahmad."

The more he thought of his idea, the more convinced he became that it could work. Surely An Mei would be pleased, grateful even, if he succeeded in rescuing the little boy. A son! And to be with An Mei again! His face brightened at the prospect. He was sure that he could bring his parents around to his idea, but now was not the time to push for it.

* * * * *

Mark walked down the lane leading to a row of single-storey shop houses that served the suburban area of Jane's house. He had to get away from the house to think clearly. His head was bowed down. He was deep in thought. He hardly noticed the people he passed nor did he realise that he had strayed off track and was in the back lane of the shops. The sun's piercing heat bore down on him. Perspiration rolled off his neck and his shirt clung, wet to his back. He stumbled on a broken brick, checked his steps and continued to stride on. He felt utterly inept in Singapore. He was among people who spoke English yet he remained a foreigner, *a gwei loh!* There was little he could do to help An Mei. He had not the foggiest idea on how he could help rescue Timothy. Uncaring and unaware of his surroundings and the heat, he walked on.

The sound of footsteps behind him caught his attention. He turned to look and saw a slender young man, perhaps around 20, walking behind him. He quickened his pace and heard a corresponding quickening of footsteps from behind. Mark turned abruptly around.

"Are you following me?" he said sternly to the young man.

The young man shook his head; his eyes darted left and right. He looked as though he was going to jump out of his own skin.

Mark continued walking. A mad hatter, he thought. Yet the man followed. Impatient, Mark whirled around and walked briskly to the man.

"Look here! Stop following me. Go away!"

"You help me," said the man, "I help you."

"What are you talking about? I'll call the police," warned Mark.

"No! No call police. I help you. You help me." His eyes once more darted from left to right. "I know where boy, you call Tim, is. I lead you to him. You help me. You help me get away. Or he kill me."

"Who will kill you? Speak to me. How do you know about Tim? Where is he?" Mark bellowed.

"Shhh! Quiet! Quiet please. I come alone. I am Ahmad's driver."

Mark stood silent. "Ahmad!" he repeated. It began to fall in place. It was just as An Mei had believed. No, not quite! She had thought that Hussein was behind this. Was he also involved? He wondered. There was no time to waste.

"Tell me, where is Tim?"

"No! No! Unless you promise you help me get away, find job, have money."

"You tell me, you lead me to Tim first. We should go to the police with this."

Aquino took two steps back; with a speed that took Mark by surprise, he ran. He vaulted over the fence that separated the dirt track from the road that ran parallel to it, and continued to run. His legs pumped; his head swirled back to look anxiously at his pursuer. Mark ran after him; his legs flying across the path; he by-passed the fence and cut across the field that separated the path from the road. Aquino thought he had lost Mark. He could see the tall grass move and sway, but there was no sign of Mark. He slowed down to a stand still and leaned over his legs, holding on to his knees, gasping for breath. Mark sprinted forward bringing to bear his years of training as a runner when he was at college, and caught hold of Aquino. Breathing hard, he held on to him.

"Now why don't you tell me everything?"

"Don't hurt me." Aquino cried out in pain. He held on to his foot. Mark could see that it was bleeding. He relinquished his hold. Aquino shot his foot out, landing it on Mark's face, knocking him over. Mark felt an explosion of red mist; blood streamed down his nose. He bounded up, but Aquino had already sprung up and bolted. He ran, legs pummelling, back towards the path they had left. Mark followed. Aquino picked up speed; he obviously knew the area. Mark saw him disappear into an alley between the shop houses. By the time he reached it, Aquino was nowhere to be seen.

* * * * *

Aquino washed himself, sluicing water over himself, letting the cold water soothe the wound in his foot. Over and over, he dipped his plastic pail into the water urn, a big brown Chinese ceramic barrel that in the past had been used for storing salted eggs. It stood at waist level in the backyard of Ahmad's house; a house that served also as Aquino's lodgings when he was in Singapore. A folding canvas camp bed in the kitchen was all that he called his own. He had nowhere else to go. From a distance, he heard a clock strike. He relinquished the pail, shook his head like a dog, spraying droplets of water all round him, and rubbed himself down with a cotton sarong. He put on his uniform and sleeked down his black hair. He would have to fetch Ahmad from the casino soon. He was told to stay with the boy they call Tim until Ahmad needed him.

In the absence of his master he had taken his chance and stolen out to look for An Mei and the white man. He had wanted to warn them and also to gain their protection. Unfortunately it had all gone wrong. Why did that white man insist on bringing in the police? If only he had not made that threat, he would have brought him here. Aquino walked to the kitchen. He buttered two slices of bread with margarine and poured out a glass of water. He laid them out carefully on the tray and carried it to Tim's room. He fished out a bunch of keys from the chest of drawers and unlocked the door. He stepped into the room as quietly as he could.

The room was stifling hot and dark. The shutters were down and the curtains drawn shut. He could see the small body curled up on the bed; the boy's chest was rising and falling rhythmically. Every so often a small groan or cry emitted from his lips, and he would thrash about as though he was trying to free himself. He saw a wet stain on the bed sheet. It seeped dark on the pale sheet, like the work of a poor artist trying to outline the contours of the boy's buttocks on the bed. Aquino's heart went out to him. He had done what he could. He just could not free him or return him to the lady unless they promised to protect and help him. He placed the tray down on the table and shook Tim gently.

"Wake up, you please eat," he said.

Tim groaned and buried his face into the bed.

"Please eat and drink. No food later."

Ahmad had been furious the previous evening when he made up a tray for Tim. "Who gave you permission to feed him? *Tak payah beri nya lauk!* There is no need to give him food!" He had yelled from the armchair where he was sitting. With one leg flung across the armrest he had waved Aquino away from the door. "*Pergi!* Go! Get into the kitchen and stay there until I call you."

Aquino had hastily backed into the kitchen. He had shut the door behind him and leaned back against it. He had seen how Ahmad had grown agitated and furious after his phone call. He had heard him say the words, *Datin* Faridah. Aquino knew who she was; a short, dumpy woman always richly clad, a person who Ahmad had visited frequently in the early days of his employment. She was *Tengku* Shalimar's mother-in-law. In the last couple of years or so, those visits had diminished. He had learnt from the other servants that there had been a fall out between Ahmad and his in-laws. He learnt that Hussein, the rising politician and Ahmad's brother-in-law, was the cause.

All through the night, Ahmad had walked up and down the room like a caged animal, drinking. He had seemed incensed. The conversation could not have gone well and Aquino felt that it did not bode well for the boy. He could feel it in his bones.

Aquino patted Tim on his shoulder. "Come, sit up and drink, even if you do not want to eat."

"I want mummy. I want daddy," Tim whimpered, pushing Aquino's hands away. Big drops of tears rolled down his cheeks.

"There, don't cry. I leave tray here. You eat, now please," he pleaded pointing vigorously to the tray and miming actions of chewing. He knew that later in the evening when Ahmad returned, he would not be allowed to bring the boy food.

"Please hide, hide tray after finish. Under bed," he said lifting the bed sheet to reveal the space underneath. "I go now."

As Aquino turned and made for the door, the boy screamed. He jumped out of the bed and clung to his legs. "No! Please stay. I want mummy. I want daddy! Take me to them." He kicked and screamed, tearing at Aquino's clothes.

"Wait. You stay in room. Eat. I come back. I think what to do." Reluctantly he pushed the boy away and closed and locked the door behind him. He clasped his hands to his ears in a desperate attempt to cut out Tim's screams. Tim reminded him of his young brothers. He had cared for them; they had been in his charge when his parents went to work. He had lost all of them now. He could not bear the thought that Tim might share the same fate.

* * * * *

The room was filled with people, old, young and the not so young. There were Chinese men and women, a few Europeans and some Malays and Indians. They were divided between two round tables, standing cheek by jowl, their attention focused on the croupiers.

The air was dense with smoke. Ahmad sat alone impervious to the fog of grey-blue cigarette fumes that reached into every corner and crevice of the room. He sat in deep concentration with his eyes narrowed, brows furrowed, jaws tight and legs crossed; one ankle resting on a thigh, the foot pointed out, the other foot jiggled and pumped in agitation. He looked so fierce that people skirted around him. Some even made it a point to cross over to the other side of the room rather than venture near him. They knew of his reputation: the man from the other side of the causeway who was not to be messed with. They were all afraid of him, except for the owner of the gambling den, Ah Cheong, so nicknamed because of his lanky body.

Ah Cheong stood in a corner of the room, one hand casually resting on the bar counter, the other hand holding a beer mug. He took a hefty sip from the mug. His eyes swept round the room and settled on the lone figure of Ahmad. The corner of his lips curled up briefly.

"Huh!" he uttered aloud before turning back to the barman. "*Pok kai!* Bankrupt!" he said in Cantonese, nodding in the direction of Ahmad. "Tell Ah Sam, our number three, to put on the squeeze. Make sure he does not leave the island without paying up. Wait until he leaves. He must not be touched in this room."

He sauntered over to Ahmad and placed a hand on his shoulder. Ahmad could feel the strength of the grip and the menace behind it even as Ah Cheong smiled and said, "*Tak main?* You are not playing?"

"*Tak! Hari ini saya rehat.* No! I am resting today," replied Ahmad. He attempted a smile.

Ah Cheong punched him playfully on his shoulder.

"*Jaga!* Careful! You owe us," he said with a smile that never left his face.

Ahmad knew the odds and had hoped that Faridah would pay up. It did not look like it now. He was angry and frustrated. He had placed such hopes on his phone call to Faridah. He had been so sure that she would come up with the money. Now he was not certain at all. He stared at the departing lanky figure and slammed his fist on the armrest of the chair.

"You will pay for this Hussein," he growled. He had no doubts that Hussein was behind Faridah's refusal to cough up the sum of money he had demanded. He stood up, brushed the creases off his trousers and followed after Ah Cheong.

* * * * *

Mark hurried back to Jane's house, running most of the way. He banged on the door. Jane let him in.

"I lost him," cried Mark. He bent over, breathless. His shirt clung wet to his back. His face was red from the exertion and traces of blood stained his upper lip.

"Lost who?" she asked.

"A young man who probably would have led us to Tim."

"Slow down. Come in. An Mei and my mum are in the sitting room." He went into the room. An Mei was sat next to Nelly on the sofa. They could tell that something was wrong. Mark was red in the face and looked sheepish, even guilty.

"What happened?" asked An Mei, jumping up at the sight of him.

He stood before them, feeling their eyes on him as he related his tale. A surge of anguish and guilt filled him. He had failed them. He could feel the reproach in An Mei's face.

"How, how could you lose him? How could you let him go? He offered to help!" she asked.

Nelly pulled her down to the seat.

"Mind what you say. Mark did not deliberately lose him," said Nelly.

An Mei fell back to the sofa seat. Her face was filled with anger one minute and despair the next. Frustration rose like a bitter pill. Their first lead and it had disappeared into thin air.

"You probably frightened him away," she said, her eyes accusing him.

"Yes! Yes! In retrospect I should have gone along with him and promised everything he asked for in return for information. But I was taken by surprise, I... I just reacted... like, I suppose like I would in a normal situation."

Mark went to An Mei.

"I am sorry," he said. "I was wrong. He came out of the blue and took me by surprise. I just am not used to being accosted in the streets by someone who I have never met and... and... be told that I have to give him protection and money in return for information. How could I trust him, let alone do a deal?" Mark tried to get An Mei to look at him but she would not look up.

"So it was Ahmad," she said after some while. "I always thought that it would be Hussein and his family. I thought that I would be safe in Singapore. I too was wrong. I should not have exposed Tim to this," she whispered.

"*Aiyah! Mo yong gong kum yeong!* No use talking like that! You wrong or he wrong what can it do? Important thing is to find Tim. We must go to the police with this new information," said Nelly.

"If it is Ahmad, the immigration department in Singapore must have a record of his entry and where he is supposed to be staying. These details must be in his immigration arrival card," said Mark, excitement creeping into his voice. "Come, let us go right now to the police." He took An Mei's hand. "I'm truly sorry. I love Tim like my own, you know that don't you?"

She nodded. She knew Mark loved Tim and would do anything for him. She knew her anger was not justified. She braced her shoulders and straightened her back.

"Let's go," she said. "Nelly is right. What happens next is more important." Turning to Nelly, she said, "Stay. Rest at home. We will be back soon. There is nothing you can do at the police station."

They stepped out of the house and made their way to the car parked out on the street. Dusk made long shadows in the street. Trees swayed and moved, their branches making intricate shifting shades on the pavements.

Aquino looked on from behind a tree. He had parked the blue Mercedes some distance away for fear that it would be recognized. His mind was still tortured, moving between anxiety for himself if he were to help An Mei and fear for Timothy if he did not. Indecision kept him stuck to the spot even when he wanted to rush forward and offer his help. He saw An Mei and Mark leave and stood still for a minute before making his way back to Ahmad's car. He would be in trouble. He had been due to collect Ahmad and he was late.

* * * * *

"Ahmad slammed down the phone on me. He said that we will pay," she cried. "I knew we should have gone along with him and given him the money. I do not know what will happen to my grandson now."

Faridah turned on her husband with fury. "You, you are to blame. Where were the police when we needed them? The police would know best. Hah!"

She brought her hands up to cover her face in anguish, then withdrew them to jab her fingers at her husband. She ranted. "They told us not to pay up, to ask for time to get the cash together. They ask us to play along because there is no guarantee that Ahmad would hand over the boy. Hah!" she snorted again. "This is what happens if we don't pay! I shall never forgive you," she cried breaking into tears.

"Calm down. We have traced the call. It is from Singapore. He is not in Malaysia. So that at least gives us a lead. The police are on to him now. Even at this very moment, they are talking to their Singapore counterparts," Rahim said with a confidence that he did not really have. He put his arm around his distraught wife in an attempt to comfort her. He had never seen her so upset before, angry yes, but not upset like this. Her longing for a grandchild had made her vulnerable and he was filled with pity for her.

"Come, come! Sit down," he said guiding her to a chair, but she pushed him away.

At the other end of the room, Hussein stood surrounded by uniformed policemen. They were gathered around the long table where they had set up the phone-tapping device. "Caught him," said one officer, looking up at Hussein with a smile.

"Not quite," said another. "He might have just borrowed a phone. Quick, get on to Singapore. This will at the very least tell us where he has been."

Hussein went over to his father. He took him by the arm and led him away from his mother.

"I'm flying to Singapore. I want to be there on the spot, talking directly to the police. I feel helpless this far away. The call might still lead nowhere. Ahmad is a slippery fellow. In any case," Hussein said lowering his voice, "I want to see An Mei. She must be in Singapore. I have already asked them," he nodded his head in the direction of the policemen, "to follow up on the lead and find An Mei. The immigration authorities must have a record of her whereabouts."

"So what will you do if you find her?"

"Father I want her back. If I can find our son, then I think that I will stand a better chance of doing so and mother might not object like she did previously. Surely the old obstacles no longer apply. I am already established."

"What if she refuses?"

"I don't know," said Hussein. "I'll take one step at a time. The most urgent matter now is to find my son."

"If An Mei refuses, it is alright with us, so long as we have the boy. Warn her. If she refuses, then we'll take her to court for the boy. I cannot let your mother suffer with another loss of a grandchild!"

Hussein looked at his father's stern and dogged face and turned away.

Chapter 40

The room was ice cold. The air conditioner was going full blast, pumping out cold air relentlessly. *Brump brump*, the machine clanked every now and then in protest at its hard labour. An Mei held on to Mark's hand, her fingers twined tightly in his. She was drawn and pale, so pale that the dark shadows of her lower eyelids looked bruised. Several times she blinked, unable to take in all that the policeman was saying to her. The many sleepless nights had taken their toil.

She turned to Mark seeking comfort. He smiled and squeezed her hand reassuringly.

"Mam," Detective Superintendent Kam's voice rose a notch higher. "Do you hear me? We know about Ahmad. Your son's father has already been in touch and he is on his way here. We might have some leads as to the whereabouts of Ahmad with his help and we will keep you informed. So far, however, our immigration records have shown up nothing. He might have entered Singapore with a false passport. There is nothing to indicate he is on the island. Neither the records in the airport nor the checkpoint at the Johor causeway, show he is here."

He looked at her sternly. He glanced at Mark and then back at her. Mark could sense his disapproval.

"In the meantime," he said, "I would like you to remain in Singapore and let us know if Ahmad or anyone else gets in touch with you. Please do not do anything on your own. Your son's life might be in danger."

She sat very still; she made no reply; her eyes turned vacant, a veil descended on her obliterating all light. Then she shook; her body trembled and her teeth chattered. She could not stop. Her greatest fear had come to pass. Hussein knows about Tim.

"Mam, mam, do you understand what I am saying. Get an ambulance! Quick!" he ordered his underlings, his earlier severe expression gone from his face. "You! Get her a glass of water!" Suddenly the room was filled with frantic activity as officers rushed to do Detective Superintendent Kam's bidding.

"No! We don't need an ambulance. We have a doctor at home. Just ... just let us be for a few moments," said Mark. He took An Mei in his arms and whispered in her ear. "It will be fine. At least we have a lead to Tim's whereabouts." He continued stroking her head until her trembling stopped. He reached out for the glass of water brought in by a policeman and gave it to An Mei, coaxing the glass to her lips.

"Hussein will take Tim away from us." Her voice was hoarse. She held on tight to Mark in an attempt to draw strength from his body. She had run from Hussein and the clutches of his family. For four years she thought she had succeeded; now it would seem all her efforts had been futile and the inevitable had happened. She blamed herself for being careless, to have thought that Singapore was safe.

He felt her despair and held her tighter.

"He won't; we'll fight that. The important thing is we now have a lead. Let's focus on that."

"Promise me, you will not let Hussein take Tim from us."

"I promise. I will do my utmost to fight him, but it is you who will have to be strong."

Mark saw the flash of uncertainty in An Mei's face; his heart sank. He turned her around gently tilting her face up until she looked at him. "You have to fight your corner. Will you be able to stand up to him?"

* * * * *

A shaft of light from the street seeped into the bedroom as the curtains blew gently inwards. It lit up the bed. An Mei turned to look at Mark. He was sleeping soundly; his chest rose and fell under the bed covers. She crept out of the bed, taking care not to disturb him. She padded barefoot out of the bedroom and made her way downstairs towards the kitchen. The clock chimed four o'clock. The kitchen light was on. She heard the humming of a kettle and the sounds of cupboard doors being opened softly and jar tops turned. She pushed open the door. Nelly turned, saw her, and then turned back to the cupboard, shutting its door firmly.

"Tea? Coffee?" she asked.

An Mei shook her head. She went to the fridge and took out a jug of water, pouring herself a large tumbler. She drank deeply from it. She felt its icy coldness rush through her and shivered.

"Did you sleep?" asked Nelly.

"Yes, a bit. I tossed and turned for some time before I finally fell asleep. What time did Mark come up to bed, do you know? I didn't hear him."

"I don't know. It must have been very late because he was still up when I went to bed at half past one. He was making many phone calls, jotting down notes and chewing on his pencil until it must be frayed. He was working so hard that I could see his exhaustion from where I was, some ten feet away." Nelly blew gently on the steam coming up from her mug of hot tea. "He loves you, you know."

An Mei chewed her lower lip and looked intently into her empty tumbler as though she was trying to fathom what else could be in the glass. "I do," she whispered.

"Jane spent some time with him after she put her baby to sleep. She told me that he was trying to check up on paternity testing. He called up some old friends in the UK who might know." Nelly placed her mug down and sighed. "He told Jane he is worried, as we are, that Hussein would take Tim from us and is desperately trying to anticipate the actions that Hussein might take."

"I won't be able to bear it," cried An Mei. "I can't even bear to think about it right now."

"You have to be strong."

An Mei stood very still; a sense of frustration grew in her. "Again that phrase," she muttered to herself. "Everyone says I have to be strong. What do they mean? How strong can I be?"

"You are not going to crumble when you see Hussein, are you?" asked Nelly anxiously. "You don't have any feelings for Hussein any more, do you?"

There was a moment of hesitation, then, An Mei shook her head vigorously, "No! I have no feelings for Hussein except pity and contempt. Contempt for someone who has sold his soul in pursuit of ambition," she said.

Nelly continued to look at An Mei, her eyes were wary. She opened her lips as though she wanted to say more. She hesitated. Then she reached out and clasped An Mei's arm and squeezed it gently.

* * * * *

Ahmad made his way to the rear of the large double story house that had hosted and fed his gambling compulsion over the past couple of years. It had seen better days. In its prime, it must have been a handsome building, more a mansion than a house. Now, age and decay marked its outer walls.

A bare light bulb lit the narrow passageway. Crates of beer, piled high, lined one side of the wall; his shoes crunched on loose tiles that were worn and stained. He stopped, and then continued at a slower pace, careful not to make any more noise. A bemused look appeared on his face as he made a mental calculation of the amount that Ah Cheong must draw in from this gambling den alone. Yet his office was little more than a hovel.

He came to the end of the corridor. A door barred with iron stood before him. Not a hole, he corrected himself, a prison. He rang the bell. He had seen Ah Cheong making his way here and he had done a recce of it previously. He was sure he would find him. The door opened and a man appeared. He wore a sleeveless thin white cotton undershirt over a pair of loose black cotton trousers. A cotton string belt was tied around his waist. Beyond him, he could see Ah Cheong seated at a desk. A portable fan stood on the desk; it turned listlessly circulating hot air in the room.

"I would like to see Ah Cheong," he said.

"Who are you?"

"Your boss knows me. Tell him I have a business proposition for him," Ahmad said raising his voice deliberately.

"Huh! Business proposition? What business proposition? *Pergi!* Go!" said the man, waving Ahmad away.

From over the man's shoulder, covered with tattoos of intertwining dragons, Ahmad could see Ah Cheong. Their eyes met. A moment's hesitation and then Cheong tilted his head in the direction of Ahmad. "Let him in," he said, lighting up a cigarette. "So a business proposition!" Switching to Mandarin, he repeated to his underling with a cackling laugh. "*Ta shuo ta yao gei wo sheng yi ji hui.*"

"Yes!" said Ahmad, "one that might be profitable for you."

"Sit! Tell Me!" Ah Cheong smiled with amusement.

* * * * *

Aquino waited outside. His master was late as usual. It depended on how the game was going. He squatted down beside the car. It was good that I gave the little boy some food, it looks like being a long night, he thought. There were other cars parked in the grounds. Minutes passed; some people were leaving the building and making their way towards the cars parked adjacent to his. He shifted on his haunches, alert.

"So the boss has agreed," Aquino heard one say. The glow from his cigarette burned bright lighting up his nose. A thin jagged scar ran from below his right ear to the corner of his mouth.

"Yes! Looks like it. It seems that if he didn't, he wouldn't be repaid no matter what he might threaten to do. You can't squeeze juice out of an empty bottle. So the boss had to go along with his proposal to salvage what he can; no doubt he has been promised a very big share."

"Where will it be done?"

"We'll use one of the small islands."

"There must be thirty or more of them off Singapore. Pulau Jong, Pulau Berani, Pulau Hantu, Pulau Busing ... which one?"

"I don't know. They are keeping it to themselves. We are only the small cogs in a big wheel with no power and influence. So mind your own business. Just make sure you have the boat ready and filled up for the journey. We will be leaving tonight. They will probably let us know at the very last minute."

The two men went their separate ways.

Aquino kept very still. He understood the gist of the conversation carried out in a mix of Chinese, English and Malay, at least enough to make him uneasy. He stood up. His legs were numb and he shook the circulation back into them holding on to the car for support. More people were coming out of the building. He saw his boss; he saw him shake the hand of the long tall Chinese man they called Ah Cheong. He waited; he broke into a cold sweat. Was it his boss, Ahmad, they were talking about? Is their boss Ah Cheong?"

He saw Ahmad walking purposefully towards him, and then he stopped half way and walked back to Ah Cheong. He saw Ah Cheong gesticulating in his direction, shaking his head in an emphatic manner. He waited. Ahmad turned again and resumed his stride towards him. Aquino felt his legs tremble with fear. He tried to get hold of himself and dug his heel deep into the tufts of grass round his feet. He felt the hard dry grass scuffing his ankle.

"I don't need you this evening. I am going to give you the evening off. Go somewhere, anywhere. But I want you back by tomorrow morning," Ahmad hollered some twenty yards from him.

"But sir, I do not have a place to go to. Can I go back to the house? I normally sleep on the camp bed in the kitchen. I don't have anywhere to go," he repeated.

"Well, you can't tonight. I have other arrangements. I don't care where you go, just make sure you do not go back to the house until tomorrow morning at eight. Is that too difficult for you? You can stay here if you wish. Sleep in the car. Don't make a fuss. Other people would be overjoyed to have an evening off."

Ahmad stood for a moment glaring at Aquino, daring him to offer further words of protest. Aquino looked away, unable to hold his gaze and too frightened to utter another word. Ahmad sniffed and his eyes narrowed for just a second. Then he turned and made his way back to Ah Cheong.

Aquino watched his departing back; he waited until the two men disappeared back into the building. Then he ran towards the back of the house, keeping to the shadows, until he reached the backyard. All along the wall were boxes and boxes of empty bottles, piled up high. He crept towards the wall. Light poured out through an open window. He slid deep into the shadows between the boxes. He kept very still, anxious not to topple any of the crates. He could hear voices from within. He strained to hear what was being said. He knew that Ah Cheong used one of the back rooms as his office. He had seen his men go in and out through the back door. He looked anxiously at the door. It was shut tight.

He could not hear what was said although he could recognise Ahmad's voice. Suddenly the backdoor crashed open; the boxes round him rattled with the impact. He shrank further into the gap between the crates. Someone came out. Then he heard Ah Cheong's voice.

"Take the jeep, make sure you have a tarpaulin that you can use as a cover. Once you have got the child, go straight to the jetty. The two boys will be waiting for you. Tell them to take you and the kid to Pulau Hantu."

The word *hantu* upset the man. "Pulau Hantu! Someone said that it is just mangroves and black waters. It could be infested with snakes," he said.

Aquino could see the man clearly now; thin, sinewy with a tattoo of coiling dragons that ran from shoulder to elbow. Aquino could see the agitation on his face even from where he was hidden.

"Yes! *Hantu!* Ghosts! Mangroves and snakes! *Mong!* Stupid! *Diu lei loh mo!* F ... your mother! That is why it has been chosen; and the name *Hantu* helps keep people away. Probably like you they fear the devil," said Ah Cheong, hurling more expletives at his underling before returning back to the house.

Aquino waited until the man left and then crept quietly in the shadows until he was some 20 yards from the house. He then ran down the dirt road in the direction of the main roads lit by streetlights. He kept going until he reached a small housing estate. Exhausted, he stopped, gasping for breath. Before him were a row of single-story terrace lodgings; they backed onto a small lane. He saw bicycles parked in the lane. He moved quickly towards them; he snatched one and pushed it forward in a trot; he flung his right leg over the seat and pedalled furiously, swerving dangerously out of the lane, to skid down the hill.

*****

The plane landed with a thud and grind, its twin engines roaring loud on the runway. Over the intercom, the speaker announced. "We have now arrived at Changi airport in Singapore." It droned on about the airport facilities, the penalty for smuggling hard drugs...

Hussein unbuckled his seat belt and stood up, ignoring the request that everyone should remain seated until the seat belt sign was turned off.

"Sir, wait. Please sit down. The plane has not come to a final stop," said the hostess making her way down the aisle, her tight sarong clung to her swaying hips as she made her way towards him. He caught a glimpse of her long legs with each stride she made. He turned away, pulled open the overhead luggage holder and pulled his bag out with force.

"Sir, we are not disembarking as yet. Would you please sit down?" she commanded.

He ignored her and made his way to the exit. She followed in pursuit. He spun around in anger. She stopped mid-stride and looked at him; her eyes wide, filled with apprehension in anticipation of the stream of abuse that normally accompanied irate passengers. She saw a brief flash of anger cross his face and stepped back, but it vanished as fast as it appeared. He smiled, his lips parting to reveal white even teeth. He looked apologetic.

"Sorry," he said. "I just want to be first at the door. I have to leave the plane urgently. Could you help me? Please? I need to be first out when the door opens, that's all. I'm sorry," he repeated.

She was completely disarmed. "Of course sir. Come with me. I'll tell the other flight attendant. We are breaking rules and I don't wish to get into trouble. I shall explain that you need to go to the toilet urgently and that is why I am allowing you to get up before the seat belt sign is off. The door will be opened soon. Come with me."

Hussein saw Ghazali rising from his seat and walking towards him. He followed the hostess and she, ignorant of what was happening, led the way to the exit.

* * * * *

Aquino wheeled the bicycle into the grove of bushes and laid it gently on the ground. He saw the truck, a dark green affair with a tarpaulin thrown roughly in the back. Thick clogs of mud caked the tyres. No one was in the truck even though the engine had been left running. He could hear its hum from where he hid; diesel fumes hung on the night air.

The house was cloaked in darkness, but through one of the windows, he could see a streak of light. It flicked from left to right and then top to bottom. He inched closer, squatting low on his heels. His eyes followed the light as it progressed from one room to another. He knew the house like the back of his hand. Shadows of two men holding torches appeared and disappeared on the wall. Suddenly the lights swivelled and dipped, a cry pierced the air and then silence. He felt his heart quicken, his mouth turned dry. It felt as though dried sawdust had soaked up every bit of moisture in his mouth. Two men came running out carrying a bundle between them. It looked limp and lifeless as it bounced with little resistance to the rough handling by the two men. Aquino shivered; his mouth worked silently in prayer. He waited until the truck drove off. He understood now what had been said outside Ah Cheong's gambling den. He clambered back on the bike and once again pedalled off furiously.

* * * * *

Bang! Bang! Bang! The loud knocks on the door reverberated throughout the house.

Nelly dropped her spoon with a clatter into her bowl of congee; thin twirls of the pale grey rice gruel splattered across her blouse top. She looked across the breakfast table with its boxes of cereals, juice, toasts and fried *yow char kuay* at An Mei. They had risen before dawn, restless, and Jane had prevailed on them to eat because they had not eaten at all the previous day.

An Mei took one look at Nelly and pushed her chair back. She ran to the window, straining to look in the direction of the thumping noise. She pushed the curtains aside impatiently; she could see nothing. The morning mist hung heavy and greyness still prevailed, coloured only slightly by shafts of pale light from a sun that had only just risen. Bobbing heads of the red hibiscus and dense green branches, all but obliterated her view of the path that led to the front door. She ran towards the front lobby, but Mark was already there before her.

"Wait here. I'll check," he said pulling her back. The thumping grew in intensity.

Jane and Nelly joined them, the children jostling and pulling behind them.

"Go in," said Mark shooing them away. He went to the door, lifted the letterbox flap and peeped. He sprung back in surprise. "It's him! It's the man who followed me and told us about Ahmad."

"Open the door," commanded An Mei. "Quick!"

Mark yanked open the door and Aquino stumbled into the hallway.

"*Tuan! Tuan!* Sir, sir! They take little boy. You do something."

"Where? Where have they taken him? Who are they? Who are you?" asked Mark.

Aquino shook; he could hardly stop his teeth from chattering. "I... I am Aquino. They must not know I told you. *Tolong! Tolong!* Please, please you must not tell them. *Jangan chakap dengan polis!* You must not tell the police. I will be in trouble."

Mark took hold of his shoulders bewildered by the mixture of English and Malay. "Get a hold of yourself. You are not making sense. Has Ahmad taken Tim? Is this what you are saying?"

For a few seconds, An Mei looked on, frozen in surprise. Then a cold calmness took over her. At last, the lead to Tim was back. Last night, nothing tangible could be done. She had gone to bed only to jump out of it like a tightly sprung coil. She had tossed and turned. Her mind had been cluttered then. Worry and fear for Tim had chased through her head and with it her fear of meeting Hussein, of what he could do to take Tim away, the power he might still wield over her and a fear of her own weakness. She had so many doubts that she did not know which she feared most. She had felt completely helpless; there was nothing to do other than wait. So her mind had gone in circles, one thought after another. She had lost focus. Now at last they could do something. First they had to get to Tim with this man's help. Then they had to leave the country before Hussein could find her. She felt empathy for the man before her. She understood his plight. She had been through such fears herself.

"Mark!" she said, taking his arm, "mind what you say! Be gentle!" She stood on tiptoe and whispered, "If you do as you did before he will run. You will scare him and he will not help. He is our lifeline. Don't you see? He wants to help despite being clearly very frightened."

Mark saw the change in her. His heart gladdened. This was more the An Mei he knew. He turned back to Aquino. "Look no one is going to the police. No one is going to harm you. Sit down," he said taking hold of a stool, and gently guiding Aquino to it. "Just tell us from start to finish what has happened."

"*Minum!* Drink this," said Nelly handing Aquino a glass of water. He took it and gulped it down. He took a few deep breaths and then told them what he had seen and heard.

After leaving the house, he had pedalled in the direction of the jetty that he had heard Ah Cheong and his underlings speak about. He had no hope of following the jeep. It was too fast for him. But he knew the jetty. He had heard talk of it during the days and nights spent waiting for his master in the car park outside Ah Cheong's gambling den. He knew that murky dealings went on there. He had assumed it involved smuggling of some sort. He had always steered clear of the people involved, pretending a dumbness that earned him the nickname of *tai fan sui, chon chai*, thick like a big sweet potato and stupid boy. So stupid and dumb that they talked freely when he was around. He had to make sure that his guess was right. By the time he arrived at the jetty, the two men and the boat had gone; seemingly vanished into the thin air. The jeep, however, was parked alongside a dirt road, just a hundred yards from the jetty itself.

"I think they took Tim to Pulau Hantu," he said. "I don't know place but I know someone to help us. We need boat.

I have a friend. We are from same island in the Philippines; came on same boat. He knows Pulau Hantu and he says he help."

Mark turned to An Mei and then Nelly. He was wary. He did not feel that they should mount a rescue on their own. He wanted to go to the police. "An Mei?" he asked. He silently mouthed the word police.

An Mei saw the flash of fear in Aquino's eyes. He looked ready to take flight. He shook his head, and pleaded silently with her.

"We don't have time," she said. "Will you go with him? I'll go too."

Mark hesitated. He saw that An Mei wished him to go. He made up his mind.

"No! It's best I go alone with Aquino. It will be dangerous. You stay."

An Mei's agitation grew. She knew that she was putting Mark in danger. Her earlier decision not to involve the police seemed fraught, but she also feared that time would be lost if they went to the police. She had not been impressed with them so far; they had waited hours just to report the incident. She also detected a certain disparagement when they spoke to her. Snippets of their conversation had drifted to her whilst she was in the police station. They had referred to her as that woman with the *ang moh,* red-haired devil. She recalled the Detective Superintendent's face, snide and unfriendly, when he told her he had spoken to Hussein. He referred to Hussein as her husband and had completely ignored Mark.

She grabbed Mark's hand and held on to it tight, not wishing to relinquish it. She prayed that she had made the right decision. She could not bear the thought of something happening to him. She could not bear the thought of Tim in the hands of his kidnappers.

"Go! Go!" said Nelly to Mark. "Decide quick. Time going." She switched to Cantonese addressing An Mei. "*Bei hui dei hui!* Let them go! Think of Tim. I trust Mark. He is a resourceful man and loves Tim."

* * * * *

The sun shone fiercely into Jane's sitting room. Its dazzling rays lit up the white walls and book-lined shelves and filled every corner of the room with a heat that the ceiling fan struggled to disperse. Nelly sat slumped in an armchair. Her shoulders sagged into the back of the seat as she laid her head back. Dark pouches underlined her eyes and her face was a cobweb of tired lines. An Mei, restless, her body tense and stiff with pent-up energy, was like a jack-in-the-box. She stood up to walk only to sit down again as, hemmed in by four walls, there was nowhere to go. She chewed her fingers, biting them until they tingled. Jane had tactfully left the two women and taken the children upstairs to play. She had taken leave from the hospital to stay at hand. Her husband was abroad.

No one spoke. Only the whirring of the ceiling fan broke the silence. An Mei pushed her hair impatiently off her face and with a quick flick of her hand tied it up with a rubber band she had snatched off the shelf. Finally, she sat down, chin hunched into the collar of her tee shirt. Nelly opened her mouth to speak then refrained. She could say little to comfort An Mei; she could say little to comfort herself for that matter. She continued to reproach herself for taking her eyes off Tim when he was in her care in the playground. So both ladies retreated deep into their own thoughts and fears.

The clock chimed mid-day.

"I shouldn't have asked Mark to go. I should have called the police. What have I done? Where are they? What is happening?" An Mei turned to Nelly. "Have I done right?" she asked knowing that there would not be an answer. "Shall I go to the police? They have been away for hours now."

"It's anxiety that makes time go so slowly," replied Nelly. "They need time to go to the jetty and that is a fair distance; then they have to find the Aquino's friend, get a boat and some help to ferry them to the island. Jane has been looking the island up on the map and it is to the south of Singapore. Then, of course, they will have to locate the two men and Tim and even when they do find them, they probably will not be able to rush in and rescue him. They will probably have to wait till dark."

"I was not thinking, was I, when I asked Mark to go? What can he do against two gangsters? Mark has done so much for me and I have so much faith in him that I expect miracles from him. Have I put Mark in danger? Have I put Tim in greater danger?"

She pushed away the lock of hair that had fallen across her eyes and placed both arms around the little bolster that was Tim's bedtime companion; she hugged it tight. He had it since he was a baby, a round soft sausage like pillow with it's white cover and embroidered teddy bears and a drawstring at the end which he chewed to sleep. She buried her nose into it drawing deeply on his scent. She longed to have him back in her arms.

The phone rang. Brrrrrng! Brrrrrng! It's insistent ringing cut through the tense silence.

She snatched up the phone.

"Hello!" she said, her voice hesitant and guarded.

"To whom am I speaking?"

"An Mei."

"This is Kam here, Detective Superintendent Kam. We have met. We have your husband here, Datuk Hussein. We would like you to come to the police station. We will send a car to collect you, say in half an hour."

"He is not my..." but the line was dead. She held the phone some distance away from her, recoiling from it as if it were a serpent. The phone fell from her hand; it dangled from its cable, quivering in protest at its harsh treatment. An Mei stared at the phone, black, ominous writhing at the end of its coiled cable.

She looked at Nelly.

"Hussein is here! So soon!" she said. Her voice was barely audible. "I had hoped that we could rescue Tim and be out of the country, away from his clutches and that of his parents before he had time to find me."

* * * * *

Mark got out of the car. He followed Aquino. They walked quickly along the dirt path. Aquino was almost running to keep ahead of Mark's long strides. Potholes like large washbasins filled with yellow muddy water dotted the way. Here and there clumps of couch grass grew, their broad blades stained a mustard-green. A stray chicken crossed their path; it clucked and protested and then ran tottering towards the bare patch of land that skirted around a cluster of small, dilapidated wooden houses. They were fishermen huts. No one was around, at least not out in the open yard. The fishermen were out at sea and the women were either inside or working in the fish-drying yard in the next village. The salt-filled air blew hot. Brightly coloured sarongs and garments, strung across a makeshift clothesline tied between two coconut palms, danced and fluttered in the air.

"My friend," explained Aquino, "*dudok sana!* He lives over there." He pointed to a small hut built on stilts, situated at the beginning of a small incline. "He mend nets. We came same boat from Philippines many years ago. We got parted when I left detention camp."

Aquino stopped to mime his words with hand gestures. He spoke English well enough although over the years he had become used to mixing his English with Malay words. It made him feel closer to his homeland, nearer the Tagalog he had spoken in the Philippines. The more excited he became, the more jumbled his words became.

"He from fishing family. We close in the camp. We help each other in camp. When I start driving my master to Singapore, I find him. He has a son and he took him to city *makan angin*, for an outing. I wait-wait for my master and see him at bus stop. Since then, we meet up when we can. He'll help us," he said proudly. "He speak good English. His father, teacher, only one not fishing; other uncles all fishing."

"Please, we must hurry," said Mark, impatient to be on his way. "We'll talk later."

"Yes! Yes! Sorry! Sorry!"

They hastened towards the house. Mark felt the sweat pouring off him; his shirt was drenched and the binoculars he had snatched from the house, hung heavy round his neck. When he had set off with Aquino, he had no clear plan of how to rescue Tim. He still had little idea of what to do. He had set out with Aquino on the rescue because of An Mei. He could not fail her. He loved Tim like his own and he could not bear the thought that he might be harmed or frightened. Yet, he was aware of the perils of setting off with someone he did not know and going against the advice of the police. He clenched and unclenched his fists to reduce the tension in his arms, and pulled his cap firmly over his head. He needed that symbolic gesture to stop himself from being distracted by thoughts of what he might or should have done. He strode forward, each stride bigger and faster than the previous one.

"I have to stay on this course now. There is no turning back," he mumbled to himself. They were now cut off from everyone, even An Mei. There did not appear to be a phone line anywhere.

As they approached the hut, a man with cut-off shorts, torn and ragged at the fringes, appeared on the top of the short wooden stairway that led to its doorway. He smiled and waved, gesturing with his hand for them to come over. He waited a few minutes and then turned and went back into the hut. By the time Mark and Aquino reached the bottom of the stairway, he had joined them holding two bottles of Coca Cola.

Mark took the lukewarm bottle and drank thirstily. "Thank you," he said holding the bottle up.

"Good?" the man asked, revealing a row of uneven teeth. They shone white against the dark mahogany of his skin.

"Yes! Very good," Mark replied with a smile. He wanted to ask immediately if the man would help them get a boat to Pulau Hantu, but he held back, unsure of the local etiquette. He looked at Aquino for guidance.

The man sensed the urgency in Mark's eyes. "I'm José," he said. "Aquino has told me. He came to me last night and asked me for help. And I made him go to you. You should decide what to do. We will help. I have a boat ready. I know the island. You tell us what you want to do."

Mark was at a loss. He had no plan. He could not form a plan when he did not know the odds; he did not know the layout of the island, where and how Tim was being kept captive, how many guards there might be. There were so many unknowns.

"Tell me more about the island."

"Come, see here." José took a long stick and began drawing lines on the surrounding sand. He drew two land masses, one bigger than the other, separated only by a small stretch of water. "They are not big islands; the biggest is only two hectares and the small one less than one. Plans are underway to reclaim the surrounding land to enlarge the islands. I know this from the local fishermen; they have been told about the plan by government officials."

He pointed to the gap between the two islands and drew wavy lines to demonstrate. "If they mentioned mangrove swamps, it would probably be here," he said pointing his stick to his roughly drawn map. "The rest of the islands' coastlines are beautiful beaches with wonderful corals and sea life."

Mark looked at him in a new light. José's command of English and the efficient way he described the island kindled his curiosity about the man. He stifled his interest; there were more urgent matters at hand.

Mark stabbed the area between the islands with his finger. "If these are mangrove swamps, how can they hide Tim there? Surely they would have to place him in a house or shelter of some sort? Have you come across any sort of shelter, hut or anything that could be used to hide a little boy?" He felt the hair on his arms rise as he imagined how terrified Tim would be.

"No! Although that does not mean there isn't. I don't fish around that area, but I have been over to the islands with other fishermen. I cannot recall seeing any huts or shelters in the mangrove swamps except here." He pointed to the surrounding sea just beyond the beach adjacent to the swamp. "Here, there are some fishing huts built on stilts in the sea. Some of the huts are connected to the beach by jetties. Any one of these could easily be used as a hideout. There are no other shelters near the mangrove swamps."

"How can we be sure that Tim is in one of these huts?" asked Mark. "Are there any other places that they might use?"

"We cannot be sure unless we get over there and stay and watch out for whoever took the little boy. Aquino, you will recognise them won't you?"

Aquino nodded.

"It's so open. They would see us if we were to try to land on the beach during the day and attempt any sort of reconnaissance or rescue," said Mark.

"Definitely! We should not go on those beaches," agreed José.

"What about at night? Is the visibility good on these islands?"

"It can be poor because of the humidity. Condensation of the moisture in the air when it cools can create a lot of mist."

"Then we have to rescue Tim at night. We have to use the time from now until then to pinpoint the spot where they are keeping Tim captive and work out a detailed rescue plan. How can we keep watch on them?"

"From the mangrove swamps," replied José.

"Is it near enough the beach and the huts? Can they see us if we station ourselves here?" asked Mark pointing to the map.

"They will not see us if we are careful. It is quite dark if you keep well within the bowers of the black mangrove; the cover is quite dense in parts. We cannot take a boat into the swamps; we have to leave our motorboat some distance away. Here, we'll beach it here," José said pointing to a spot on his improvised map, almost opposite from the mangrove. "From here, we would have to use a small canoe and paddle along the coast to the swamp. We can't take a motorboat in because of the mangal roots. The advantage we have is that tonight's visibility will most likely be poor and it will be low tide. It will be shallow enough for us to walk from the mangrove swamp to the huts."

"Then can we go now? Do you have the boats?"

"I have a outboard motorboat and a small canoe which we can tow. They are not mine, but I have use of them. I made all the arrangements after Aquino left me in search of you last night. It will not take long to reach the islands. If they do spot us they would just mistake us for fishermen in search of crabs and prawns. Don't wear that cap; I'll lend you a fisherman's hat. We'll need to darken your skin."

José disappeared into the hut and came out with a jar of brown goo. He smiled sheepishly. "I concocted this in anticipation that you would need some form of disguise. Probably not very good for the skin. Coconut oil and thick dark soya sauce."

"So we are set," said Mark taking the jar. He looked at the two men before him. "Let's do it."

Chapter 41

An Mei closed her eyes and tilted her head to let the hot water stream over her head and face. The surrounding glass panel of the shower misted with the heat. Drop after drop created a tracery down the glass. She turned her back and pressed her forehead on the opposite wall, longing to find comfort in the pelting hot water. The tight knots between her shoulder blades screamed for relief and her head felt tight. Minutes passed. The steam grew in intensity. Yet her head would not clear nor her muscles yield. A sob rose from her throat. She tried to stifle it, only to find herself shaking and breathless. Her legs gave way and she slid down, her back gliding over the wall until she ended sat on the floor of the cubicle.

"Please, please let Tim be returned to me safely," she cried aloud. If someone were to predict, when she was young, how her life would be, she would have thought it a tall story. Every ray of hope she had seemed jinxed. Even the prospect of Tim returning to her was now threatened by the possibility that she would lose him to Hussein.

"An Mei, An Mei! They are here. They have come to collect you," called Nelly. She knocked on the bathroom door loudly, urgently.

An Mei forced herself to rise from the floor. She turned off the tap and using both hands, squeezed her hair dry before stepping out of the shower. She dried herself and carelessly pulled on a pair of trousers and a shirt.

"Please tell them to wait. I am not ready." She wanted time to think, to prepare herself for her meeting with Hussein. How much should she tell them? What would be the consequences if she were to tell them that Mark had gone off in search of Tim? Would it help find Tim or would it reduce Mark's chances of rescuing him?

She stood for a moment to look at her reflection in the mirror. The woman who returned her gaze looked hollow-eyed and pale. "Weak," she said as she grimaced at herself. "How are you going to prevent Hussein from seeing Tim if Mark manages to rescue him?" she asked her reflection. "Won't he recognise Tim as his own?" She took a deep breath.

Her heart to heart talk with Nelly had not eased her other nagging fear. She did not know how she would react when she saw Hussein. Nelly had suspected her unease.

"You have to be strong," Nelly had said. "Think of all the things he did to you, casting you aside without even the decency of saying it to your face. Think of how his family treated you. You must steel your heart! You have to stay firm; you have to fight for Tim and keep him from their clutches."

* * * * *

Detective Superintendent Kam's office was exactly as she had remembered it: bare white walls, brightly lit by fluorescent strip bulbs, and cold. The air conditioner made no concession to the heat outside. Detective Superintendent Kam came out from behind his desk.

"Good to see you," he said, shaking her hand. He gestured in the direction behind her. "I don't have to introduce you; this is Datuk Hussein from Malaysia."

An Mei started. She had not noticed Hussein. She had walked straight into the office and headed straight for Detective Superintendent Kam's desk. She sensed Hussein's eyes boring into her back and she imagined a thousand spidery fingers crawling over her.

"Come," said Kam, "let us sit around the low coffee table, it is more comfortable." He walked over to a coffee table indicating that An Mei should follow him.

She turned to do his bidding and came face to face with Hussein. He was looking at her intently, so intently that she had to turn away briefly to regain her composure. She squared her shoulders and smiled, a merest quirk of her lips, to acknowledge his presence and sat down. She crossed her legs and looked up. He did not let up; he continued looking at her, this time with a smile, half-apologetic. "How are you?" he asked. He tried to engage her eye.

"Shall we get on with why you asked me to come," she said instead turning to Kam.

"Datuk Hussein is here because Ahmad contacted his parents, his mother to be precise, and told her that he has Tim. He asked for a ransom," said Kam. "Ahmad is expected to call again. Datin Faridah, following the advice of the Malaysian police, asked for time to get together the cash he demanded. It apparently irritated Ahmad and he hung up on her. He has yet to make another call. The Malaysian police have now asked for our cooperation and Datuk Hussein is here for this purpose. Of course, you must be aware that the crime has taken place under our jurisdiction and we remain in primary control of the investigation. The call was made from Singapore and so we can assume, until otherwise proven, that Ahmad is still on the island."

"But Tim has nothing to do with my former husband. I do not know why Ahmad called Datin Faridah," said An Mei, still refusing to look at Hussein. "There is no necessity for his involvement."

Detective Superintendent Kam looked from An Mei to Hussein.

"Come, come An Mei," said Hussein, "Ahmad said the boy is the spitting image of me. Surely you are not going to deny that he is my son. Of course, I am involved in this case."

She turned and looked straight at him. "He is not your son. I have not borne any child with you in our short marriage and you know it. If he called your mother, it is to make mischief. I don't think you need to involve yourself in my affairs."

"Even when Ahmad has demanded a ransom from us and he might harm your son, *our* son, if I do not concede to his demand? Would you still insist that I do not get involved?"

She gripped the arm of her chair. "If it is a matter of ransom, we will raise the money."

"But Ahmad did not contact you. If it were just about money, surely he would have got in touch with you first."

Kam placed himself between the two of them. An Mei could picture him as a referee, making a ruling between squabbling players.

"We are here to cooperate for the sake of the child. Whether Datuk Hussein is his father or not is not the immediate or crucial issue here. If Ahmad were to get in touch with Datuk Hussein's family, we would still have to use whatever lead it provides us to trace the child. Hence his cooperation is important. Is that not so? You can sort out the question of paternity afterwards. It is not my concern at this point. Agree?" Kam asked.

An Mei nodded with some reluctance.

"One more question. Where is Mr. Hayes?"

"Mr. Hayes? Who is Mr. Hayes?" asked Hussein, his eyes flashed from one to the other.

"My husband. Tim's father," replied An Mei. She saw the glitter of surprise and anger in Hussein's eyes. She ignored it and turned back to Kam.

"Mark is trying to find Tim. He is out there, looking for people who might have seen our son." She clenched her fist tight and felt her fingernails biting hard into the palms of her hand. It was not quite the truth, but not a lie either.

"You are sure you are not hiding anything from us?" Kam asked.

She nodded, unable to answer in case her voice failed her. She was sure that Kam did not believe her.

"Just keep us informed of anything, anything at all that you hear, see or read. Okay?" asked Kam.

She smiled gratefully, unable to believe her luck to be let off so lightly. She did not know if she had imagined it, but she saw a ghost of a smile from Kam. It was there and gone in a flash. She turned and with a brief nod to Hussein made her way to the door. He was there before her, opening the door for her. She walked purposefully towards the exit of the police station. He followed her, walking by her side, matching her pace.

"An Mei! Can't you look at me? Can't we talk like two civilised adults? I miss you," he said taking her arm to restrain her.

Heads turned to stare at them. A tall, well-dressed, dark Malay man, pursuing a young Chinese lady in trousers. They could see that he was begging and pleading with her; she seemed impervious to his entreaties, angry even. His entourage of what could only be security guards looked on with impassive faces.

She wrenched her arm away and leaned back from him. "We have nothing more to say to each other," she said. "More specifically, I have nothing to say to you. I don't wish to see you again."

"I miss you," he persisted. His voice was soft and cajoling. "Whoever this Mark is, he cannot be as important to you as we were to each other."

"Mark is my husband. You are not fit to mention his name!"

Hussein was stung to the core by her reply. "You cannot mean it. You are just saying it to hurt me. We are soul mates," he continued. "Remember, you are my first and only love and I hope that I am the same way to you."

She turned to walk away. He reached forward to catch her arm again.

"I am here to ask if you would take me back," said Hussein.

She felt herself tremble. She bit her lips to stop the trembling. She knew that if she gave in to herself, she would weaken. She had, for days, this nagging fear of failing herself as she had failed herself so many times before when she was with Hussein. "Retreat into your anger, your pride," Nelly had counselled her over and over again. She thought of her past humiliation. Suddenly her anger flared. The cheek of him! She rounded on Hussein.

"Don't you understand? I don't miss you and I don't want to have anything to do with you," she said. She locked gaze with him for a second. He stepped back, startled by her vehement reply. Without a glance backwards, she hailed a taxi, shutting her ears and mind to his voice.

In the taxi, An Mei sat dry-eyed in the corner. Her body was stiff and tense. She clamped her jaws. She stayed like that all the way back to Jane's house. She had prepared and schooled herself for her encounter with Hussein. It was only when he said he wanted her back that she nearly lost the defence she had created round herself. She could not afford to allow her weakness to show. She was glad for Nelly's advice. If she had not drawn on her anger and pride, she would have shown her weakness. She wished that Mark were with her; she needed his strength, his sensibility and his love. "Mark!" she whispered, "where are you? Where is Tim?" She bowed her head in prayer for their safety, murmuring her prayers over and over again; something she had not done for years.

*****

Ahmad sat alone in the armchair, one leg was slung across the armrest and the other jiggled furiously. The die was cast, he thought. He had broken all ties now and would not be able to return to Malaysia. He would probably not even be able to return to his house in Singapore because his cover must have been blown. Otherwise why had Aquino disappeared?

He mulled over the events that had led to his present predicament. He looked at the bare room with its two tiny iron-barred windows that now served as his safe house, one provided courtesy of Ah Cheong. He closed his eyes in disgust at his surroundings. The unwashed odour of previous inhabitants persisted even in the air he breathed. He had no choice. He had nowhere to go until the ransom money materialised and arrangements for his flight to Indonesia were completed. He had not wanted things to turn out the way they had. He called Faridah, his old ally, in the hope of winning her favour. After all, he would be returning her grandson to her. He heard the joy in her voice, even when he raised the issue of money. She was receptive to his proposal. She believed he had taken the child for her sake. Then it had all changed the second time he called. He had hung up and in anger sought Ah Cheong's help. He realised now that by calling Faridah, he had placed himself in serious jeopardy. He had committed a criminal act, kidnapping. He preferred to think that he had taken Tim to rescue him from the clutches of a wicked infidel, a woman who had cheated her husband and in-laws of a lawful child and grandchild. He had been so sure that Faridah would support him. He even thought he might regain favour in Faridah's household. It must be Hussein's doing that he was now on the run and forced into the hands of Ah Cheong. Anger stirred in him. His involvement of Ah Cheong meant that he had to share his takings.

"I will just have to double it," he said aloud. "I will have to call the boy's mother! Make her stew! Make her pay as well."

Having decided on this new course of action he picked up the phone. He dialled and waited.

"Call this number," he said repeating the number twice to make sure that his accomplice had it correct. "Say that you have the boy. Say you want one million in used notes. Say you will call again to tell them where to deposit it. Warn them of the dire consequences for the boy if they involved the police.

Speak in Chinese and disguise your voice. That should confuse them because by now the police will have been told that I have kidnapped the boy. They will not understand why a Chinese is involved. They expect me to call. Do not make your call from Singapore. Call from Malaysia; call from the state of Johor. That will make them more fearful. An Mei must know that if the child is in Malaysia, her chances of losing him to Hussein and his family will be that much greater since her claim would be challenged in a Shariah court. That should make them more receptive to my demands. It will also stop them from looking in Singapore."

He placed the phone down. There was nothing more he could do. He would have to sit tight and wait.

* * * * *

"For you," said Nelly. She gestured to An Mei to take up the extension. She continued holding the phone to her ear; hardly daring to breathe for fear that she would be heard.

"Who is this?" asked An Mei, her voice anxious.

"Never mind who I am," came the reply. The voice was high and the words clipped and metallic. "All you need to know is that I have your son. And I want you to put together one million dollars in used notes for me. I will call you again in twenty-four hours to tell you where to make the drop. If everything proceeds the way we want, you will have the boy back."

"Who are you? Is this a joke?" asked An Mei bewildered by the voice.

"Joke?" the voice asked. "Here, listen to this."

An Mei heard a scream in the background and Tim's voice shouting, "Mummy! Mummy!"

"Please let me speak to him. Is he alright?" she pleaded. "Don't hurt him."

"If he gets hurt, it will not be because of me. It will be because of you." The voice was teasing; the undertone was full of malice. "You decide whether he should be hurt. An ear off would do nicely. You know the consequences if you do not do as we tell you or if you go to the police. I will call you again."

"Hello! Hello! Please! Please!" pleaded An Mei. She looked up to see Detective Superintendent Kam indicating with his finger rotating around his ear. "Keep talking," he mouthed silently.

"I will do as you say. You say in used notes. Does it have to be a particular denomination? Are we talking about Singapore or Malaysian Dollars?"

Silence.

"Hello! Hello! Are you there?" asked An Mei frantically.

A string of curses followed. "Singapore dollars of course! What do you take us for? Small denominations, twenty and fifty dollars, will do."

"But it will be bulky."

"Do as you are told!"

The phone went dead.

An Mei stared gaunt-eyed at Nelly. "What shall we do?" she asked. Strands of hair came loose from her ponytail. They fell forward making an untidy halo around her pale cheeks.

Detective Superintendent Kam came forward. "You did well. You kept the person long enough for us to trace the call. We will try to unscramble the voice. It did not sound natural, too high pitched, too clipped, too much resonance in the background and what a strange accent!"

Suddenly, An Mei began to feel grateful for his presence. Detective Superintendent Kam had arrived not long after she returned home to Nelly. She had been vehement in her protests. She did not want his intrusion and feared that he would continue questioning her about Mark's absence. She feared that she would not be able to continue with her deception. Kam had calmly ignored her protests and set up a surveillance team in anticipation of a call from Ahmad. Telephone lines were rigged and a host of equipment was set up in the living room. His manner towards her, although distantly polite, did not have the scorn he had shown when he first interviewed her.

"What about the money? We need time to raise that amount and to have it in cash," said An Mei. "Jane and her husband have agreed to put up some and Jeremy, my aunt's son, has contacted the bank he used to work for to stand as surety for a loan."

"We'll take care of it; we'll speak to the bank as well," Kam said.

An Mei took a deep breath. She turned and collapsed into Nelly's arms. All energy sapped out of her.

"Don't worry," whispered Nelly. "I think Kam is now on our side."

"Why? Why did he change his mind?"

"I am sorry but I told him your background, the whole story. I had to, to win him over."

"Was that why you cornered him as soon as he arrived and took him to the den?" said An Mei.

"I told him before that. In fact, soon after you left for the police station to meet with Hussein. I called him because I thought you would need help when you came face-to-face with Hussein," said Nelly.

An Mei looked over Nelly's shoulder at Detective Superintendent Kam. He caught her eye.

"Will you please tell us where Mr. Hayes is? We cannot believe that he would leave you on your own at a time like this," said Kam.

* * * * *

Mark sat cramped in the canoe with Aquino. Just over two feet wide, there was hardly any space to move. They did not speak. The heat enveloped them. The soft sound of water lapping against the side of their boat mingled with the distant calls of seabirds and waves crashing on the adjacent shores. They sat watching the fishermen's huts on stilts. Each hut was connected to the beach by a long wooden jetty. The front of the huts looked out to sea. Everything was still. Water rose high on the stilts of the huts, leaving them barely two feet clear of the waves. The hours passed. There were no movements, no sign of people. A strong wind blew, clouds gathered to form big foams of cotton wool. Suddenly, the weather changed. Purple clouds gathered, turning darker and darker. A red tinge of fire outlined their burgeoning form. Then a flash of lightning was followed by a burst of thunder. The skies opened releasing a deluge of torrential rain that obscured their vision. They lost sight of the huts. Then as suddenly as it started, the rain stopped. Water dripped down from the mangrove bowers. Drip, drip, drip!

Mark saw a figure appear from the hut nearest to them. He looked through the binoculars. He watched as the man lit up and smoked; halos of smoke puffed and disappeared into the air. The glow of his cigarette burned bright.

Mark turned to Aquino and gave him the binoculars. "Do you recognise him?"

"Yes! That's one of them," said Aquino.

"Are you sure?"

"Yes! He had tattoo on shoulder and arm. I saw when he lifted arm to smoke."

Suddenly, the man flipped the cigarette butt over the jetty and sauntered back into the hut.

"That must be the hut where Tim is being held," whispered Mark.

Aquino tilted his head skywards. "Night soon. Sun already setting," he said, pointing to the horizon.

Mark looked in amazement at the sunset: red, fiery with little sign of the tropical storm of just minutes ago. Still they waited, cramped together in the canoe. They watched as the waves retreat from the shoreline. Each wave smaller than the next until they were just ripples lapping on the fine sand. Low tide! His heart thumped faster and faster. It would soon be time to make their first move. The canoe settled lower and was almost touching the bottom. Thick roots of the black mangrove emerged, gnarled, contorted. Some distance away, he saw a snake slither away.

"Look!" whispered Aquino. A man appeared outside the hut. Mark snatched the binoculars from Aquino.

"It is not the same man! So there are at least two of them."

Mark panicked. He had hoped that there would only be one guard. José had told him that the truck that had been there earlier had left the jetty sometime during the night. From this, he had assumed that only one of the men had stayed behind with Tim. It was clear now that someone else had come to pick up the truck. Mark reached into the depth of the canoe and took out a knife and an axe that José had given him. "I hope we do not have to use these," he said with a grimace.

A noise came from behind them.

"Did you hear that?" asked Aquino, turning sharply round to face Mark.

Mark sat still straining to hear. Then almost imperceptibly he heard the rhythmic sound of movements; people ploughing through thick slush and mud. The sound got closer and closer. Figures emerged from the direction where they had left José and the boat. He crouched into the canoe, making his body flat. Aquino followed suit. The canoe wobbled dangerously. He could hardly breathe as his knees dug into his ribs; his back strained and stretched in the unfamiliar position.

"Heh! Heh! It's me, José."

Mark straightened up immediately. He saw José. With him were five other men. They carried arms and were holding them chest high well clear of the muddy slush of the swamp they were threading through.

"What...?" Mark, taken by surprise, did not finish his sentence. His eyes narrowed as he examined José's companions. He recognised one of them: Kam, the Detective Superintendent. He held his breath. Why was Kam with José? How did José bring him here? He glanced at Aquino trying to read his expression. He did not see anything beyond surprise in his face. So, had he been duped by his friend? Did José have a prior arrangement with Detective Superintendent Kam to trap him? How did Kam know of their whereabouts?

Mark was disconcerted by the turn of events. He had hoped to rescue Tim and flee with him and An Mei back to England. There he believed they would have greater legal leverage. From what he had heard, they would have a hard time convincing a

Shariah court in Malaysia that An Mei should have custody of the child. He was hopeful they would fare better in a civil court and to fight in a civil court they had to be away from the Malaysian jurisdiction. He feared that with Kam's intervention, they would not be able to leave quickly and easily. Yet at that very moment, despite his apprehension that he would not be able to spirit An Mei and Tim away, he was secretly relieved. He was glad to see Kam and his reinforcements. He knew deep down that their chances of rescuing Tim would be significantly improved with them and the law on their side. He would just have to take one problem at a time.

"So," said Kam as he approached the canoe. He studied Mark at length, opened his mouth as if to speak, then closed it again. He shrugged his shoulders. "I'll keep what I wanted to say until later when we have got the boy. I want you to stay here. We'll surround the hut. It is already dark and the water has receded almost completely. In this low tide, it will not be difficult. The soft sand will muffle the sound of our footsteps. We have a helicopter as back up. It will keep some distance away so as not to attract attention. It will come in only at the last moment."

"No! Please let me come with you," pleaded Mark, "I will not be in your way. Tim will not be as frightened if he sees me coming to the rescue. He might scream if he sees your men and that would alert the two men, even if you succeed in getting to the hut."

Kam hesitated for a moment. "Right, let's go! You just follow and keep out of the way. Do exactly as I tell you."

* * * * *

Kam and his police commandoes spread out, moving in a pincer-like formation towards the hut where the two men had emerged earlier. They walked soft-footed across the sand, carrying their arms. Footprints formed and vanished, washed away by the lapping waves of the receding tide. Their bodies cast long shadows in front, like shadow puppets mimicking and pre-empting their every movement. Mark kept close to Kam. They crouched low as they moved forward. They kept their eyes fixed firmly on the hut in case one of the occupants should come out and somehow manage to spot them in the dark. The distant roar of the sea camouflaged all sound. Within minutes, they reached the base of the stilts. Kam motioned everyone to move into position. Two of the commandoes clambered up a stilt with the aid of a rope thrown around an anchor post on the jetty. Once on top they laid belly down on the jetty a short distance from the hut, their guns pointed at the doorway. In the meantime, the two other men clambered up a pair of stilts directly below the hut itself. They moved quickly and climbed with simian-like agility. They grasped the stilts as high as they could, then drew up their knees. Clutching the stilts firmly with their feet, they straightened their legs pushing their bodies further up the stilts and reached upwards with their arms. Once again they grasped the stilts, drew up their knees and repeated the climbing sequence. The movements were fast, graceful, effortless. They pulled themselves up and clambered onto a wooden platform that ran around the hut, then made their way towards the doorway. Once there, they drew their firearms and stood with their backs flat against the wall.

The sound of music drifted from the hut, interspersed by harsh guttural swearing. Dice were thrown and cards were unveiled. Slap! Slam! A child whimpered. A string of expletives followed, "*Diu lei loh mo!* F... your mother! Stop crying!"

Mark placed a foot forward, ready to sprint to the jetty. He looked at Kam who shook his head and silently mouthed, "No! Follow me."

Kam moved round the stilts supporting the hut with Mark close on his heels. Kam knew these fishing huts would have another exit in addition to the main one that led out to the jetty. To the front of the hut, facing the sea, there was a door that opened on to a platform used for casting fishing nets. Now, with low tide, the drop from the platform to the ground was great. It was unlikely that anyone would choose to jump from that height, but, still, precautions must be taken, thought Kam. He could not spare any of his men to keep watch here; he needed them to guard the front exit, which the two thugs were most likely to use to escape. He motioned Mark to station himself below the exit that faced out to sea, pointing upwards to tell him to keep watch. That should keep Mark out of the way, he thought, and he might be useful in the unlikely event that someone did decide to jump. He left Mark and made his way towards the jetty, to the men he had left there.

Suddenly one of Cheong's men appeared at the doorway leading out to the jetty. He sauntered nonchalantly out of the hut, one hand dug deep into his trouser pocket fishing out his pack of cigarettes. He turned to speak to the man within. A sudden movement by the doorway caught his eye. He opened his mouth to shout a warning, but the policeman who had been laid on his belly was already moving forward. He took him from the behind, pressing one arm around his victim's throat in a stranglehold and using his free hand to twist the man's right arm behind his back. They fell with a thud! Immediately the rest of the police force rushed forward. The lights went out in the hut and it was engulfed in darkness momentarily before the powerful torches of the police lit the area.

"Give up! You are surrounded! Hand over the boy!" Kam's voice boomed through a loud hailer. "Walk out with both hands on your head."

"I have the boy and I have a knife to his throat!" shouted the accomplice from within.

"You would not wish to harm the boy. It will only add to the seriousness of your crime. Hand over the boy peacefully and we will take this into account. This is your only chance for reprieve."

Silence followed.

At the opposite end of the hut, Mark stood below the platform and the seaward exit, every sinew in his body ready for action. He was half-hidden by the protruding planks as he peered intently through the gaps between them at the exit. Suddenly, the shadow of a man appeared barely visible against the dark night sky. Like lightning he leapt clear off the platform. He landed badly on his back with one leg caught twisted beneath him. Mark saw the struggling bundle that the man was trying to hold. Mark stepped forward and quickly grabbed the bundle from the man and embraced it in his arms. Within seconds, Kam's men surrounded them.

Chapter 42

The book lay open on An Mei's lap, unread. All around her was darkness except for the light coming from the solitary table lamp behind her. She flipped through the pages at random; the text appeared like meaningless squiggles. She snapped the book shut. She could not read. She could not concentrate. Torturous thoughts tormented her ever since Detective Superintendent Kam left. She had told him all she knew of Mark and Aquino's whereabouts. Now all she could think of was Tim and Mark. Has Kam found them? She could not bear to think of the danger they must be in, danger that she had put them in. She could not dismiss from her mind visions of what might be happening. She worried and fretted. Over and over again, she prayed. "Please, please, let them return safely."

The door opened. Nelly came in. She took one look at An Mei and said, "Go to bed. Take a rest. I'll sit up and wait."

"I can't." An Mei looked at the clock. "You go back to bed. There is absolutely no need for you to be tired as well.

"I'll make some tea," replied Nelly. "Why don't you lie ... look!" A sudden flash of light caught her attention. She pointed to the window. Two cars had swerved into the street. The rotating beams of the lights perched on top of them lit up the road and penetrated into the room. An Mei rushed to the door. The doors of the cars opened. A policeman came out of one of them, followed by Mark, holding Tim.

"Mummy, Mummy!" shouted Tim.

Mark released him and he ran as fast as his little legs would take him to An Mei. She scooped him up into her arms and snuggled her nose into his little body, covering his face with kisses. Tears rolled down her face. Mark reached her and took her in his arms, with Tim squashed between them. They laughed. Joy, pure joy bubbled out of them. Yet, they cried. Their eyes streamed. Nelly looked on and reached for her shirt ends, bringing them to her eyes as she too joined in their happiness and relief.

Kam came forward. He did not wish to interrupt their joyful reunion, but he was in a hurry. He stood aside for a moment watching them. He cleared his throat. They were totally wrapped up in each other. They did not hear him. He was forced to interrupt them. "Mmm! Excuse me, but I have to leave. The two men have been taken straight to the police station for questioning and I have to be there. I hope that it will not be long before we catch Ahmad. I am sure we can make them talk. We'll take Aquino with us. He will be useful."

The smile on An Mei's face vanished. She had forgotten about Aquino. A feeling of guilt and apprehension crossed her face. She looked at Mark and then at Kam. "Will Aquino be all right?" she asked. "I have reneged on my promise not to tell the police. He fears the police. He fears that he will be deported. We promised him he would come to no harm and that he would be able to stay. At least, let that promise be kept."

Kam looked at her sternly. "It is not your place to promise him something that you have no authority over. As far as we are concerned, if he is a bona fide visitor in Singapore and not an illegal immigrant he will not be deported from Singapore for illegal entry. I have no idea of his status in Malaysia. That would be a matter for the Malaysian authorities. However, as to the role he played in the kidnapping, it is a different matter..." Kam let his sentence hang.

"If it were not for him we would not have found Tim. I would hope that will count for something. In any case, he was forced into the situation and came to us as soon as he could," protested Mark. He looked beyond Kam's shoulder. Aquino was looking at him, his face, white with fear. "Please sir, if there is any leniency that can be applied to his case, I would appreciate it. I'll stand guarantor."

Kam swept his eyes over Mark. "You sir will also need to come to the station to make a statement. There are many questions to be answered. Your interference with the law, trying to take the matter of rescue into your own hands, obstructing police work are all serious matters."

Mark kept silent.

"It's my fault," said An Mei. "I persuaded him to do it."

Kam regarded her with his steady gaze. He had been struck by what Nelly had told him about An Mei's situation. His view of her had changed dramatically since then. When he first saw her with Mark, he had allowed his own bias to see her as an *ang moh* lover, a woman that prefers white skin. He had been contemptuous then, especially when Hussein called to say that he was her husband. Now he saw her differently and with compassion. So he softened his stance and returned his attention to Mark.

"However, Mr. Hayes has also shown exceptional courage during the rescue. We'll leave this for tomorrow because we have more urgent matters to attend to. But both of you are not to leave the country. We'll call for you tomorrow."

*****

An Mei tucked a blanket around Tim and straightened his bedclothes. She kissed his cheek, stroked it and bent once more to kiss it, lingering on to smell him, his little boy scent. It was a habit that she had not been able to cast aside. She had to restrain herself from picking him up and pulling him close to her again. Mark placed his arm around her shoulder and took her hand. "Let him sleep. He is exhausted and so are you," he said, leading her away.

They had made up a little bed in their bedroom in Jane's house, unwilling to let Tim out of their sight. They walked to the far end of the room and sat down, sharing a low seat by the bay window. An Mei placed her head on Mark's shoulders. She felt safe when he was around. It felt like he had taken on her burden and worries, and made a cocoon for her to nestle in. She felt loved and needed. It was sufficient that he was there. She sighed and closed her eyes and began to drift off.

Out of nowhere, Hussein's face came to her mind's eye, another love, a different love, a different time. For a split second, she felt its pull and was confused. She struggled, shaking her head to will the image away. She woke herself up. She opened her eyes wide and turned to look at Mark. She needed to affirm that it was a dream. He looked at her mystified. "What's up?" he asked.

"Nothing," she replied. She drew her finger along his face, down his nose and jaw line seeking to imprint his face in her mind. She sought to wipe out the image of Hussein. She kissed Mark, gently on his lips and his eyebrows and then more fervently. He held her tight. They sat not speaking, his arms around her. Her serenity returned. With it came complete relaxation; then exhaustion hit her. The room fell quiet. Her eyelids grew heavy and she dozed off. Mark saw her sleep; his eyelids began to droop and within minutes he too fell fast asleep.

At the break of dawn, An Mei stirred. And with that awakening came a crush of all the worries that had been temporarily pushed aside by sheer exhaustion. She squirmed from under the weight of Mark's arms and sat upright, the tension in her body returned as though she had never rested. Every muscle in her body felt tight. She could feel it in her neck, between her shoulder blades. Mark woke up and rubbed his bleary eyes. When he opened them, he could see the anxiety on her face.

"We did not have a chance to talk last night," said An Mei immediately. Her voice was urgent. "Hussein is here, in Singapore, and I met him. He believes that Tim is his. I told him Tim was yours, but I do not think he believed me." She broke off. A heat seemed to have risen from the depth of her to fill her chest and lungs. She had no tears. She had used them all up. The inevitable had arrived and she would have to face up to it. "Now, begins another battle," she said. Her voice was resigned.

Mark moved closer to comfort her; he felt deeply her despair.

"I so, so fear losing Tim. Tell me, what shall we do?" asked An Mei.

"We will have to wait to see what Hussein wants. He might not pursue us if we can convince him that Tim is not his. After all he has not made any effort to look for you all these years." Mark was wary whenever he spoke of Hussein to An Mei. In the past he had not wished to delve too closely into An Mei's feelings for her former husband for fear that he might discover something he would prefer not to know. The past was the past. The circumstances had changed now. Hussein was with them and Mark felt he had to tackle the issue headlong. He watched his wife intently to see how she would respond.

An Mei looked away unable to bring herself to tell Mark what Hussein had said to her; that he wanted her back. A hatred and anger rose in her when she thought of what Hussein had said. It was not only anger against Hussein but also an anger directed at herself. She was angry that he had managed to stir something that she thought was long dead. He had managed to disturb her peace with a mere sentence. She still thought of what could have been. She despised herself for her weakness. She could not understand why she was doing this to herself. Was it because she hankered for what she could not have and in the process prized too low a love that she did have?

Mark withdrew his arm from around her; he sensed that she was withholding something from him. Her face was an open book. The wistfulness had lit her eyes for but a second when he mentioned Hussein, but he saw it as though it was written in bold letters. Hurt and anger took over. "Huh! Where is this Chinese inscrutability that people speak about," he mumbled to himself. He went to Tim's bed and bent over to kiss him lightly. He grabbed a shirt and headed for the door. Jealousy filled him; and fear, fear of losing her.

"Mark!"

"I'm going for a walk."

"We need to talk."

"Yes! We do, but I need to think first. You do too."

"Please!"

He went back to her. "I'm not angry, just hurt. Until you tell me everything we cannot be talking truly. I am leaving you some space to think, as I need to think myself. If you wish to keep Tim, if *we* wish to keep Tim," he corrected himself, "we must not return to Malaysia where we will immediately come under a legal jurisdiction about which we know so little. I have been doing a bit of research and have called up old friends in the UK on claims of paternity. We'll discuss this when I come back."

He hesitated a moment and then planted a kiss her on her forehead and left. She watched his departing figure, the slump in his shoulder. A deep remorse welled up in her. She went back to Tim. She stood looking at her son, trailing her finger on his sleeping form. "Mummy is a fool," she said to him. "What an idiot I am." For in that instant when Mark turned away and left, she knew that between the two men, she valued and loved Mark more. What she felt for Hussein was nothing more than nostalgia for something that never really was. She suddenly felt afraid. She feared she might lose Mark.

A shadow fell across the bed. She looked over her shoulder.

"An Mei," said Nelly. "Why did Mark leave? What have you said to him? He looked so sad, so bewildered."

"I have been stupid."

"Is it Hussein? Think carefully. He is not worth it."

"I know, I know. I keep thinking of the past, of the good times, the love that Hussein and I had when we were young and a sense of regret keeps returning to my thoughts. It keeps drawing me back. At the same time, I feel anger and shame; I am ashamed of myself. I feel that I am betraying Mark even by having these thoughts."

An Mei pressed her fist between her breasts. She needed the physical pressure to relieve the pain building within her. "I am all muddled up. Deep down I know Mark loves me. I trust him. He would not betray me like Hussein has done. And I do love Mark. I will not trade him for Hussein. Believe me. Now I have hurt Mark. He knows that I am keeping something back from him. I did not tell him about Hussein's proposal that we get back together. If I tell him now, he will be suspicious; he will think I am contemplating that possibility. I have made him distrust me by holding back information from him."

Nelly walked round the bed to face An Mei. "I think you have to be clear and truthful to yourself. Love is not just sexual love; it goes deeper; it is about friendship and trust as well. The first may decline with time. Friendship and trust, however, last and will stand the test of time."

Chapter 43

Hussein marched, with Ghazali close on his heels, into the Detective Superintendent's office without knocking. He went straight to the desk. He spread his arms out wide and gripped the edge of it. His knuckles, little bony protruding hillocks, waxed white with the hardness of the grip. He stood for a moment bent over the desk, shoulders hunched up, aggressive, his eyes glaring at Kam's bowed head. Kam looked up in surprise. Before he could say anything Hussein sat down; one leg crossed over the other to reveal the sharp crease of his trouser leg; his elbows resting on the armrest, hands linked together in front. He looked in utter command of himself. He wanted to convey that message. He wanted Kam to know that he expected him to obey his commands.

Kam's displeasure was thinly veiled. He made no effort to get up from his desk. He knew that he should have stood up to acknowledge the presence of a Minister, even if this was an unofficial visit. Resentment made him pose a counter argument. Hussein was a Minister but not in Singapore; he had not made any attempt to follow any rules or code of behaviour and could not swagger in and expect everyone to be at his beck and call. He reflected on his conversation with his superior. He had said, "Grant our neighbour help, of course, but I leave it to you to show judgement. On no account, should you give the impression that our police force is subservient to theirs."

Kam knew that relationship between Singapore and Malaysia had its up and downs. He knew that in the past month, it had soured somewhat. He knew also that this decline was transitional and would pass, just as in the past. Singapore had made rapid progress in its manufacturing industry and its northern neighbour remained a major source of raw materials. It also provided a major market for the manufactured products. In fact, it was impossible not to be aware of the ties of geography, economics and kinship. Even his Prime Minister, Lee Kuan Yew, had made reference to it. Yet, his resentment at being treated like a flunky clouded his thoughts, even though he knew that his job could be at stake if he made an undiplomatic blunder. No wonder, he mused. His thoughts strayed to what Nelly had told him about An Mei and his sympathy for her became doubly reinforced.

Kam nodded to the police officer in the doorway, indicating that the situation was under control. It was necessary. He had lost face even in his own office. The officer had hurried after Hussein in an attempt to stop him from barging into Kam's office and had witnessed his superior's helplessness in handling the situation.

Hussein fumed, impatient with Kam's slow acknowledgment of his presence; he was taken aback by what he considered a lack of courtesy. Over the past few years, he had grown accustomed to having his words hung onto by all and sundry.

"You have found my son?" he growled.

"We have found Tim, the little boy."

"Why was I not informed immediately?" Hussein glared at him.

"We informed our Malaysian counterpart, the police, immediately. We would have called you this morning but you have already pre-empted us." Kam looked at his watch to illustrate the earliness of the hour. It was, after all, only just after eight in the morning and he had been up all night.

"Where is he now?"

"With his parents."

"Mind what you say!" Hussein's voice grew louder. He half rose from his seat and wagged his finger. "Mind what you say. I am the father. You remember that."

"Sir, Datuk," said Kam, his tone conciliatory, reasonable, "all I know is that I returned the child to the mother. The mother says that the father is Mr. Hayes. I am not here to judge. Both Mr. and Mrs. Hayes reported the kidnap to us and we, the Singapore police, executed the rescue successfully. You, sir, reported that someone called Ahmad had kidnapped a child, whom you believe is yours. You have not met this said child. The mother has said it is not yours. We are in the process of interrogating the two men found holding the child. We will report to you the progress we make in the case. If there is a link between the two men and *Encik* Ahmad, I will keep you informed."

Kam stood up. He extended his hand.

"Sir! Datuk Hussein! Thank you for coming to our office."

"I have not finished with you," growled Hussein. "Who are you to keep my child from me. Why was he not returned to me?"

"Sir! It is not my position or responsibility to return the child to you. It is a matter for a court. And now, if you will excuse me, I have to attend to the matter of the two men we caught. I am sorry I cannot be more helpful; it is not my intention to offend."

Kam bowed briefly and walked to the door. Hussein got up crashing the chair behind him and brushed passed Kam without a glance, leaving Ghazali to pick up the chair.

*****

They marched through the long corridors flanked by security guards. People stepped aside as Hussein's men barged past them, an early morning throng of people who were arriving at the station: officers reporting for duty, people coming in to report all and sundry, cleaners, clerks, secretaries, drivers. They looked on in astonishment and pressed against the wall to free the passageway. Some clucked their tongues and wagged their heads in dismay. "Disgraceful!" they said. "Who is he?" they asked of his departing back. Someone whispered in Cantonese, "*Gon mmn cheet, hui san fun!* Hurrying to his graveyard!"

Hussein ignored their talk. He stepped out on to the pavement. His car was waiting; his driver held the door open and he slipped in followed by Ghazali. The car rolled smoothly forward. Ghazali stole an anxious glance at his boss.

Some twenty minutes into the ride, Hussein sighed, "I behaved badly, didn't I? I shouldn't have gone in and made all those demands. No way to conduct diplomatic relations or to gain the help of the other party." He glanced at his secretary, huddled in a corner, holding his brief case. "You are free to speak. Tell me the truth."

"No sir! You would not have done this in the early days." Ghazali reflected on Hussein's early days of political campaigning. Young and old had warmed to his charm. He showed care and respect for all who he met.

"What has happened to me?" Hussein said to his reflection in the driver's rear mirror. "Too much power," he said to himself, grimacing at his own image. The anger lines seemed engraved on his face, making deep grooves from the side of his nose to the corner of his lips. He looked again and saw the furrows on his forehead. He knew the answers. It was this big, big void, this emptiness that was eating him up. It had grown steadily since he divorced An Mei. He had filled it with political success. He had almost got used to this void until Ahmad's call. Remorse and regret gnawed at him afresh. He wanted to make amends, ask her to have him back. He thought he would win her back by rescuing their son. Her denial that the boy was his was bad enough; then to find that she had remarried! He winced. Her rejection, especially her off-hand dismissal of his overtures, offended him. He could not let her go. He must see this boy to verify for himself if there was any truth in Ahmad's claim.

"Turn around," he instructed the driver.

Chapter 44

The field was parched dry, more yellowy brown than green. An Mei ran down the slope, ignoring the sharp blades of *lalang,* and their plumes of dried seed heads. They brushed against her, leaving fluffs of seeds, whispery white trails of cotton that dotted her long indigo-blue skirt. Lifting a hand to her brow to shield her eyes from the dazzling sun, she looked towards the river. No one could be seen. She quickened her footsteps; her sandals crunched against the dried stalks of grass, flattening them to the ground. Until the monsoon breaks, the heat would continue to build. She felt the trickles of sweat on her body; her face burned with the heat. She placed both hands around her mouth and hollered, "Mark, Mark! Where are you?"

Her voice echoed across the field, and then tailed off with the wind; hushed whispers that had no form, just resonance of sound. The maid had told her that Mark went out by the side gate of the back garden. She waited and waited for his return and when he did not come back, she grew alarmed. She decided to go in search of him, leaving also by the side gate, fighting her way through the undergrowth that had choked the narrow path leading out to the fields beyond. She remembered Mark asking her if the path was equivalent to public footpaths in England, which would end up normally in good walking grounds. She had laughed. "People," she had said, "do not usually walk for pleasure in Singapore. It's the same in Malaysia and I daresay elsewhere in the region. It is too hot."

She did not know if the fields were good for walking. Jane had mentioned that they used to be divided into vegetable plots. A few families had planted and tended them with care, growing vegetables for the local market. Each morning would find them watering and hoeing the ground, their faces hidden under wide woven hats, making ridges of rich black earth from which would sprout delectable greens, *choi sam*, mustard greens, *kai lan,* kale, and fat Chinese cabbages, their white tubular forms and wrinkly lime green leaves, bursting from the earth ready for harvesting. Now, the fields were barren, left unattended, wild, waiting for another residential housing estate to be built on the land.

She made her way down the gentle slopes to the river. It was brown and in places, almost silted up. Dry outcrops of rock stood at the side. Many days had passed without a single drop of rain as the season built up to one giant ball of heat before the onslaught of the monsoon. She looked to the left and right of her. Which way? she wondered. She turned to the right and broke into a run. She followed the dirt path, kicking up dried earth as she ran. Soon her skirt was plastered with pellets of brown earth. She rounded a bend, following the lazy meandering of the river and came to a stop. For there, seated on a rock, was Mark.

He saw her and waved. Her heart lifted. He was not angry with her. She smiled walking up to him and he returned it with a tiny quirk of his lips, but as she got closer, she could see the wariness in his eyes. She guessed he was expecting her to say she wanted to leave him for Hussein and he was steeling himself to take it on the chin. She could see his hurt. She ran, ignoring the dirt, her skirt trailing, and her sandals, their straps slipping down on her heels and becoming unfastened under unaccustomed use. She reached him. She looked at him for a second and then put out both her hands and took hold of his and hauled him up. Then she kissed him, a gentle kiss that grew in intensity, murmuring all the while that she was sorry. She told him of her dilemma, of Hussein. He listened. When she finished, he asked, "Are you sure? Are you sure you wish to be with me?"

She buried her head into his chest. She had thought and thought the whole morning. She loved Mark. Hussein was the past, a love that she had imagined to be more than it had proved to be.

* * * * *

Hand-in-hand they walked, retracing their steps along the river, up the gentle slopes of the brown fields and onto the main road. They saw Jane's house from afar, a white detached house with a portico and a white gate on a tree-lined road. An ice-cream van was parked at the top of the road. She could see Nelly coming out with Tim, making their way to the van. From across the road, someone came out of a parked car. He headed towards Nelly and Tim. An Mei broke into a run, followed by Mark.

"No! No!" she cried.

Mark picked up speed, his legs moving fast, sensing danger. "Nelly!" he shouted.

Nelly looked up. Hussein waylaid her. He stood in her path. "Ah! The dependable aunt!" he mocked. "And ... my son?" he asked raising his eyebrows like a question mark and looking at Tim.

"No! I am not your son," said Tim looking up, his eyes wide, appraising this stranger. He stuck a finger in his mouth, withdrew it and, with a gravity that both pained and captivated Hussein, said, "My mother said I am not to talk to strangers. We are going to get an ice cream." Nevertheless he smiled, his little teeth, white against his brown skin, proud that he remembered his mother's instructions, delighted that he was going to get an ice cream because he had been bored staying in the whole morning. "Daddy says it is very important to listen to mummy," he added.

Hussein looked at the little boy. Such a beautiful boy! He had an overwhelming desire to pick him up and claim him as his own there and then.

"What's your name?"

"None of your business. Will you please stand aside?" demanded Nelly. She tried to shield Tim from Hussein.

"Go in Tim," said Mark, arriving with An Mei closed at his heel.

"No! No! I want an ice cream." He struggled flaying his arms as he tried to free himself from Nelly's hand and run towards the van.

"We'll get it for you. Just wait a little," coaxed Mark. He squatted down on his haunches and patted Tim on the head.

Nelly gathered the struggling Tim to her and retreated back into the house.

Hussein could hardly contain the jealousy that surged within him. His face turned pale with anger: to witness the authority that this, this *mat salleh,* dared to wield over his son. His thoughts became incoherent. Grudges that had no connection with the present, flashed through his mind. *Mat salleh!* A white man, no better than the mad sailor boys arriving in the past at our shores to wreak havoc on our women. It reignited his anger against those who had been responsible for Malaysia's past subservience as a colony. He had not felt like this when he was a young graduate in Oxford. Since taking up politics, however, it had grown like a boil in his gums, fierce, ready to burst. He glared accusingly at An Mei, "So this is him."

"I know who you are," said Mark, moving protectively to An Mei's side. "An Mei has told me about you. I do not know why you are watching our house and stalking us, but I would like to make it plain that we do not wish you near us and our family."

The two men glared at each other.

"Please leave," said An Mei, appealing to Hussein.

"Leave?" Hussein asked. "He is my son. You need only to look at him."

"Please leave. He is *not* your son," An Mei insisted.

Hussein stood still. He stared at her, ignoring Mark's presence. The air was filled with all the recriminations that though unsaid were omniscient and real.

"You'll hear from my lawyers," Hussein said quietly and confidently. He turned and returned to his car. An Mei reached for Mark's hand and he took her trembling hand into his own.

* * * * *

She sat on the floor, legs tucked beneath her, her skirt spread out. The blotches of dried earth stood out from its indigo blue like giant disfigured poker dots. On her lap lay Tim's head, his little body curled up on the floor, his knees to his chest, deep in sleep. She had one hand protectively on him while the other brushed the tendrils of hair that had fallen over his eyes. Now and then she would stroke his cheek, marveling at its smoothness. I cannot lose him, she thought, looking down at his small defenseless body and instantly panic engulfed her. Hussein's threat! She recalled how he had looked at her, stripping her naked, forcing her to bend to his will, to reveal her soul. The hammering in her chest increased. Her eyes sought Mark's.

"We must leave," she said, "I am frightened of what Hussein might do."

Mark turned to look at her upturned face. He wanted to be strong for her, but felt nothing other than frustration and a sense of helplessness. "Yes!" he said, "the problem is how to do it? We have this unfinished business with the police. Kam has warned us not to leave. I might still be charged for obstructing the police."

He dropped to his knees beside her. "What we need is good legal advice; not only with regard to the police, but also with respect to Hussein's threat. Are we dealing with Hussein's bluff or can he build up a real case against us? Can he prove Tim is his own?"

"The solicitor I saw for my divorce," said An Mei. Her face brightened. "Mr. Tan. Jeremy introduced him to me. We could talk to him."

"Unfortunately he is in Kuala Lumpur. It is of the utmost importance that we do not go to Malaysia. It will make it easier for Hussein. I think he would find it easier to serve a writ against us."

He slipped both hands under Tim and stood up, cradling him. He walked to the bed and laid him down. An Mei watched him tuck the bedclothes with care around Tim and she felt a calm descend on her.

"The best thing we could do is leave now for Rome," he said, turning around to face her, unaware of being appraised.

"Shall I call Kam? At least we would know where we are with respect to the police."

"Yes! And we should call Jeremy to ask if he knows anyone in Singapore who could explain the legal system and advise us on what to do. I wonder if Jane knows any one?"

* * * * *

Mark looked through the glass window into a small cell. It was stripped of everything except for a table, with a recording machine set on one side of it, and some chairs. A guard was posted at the door. One of the two men who had been apprehended by the police commandoes was in it. He sat in a chair; his elbows on the table with his hands laid cuffed in front of him. Mark recognized him as the one with the tattoo who had emerged from the hut for a smoke and who had jumped carrying Tim bundled in his arms. He looked nervous and agitated. His eyes were sullen and defiant. Across the table, two men sat facing him.

"Come," said Kam, "let us adjourn to my office and leave my officers to their work. I am sure we can break him; the other has already confessed. My men are already out there looking for Ah Cheong. And through him, we should be able to get to Ahmad."

He went ahead, leaving Mark and An Mei to follow. Mark wondered at the methods they might use to break a person under interrogation. In this case, the detainee was a criminal, caught red-handed. Yet he wondered how he, himself, might be questioned. An Mei sensed his anxiety and squeezed his hand.

They walked through the maze of corridors and eventually found themselves back once more in the Detective Superintendent's office. Kam took his time going round to his desk before indicating that they should be seated. He sat and rifled through his notes; his movements were slow, keeping them in suspense.

"Detective Superintendent Kam," said Mark, "are we free to go?"

Kam looked up, seemingly surprised by the direct question. He took time considering it, looking from one to the other. An Mei, who had earlier relinquished Mark's hand when they sat down, reached out for it again. Kam saw her anxiety. He chose, however, to ignore her, turning his full attention on Mark.

"Why are you in such a hurry to leave? Are you not interested in catching the culprit, the man behind the kidnap?"

Mark racked his brain to compose an answer that would be the least compromising. Kam did not give him a chance to reply.

"Then there is still the question of your attempt to withhold information from the police." Kam tapped his mouth with his pen; his lips pressed tightly together, the lower lip jutted slightly forward in bemusement. "You have also not asked after Aquino."

They look guiltily at each other at the mention of Aquino. They had forgotten him again in their anxiety and they looked ashamed. They had promised him their protection. All they had been thinking about since Hussein's threat was to secure their own escape.

"Where is he?"

"In one of my cells."

"Please would you treat him with leniency because without his help we would not have found Tim. He placed himself in great danger to help us," said Mark.

"Ahhh!" Kam seemed to be enjoying their discomfort. He leaned back in his chair, still tapping the pen on his lips. "You know as well as I do, he also played a part in the kidnap. He was the driver; he was with the boy in the house and therefore an accomplice in holding the child there. So on those grounds we can continue to detain him. If he had been innocent, then we would, of course, let him go free."

Kam leaned forward and gripping his pen between his index and middle finger, twiddled it on the desk to emphasise his next words. "You see, like the laws of your own land, we cannot detain people beyond a certain number of hours, in our case 48 hours, without a charge. We are not uncivilized. However, we will charge him although, at present, I cannot tell you what exactly the charge will be."

Mark felt himself being toyed with and he did not know quite how to respond. Why, he wondered, had Kam felt it necessary to compare the two countries? He had been warned that in his travels to former British colonies he was likely to encounter two very different types of people. Those very compliant and respectful of people from the west, because they believe them to be powerful and superior, a remnant of a past when the white men, or *orang puteh* as they called them in this part of the world, were their colonial masters. Then there were those who would be resentful of anything that might remotely remind them of the colonial past. This second kind of person would not miss any opportunity to demonstrate they were equal if not better than their former colonial masters. Mark pushed aside these thoughts. He might be oversensitive himself. In any case for the sake of Aquino, he would not rise to the bait if it were one. Instead, he asked, "Can you release him on police bail?"

"And who would stand bail for him?"

Mark looked quickly at An Mei. "Us?" he asked.

"Ahhh! To be a bailer, you have to be a Singapore citizen or at least a permanent resident."

"Aunt Nelly!" said An Mei. "Jane," she added.

Mark looked doubtful at committing the two ladies without asking their permission but he did not want to leave Aquino in the lurch, not after all his help. He was convinced that the young man was not a willing partner in the crime; he was just a victim of the situation. He leaned over to An Mei and told her they needed to discuss this alone and consult with Nelly and Jane.

"Can we get back on this matter? We need legal advice and, of course, we need to discuss it with our Singaporean relatives," Mark said.

"Fine! I can do that. Let you have a bit more time."

They look expectantly at Kam.

"What about... what about us? Can we leave Singapore?" Mark asked again.

Kam looked gravely at them. He compared Mark's response to that of Hussein. *At least he does not throw his weight around.*

And he has integrity because he seemed genuinely concerned about Aquino. He had enjoyed teasing him and had almost laughed out aloud when he was doing so. He had discussed the situation with his superiors. They had been pleased with the rescue. If they had not succeeded, then it would have been very bad publicity for the island's efforts to establish itself as a tourist spot or financial centre.

The general consensus was that there was no necessity to rake over the fact that Mark had tried to undertake the operation on his own. A good warning would be sufficient chastisement because, in the end, An Mei did tell them and Mark did not do much beyond watching the hut where the criminals were. He did lead the police to the criminals and did in the end play an important part in the boy's release. The fact that he would have tried to save the little boy on his own was still a supposition, his superiors considered, because the police did not catch him in the act. Kicking up a fuss would detract from the bigger issue, the kidnappers themselves. Above all, it might lead to bad publicity. Kam had agreed wholeheartedly.

Out of the corner of his eyes, he stole a glance at An Mei. He saw the fear in her face. He had developed a soft spot for her since Nelly had told him of her situation, but he was not going to let them off so easily without a warning. He summoned a stern expression.

"When we catch the mastermind behind the kidnapping, you will have to attend court as witnesses. We will need you to identify formally the criminals we have so far apprehended and hence you can't..."

The phone rang, its ring shrill and sharp. Kam picked it up impatiently. He listened. His eyes widened. Mark could not read the expression. At times, he broke into Cantonese.

He nodded sympathetically at intervals. He turned his back to them, and spoke softly into the phone. An Mei and Mark looked in wonder as they waited to hear their fate. They looked at the clock on the wall and then at their watches. Every minute of delay could make more real, Hussein's threat. Their unease grew. They waited. Finally, Kam placed the phone down.

"Excuse me. That was an important call. Where were we?" he asked.

"You were saying..."

"Yes! Yes! I remember. Let's say that we do not bring any charges against you for obstructing the law. Mind you this would be purely an amnesty on our part. You will not attempt to withhold information again. You will liaise and keep us informed on all matters relating to this crime. We will need you as witnesses. As to whether you have to be physically present," his voice softened, "you might wish to take legal advice." Kam drew open his drawer, flicked through a stack of cards and pushed one across the desk to them. "You might like to be advised by this gentleman."

Chapter 45

The road wound round the mountain range. On one side of it was the steep rise of the mountain and on the other side a sheer drop, concealed by dense rain forest. Tall tree ferns rose high, their lime green fronds spread and interlocked to form a canopy of shades. Through them, rays of sunshine filtered; first golden and then pearly white as a haze of dewdrops spiralled round them until they reached the ground. They struck the stems of the giant ferns, accentuating their craggy brown bark and the unrolling fronds of smaller plants growing closer to the ground. The buttress roots of the banyan trees loomed large. Everywhere was the lush green of the forest. At a distance, deep in the jungle, wild orchids hung precipitously down from their hosts; their large waxy blooms a colourful contrast to the surrounding green. Long-tailed monkeys swung from tree to tree, their cries echoing across the mountain. Then suddenly the car was descending; the road began to bend and twist more gently, each meander further apart than the previous one. Gradually, warm air supplanted the cold dampness of the rain forest and the flora changed. A stream emerged, drawing water from its source, hidden behind boulders in the hinterland. The car left the Main Range and they were back in the lowlands that run the length of the east coast of the Malay Peninsula. They were returning to Kemun and Hussein's parents.

Hussein sat at the back of the limousine with one arm sprawled along the top of the back seat, the other resting on his knee. He stared unseeing as they drove past oil palms, row upon row of them. They were heavy with fruits; reddish berries the size of plums hung in thick huge clusters beneath the crowns of spiky fronds. In normal times, he would have looked eagerly at the landscape, marvelling at the progress that had been made even in the short time he had been in politics. He had seen the growth of the palm oil industry. Since its arrival from Africa in 1910, palm oil had flourished, but its development was, he believed, secured by the creation of the Palm Oil Research Institute of Malaysia, which he fondly called PORIM. And he was proud of it, proud to be associated with a government that had made it possible. For with the help of PORIM, palm oil had been made one of the country's biggest export earners.

He looked at the neat houses amidst the estates. Ghazali who was sitting next to Hussein detected a tiny lightening of his boss's mood. He half expected him to announce, as he had done many times before, the word "FELDA", the Federal Land Development Authority. It was a pet topic of his. Ghazali remembered the early days, when fresh from university and fired with an ambition to alleviate rural poverty, Hussein had been all for the scheme established to resettle poor rural Malays on smallholder farms growing cash crops. He had canvassed with his boss through many of these holdings and enjoyed the welcome of farmers and their families, and appreciated their salutations, hand to heart and then to lips, with a bow of acknowledgement and thanks. The tiny elevation of mood proved to be short lived. Ghazali could see that Hussein had retreated into himself once more as they flashed past the palm oil holdings.

Hussein looked wistfully at the passing scenery. "Was it worth all the personal losses I have suffered? Was it worth my loss of An Mei?" he asked himself. "I would never have given her up if I had known she was pregnant." He recalled the intimacy between Mark and An Mei, how they held hands as they walked towards the house. His bitterness grew like bile. He looked up at Ghazali, more a confidante and friend than a personal assistant.

"I want my child back. Would you look into the matter for me? Make an appointment with my lawyer."

"May I say something?"

"Of course!"

"Are you sure, the child is yours?"

"How can he not be? Who else then could be the father? He looks like me; he is about four, which makes the timing about right. He certainly is not a white, an *orang putih*! Are you telling me that An Mei, Noraidin, had an affair while married to me?" He grew angry, even as he contemplated the possibility.

Ghazali smiled, "No! Nothing of the sort. Just that an old bachelor like myself cannot see a likeness. I cannot tell one baby from another; the boy Tim is not particularly pale, but I have seen Europeans who are also of that colouring. And I just wonder whether at this point in your career it is worth the inevitable acrimony. It is bound to create a lot of unwanted publicity and allow the opposition to make hay from the situation. Unless, of course, you are absolutely sure he is your son."

"To hell with it. I spend half my time now thinking about what people might say."

"Yes, I agree, even so, are you absolutely sure? How did she hide her pregnancy from you? Remember! You divorced her. Within months of marrying An Mei, I mean, *Puan* Noraidin, you married *Tengku* Shalimar! Won't people's sympathy swing towards her? Your divorce did not make the headlines only because *Puan* Noraidin conceded without a challenge and left the country. If you take her to court now, it would all be raked up. In the four years since then women's groups have been making themselves heard."

Ghazali had seen how the recent affair had affected Hussein and he did not want to see him hurt. He felt it would be better for his boss to start afresh rather than risk everything they had built in pursuit of a child, whose paternity, in his eyes, had yet to be proven.

"Then find out how I can prove parenthood. I don't want them to flee the country. I would like them subpoenaed. Now! I would like them extradited to Malaysia and I want the matter settled in a Shariah court because it falls under family matters."

"On what grounds? You can accuse and take them to court but you have to prove parenthood to win. It is a very complex case. She is not a Malaysian any more. I checked when I went to the immigration department to find out about her entry into Singapore and her whereabouts. There will be an element of international law that is bound to make it even messier."

"Then do it fast while she is in Singapore. Singapore is bound by agreement as a commonwealth country to extradite her to us."

"This is not a straight forward case. If it is not a criminal case, are they still bound to extradite to us? Are you sure that the matter would fall under family law, if the family unit, you and her, no longer exists."

"Then find out!"

Hussein turned away and stared out of the window. All of a sudden, he was less sure of his chances. He began to feel the strain. The muscle in his neck twitched. He felt a dull pain spreading in his brain. He reached into his pocket and drew out a packet of pills. He picked two out from a blister and popped them into his mouth. He laid his head back and closed his eye, waiting for the ache to go. An incredible sense of sadness enfolded him.

* * * * *

The drawing room was huge with tall windows stretching from floor to ceiling on one wall. Outside a tropical storm raged. Big drops of rain pelted down, hitting the windowpane. Trees bent under the force of the wind, their branches whipping in frenzy like coiled springs catapulting back and forth.

Rahim stood facing the window. He had both hands behind his back; one held the other wrist. He was deep in thought, going over and over again what he had heard from Ghazali. He had not bothered to turn on the lights. The room, filled with ornaments and artefacts collected from their travels, was cast in almost total darkness by the storm. He shifted his weight from one foot to the other, undecided what to do. Faridah had gone to her bedroom, upset by Hussein's failure to bring home her grandson. She had waited impatiently for their return and when Hussein arrived empty-handed she had burst into tears.

Hussein had left immediately, unwilling to speak any more. He had professed his intention to take An Mei back before he went to Singapore. Now he had returned home to inform his parents that not only had she rejected his offer but she was also married to another.

Rahim turned away from the window and walked to an armchair. He sat down, his body heavy with care. He too would have wished for a grandson, although he agreed with Ghazali that it would be better for Hussein to start afresh with someone new. He also knew that he could not influence his son like in the past. Hussein was now a man, a successful politician in his own right. He could only counsel him and even then he had to tread very carefully.

Chapter 46

Mark turned into the makeshift car park, a patch of rough ground that still had the scattered remnants of rubble from buildings that had just been pulled down. A rush of dust bloomed. It filled the air and covered the bonnet of the car.

A young man came over. He was neatly dressed in a white shirt and dark khaki trousers. A money pouch was slung over his shoulder and hung at his waist. He tapped on the window and pointed to a crudely improvised sign at the entrance. It had a list of parking fees.

"Goodness! Is that how it is done in Singapore? I thought there would be parking meters," said Mark, as he was about to open the door.

"Wait! Let the air settle," said An Mei putting out her hand to stop Mark. "This is a temporary car park. The owner must be trying to earn some money before building begins," she felt obliged to explain. "Look around you. Only the shop houses in that street to the right of us are intact. Soon this car park will be transformed into a multi-storey complex."

Mark turned. To the left of them, between the gaps in the fence, painted a bright green, he could see the façade of a row of shop houses. Nothing of their structure remained to the rear of them. Like a film set, they stood almost comical in their completeness in front, down to details of the name of the shops and the date when they were built. Everything was neat and orderly.

"The whole area is going to be re-built and improved, but to retain the character and history of the place, the façade of the houses will be kept. Come! The dust has settled. Two hours should be sufficient. Let's pay him. We go to the right." An Mei was in a hurry and anxious to get to their destination. She felt energised, more in control now that they were at least going to see a lawyer.

They set off with An Mei leading the way. After the air-conditioned car, the heat was oppressive. She pointed to a signboard on the upper floor of a two-storey shop house. It was one of many terraced shop houses on the street. The ground floors consisted mainly of shops while the upper floors were either living quarters attached to the shops below or offices. A covered way linked the shop houses offering protection for pedestrians from both rain and sun. Grasping Mark's hand, An Mei crossed the road and hurried towards the shaded passage.

Mark could not help looking around him, temporarily distracted by the newness and quaintness of everything he could see. The old and the new, juxtaposed to form a seamless area of contrasting buildings with the people weaving in and out of the streets as the main connecting force. They stopped in front of a coffee shop. It was old and painted rose pink. A sign read "*Kopitiam*". He peered into its dark deep interior. He could see an inviting courtyard within, lit by a shaft light from the sky above. An Mei shook her head. "No time," she said, pointing instead to a narrow cement stairway to the side of the coffee shop. It had a wooden door, thrown wide open, and over it was another sign. It read, Tay Solicitors.

"Are you sure?" he asked looking dubiously at the bare steps.

"Yes! Not all solicitors have big offices although most have moved to more modern accommodation. You probably won't find this in years to come. Still it is the address that Kam gave us. I called to confirm it and make an appointment. Don't worry. I am sure Kam would not have referred us to this lawyer if he were not good at his job. I have been to worse-looking offices," she said reflecting on her visit to Mr. Tan in Kuala Lumpur. Immediately, a frown crossed her face. She had gone to Mr. Tan's office to find a way of keeping her unborn child. She was now in yet another office to fight for him. "Come!" She set off up the stairs. Her shoes clacked loudly on the bare cement. Mark followed.

There was little formality. A young woman, neat in a dark skirt and white blouse, smiled and showed them to a small waiting room. A Van Gogh print hung on one wall; its vase of yellow sunflowers looked benignly over synthetic leather armchairs, blue, beige and black, arranged alongside the opposite wall. Pushed into one corner was a table piled high with magazines and newspapers.

"Please wait," she said and pattered off, only to return almost immediately.

"Please come this way," she said indicating another room to the top left-hand side of the stairway, "Mr. Tay is waiting for you."

Mr. Tay was in his late thirties, earnest and bespectacled. His jet-black hair was parted to the side and combed to the back, accentuating his clean-shaven and pale face. He stood up briefly, shook their hands and invited them to be seated.

"What can I do for you?" he asked, sitting forward and clasping his hands together, his elbows rested on the desk. He looked ready to spring. Behind him shelves lined the wall from floor to ceiling. Books, leather bound in black, red, deep blue, packed the shelves.

They explained, haltingly at first and then more animatedly, the kidnap, their situation, Hussein's threat and their fears. An Mei began and Mark joined in, sometimes elaborating on a point, sometimes asking a question. Mr. Tay listened and jotted down notes. A concentrated frown appeared on his forehead. He interrupted to clarify a point and then bent over to scribble. At times, he would seem to have a sudden thought; his eyes would widen behind his spectacles and he would swivel his chair to look at the volumes of law books on the shelves, only to turn back to his desk and to scribble again. "Needs checking! Continue," he would mutter, putting asterisks next to his notes.

At last they finished. An Mei looked exhausted. Mark who had had little sleep the previous night, looked longingly at the cup of coffee that had been placed in front of him earlier. It had gone cold, yet in his thirst, its milky brown still looked inviting. "May I?" he asked taking the cup from its saucer and drinking its contents in one go, the sweetness taking him by surprise. He wondered how much longer he could retain his English reserve; he felt at times it would be better to throw in his lot with the very emotional Asians. The so-called inscrutable Chinese who nevertheless seemed willing to lay bare their souls for all to see. At least they enjoyed some relief. They waited for Mr. Tay to speak.

Mr. Tay took his time. He flicked through some pages of the notes before him, absent-mindedly. His eyes were unseeing; he just needed something to occupy his hands. He was deep in thought over what they had told him. Finally, looking up, he asked, "What do you want out of all this?"

They look at each other and answered almost in unison. "We want to protect Tim, our son. We don't want to lose him."

"Sorry, but I have to ask this. Is Hussein the biological father?"

An Mei hesitated. Once again, she found herself wondering how much respect would be given to client confidentiality. She had been told before that a breach of confidentiality is highly unlikely but she still had a problem trusting the lawyer. If she told Tay the truth, would he be bound to reveal it? Would it reduce his inclination to defend them? She was in a dilemma. She clutched Mark's hand.

"How easy is it to prove parenthood?" interrupted Mark.

"I had a recent case. My client had an affair with a wealthy businessman. She became pregnant with his child. She took him to court. The man denied the child was his. The lady had the blood of the child matched to the man to prove that he was the father. But the case was not conclusive."

"Why?"

"Well, the man contested it. You see, if the blood does not match, you can prove conclusively that he is not the father. However, if the blood matches, as in that particular case, you can only prove he could have been the father."

"So it is not possible to prove conclusively if the blood matches," repeated Mark. His heart leapt at this piece of news.

"This is what makes it such a fascinating case. Scientists have made vast inroads into the matter of paternity testing. You not only need to match the blood type, you also need to match the tissue. Scientists have discovered a protein — human leukocyte antigen or HLA — prevalent in human cells, especially white blood cells, though not in red blood cells. If you can match this and the blood type, then you can have a 90 per cent chance of proving biological relationship."

"Then why hasn't your client done this?"

"Well, it is a relatively new method, especially in this country. It requires very large blood samples that might prove dangerous for infants. So the mother hasn't pursued it. I am told, however, that work is underway now that would make HLA testing a thing of the past. It's called DNA testing and from what I hear, it will be almost 100 per cent conclusive. So it may well be best for her to bide her time."

Tay leaned back in his chair. He wondered at Mark's fascination and interest of how paternity could be proved. His eyes wandered to An Mei and he saw how agitated she had become since he asked her if Hussein was the father. He surmised that Hussein was probably the father. Detective Kam had called to tell him that he was sending over two people who were desperate for help and that the lady in particular had had a terrible experience in her previous marriage. Mr Tay wanted to help them but they seemed to be holding back from him. He waited patiently. The minutes ticked by; Tay looked at his watch and asked again, "Who is Tim's biological father? Is it Hussein?"

An Mei looked desperately at Mark. Mark had been elated when Tay said that blood testing was not conclusive. His hopes were dashed immediately, however, with the mention of HLA and, worst still, the future possibility of a foolproof way of establishing paternity using DNA. It could only be a matter of time before Hussein would stake his claim on Tim, even if they managed to avert it now.

"Can my wife and I have a word in private?" Mark asked.

Tay nodded, "Of course! But please note that I am not here to judge. If you would like me to act for you, then I will do so to the best of my ability. But I have to know the full story in order to advise you on the best options available. I think sir," he said looking at Mark, "that you know you cannot evade the truth. It will come out sooner or later."

Mark glanced at An Mei. "What we would like to know is whether we are free to leave Singapore."

"It depends on the police. They might wish you to take the witness stand when the kidnap trial begins, but, unless they have specific objections, you should be free to leave. It is unlikely that the case will begin immediately, especially, if, as I understand it, not everyone has been caught. However, the Court might ask you to return in the future for the trial of the kidnapper."

"Are we obliged to return?"

"Normally, a parent would wish to see the kidnapper punished and, therefore, would return. But note that a court's order to a witness to attend is valid only in the country concerned, in this case, Singapore. If a witness were to live abroad, then he or she would be entitled to refuse to come in person to attend court. The witness could opt to give evidence and be cross-examined remotely. So a court in Singapore would not have jurisdiction to order an overseas witness to return here."

"What about Hussein's threat to take legal action against us? Can he subpoena us and could we be extradited to

Malaysia? We would rather have any legal action settled in a country where we are more familiar with the legal system."

"Ahhh! You use the word extradition. An extradition order can be issued only in criminal cases. And if we are talking about a criminal case, it really depends on where you are located. If you are a resident in Singapore and, say, the gentleman in question is in Malaysia and he subpoenas you, then Singapore as a member of the Commonwealth is obliged by treaty to extradite you to Malaysia. I would imagine, and I would have to check this, the same would apply if you were in the UK."

"What if we reside in a country without such an agreement with Malaysia?"

"Could you be more specific?"

"Say, Italy. We both live and work in Italy."

"Italy does not have such an agreement with Malaysia. So it is not legally bound to surrender an accused to Malaysia."

Tay looked at the couple before him. He wondered if they were asking him the right questions; they seemed not on track with the real issues at hand. Both of them looked so desperate. He leaned forward and said, "Let me qualify this. You asked me about extradition. And I have answered accordingly. Extradition law is extremely complex and has to be taken almost on a case-by-case basis although some general rules apply. Are we, however, talking about a crime? There is no question of extradition being applied in civil matters."

An Mei had said little. Her head was reeling. Every answer Mr. Tay gave seemed to open up ever more avenues to the unknown. Was her deed, concealing from Hussein that she was pregnant with Tim when he divorced her, a criminal act? She had so many questions, yet each of these would reveal her situation a bit more and she couldn't bring herself to tell all. She felt, knew, even, that Tay must have reached a conclusion as to who the father was but still she held back on the answer. I have not confirmed it, she thought, and hence it would remain a suspicion rather than a certainty. She did not know whether confessing would help or undo her case. She was still not sure how far a lawyer would or could protect his client's confidentiality despite all their assurances. Could she deny that Hussein was the father if she were put on the stand, if she had confessed to Tay? Would it mean that Tay would be forced to abet in her perjury? She felt the thump of her heart; it was beating so violently she felt sure the palpitations must be noticeable.

She recalled the decision she had made in Mr Tan's office in Malaysia many years ago. She was not prepared to take the risk of telling the truth to a solicitor then; she felt the same now. She could not breathe. The fear of losing Tim overwhelmed her. She clamped her bloodless lips tightly together and looked to Mark for help.

Mark seeing her suffering turned to Tay, "Please would you excuse us? My wife is not feeling well. We will come back to you and make another appointment."

"Of course. As you please."

They stood up, awkward and embarrassed to abandon a consultation that they themselves had requested. Mark put out his hand and Mr. Tay shook it. He then took An Mei's outstretched hand and shook it. Her hands felt small and cold. Tay held on to her hand and placed his other over it.

"Mam," he asked, "are you sure you wish to go? Would you please stay for a little while and let me explain some matters to you."

An Mei felt as though her knees would give way. Mark put his arms around her. "Shall we sit down and hear what Mr. Tay has to say?"

"Please, Mrs Hayes," said Tay.

They sat down, she reluctantly and he expectantly.

"You said that Hussein has threatened to take legal action against you to retrieve Tim who he alleges is his son. Such a matter is a family issue and hence falls under family law. As Hussein is a Muslim, if the case were to be heard in Malaysia, it would most likely to be presided over in a Shariah court. You might be right that if you were to contest the case in a Shariah court, the ruling could favour Hussein and, if it were proven that he is the biological father, he might gain custody of the child. In a Shariah court, custody is normally awarded to the person best able to bring up the child as a Muslim."

"That is preposterous!" exclaimed Mark.

"Not really. It is not uncommon for each nation to have its own peculiar bias when it comes to awarding custody. In the UK, the bias is towards the woman. In Germany, it is towards their own nationals. So if an Englishwoman were to marry a German man, then a German court would award custody to the man whereas an English court would probably favour the woman. So you can understand that in Shariah law, the bias is in favour of the Muslim."

Tay paused to let his word sink in. "But," he said with a resounding voice, "but" he repeated for emphasis, he hit his palm with the ruler with a flourish, "if a Malaysian civil court issues an order against you, it has only jurisdiction in Malaysia. You are not obliged to come to court in Malaysia to contest it, even if he attempts to summon your return."

"So it is of utmost importance that we do not enter Malaysia," said An Mei.

"Yes! And you have not done so."

"What if Hussein takes criminal action against us and calls it a crime?"

"He might well make that allegation and call it kidnapping, but it is unlikely to succeed. The abduction of children by parents is a civil and criminal offence, but, generally, the criminal law is not evoked. The parent who has lost the child will normally have to resort to the civil courts to get the child back. In deciding whom to award the custody of the child, the court will consider how the child is affected by the abduction. If the child has been abducted recently, the court tends to favour the parent who lost the child in order to return to the 'status quo' of the child. If, however, the abduction took place a long time ago, especially if the child has adapted well to the circumstances of the environment he or she was brought up in, then it is unlikely the child would be taken away from the parent-abductor. To remove the child from the abducting parent and restore him or her to the other parent might be deemed as causing trauma to the child. According to the Hague Convention, it is habitual residence that matters, essentially what is best for the child, rather than the rights and wrongs of the contesting parents."

A glimmer of renewed hope appeared in An Mei's face. The fatigue that so marked her face just moments ago, went. Mark grinned broadly.

"It would not be easy for Hussein to succeed in his legal action," added Tay. "If he does it through a Malaysian court, he has no legal jurisdiction to summon you to Malaysia. He could take legal action through an English court. Past cases have shown that an English court generally favours the mother unless it is to the detriment of the child's welfare. And of course, as a member of the Hague Convention, what I said regarding habitual residence would apply and that too would favour your situation."

"Thank you! Thank you," cried An Mei.

"Yes! We really appreciate your help. That has cleared a lot of things in our mind," said Mark.

"Not at all. It is my work. A word of caution! Malaysia is not, I believe, a signatory to the Hague Convention. So if Hussein did take his case to a Malaysian court, it might not be so guided by the rulings of the Hague convention. But you know, I think, what you must do. You must ensure that Tim never enters Malaysia while he is a minor."

* * * * *

An Mei held on to Tim with one hand and carried a tote bag filled with books, crayons and toys with the other. Mark walked alongside An Mei carrying the cabin bags. She felt surreal walking amidst the surge of people all rushing to catch their flights.

A man brushed passed An Mei. She jumped.

"Sorry," he said.

She moved away as though she had been stung. Seeing her reaction he glared at her. "*Gila!* Mad!" he muttered.

The three of them made their way towards the departure lounge. They had two full hours before their flight to Rome. Long queues had formed behind the security check. It was not quite a queue; sometimes two or three people stood side by side. The line curved and wound at random, like a snake inching forward. She held on to Tim's hands. Her eyes were wary. They darted nervously, checking everywhere.

At a distance, she saw a man. He seemed to be watching them. When she stared at him, he looked away, seemingly preoccupied with the notices on the board. She blinked. She thought he looked familiar.

"Mummy, let go of my hands. I'm hot!" Tim was getting tired. He wanted to play. He pulled away. She hurried after him.

"No! Stay with mummy."

"I want to see what's there, I want to see," he yelled. He ran towards the conveyor belt carrying the bags through for security checks. She followed, her body loping forward, banging her bag against others in the queue.

"Madam," said an officer, his face bristling with indignation as he saw how she had tried to by pass the others in front of her and push ahead towards the security checkpoint.

"Sorry, I am not breaking queue. I am running after my son," she answered. She took her eyes off Tim for a moment to speak to the officer. She looked back towards him. He was not there. She turned wildly to look at the people around her. They were pushing forward towards the checkpoint. She could not see Tim. She turned back to where Mark was. "Where did Tim go?" her voice was hoarse.

"Mam, please put your bag on the conveyor belt and walk through this door."

"No! My son! I can't find him."

"Then you have to wait your turn. Next please!" He glared at her.

Mark hurried forward towards her, his cabin bags swung perilously close to others in the crushing crowd. People glared at him. "What cheek!" they exclaimed.

"It's not your turn. I was here first," said an old lady blocking his passage. She looked at Mark; her voice was querulous, accusing. She pointed her finger at him. "Don't try to take advantage of an old lady."

"We are not trying to jump the queue. We are looking for our little boy," he explained. He looked apologetically at the lady. She tried to engage him in a discussion, but he was preoccupied by the search for Tim.

She turned to her companion and said, "*Gwei loh!* Foreign devil! No manners."

He ignored the barbed comment. He recognised the word "*gwei loh*. A commotion caught his attention. People parted like swaying corn.

"Do you mean this little boy?" asked a young man walking quickly towards them with Tim in his arms. "I found him hiding behind that lady," he said turning around to point at a large lady wearing a long voluminous skirt that almost trailed the floor.

"You could not find me," Tim said with a wicked grin. He kicked his legs, thrashing the young man's side. "I hide. You have to find me."

Mark took Tim from the young man and thanked him. "Sorry! Sorry! Thank you! Thank you so much. Please excuse us," he said to the crowd of people returning to where they had been earlier. An Mei followed, relief on her face. She had been near to tears. Her nerves were frayed.

"I think it is better if we keep Tim between us," she said walking round Mark to position Tim so that he was securely sandwiched between them. "More secure," she added. "Do you think they would let me through that security screen with Tim?"

"Probably not! I shall go ahead, and wait on the other side. Then send Tim through. You go last." Mark placed the cabin bag on the floor and placed his arm around An Mei. "It will be fine. I don't think anyone will try to take Tim from us here."

"How can we be sure?" This is the last chance they have. They might try."

"Once we get into the departure lounge, it should be alright."

"Yes! I hope so." An Mei turned to look for the man whom she was sure had been watching them. He had disappeared.

Chapter 47

An Mei stepped into the entrance foyer, some twenty metres in length and about ten metres wide, clad in marble and with a ceiling as high as a two-storey building. It was busy. A long queue had formed in front of a glass booth set in the centre. The booth manned by security guards separated the foyer from an equally large but dimly lit lounge. The flags of nearly 170 member nations were displayed on the walls of the lounge, creating a tapestry of red, blue, yellow and green. In the queue were men in grey suits carrying leather briefcases and women in dark skirts and jackets, one hand clutching a handbag, the other a briefcase. The sombre colours of their clothes were interrupted here and there by brilliant flashes of scarlet, turquoise, green, yellow and ochre worn by people who had chosen to arrive in their traditional national dress.

They were all visitors to the Food and Agriculture Organization, waiting patiently for their turn to be issued with a building pass to enter the premises. First the passports and identity documents were handed over to the uniformed guard, then a phone call to verify that they had an appointment, then a welcoming smile and the issue of a building pass. Many of the visitors, once cleared, went into the lounge and sat waiting to be collected.

An Mei smiled briefly at some of the visitors and walked into the inner confines of the building. She used the doorway to the right, flashing her own pass as a staff member to a guard, and walked passed the corner bookshop towards a broad marble staircase. She stopped and turned around, her eyes lingering over the familiar scene behind her. To the right was the bank, the *Banca Commerciale Italiana*, or BCI. Next to it, the post office, and further beyond was the corridor to the Staff Commissary, an enormous neon-lit commercial area. She smiled, reminded of how thrilled she had been when she first joined the Organization to discover the Commissary. It was like an Aladdin's cave piled high with exotic goods — goods that were not available or were difficult to find in Rome, goods that staff members pined for from their homeland. She caught the eye of a colleague and smiled at his gesture to join him for coffee during the break. She indicated with her wrist that she was late and would catch up later. She had just returned from Singapore. She walked quickly up the marble staircase.

She had been away for more than a month, but it was as though she had never been away. She walked on, her mind going back to the day she first joined the UN agency. She had been nervous then, eager to have a job, delighted that she had been selected. Her work gave her a sense of direction and economic independence. And she had loved it and still did.

She continued up the stairway, ignoring the lifts at every floor. She needed to move to calm herself. She shrugged her shoulders and shook her head to relieve the tension. She arrived on the third floor. The lift door slid open and someone from within waved her in. "There is room," a passenger called, stepping aside to make space.

"I'm fine, thank you. I'll walk," she responded and pressed on. She turned off the staircase into a long corridor with offices on either side. She peered into one. Two secretaries shared it and their desks were set facing each other, the walls were lined with filing cabinets. A potted plant by the windowsill was the only attempt to liven up the room. She recalled a visitor's comment. "Such small grey rooms! I expected more glamorous offices in a UN building."

"Not where the real work is done," someone had volunteered with a laugh.

She stopped in front of a door and knocked hesitantly and then more firmly.

"Come in," said a voice from within.

She walked in.

"An Mei! Welcome back! How was your trip? I gathered that it was work, but you took some leave as well. Was the family there with you? How are Mark and little Tim?" asked Sandra Pool.

Sandra came from behind her desk and took a chair for herself and pulled another alongside for An Mei. She was the personnel officer for the department where An Mei worked. A large woman, she had taken an instant liking to the petite small-boned An Mei and had helped her settle in Rome. An Mei sat in the proffered chair and Sandra plumped herself down in the adjacent one. The folds of her skirt cut in an A-shape, fell on either side of the chair like a tablecloth trailing the ground.

An Mei hesitated. She wondered how she should answer. How to say fine, which was expected of her, when it was not fine? She recalled the comment of a friend when she had voiced the same question in the past.

"When people ask you how you are just casually, you are not expected to go into any details or even tell the truth. You are expected to say, fine, and pass on. If you go into details then you should not be surprised to find that some people will shy away from you in future."

An Mei steeled herself. "My work went well," she said, "but unfortunately, the trip as far as the family is concerned was an absolute disaster and a very frightening experience." She was not going to say that everything was fine when it was quite the opposite. It would be incongruous given what she was going to say next. "In fact, I have come to ask you for advice. I intend to hand in my resignation."

Sandra took in the information without a comment. She sat with her hands on the armrest for a moment and then hauled herself up, pressing hard on the chair to get up.

"I gather this is just an informal sounding out and that nothing has yet been done or decided." She looked curiously at An Mei. Her brown eyes were serious.

An Mei shook her head. "I've not spoken to anyone. I came to you as a friend."

"Ahhh! Then as a friend I invite you for coffee at the terrace bar." She looked at her wristwatch. "You came just at the right time. I'll let my secretary know."

She walked to the adjoining door and put her head round the doorway. An Mei could hear her speaking in her low melodic voice. Sandra had the most calming effect when she spoke. Her voice sounded like the strumming of a harp.

Although she was not beautiful, she gave an impression of beauty and calm when she spoke. An Mei found herself responding to its beneficial effect.

They said little as they took the lift to the top floor. They stepped out, rounded a corner and went into the bar, a large room with a long counter, and were immediately accosted by the loud clatter of cups and saucers.

"*Un caffè macchiato! Un caffè latte, Due cappuccini! Un lungo! Doppio! Espresso! Caffè latte fredo!*" The barmen, smart in their black and white uniforms, yelled the orders in loud voices that reverberated across the counter. Queues formed and dwindled. Cigarette lighters popped, a flare of light was followed by spirals of smoke.

"Would you like a pastry? Which would you like, plain, chocolate or custard?" asked Sandra, looking longingly at the basket piled high with *cornetti*.

"Not for me, thank you, but you have one."

"Are you sure?"

"Yes! Yes!"

Loaded with cups of steaming coffee, they stepped out onto the roof terrace that ran the entire length of the building. They were temporarily blinded by the bright sunshine and a clear blue sky.

"Let's go over there, the corner that overlooks the *Circo Massimo*. There is some shade and not many people so we should be able to talk undisturbed," Sandra suggested.

They stood companionably sipping their coffee in silence; steam rose from their cups like little puffs of smoke in the cool dry air of the autumn morning. They leaned on the stone balustrade and looked out on to the *Circo Massimo,* two figures looking at the remnants of the ancient Roman chariot racetrack.

"This is so beautiful. It hits me every time I come up here, even after seeing it for all the 20 years I have been in service. Look at the old Roman Baths over there." Sandra pointed to the crumbling stonewalls and arches of the *Terme di Caracalla* to the right of her. The bright sunshine lit up the walls turning them fiery brown against the sapphire blue of the clear sky. Canopies of the aptly named umbrella pine trees rose above the walls.

"Can you bear to leave us? And what has brought this on?" asked Sandra turning to look at An Mei. She rested one elbow on the top of the low wall. "You know how difficult it is to get into the organization. You love your job and you are good at it. Every performance appraisal has marked you out as, as ... excellent. "

"I have no choice. You see..." In a quiet voice, An Mei told her about Tim's kidnap, Hussein's threat and what Mr. Tay had told her. "It means that should Tim fall into their hands again and be brought to Malaysia, the chances of my getting him back would be minimal. I need to be with Tim all the time to make sure that he can never be abducted again."

"Where is Tim now?"

"I left him with Mark. Mark took the day off. I trust no one else."

"I don't quite follow, all the legal bits I mean," said Sandra.

"My former husband cannot compel me to appear before a Malaysian court, but, by the same token, if he abducts Tim, I cannot compel him to attend an English or Italian court if I were to take legal action against him for the return of Tim. If I take a case against him, I would have to fight in a Malaysian court and I doubt whether I would be deemed as a suitable mother for bringing up Tim as a Muslim."

She looked out over the ruins. Her voice caught and wavered. "I was so happy when I heard that Hussein had no legal power to make me return to Malaysia. I thought that if I brought Tim back here we would be safe. But that is only so if I can make sure he is not abducted. The warning that the solicitor gave me at the very last did not sink in. I was so elated that we were able to leave. It was only in the airport in Kuala Lumpur that the full significance of his parting words became clear. He said that Tim must not return to Malaysia while he is a minor. That is why I have to resign so that I can be near him all the time."

Sandra looked away. She could not bear the anguish in An Mei's eyes. "Are you sure Tim would be in danger? Do you think that they would actually come here to take him?"

"That's the problem. I am not sure of anything. I am jittery all the time. I suspect every passer-by who shows any interest in him. I fear strangers looking at us. I jump at every corner. I worry when he is in bed and I am not near to him. I thought that I could trust leaving Tim with my aunty, but, ever since the kidnap, I worry when I do. Not because I do not trust her, but because I fear the long reach of my former husband's arm. I know he hates me; he hates me not only because of Tim but because I have rejected him for Mark."

"Are you exaggerating this, building up this fear in yourself?"

"Perhaps. Nevertheless, to me it is real enough. In the immediate days following the release of Tim, I was not so afraid. Since then the fear has grown in me like a cancer. My mind keeps going back to the day when I caught Hussein accosting my aunt and Tim."

An Mei reached into her bag and fished out an envelope. She pushed it towards Sandra. "This is a copy for you. I am

392 Chan Ling Yap

going to see my boss now." Her eyes were bright with unshed tears.

"Wait! There might be a way out. Let me explore this. Meanwhile, hold on to this," said Sandra pushing the envelope back into An Mei's hands. "Go to your office and ask for a day's leave. Go back to Tim. I'll take the matter up with your department."

"What are you going to do?"

"I am going to find out if you could have extended unpaid leave under these extraordinary circumstances."

"No! I have made up my mind to leave. Thank you."

Chapter 48

The fishing boats were lined up on the volcanic beach. There were fifteen of them, long narrow-bodied canoes, each tied neatly to a log hammered deep into the black ash. The *jukongs* were all painted, some were red with white stripes, others blue and yellow and yet others in hues ranging from orange to deep mauve. Their jutting bows, carved in the shape of the mythical elephant fish, had painted black eyes that glared fiercely. The wind blew hot from the ocean lending to the air a salty scent of the sea. Ahmad could see fishing boats coming to the shore, their beautiful sails unfurled, balanced gracefully on the outriggers. He heaved himself from the empty barrel. He felt stiff. Black ash and sand encrusted the sides of his shoes like granulated sugar. He pushed a fist into his lower back to ease the pain. He had lain cramped at the base of a boat for hours, staring into the pitch-black sky sprinkled with stars. Every bone in his body had protested with each creak and sway of the boat. The journey from Singapore to these Indonesian shores had taken three weeks. They had stopped at many islands and fishing villages to replenish supplies and the nine hundred nautical miles had seemed endless as they sailed close to shore. He sniffed, repelled by his own unwashed odour and then, stamping his feet to awaken his aching muscles, lumbered laboriously towards a hut. At the top of a short flight of stairs that led to the entrance to the hut, a lady stood waiting. She smiled revealing a gap in her front teeth and waved him to the back of the hut. With a quick motion of her hands, she indicated that he was to wash. She cackled pointing to his shoes and clothes.

"*Sana*! There!" She pointed again to the back yard. "*Cuci*! Wash!" She threw him a sarong.

He hardly looked at her but grudgingly grunted a thank you. His shoes, battered and scuffed, dragged on the ground leaving a trail in the dirt as he walked towards the backyard. A large stone urn, with a wooden ladle hung at its side, stood behind the house. The courtyard was small, hemmed in by fruit trees. A mangosteen tree grew to one side, laden with dark purple fruits the size of apples on branches that harboured masses of thick elliptical glossy leaves. Some twenty yards apart was the *cempedak* tree. A few *cempedak* clustered low on the tree trunk. Someone had placed a white cotton kerchief around the fruits to protect them from insects. They were large and globular, a foot long, and heavy in their ripeness. He could imagine the turgid, sweet, butter-coloured, fleshy seeds embedded in the large pineapple-shaped fruits. Stricken with hunger, he swallowed and took a deep breath of the rich aromas of the fruits.

A woman stared at him from across the yard. She sat with a trestle between her knees. Her hand held a stone pestle. She was pounding the contents of a mortar with vigour; a light sea breeze carried the smell of fermented shrimp, onions and chillies to him. It smelt so much like home, but this was not home. He was in a village somewhere near Bali. He had been dropped there and told to make his way to the hut where he would be fed and sheltered until someone came to collect him.

He turned his back to the woman and stripped off his shirt. He took the ladle dipping the coconut half shell into the cool water and sluiced it over his head. Someone had sprinkled rose and jasmine petals and kaffir lime leaves into the urn. They fell with the water around his feet. He washed himself vigorously, rubbing his limbs and body, washing hair that had grown long and lank, ridding himself of the stench of fish and grime.

He heard a laugh and turned to see the woman with the pestle and mortar gesticulating towards him with a grin so wide that her eyes disappeared into the folds of her cheek. A group of little boys gathered around her laughed. Their little brown bodies writhed and shook as the woman said, "*Kotor*! *Kotor*! Dirty!"

He turned his back to them, pulled the sarong over his head and tied it around his middle. He then dropped his trousers, struggling with his underpants, tripping as he tried to disengage from them without losing hold of the sarong. He held on to the urn to steady himself. He gestured fiercely at the children. They ran off. He walked to the front of the house. He felt whole again and he was hungry. He smelt wood burning and cooking smells. Hot, spicy, pungent. He had not had a proper meal for weeks. He walked up the short flight of wooden steps. The woman who had pointed him to the backyard was again waiting for him. She gestured with a folding of her fingers pointing towards her mouth. "*Makan!* Eat," directing him to a small wooden table. It was decked with a plastic tablecloth decorated with green and red flowers. On the table the woman had set an enamel plate piled with white rice and an assortment of small dishes. He ate, barely waiting to stop between the balls of food that he doled into his mouth with his fingers. His fingers gathered and moulded rice and meat, rice and vegetables, over and over until they grew slick with oil and spice. Finally replete, he sat back and dipped his fingers into the finger bowl. Then he got up and walked out to the front of the house and back on to the beach.

He had done everything like a robot since he landed. He had no thoughts in his head, no feelings either. His whole being was geared towards the basic primal needs of food and rest. During those short hours he had almost been at peace with himself in a way he had never experienced before. He saw the beauty of the backyard, despite the obvious poverty of its surroundings. A broken bicycle with rust-encrusted wheels leaned on a wall. A few scrawny chickens pecked away in the dirt yard. He heard the laughter of the children. They were barefoot and their clothes were mere rags, patched and re-patched. Yet there was joy in their play.

He stepped on to the beach, his shoes crunching on the black volcanic sand, and walked on until he found the barrel where he had sat when he first landed. Lowering himself on to it, he stretched his feet out in front of him, and looked out to sea. The sound of crashing waves filled the air. Darkness approached. In the distance a flash of lightning lit up the whole sky, tingeing the cumulous balls of dark clouds. The wind picked up speed. He heard the wailing of the elements. His thoughts seemed to mimic the approaching tempest. They began with a flicker of resentment and grew into a storm of hate. They crowded his mind. He thought of all that he had been forced to leave behind. He looked at the small wooden houses behind him. The beauty and calm he saw just moments ago vanished. He did not belong here. He had to find a way to return to his homeland.

* * * * *

Two men collected him the following day. They came in a jeep. Beyond a curt nod and an instruction for him to get in, they barely spoke. He clambered into the back of the vehicle and sat amidst an odd assortment of ropes, oilcans, and baskets that reeked of fish. The jeep rolled forward, bumping along the dirt road; the cans rattled and the baskets slid around. They passed villages similar to the one they had just left behind: a group of huts, some vegetable plots, fruit trees, a well, a school and children playing *sepak takraw*. They ran in pursuit of a rattan ball, kicking it high in the air. Every now and then, anguished cries of despair rose from their midst; someone had failed to keep the ball in the air. He looked at the passing scene. He did not register the images. He was impatient to reach the city. He needed new clothes, money and, above all, he needed a telephone.

The jeep turned on to the main highway and the dirt road gave way to sizzling tarmac. Soon he was leaving the countryside; the green smell of the forests and plantations gave way to smoke fires and diesel fumes. The traffic grew denser. By the time they reached the city, the roads were thronged with bicycles, cars and three-wheeled vehicles. *Bajaj* and *bechak* competed for space. Passengers crowded into them, sheltering behind the plastic covers of the brightly coloured three-wheelers. The noise of the streets rang loud. Ahmad's spirit rose; he felt at home, alive. There were people; there were nightclubs, cinemas. The city smelled of activity and money. The jeep came to a stop. The driver jumped out and indicated that he should alight. He pointed to a shop with a neon-lit sign and said, "*Boleh tukar wang sana.* You can change money there. You will be met by someone."

Ahmad walked towards the shop, a small unpromising edifice with an enclosed glass counter behind which sat a young man of Indian origin. He had not come to change money; he had none beyond the few crumpled Ringgit and Singapore dollars he had in his pocket when he fled. He needed some cash and he had come to collect. He waited his turn at the counter. The man looked at him. Ahmad pushed a piece of paper across.

"Please wait!" the man said. He reached over, the baggy sleeves of his white cotton shirt flapped as he rang a bell. A side door opened and he signalled Ahmad to enter.

Ahmad stepped through the doorway and instantly, the door slid shut behind him. He walked on down a narrow dusty passage and came to a room. There was no one. A small suitcase stood on the lone table in the room. He looked around expectantly. He waited. Still no one! He circled the table, looking at the suitcase. He reached for it, snapping open the catch. In the case was an assortment of clothing, a small wash bag and a parcel wrapped in brown paper with a further outer wrapping of plastic film. He tore it open. *Rupiahs!* Wads of the Indonesian currency, all neatly accounted for and in bundles tied with rubber bands. On top sat a note with an address. He smiled, pleased at his own ingenuity in having made prior arrangements for his flight here. He pocketed the address and pushed the money back into the parcel. He locked the suitcase.

Grasping it firmly in his hand he went back to the door. Within minutes he was out of the shop.

* * * * *

"I did it for you," said Ahmad. His voice was muffled and low. "If you had done what I had asked, your grandson would have been with you this very moment. Instead, you let it all slip away, landing me in trouble."

Faridah clutched the phone. The temptation was strong. Her longing for her grandson had grown by the day, ever since Hussein returned empty handed. She was starting to doubt that she would ever be able to see him, let alone have him returned to her and this seemed a Godsend. "Can you ... will you help return him to us?" she whispered holding the receiver close to her lips.

A long silence followed.

"It depends. It is going to be much harder this time. It will also cost more. More importantly, can you get me off the charges? Can you arrange for my return to Malaysia?"

"I'll see. I'll try," she corrected herself. She wanted to promise, but she could not do it without help and was reluctant to commit herself.

"Not good enough. I need more than that."

Faridah looked at the phone in her hand. He had hung up on her. She dropped the receiver back into its cradle and backed away from it as though she had been stung. She heard a movement. She turned. There was no one.

* * * * *

Ghazali was appalled by what he had overheard. He walked soft-footed along the corridor to Rahim's office. He stood outside the closed door wondering if he was doing the right thing. He raised his hand to knock, hesitated and then turned to walk away. Was he overstepping himself, if he were to tell? He asked himself. What if it was not taken as it was intended? Is it possible that Rahim himself was in agreement with his wife's actions? It would be a catastrophe for his master Hussein if it were to be discovered. He turned and walked back to Rahim's office. Driven by concern for Hussein, he did not stop to think further about the possible implications of his actions for himself. He knocked; a purposeful rap that echoed in the corridor.

"*Masuk*! Come in!" Rahim said.

Ghazali entered. It was dark in the room. Only the desk lamp was on, lighting up the dark wood of the desk with its yellow glow. Long shadows masked the paintings on the walls. Rahim was sat at the desk, his body half submerged in the shadows.

"Good! Just the person I want to see," he said. He leaned further back into his chair and the shadows. With a wave of his hand, he indicated that Ghazali should sit, a gesture that took Ghazali by surprise. Despite the number of years he had worked for Hussein, his parents had never treated him as anything other than a member of staff. He sat down on the edge of the seat, knees closed together and hands folded on his lap. He did not want to be the first to speak now that he knew Rahim wanted to see him. So he waited in silence.

Ghazali wondered why Rahim wished to talk to him. He wondered too why Rahim had chosen to sit in darkness. Things had not been the same since Ahmad had contacted them. Everyone was behaving strangely, going his or her separate ways. Hussein's family was no longer a family. They were disunited. He squirmed in his seat, wishing that he had not come. He felt himself at a definite disadvantage because he could not see Rahim sitting there in the shadows.

"Tell me," said Rahim. He moved forward, coming out of the shadows to lean his elbows on the desk. His leather seat groaned with the shift of his weight. His dark eyebrows, peppered white, were raised, but there was no fire in his eyes. He looked tired, haggard. The jowls in his face seemed to have lost their firmness and strength, leaving his cheeks loose. Long deep lines broke on either side of his mouth when he spoke. It had been more than a month since Ghazali had met with him in this very room. Then Rahim had struck a commanding and decisive figure. That figure was gone replaced by a shadow.

"Please sir, why do you wish to see me?"

"This," said Rahim, waving some sheets of paper at him. "Mutterings of dissatisfaction from our constituency in Kemun and not so gentle complaints from the capital. Apparently Hussein has been distracted. He is not working well; he has missed appointments and deadlines; he says the wrong things... you name it... its all here." He threw the papers down on the desk. "What is up?"

"He is completely wrapped up with the idea of retrieving the boy, 'Tim' I believe he is called," Ghazali explained. "He is convinced that the child is his son. It has consumed him, sapped all his energy. He spends hours talking to lawyers and looking into the possibility of getting Tim. I did warn about this before. He is in Kuala Lumpur at this moment. He sent me here to deal with some constituency matters on his behalf."

"I am very worried about Hussein. He was doing so well until that ill-timed, cursed phone call from Ahmad. I wish he had never called. It has stirred up the past, a past that is best forgotten. My son is obsessed with his former wife. I don't understand it. He would never have got this far if she had remained in his life."

Over the past month, Rahim had become increasingly convinced that Tim was not his grandson. He had spoken to all the women folk, including the servants, and none had any inkling that An Mei was expecting. He had questioned in particular Fawziah, An Mei's maid. Only she amongst all the others had hesitated in her answer. In the end she too had affirmed what they said. It must be Ahmad's way of getting back at them and to get more money. A grunt of annoyance escaped him. He stood up, pushing his chair away. He walked towards the windows and looked out to the distance. "Any news of Ahmad? Have they captured him?"

"No! I do not believe they have captured him. Neither did they manage to catch Ah Cheong, his accomplice. The Singapore police blamed it on the porosity of our borders allowing criminals to move with ease between countries."

Ghazali had stood up when Rahim walked to the window. He now walked to stand behind him. He lowered his voice. "Sir!" he said hesitantly.

"Yes?" asked Rahim as he spun around to face Ghazali.

"Perhaps *Datin* would know the whereabouts of Ahmad. I heard her speaking to someone on the phone. I think it could be Ahmad. She was asking the person to help get her grandson." Even as he spoke, a dread descended on him. He ran his tongue around his lips. He was on surer grounds when he spoke about Hussein. He felt that Rahim was of the same mind as him. But this, this telling on Faridah, Rahim's wife was another matter.

Taken aback, Rahim glared at his son's short bespectacled loyal assistant. "Are you sure?" he asked, his voice reflecting his disbelief.

"I heard her. I cannot be absolutely sure, but I think she was talking to Ahmad," insisted Ghazali.

"There is only one way to find out. Send for her! I'll ask her myself. If what you say is true, I will put a stop to this nonsense once and for all. But if you are lying ... you will not be working for Hussein much longer. Understand?"

* * * * *

The car stopped in the portico and Hussein got out. He climbed up the stairway to the entrance of the family residence in Kuala Lumpur. He stepped into the house and was overwhelmed by its silence. He remembered how An Mei had complained that she felt like a prisoner there despite its grandeur. He had never felt that way. In the past, the house was always filled with people. His parents or kin were always there. There were always guests. Not this time. It was deserted except for servants. They were quiet like they were told to be. How he wished he had not sent Ghazali to Kemun. At least then, he would have had someone to talk to.

He walked up the spiral stairway, past the inner courtyard to his room. He lowered himself onto the couch. His hand went to his chest. He felt a tenderness lodged deep in it as if he had been wounded. It was like the aftermath of a knife wound, an initial sharp stabbing pain followed by a dull throbbing ache. His head pounded sending a sharp signal to his left temple; it spread all round the socket of his eye. He felt unbalanced. He was aware only of the left eye and its discomfort. He rubbed and tapped his head to rid it of the all-consuming pain, but it remained. He groaned; he thrust his legs out in front of him to slide deeper into the couch. He looked at the papers and reports strewn around him. He could not read them; he could not remember what they were; he could not concentrate, he did not care. All he could think of was the file the lawyers had prepared for him. They had not given him much hope. They said such civil cases were notoriously long-winded and damaging. They were willing to take the case, of course, but had hastened to add so many caveats that he had wanted to scream at them. Perhaps, he should have gone with Ahmad's suggestion, but at that time he had thought he could win An Mei back.

He closed his eyes willing himself to rest. He took a deep breath, releasing it long and slowly. The doctor had warned him that his blood pressure was dangerously high.

Fawziah came into the room with a tray laid with teacups, saucers and a plate of pastries. She placed it on the coffee table, careful not to make any sound. She stood unsure whether she should wake him or remove the tray. His breath came in rasps. Suddenly his head jerked. She stood ready to run before he woke, but his eyes, rimmed with dark shadows, remained shut. She stood looking at him. The cook had sent her up because he had not eaten. The previous night's dinner had also remained untouched. The dishes the cook had prepared for his lunch had been left to cool and congeal. The cook had exclaimed, "*Nak tinggal dunia!* He wants to leave this world! But I do not want to be blamed. So take him this," thrusting on Fawziah the tray of food.

Fawziah bent to take a closer look at Hussein. His cheeks were hollowed throwing into relief the sharpness of his cheekbones and jaw. She could feel his breath, warm, ragged. She wanted to touch his face. She put out her hand and imagined touching it. His hand shot out and grabbed hers.

"What are you doing?" he demanded, his eyes wide-open. He recognised her as the maid who had helped him find An Mei when he first brought her home and she fled. He held Fawziah's hand tightly, almost twisting her arm, and brought it down even as he struggled to stand up to tower over her. She bowed her head with shame and embarrassment. She did not know what made her reach out. She did not know why she did it, only the compelling urge to touch this man, an urge grown out of compassion. She had been a witness to the trials and tribulations of his pursuit of her mistress An Mei and the misery he was in now.

"*Minta maaf*," she whispered. "I did not mean anything. I was not thinking. Please do not tell *Datin*."

He dropped her hand. He swayed unsteadily. An explosion of pain went through his temple and, for a minute or two; he did not know where he was. It had happened before; a few moments of complete blackout, of not remembering, conscious of nothing except for the excruciating pain in his temple. He looked wildly around him.

"Please, I'll help you sit down." She placed her arm around him and guided him back into the couch. "I'll call the doctor."

"Stay with me," he said.

"Yes, I only need to reach the phone to call the doctor, then I will return. I'll be back."

* * * * *

"I am afraid, we have found a tumour in his brain. I am sorry to have to tell you this." The doctor spoke gravely.

The walls receded from Rahim's vision. He stared blankly at the doctor unable to take in the news. Only Faridah's muffled cries brought him to the present. She pressed her face into his body and he could feel her tears soaking his tunic.

"Can anything be done?" asked Rahim.

"There are a number of drug trials being carried out. One in particular, Temozolomide, looks interesting. The drug is being developed at Birmingham's Aston University in the UK, but it will take many years of trials and refinement before it comes onto the market. Even then, I suspect it will only buy the patient more time. Chemotherapy would still be the main treatment in this case. Then, of course, there is surgery, but it is extremely delicate. For that, perhaps, it might be advisable to take him to a hospital that has had experience of the operation."

"How much time do we have?"

"I can't really tell you. Each person responds differently to the treatment."

Rahim was not listening anymore. He could not absorb the enormity of the news. He heard his wife's whimper; he held her trembling body close to him as much to get comfort as to give it. He recalled his son's pallor, his body on the narrow hospital bed, hooked up to machines and monitors, tubes hanging like tangled snakes coiled around his body. The hopes, ambitions and pride that he held and felt for his son, all dashed to smithereens. Was he to blame? Had he pushed Hussein too far? How did he fail to notice the changes in his son's behaviour, his sickness? What kind of a father was he?

"Perhaps sir, you might wish to go home and take some rest. There is little you can do here. We will call for you when he wakes up. We can discuss this again. It is difficult to take in all at once."

* * * * *

Fawziah sat in a chair in the corner of the hospital room. The smell of disinfectant rose from the floor, suffusing the air with its stringent odour. She felt encased in the whitewashed walls of the room. The panoply of apparatus meant little to her. Monitors that flashed numbers and graphs; the beeps and sounds coming from them. She was wary and bewildered by the tubes that hung from high and dripped viscous liquids down into the vein of the unresisting patient. She had been left to make sure that the medical staff could be summoned if the need arose and in order that his parents could be contacted the minute he became conscious. She looked at Hussein anxiously, afraid that she might miss something should she so much as blink. The ticking and murmurs of the machines were soporific. She pinched herself to keep alert.

A small movement caught her eye. She went over to him. She could see his eyes flickering behind his closed lids. His lips, parched and dry, moved soundlessly. She hurried over. Her hand reached for the bell.

He caught her wrist. "An Mei," he said. "Stay."

She knelt down, her wrist caught in his grip. She could feel his hand, hot, feverish, and clammy.

"She is not here. I am Fawziah," she whispered.

"Don't leave me." His eyes moved rapidly behind closed lids. "Where is our son?"

"I am not An Mei," she said. He moved his head. His eyelids remained shut but, behind them, his eyes continued their restless twitching. She gently stroked his hand. His jerking stopped. Slowly his hands grew limp and the flickering of his eyes stopped. She could see the rhythmic rise and fall of his breath. She stood up and went out to call the nurse. Then she made her way to the telephone booth in the corridor. She stood for a moment outside the booth. No good would come out of his hankering for *Puan* Noraidin and the boy. He needs peace and she, her newfound freedom. Fawziah took up the phone and whispered with her eyes closed and face looking upwards, "Forgive me my lies."

She dialled and waited.

"*Datin*," she said, "your son is sleeping and I have called the nurse to check if he is all right. I have something to tell you. *Datuk* has been asking if *Puan* Noraidin was pregnant before she left us. I am afraid I might not have been sufficiently clear. I did not explain why I believe that she was not with child. I would like to tell you why I know. I tended to her clothes. She did not miss her moon. She was not pregnant when she left."

Chapter 49

From where they stood, the hill sloped down on both sides. On one side, the hill contours followed the rough car track. On the other, it fell steeply into a deep valley. A river wound through fields. At intervals, diverted eddies of water gushed and tumbled around boulders, seeping between the rocks, before re-joining the main flow. In other places the rushing river seemed to check and stall giving way to peaceful stretches of deep emerald water.

An Mei stood on the hilltop, one hand holding Tim, the other clutching a bunch of wild pink cyclamens and yellow primroses. Everything was still. Under the clear blue sky, the long grass, heavy with morning dew, lay flat where Tim had been rolling his little cart. Wild anemones sprinkled the fields with blue and white. In the distance, a cuckoo called. She breathed in deeply the scented air and tilted her head to the sky. "Thank you," she murmured, "for all this."

She dropped Tim's hand and stretched out both arms to embrace the air. She felt free, liberated. She spun around. Her chuckling and joy infected Tim. He too laughed, his delight bursting out of him as he too spun around. It was lovely to see his mother so happy. He turned and turned, both hands held up high, his jacket bonnet slipping behind him, until An Mei caught him in her arms. "Stop! You will be dizzy," she laughed.

She set him down on the grass and pointed to the car track. "Let's walk on the Golly Gosh road. Be careful not to fall into Golly Gosh's holes. Daddy is waiting for us in Mr. Giuseppe's house. The *festa* must have started. There will be a big fire."

She held on to his hand and took the cart from him, tucking it under her arm. He skipped and flapped his arm, yanking hers as he went.

"Golly!" he shouted as he jumped over a small pile of gravel and stones. "Gosh!" he exclaimed as he deliberately landed in a shallow hole. Tim had been the first to name the road as the car bounced up the track when they were searching for the house they now owned just fifty-eight kilometres from Rome. It had been love at first sight for all of them when they saw the house with walls built of volcanic *tuffa* and a roof of traditional terracotta tiles. The main sitting room had a large open wood fire while French windows on each side opened on to terraces that adjoined the garden. To the east was the orchard, a gentle sloping incline that inched upwards to join another hill. To the west, was another terrace that looked out over the valley and the river.

She stopped to turn and look at the house. Tim pulled impatiently at her hand and she continued down the rough road. She did not want to rush. She wanted to take in every minute of the day, dawdling at times to look at the wild flowers that grew in profusion by the roadside. Bees droned, humming their tune, as they dipped and flew from flower to flower.

Buttercups and mustard yellow primroses, flowers that she had long associated with England, grew in even greater abundance here. She stooped to pick some buttercups to add to her bunch.

"Mummy! Hurry! I am hungry," pleaded Tim.

In the distance she saw smoke rising from a fire. Across the field came the sweet, rich aroma of *porchetta* and *abbachio*. She could see a huge pig, stuffed with fennel, garlic and rosemary, laid out on a trestle table. Close by a lamb on a spit was roasting over a fire pit. A man, his sleeves rolled up to reveal strong brown arms, dipped and brushed olive oil scented with rosemary and garlic on the lamb, while another patiently turned the spit. The fire cackled and spat as the fat and juices oozing from the lamb hit the hot ashes. Tim ran and she hurried forward to keep up. Another huge trestle table covered with a white cloth had been set up under the shade of a fig tree, its wide palmate leaves offering much needed shade. A woman stood with a huge loaf of *casareccio* bread held tight against her bosom, cutting thick slices and dropping them neatly into woven baskets. Another woman busied herself filling up bowls with glistening fat black and green olives slicked with olive oil, to be taken to the table.

"*Signora*, just in time to help with the *bruschetta*. We need someone to help chop up the tomatoes and the garlic and basil. Here, I'll take Tim over to the other children. He'll be safe with Simonetta," said Giuseppe's wife, Claudia, taking Tim by the hand. "Go!" she commanded, pointing An Mei in the direction of another table set by the kitchen door.

"Where is Mark?"

"He will be here soon. *Non ti preoccupare!* Do not worry. We sent him to chop more wood. He is *forte*, strong," she chuckled flexing her own biceps to make her point.

An Mei looked anxiously at Tim's back. He had broken free and was running and skipping part of the way to join a group of children assembled around Simonetta. A little boy had his eyes blind-folded. The game of blind man's buff had just started. Shrieks of laughter filled the air as the children gave chase, running close to tease the boy before escaping with shouts of glee.

From the corner of her eye, Giuseppe's wife saw the anxiety that drifted across An Mei's face. "Go! Don't worry," she said. She reached out to squeeze An Mei's arm. "You are with friends."

An Mei smiled, embarrassed. "Yes! I'll go over to help."

Two women had stationed themselves behind a long travertine table and were preparing *bruschetta*. A big pile of bread had already been sliced ready for toasting on the open barbecue. One woman, her hair tied up with a scarf and an apron knotted hastily round her waist, was laying out braids of dried garlic, ready to be peeled and minced. The other had begun chopping up tomatoes. "Here, just in time. You prepare the *basilico*," the woman with the scarf said, handing her bunches of green basil. "Shred the leaves finely and we'll mix them with the tomatoes. With some garlic, a big glug of virgin olive oil, salt and pepper, they will provide a wonderful topping for the toasted *casareccio.* "

An Mei smiled. Ever since her first days in Italy, she had been familiar with the recipe, "*alia, olio, un po' di pepe, un po' di sale*: garlic, oil, a little pepper and a little salt, that more or less covered the basic flavouring of most dishes.

"Shred a bit more," said one woman observing her smile and wishing to impress on her that much more chopping and preparation had still to be done. "We'll need some extra basil for the *caprese, un insalata merivigliosa*, a wonderful salad. Have you eaten mozzarella and tomatoes served with olive oil?" she asked, stopping to hear the answer but not before adding a further advice. "You must only use *mozarrella di bufala*, made from water buffalo milk."

An Mei nodded towards the bowl of mozzarellas, round white globular cheese, standing in lightly salted liquid. "You mean those? I love them."

The women beamed, pleased with the reply. They worked and chatted. The smell of tomatoes, garlic and basil filled the air. Time rushed by and she found herself caught in a time warp of just chopping, shredding and peeling.

Shouts echoed across the field. The men were coming back. She saw Mark making his way towards her. He waved and she put her hand up to wave to him. The women nudged each other. "*Che belli! I giovani!* How beautiful! The young! Go to him, we'll take care of this," they said.

But she stood waiting. A warm glow spread over her, starting from her face, down to her neck and her body. She watched him walk toward her. She lifted her face to receive his kiss.

"Alright?" he asked.

She nodded.

"Happy?"

She tiptoed and whispered in his ear. The women stopped to watch, their eyes round. Mark lips broke into a broad grin. He picked her up and hugged her. "Can I tell them?" he asked. She nodded.

Still holding her close against him, he announced, "You are the first to hear our news," he half shouted with joy, "my wife is expecting a baby." Cheers and claps followed. The women pressed forward, claiming their kisses, one on each cheek. The children ran over to see what was happening. They could see Tim running towards them. Mark ran to meet him. He lifted him high and then placed him on his shoulders. An Mei stood watching them; her happiness complete.